I0831137

INCENDIARY

INCENDIARY

CLAIRE DOWLER

First Printing, 2021

For my sunshine.

Contents

One

THE SEER

"He says you look beautiful this evening."

She was quite deliberately rephrasing the man's comment that his widow looked more like a bearded goat than ever.

The woman arched an over-plucked eyebrow. "That doesn't sound like Ralph."

Charlie shrugged noncommittally. "People change in the hereafter. We're divested of all our earthly worries and preoccupations. What we're left with is simply peace and love."

Ralph snorted from where the blurry edges of his bulging backside enveloped the stool at the side of the room. "What a load of rot. She's as irritating to me now as the day I married her – which coincidentally was the first day I wanted a divorce. I was looking forward to an afterlife without her yipping at me like a Chihuahua, yet here I am. Summoned by *you*." He drew out the final word with contempt, glaring at Charlie bitterly through beady grey eyes.

"Do you have any questions for Ralph?" Ignoring the daggers being thrown her way, Charlie focused on the portly fifty-something-year-old sitting before her.

Red waves bounced voluminously to her shoulders, the faintest line betraying the grey lurking beneath. A daffodil-yellow handkerchief was pressed to her cheek which, despite her frequent dabbing, was still mysteriously dry.

"Well, I want to know... Ralph and I didn't always see eye to eye on much, really. One of the last things he said was that he never wanted me to remarry... does he still feel the same way?" She peered up at Charlie from behind red-horned glasses.

"Ha!" Ralph let out a triumphant cry and slammed his fist on the table, or he would have, had his hand not passed cleanly through the wood. Evidently, Charlie observed, he hadn't been dead long enough to learn how to control his energy.

"I knew that tramp would be barking up the next tree before I was cold in my grave! Yes, I did bloody mean it. If I had to spend the best of my years in misery with her, then why the bloody hell should she get to enjoy herself because I carked it before her? No cigar, sugar."

Charlie hesitated. What was she meant to do with that?

"Ralph is conflicted," she said slowly, ignoring his colourful protests. "While he loves you very much and wants to have you for himself, he also wants you to be happy."

At this, the woman could not conceal her incredulity. "Are you sure you've found the right husband?"

Casting an eye in his direction, Charlie drew upon some of his more distinguishing features; "receding hairline with a combover which surely didn't fool anyone, well-fed belly, more rings on his fingers than are circling Saturn and—" she sniffed, his cologne smelling familiar. "Is that *Rochas's Moustache*?"

The woman pursed her thin lips, dabbed again at the bone dry corner of her heavily lined eye and, collecting herself, rose demurely from the chair.

"Yes, I suppose that's all the proof I need." With the pretence of collecting herself, slinging her fur-lined purse over her shoulder, she made to leave.

"Oh, ma'am— there's just the matter of the— um," Charlie stammered unnecessarily. She'd been doing this quite long enough to say 'excuse me, you owe me coin', but the helpless young girl card always played nicely.

"Oh, yes," the woman replied with a tone that revealed she hadn't forgotten at all. Rustling in her purse for a moment, she produced a crisp $10 bill and laid it on the white tablecloth. "Do keep the change. Try not to spend it all on liquor."

With that, the woman clutched her purse to her buxom breast and, oblivious to her dead husband now following her with a trail of vulgar analogies, showed herself to the door which clunked dully behind her. As usual, it hadn't shut properly – it needed a firm shove to cooperate.

With a heavy sigh, Charlie put her hip into it, hearing the latch click into place before silence descended.

Whilst the woman may have believed she was giving some harsh advice, Charlie felt quietly vindicated knowing she was the exception to the rule in downtown Blanford, where beggars lined the streets and fought over a dollar. Even so, as she looked around her dilapidated flat, it was a grim reminder she was still there.

The front door, where she stood, opened immediately into the living room, only just wide enough for a moth-eaten two-seater couch the former tenants had left behind (which she had attempted to cover with a throw) and a small black and white television set she'd found in the dumpster behind Polk Brothers. Most of the channels worked; that is, until she actually wanted to watch them.

A thin wall separated the lounge from the kitchen, just big enough for one person to swelter in front of the hot plates. She had squeezed a tarnished fold-out table between the counter and the window, which offered premium views over the dingy street featuring Joe's Gun and Lock Shop, the Loan Bank, and Rothschild Liquors. The latter bore a peeling sign touting 'Country's best old brew beer' and, below it, the weekly special; a full pint of wine for 29c.

The bedroom was an equally sorry state of affairs; the double bed squashed up against the water-stained wall allowed only just enough space to scrape past. Her clothes were still in boxes which she rummaged through daily but had never been able to bring herself to unpack, despite now having been there for over a year.

Please, don't talk about the bathroom.

"Is your unblinking stare an attempt to blind yourself?"

A weightless body had oozed through the door next to her, following her weary gaze to a stubborn stain on the old shag pile carpet.

"Do you think it will work?" Charlie muttered as she pushed herself from the door and collected the crisp bill from her working table.

"Don't wish away life's joys, child."

Charlie scoffed. "What's joyful about being able to see the cesspool I live in?" she asked, gesturing half-heartedly at the flat that seemed to be decaying around her even as she spoke.

"If you couldn't see the ugly, how could you see the beauty? There are many undesirable characters in this city, yet they made it all the easier to find you."

Charlie saw the back of her head as she snorted, but her resentment dissipated in spite of herself. Only Hudson could break through her defences. A kindly ghost on the cusp of sixty-something, he had a gentle English accent and wore a coat with a fresh-pressed handkerchief in the pocket, still ready for the ball he had been on his way to attend about half a century ago.

"So you're just hanging around me because I compare favourably to the other wet rags in this city? You're too kind, Hudson," she quipped, letting the ghost know she was joking with a twitch of her lip as she busied herself with resetting the reading table.

Clutching the $10 bill, she prised the air vent from the wall where she added it to a thick wad of identical notes. *Spend it on liquor... please.* Her clients fell into two categories; those with more money than sense, and those whose desperation outweighed their sense.

"You've gathered a tidy sum," Hudson remarked from over her shoulder as she shoved the vent back into place. "How much longer do you anticipate?"

"Too long," she lamented, moving with one short step from the living room to the kitchen, where she busied herself with peeling potatoes for dinner.

She had been desperately squirrelling away money for the better part of five years with a vague but hopeful dream of moving as far away from Blanford as she could.

There was a quaint cottage in the country somewhere waiting for her, with a rocking chair on the front verandah and a few farm animals she would come to love. Somewhere she wouldn't be probed and scrutinised by the city crowds. Every day she was reminded she was an outcast, and every day she prayed she would not wake to find herself in a prison or, worse, an Enlightenment facility.

Charlie's mother, Florence, had been able to See. Her childhood had been spent sitting on her front porch, often with the guise of a doll in hand, while her mother took clients.

Each night before dinner, with the curtains drawn, her mother took her hand and prayed. She prayed that God would keep them safe, for forgiveness for Charlie's father, and for the broken world they lived in. This would be followed, without fail, by Florence reminding her firmly that no one needed to know.

"What's it like, Hudson?" she asked, dropping the potatoes into a pot of boiling water.

"Marvellous, I'm sure, but what exactly?" he asked while perusing her small collection of books gathered on the disused mantel.

"Being dead."

He turned and looked past her with a considered stare, contemplating. "I suppose it would depend on who one asks. I have heard it is peaceful, among other things."

"And for you?"

He gave her a small smile. "I would not want to be anywhere else."

"That's not what I asked."

Picking at a strip of yellow paint curling off the cupboard door, she eyed the potatoes bobbing lethargically in the discoloured pot. "If I were you, I'd be anywhere but here."

The sigh from behind her told her he'd moved closer and the familiar warmth of his energy radiated over her back like the morning sun.

"It's amusing that we humans have a preconception of belonging in a certain place and equate our happiness to either being in it or being separated from it. Some of us are fortunate enough never to learn we are wrong. The rest, however, discover that without the people we love, those places mean very little after all."

It was a painful truth she knew well.

Charlie hadn't always regarded the dilapidated buildings of downtown Blanford and its flocks of blind servants with such disdain. It had been a different place when she had been able to see it through her mother's eyes.

"They are only human," her mother would answer when Charlie complained about some blight in her day. With an understanding twinkle in her crystal blue eyes, her mother would gently ask, "In the grand scheme of things, does it really matter?"

And with that, Charlie's grievances would melt into the tomato soup she, her mother and grandmother shared for dinner.

"There is nothing for me here, Hudson."

"I know that, my lady. But a change of scenery can only do so much. The rest, I'm afraid, relies on your new abode being in close proximity to a decent coffee shop."

Charlie let out a burst of laughter as the pot overflowed. The hot plate hissing angrily, she began mashing the potatoes into a lumpy sludge.

She still had a slice of vegetable quiche in the refrigerator to add to her meal which, she reflected, was about as balanced as it had been in months.

Reticently, Charlie stabbed her quiche which posed far too much resistance to her fork to be considered fresh.

"A group of incendiaries were arrested today after a public display in which they spouted theological falsehoods on the steps of Town Hall."

Charlie's eyes flickered to the grainy image on her cube-like television where a slick middle-aged man in a blazer was staring down the camera.

"The group caused alarm with claims of impending judgement,

attempting to convince innocent citizens to seek forgiveness before it's too late. The following footage may be distressing for some viewers."

The scene unfolded like one of Charlie's nightmares. An elderly man in a cassock held a picture of Christ above his head, begging the onlookers to repent and see the light.

"He does not blame you," his voice trembled as he yelled. "He sees you. He loves you. He is waiting to welcome you home, but first, you must welcome Him into your heart."

A few beleaguered supporters stood by his side, dressed in everyday attire with expressions of resigned fear. One held a bottle of oil, another held some sticks that looked like incense and the last held a gold chalet to her chest.

The Enforcers didn't give a warning – they didn't need to. Twenty armed officers descended on the unarmed group, kicking and striking the backs of their knees so they fell heavily to the ground, twisting their arms until they cried out in pain.

Oil and glass shattered on the pavement in a glistening mosaic. One Enforcer took the opportunity to push the priest's head into the mess.

The camera zoomed into his bloodied face, sandwiched between a knee and the concrete, as he searched imploringly for help that wouldn't come. Charlie's heart wrenched as her eyes met his before the scene ended abruptly.

"Thankfully, no civilians were hurt and the incendiaries are expected to face court later this week."

Charlie's fork clattered to the plate as she dropped it in disgust. She knew what awaited the believers in the court. If they were lucky, it would be quick and painless — unlike the fate her mother had met.

Two

THE BOY

Charlie was "different", her mother had assured her from the time she was old enough to talk to the fuzzy-edged people she could see hovering around her.

She hadn't been old enough to discern between the people who knocked on their door, seeking answers from their beloved departed, and the people who appeared uninvited at odd hours of the day and night, seeking someone who could affirm their existence.

The world was a dangerous place for people like them. Religion and belief in any higher power had been outlawed for the past half a century after it was unanimously agreed by the Assembly of Nations that it separated cultures and sparked more violence and hatred than uniformity and structure. The movement had been spearheaded by the leader of the free world, President Edgar Cormback – a man of the belief that the concept of a deity distracted the populace from serving their country and 'true' leader.

Legislation had been lenient at first. Fines were issued to defiant worshippers and clerics who, regardless of denomination, were ordered to integrate with society through 'Enlightenment Camps'. These month-long brainwashing sessions were said to be educational and informative, focusing on the detrimental impact of religion throughout history, the scientific reasons that a deity could not exist, and how they might be able to support the State and redeem themselves.

Punishments became more brutal with each successive President and his appointed Chief Enforcer. Preachers were soon being beaten in the streets. Parents who covertly attempted to baptise their children saw them taken by the State. Religious leaders who made any effort to gather a following were incarcerated.

Her mother's fate had been worse.

Charlie slept fitfully that night, waking up several times in a cold sweat, remembering the way the priest's eyes had begged her for help. It was only after she felt a knee pressed into the back of her own head and the glass pricking painfully against her skin that she threw the blankets back and decided a strong cup of coffee was more attainable than a restful sleep.

Steam meandering up her face as she raised the mug to her lips, she peered thoughtlessly out the discoloured kitchen window. A patchwork of crested ochre and mahogany roofs stretched out into the distance beneath her lofty perch. She had often imagined running across them, leaping from rooftop to rooftop until they dropped away into undulating hills, and the crisp country air welcomed her like a new friend.

The walls around her suddenly felt stifling, pressing in like an iron-clad coffin. The coffee dregs now peered up at her with gluggy brown eyes. Her legs carried her without conscious thought to her coat, which she threw on in a daze before abandoning the claustrophobic unit.

She had always taken the stairs of her building as fast as she could. The eleven flights of an archaic spiral were her only route to and from her unit. The wooden steps curved compliantly under the weight of their many years of service and the bottle-green wallpaper was gradually retiring from its post.

The pounding of her racing feet did little to soothe her increasingly frantic mind, now desperate for the smell of cigarette smoke and petrol fumes waiting for her on the street. The air grew colder as she neared the front doors and her lungs began to fill with the freedom of the chilly morning outside, but a figure blocked her escape.

"Charlie. Where are you going in such a hurry at this hour?" A bulbous man peered up at her from the landing below, the cigar still skewered beneath his moustache, causing his usual drawl to lengthen horribly.

Fred lived on the eighth floor with his sad and mistreated wife, Dot. He came home at all hours of the morning, often stumbling up the stairs with the distinctive aroma of bourbon trailing behind him. The shouting arguments between the couple had gradually petered out in recent months. They now lived in un-companionable silence with a deep-seated hope the other would die in their sleep.

Or so Dot's deceased mother had told her. She had hung around for several months, worrying over her melancholy daughter and fuming at the bruises she kept hidden beneath long-sleeved blouses. Eventually the trauma was too much for her to have to witness and she stepped quietly over to the Otherside, waiting to welcome her daughter with loving arms.

"Just for a walk, Fred," she puffed, the rapid descent having stolen her breath. "Have you already been for one too?"

He swayed uneasily and reached for the hand railing to mitigate a fall. "A walk – errr... yes. I've been for a walk."

His mouth moved awkwardly around the word. She thought she detected a different scent on his person – something sweet, a perfume perhaps. Blinking blearily up at her for a moment, his eyes raked down her coat, letting them linger where her chest and hips filled out the fabric. He licked his lips.

"Why don't you have a husband, girl? You too busy eh... working?" She didn't like what his tone implied.

"Not that I think it's any of your business, but I am simply not interested in dating," she replied curtly.

He snorted. "That's what all the old spinsters say. Truth is, you're all just filthy tramps who never learned to cook or clean." His beady eyes narrowed, becoming predator-like. "There is another use for you though..."

Charlie hastily backed up a stair as Fred staggered toward her, not bothering to ask if she gave her permission or even if she was remotely interested. He was an adulterous drunk who had stumbled upon an attractive girl alone in the dark hours of the morning.

Considering whether she should run back up the stairs or past him and out the front door, her answer presented itself as the toe of Fred's boot caught on the stair and he crashed forward.

"Blast it!"

She slipped past him. "Better watch your step, Fred." Not waiting for a reply, she now found her exit unhindered and burst from the vestibule into the crisp early morning air.

Her breath rose before her in a wispy cloud as she tightened her coat around her slender frame. Cars were scattered along the street, their owners still tucked in their beds. The sallow light seeping from the lamp posts faded into the sky as the night gradually released its grip.

Charlie began walking in no particular direction and with no particular ambition, other than perhaps to pretend she would find herself somewhere more pleasant. She had often been told the downtown streets were no place for a young girl to be wandering alone, particularly at night (or in the early morning hours). Her inner voice usually answered back, 'I could not possibly lose more than I already have.'

Buildings hulked over her, more intimidating than reassuring, but she kept her eyes on the pavement and imagined where it might take her.

Charlie walked until she lost track of time, but when the sun glared down on her and the morning onslaught of businessmen and school children began shouldering past her, she realised it must nearly be 9 o'clock.

Her mother had never Seen for people on the same days, or in any discernible pattern, in an effort to dissuade unwanted attention, a rule Charlie followed too. So with nowhere to be that day, she took a side street she knew well, away from the noise and judgemental eyes of the city crowds.

Cemeteries offered her reprieve as they were a place in which neither the living nor the dead liked to dwell. Elm Woods Cemetery was nestled snugly between the buildings, which even themselves seemed to purposefully look past the small, peaceful resting place. Wrapped protectively within an elaborate wrought iron fence, most people quickly skirted around the perimeter, as if one wrong look could see them convicted of faith. Which, if Charlie was honest with herself, it probably could.

The gravestones bore no reference to God, Heaven or a life hereafter. Instead, they wore inscriptions like 'Dearly loved father, brother and son who served his country and his people', and 'A precious daughter we will remember, may she rest and suffer no more'.

People still grieved, but it was a hopeless, despairing kind of grief. It used to be different, her grandmother had told her. People had held hope they would see their loved ones again. They would cry and laugh, reminisce and talk to their lost family members as if they were standing beside them. Which, of course, they often were.

Grief now was hollow, meaningless. People cried for their loved ones who would never know reprieve from their earthly encumberment, nor see their children grow and prosper. They were simply gone, disappearing into time, and the living waited until they would do the same.

Charlie felt the tension in her bones ease slightly as even the noise of the city seemed to respect the cemetery's plotted boundaries. And yet there was a noise – not one she was used to here. Someone was talking. Two someones were talking, and not in the hushed tones one would expect in the presence of the dead.

Charlie stepped into the shadow of a crypt, casting furtive glances between the headstones. She was in no real danger, she tried to placate herself. She had as much right to be here as these people did. The only danger lay in it becoming known how often she frequented this hallowed place.

Laughter drew her attention and she found the perpetrator; a boy no older than fourteen was kicking his heels in the dirt while grinning playfully at a girl about the same age.

He looked quite ordinary in his matching grey school trousers and jumper, with a maroon collar framing a pale neck. At first glance, the girl was similarly ordinary with a blonde braid that fell down the back of a blue pinafore. Her hands were held in front of her as she tilted her head shyly at the boy.

It would have been a sweet scene of young infatuation; a couple of kids wagging school to spend time together without the watchful gaze of authority.

It would have been, if the girl hadn't been blurry around the edges.

Charlie was filled with a wave of panic that someone else would see the boy talking to thin air. After a moment of indecision, she made her way indirectly towards them while pretending to look contemplatively at the gravestones. After a few steps, she felt them watching her. A few more and, as she'd hoped, the girl waved a sad goodbye and disappeared.

From her peripheral vision, she saw the boy slump to the ground and lean back against a headstone. This was none of her business, she should turn around and go home. He wasn't her responsibility; she was her own responsibility. Yes, that was how everyone else thought. *And just look at the state of the world.*

Kneading her forehead with a frustrated groan, she set her sights on the headstone the boy had disappeared behind. Her boots crunched on the gravel, creating a sense of foreboding. She could only imagine the fear she must have been striking into his heart.

Good, she thought. *Maybe fear is what he needs.*

Rounding the corner, his wide, petrified stare made her momentarily regret her direct approach. She swallowed her clemency and stared down the bridge of her nose at the frozen child.

"Who were you talking to?" she asked, without introduction.

"No one," the boy answered too quickly. He had been waiting for the question. She thought she heard a southern accent meandering around the two short syllables.

For a moment Charlie contemplated playing the role of shrewd observer. She could convince him she knew his secret, make him believe she was going to tell an Enforcer. She could bring him to tears quite easily; even now his eyes darted back and forth under her unwavering stare. She might be able to scare him into exercising caution.

Charlie also wasn't that kind of person. "She didn't look like no one."

He wasn't expecting that reply. His head snapped back so quickly she heard it thud gently against the stone. His hand searched for the strap of his backpack.

"I wasn't talking to no one," he said again, his feet sliding out on the gravel as he tried to push himself up.

"You might hurt her feelings if she heard you say that. She looked like she quite liked your company. I had a beautiful blue pinafore just like hers when I was younger."

He sprung to his feet in alarm, arms held out from his sides and legs in a half crouch as though he were expecting her to lunge at him.

"Who are you?" His voice was small, but he raised it defiantly.

"I could have been an Enforcer. Do you have any idea how lucky you are?" Charlie was talking but it was her mother's voice coming out of her mouth.

"If you're not an Enforcer, then who are you?" Red, blotchy stains were seeping into his freckled cheeks. She may make him cry after all.

"I'm—" she faltered, realising it would be foolish to give a stranger her real name and her classified occupation in the same afternoon.

"I'm Florence. I'm a Seer. And what I saw was nothing short of reckless." Taking her mother's name seemed appropriate given she was already using her words.

"Oh." His shoulders seemed to release some of their tension. "No one comes here, but. You're the first person I've seen here. First live person anyway." He still looked panicked, but his arms slowly relaxed, allowing his hands to fall by the sides of his cotton trousers.

"That's one hell of a gamble when the stakes are your life. What's your name?"

He blinked as Charlie imagined he considered the same risk she had.

"Don't tell me," she stopped him before he could reply. "You shouldn't trust anyone, let alone me. Just promise me something: that you'll never use your gift in public again. The next time someone catches you, you can bet your freckles they won't be as understanding."

Berated, the boy wilted in front of her. "I just wanted to... I like talking to her. She's my friend," he admitted in a tone that plucked a heart-string.

Her voice softened. "If she's your friend, she'll want you to take care of yourself. Imagine how upset she'd be if you were found out! You look like you should be in school. Take this as a lesson learned and go be where you're meant to be."

She turned to leave but the boy didn't move. For God's sake, she moaned internally.

"I've never met someone like me before," he mumbled timidly.

It was hard for Charlie to separate herself from the young, blissfully ignorant young teen standing in front of her. She had only been a year or so younger than him when she had lost her mother, and a few years older when her grandmother followed. She found herself alone in a world that neither understood her nor wanted to.

"Look, kid, I'd love to help you, but it's dangerous enough for people like us to exist by ourselves, let alone when we start forming groups. The best thing I can do for you is pretend I've never met you."

The heel of her boot crunched in the shingle as she turned and left him standing there. Every step was a fresh wave of guilt which she shoved down into her socks. This world wasn't a fair one, and if this was the way he had to learn, then so be it.

But the rapid approach of small footsteps told her that the lesson had passed clean over his head.

"Don't you get lonely?" he called to her retreating back. "You have to be at least thirty. That's a long time to be alone."

"I'm not thirty," she shot over her shoulder, supremely insulted. "And loneliness is what keeps me alive."

The child was nipping at her heels like a puppy, but she didn't slow her pace.

"That doesn't sound like much fun. What about your parents? Where are they?"

"Gone." She let the answer hang in the air for a moment before adding, "Because my mother wasn't careful enough."

"Oh." The boy was quiet behind her for a minute. She would have thought she'd lost him if it weren't for his lighter crunches, slightly more frequent than hers. "I'm sorry."

"If you're sorry, you'll go to school and pretend you missed the bus." She rounded on him so suddenly he shot out his hands to steady himself. "If you're sorry, you'll be more careful from now on. Go home and be grateful that you can. And don't speak about your gift with anyone but your parents."

"I can't," he answered quietly, saddened eyes dropping from her steely gaze. "They don't get it. I'm not allowed to talk about it or act... different." He shuffled uncomfortably, the morning sun filtering through the overhanging branches of a cypress tree, casting dancing shadows on his face. "I'm not that good at acting normal. Maybe you could teach me how you do it?"

"Oh." It was her turn for words to fail her.

No wonder the boy had no discipline or common sense. He had never been taught, much less understood. He had been told to cut off one of his limbs and pretend it had never been there. Usually Seers were generational, inheriting the gift from a grandparent. Her direct inheritance from her mother was rare, but his apparent birth into a very ordinary family was almost unheard of.

She stared at the half-grown man in front of her as her mind waged war with her heart.

Three

THE DENIAL

"How old are you?

"Fourteen. How old are you?"

Christ, soon she'd have a pubescent teenager on her hands. "Old enough."

"Old enough for what?"

"Quiet. I'm thinking."

The boy peered up at her for a second through forest green eyes before he retrieved a tennis ball from his pocket and started to beat the pavement with a rhythmic thud, thud, thud.

Charlie was risking a great deal if she agreed to teach him. And there was more that went with the territory than just "acting normal". It would probably be best to return to her humble, albeit depressing, little apartment, life unchanged. This boy would go his way, likely never to be heard from again. *Except perhaps when he was the one being forcefully arrested on television*, a voice in her head reminded her.

She paced in chaotic circles between watchful sepulchres where the eyes of passersby could not pry. Diminutive flower beds lined her dancefloor, and she unintentionally threatened a trail of ants with every unseeing step.

Doing business was risky enough as it was. It had been enough to see her mother... well, dead. She had perfected a rhythm, a pattern undetectable to anyone but her. Her method of Seeing for clients meant she was able to save for her escape to the countryside without drawing attention. Would she jeopardise her future for this boy? Years of careful planning and precise execution for the sake of this young man without a name?

"Boy," she called suddenly, turning on her heel.

He caught the ascending ball and froze in trepidation.

"What do I call you?" she asked, as one might ask for the diagnosis of a disease.

The boy seemed to consider his options, eyes not leaving hers and she watched a plethora of possibilities unfold behind them. "Wynn," he said finally. "Just Wynn."

She nodded and resumed her ill-conceived ballet, muttering incoherently to herself

Charlie had readily assumed she was an able teacher, but *what* could she even teach him? Most of what she knew had been passed on from her grandmother, but she had nothing against which to measure its accuracy. Perhaps she would lead the boy into a life of paranoia and, potentially, that of a fugitive. It was all she knew, after all.

Sighing, she took a seat at the feet of a concrete woman nursing an infant, lichen scattered across them like snow. "What do you want, Wynn?"

Mouth slightly ajar in a taken-aback stare, the boy's expression indicated that wasn't a question he'd been asked before. Most families in the city were strict, capitalistic folk, raising their children to hold the same law-based values they held. She suspected Wynn had always been told what he wanted rather than asked.

"Umm... friends, I guess. I mean," he flushed, realising what he'd said, "obviously I have friends. But people I can talk about this stuff with. Who I can tell things, and they won't think I'm weird. Or like, tell my dad."

He paused, fidgeting with the ball and contemplating the pavement. "I mean, I know my parents love me and all that. Parents always love their kids, right? But I know they'll never accept me how *I* am because of how *they* are. And I don't want to get them in trouble, either. But I can't get you in trouble because we have the same secret, right?"

Having followed the chaotic dialogue, Charlie pinched the bridge of her nose between her thumb and forefinger. This would be difficult but necessary.

"You want some advice?" she asked, leaning forward on her knees. "Go to school. Pretend you never met me. Pretend you can't talk to dead people. Give your mother and father a hug; they are trying to keep you safe. In any other world, what we can do might be called a gift. But not in this world. Here we are, and it's a liability. It would be irresponsible of me to lead you into a life I know could kill you one day."

They locked eyes for several seconds but she broke the stare as his began to shine. "I'm sorry, Wynn. It was nice meeting you."

And with that, she left him staring after her, forlorn amid an army of headstones.

Her eyes stung, but she hadn't cried properly in years. She wondered idly if her tear ducts had clogged.

Oh, the barista was staring at her.

"I'm sorry – a long black, please. One sugar."

These days coffee was the only thing that could warm her insides. Without resorting to whisky, that is. She had learned to take it as her grandmother had, as one always seemed to accidentally take the other's cup. It saved the fuss.

On more than one occasion, her grandmother's wizened hand had slapped hers gently as Charlie went to dole out the coffee before the boiling water.

"You'll scald the grounds!" she had chastised. "First the water, then the coffee."

Accepting the steaming cup with grateful hands, Charlie sank into her usual armchair in the innermost corner of the quaint cafe. Too eager, her lips smarted at the scalding liquid.

A yellowed checker of black and white linoleum sprawled across the floor. Wooden panelling covered the walls from ceiling to ground, decorated chaotically with photos of the owner and b-grade celebrities he'd brushed shoulders with over the years. The tables were scattered with just enough room between them to run a mop at the end of the day.

This was where she felt gleefully ordinary; just a girl enjoying a cup of coffee. The staff usually complied with her apparent wish for solitude. Watching the other patrons drift in and out, some chattering about what was showing at the picture theatre, others as solitary as herself, was cathartic and lulled her into a relaxed state of contemplation.

Her mother was the only other Seer she'd known in her years, and she never consciously considered that the curse might not be limited to her family. It was a female gift, her grandmother had told her. She was wrong on both fronts – it wasn't only women who received it, and it most certainly wasn't a gift.

Wayne or Wynn – or whatever the boy's name was – was infinitely more fortunate to have been turned away by her than he would know until he was much, much older. If her family had ignored it and taught Charlie to do the same, their lives would have been infinitely different. Her mother may have had one, for a start. But what, then, was this hole in her stomach that she was trying to fill with coffee

The familiar fragrance of cigars and peppermint wafted over her as she became aware she was not alone.

"My lady, your brow has almost fallen into your cup." She looked up, startled, as the warm energy of a ghostly thumb pressed gently between her eyebrows and smoothed out the crease.

Glancing around the coffee shop, she discovered the only other patron was nose-deep in a newspaper emblazoned with the words 'GOD-SEEKERS FIND PSYCHIATRIC CARE'. She thought she heard a snore from somewhere behind the pages.

"You know you're not supposed to talk to me in public!" she hissed, her voice barely more than a whisper.

"I do recall," he said lightly, settling himself in the chair opposite her. "But I'm not here for conversation. You just rather looked like you were in need of company."

Her look softened and he knew her well enough to accept the small change in expression as gratitude.

Charlie was more grateful for Hudson than she had ever verbally expressed. They say you should never leave things unsaid, lest you lose the opportunity tomorrow. She assumed, though, that she wasn't at risk of losing him anytime soon.

He had entered her life while she was mourning her grandmother. Somewhere in those bleak, empty months, he had caught her sneaking a stranger's wallet from his trousers.

"I saw that, young lady," he had said over her shoulder, in the same tone a grandparent might chastise you with after you were caught stealing candy.

She turned, eyes wide, with the few meagre dollars she had earned in her outstretched hand.

He cast a discerning eye over the coins. "And it would seem it didn't pay."

She ran, weaving through the marching coats, but every time she looked over her shoulder, he was only a few steps behind.

Turning down a side street, she found herself at a dead-end without so much as a milk crate to hoist herself over the chainlink fence. She turned with raised fists and a quivering lip to face her pursuer.

With wisps of grey hair sneaking from beneath a bowler hat and a pocket watch fastened to the breast pocket of his vest, the man could have stepped out of eighteenth century England. His moustache concealed his pursed lips, and as his eyes framed by half-moon spectacles fell on her clenched fists, his features dissolved into an involuntary peal of laughter.

"Good gracious, my lady. Whatever do you think you're doing with those?"

Met only with stony silence, he blinked under her unwavering stare and advanced slowly, raising two gloved hands in mock surrender. "I mean to do you no harm. Though I was surprised a young lady, such as yourself, could—"

"It was just pocket change," she cut him off, edging backwards as he closed the space between them. "You can have it, if you want. It's only a few coins, but you can have them if you'll let me go."

"How much do you think money is worth to me, child?"

She frowned, searching his eyes but finding nothing that betrayed his intentions. As he slowly drew nearer, she realised his outline was not as sharp as it should have been. His gloves blurred at the edges as he twinkled his fingers.

She dropped her hands. He may not think much of money, but now he would definitely think of her as an idiot.

"If you're a... why did you chase me like that?" Her jaw stiffened now she knew she was in no real danger and she looked furtively past him to check no passersby had stopped for the spectacle of a girl arguing with herself.

"What would your mother say if she could see you stealing from unsuspecting strangers?"

Her eyes narrowed. "What would you know about my mother?"

"I was fortunate enough to know her. She was, in fact, quite a good friend. I was sorry to hear of her passing."

"That was years ago. And she never mentioned you," Charlie said dismissively. "While this has been lovely, I do have other places to be, so if you'll excuse me." She pushed past him and made to leave.

"I daresay there was much she failed to mention. Such as the whereabouts of her client journal."

At this, she stopped.

On her grandmother's passing and the loss of her pension, Charlie knew she would have to commence paying the rent. She had spent the past few weeks searching the house for her mother's client records so she might obtain some business. So precious was this journal that not even she was permitted to know the whereabouts, and bank foreclosure on the house was expected any day now.

"Not because I don't trust you," her soft, stout grandmother had said, patting her affectionately on her unruly hair. "But it's safer in one mind than two, for now." But then she had died, taking the secret with her.

For a humble home easily crossed in ten meagre steps, Charlie found no sign of it, and resigned herself to 'earning' what she could on the street.

As it turned out, Charlie would never have found it in the house itself. A brick below the kitchen window – three bricks down and two across, to be precise – came away from its neighbours without complaint as she pulled. Beneath it, protected from the weather in a leather pouch, was her mother's small black book.

"A novel hiding place, was it not?" the elderly ghost had asked jovially, settling himself on a kitchen chair as if he expected to be offered tea.

Hudson had visited her every day since, be it because he was lonely, found her interesting, or enjoyed her sarcastic remarks (though she doubted the latter), she wasn't sure. He had even helped her find her apartment and counselled her through the ordeal of moving – as much as a ghost could. He was as good a friend to her as one could want.

And so they sat in easy silence as the morning rush came and went, starting slightly when the barista cleared his throat and asked if she would like another cup.

"A takeaway, please," she said, embarrassed she had sat for so long while only ordering a ten-cent coffee.

"Are you Seeing this evening?" Hudson asked her softly, careful not to frighten her again and send her drink flying.

She nodded minutely.

"A new client?"

Again, she inclined her head marginally.

"Splendid. I will see you later to ensure all is well." And with that he was gone, evaporating with his scent of cigars and peppermint.

Upon returning to her apartment, however, all was not well. She detected something in the air; it smelled like metal and petrol. Closing the door quietly behind her, she searched the apartment for an intruder. There was a faint rustle from the next room. She was not alone.

Four

THE POOL

"Well, you took your time. Off scouting for more young boys to prey on, were you?" a snarky male voice called from her bedroom.

She bristled. It wasn't uncommon for her to arrive home to a spirit on her sofa, but her bedroom was off-limits to – well, everyone. Even Hudson, as long as she had known him, respected her personal space and remained in the main living areas, dismally unappealing, as they were.

Rounding the corner slowly, she found a young man of no more than twenty-five years old stretched out on her bed, hands behind his head. Much too long for the compact bed, his brown Chukka boots hung off the end, where they were crossed leisurely. His well-worn overalls were still smeared with grease and, even knowing he could not dirty her bedding, she grimaced at the sight.

"What. Do you think. You are doing. On my bed?" she ground out through gritted teeth.

"That's no way to greet someone. First impressions really aren't your forte, are they?" He smirked at her glower. "Righto, I'll get to the point, then. What. Do you think. You were doing. With my brother?" he spat in a similar tone, mocking her derision with contempt of his own.

"Who's your—" She stopped. *Wynn.* The boy in the graveyard, who else? "Oh, no, no, no! That boy was practising in broad daylight. He's lucky I'm the only one who saw him! Imagine what would have happened if an Enforcer was walking past and he was sitting there having a conversation with thin air. And get off my bed!" she finished, voice raised and a flush seeping into her cheeks.

He blinked at her slowly, seeming to enjoy her frustration for a few seconds, before pushing himself off the bed with as much enthusiasm as a spoilt Siamese. He stood over her, a full head above her black mop, but she looked back at him with equal indignance.

"If you come near my brother again, life will become very unpleasant for you. Do you understand?" He still had grease smeared on one cheek and his defined jaw was sprinkled with stubble.

"You don't know who you're threatening," she breathed, lip curling as she drew herself up to her full 5"5'.

He barked a laugh that didn't touch his eyes. "I'm sure I don't. You are quite terrifying."

"It will be more difficult for you to mock me when a few sprigs of cypress are laid across your grave in Ambrose's Cemetery." It was a guess, of course. She had no way of knowing that's where he was buried, but his faltering smirk assured her that her assumption was correct. "And while we're talking about our residences, how did you find mine?"

"I followed Wynn. I didn't realise the invitation was exclusive." He folded his arms over his broad chest, leaning against the doorframe.

She frowned. "You followed him? Here? Well then, how does *he* know where I live?"

"Oh for Pete's sake, spare me. Don't play dumb. You found a vulnerable boy in a graveyard, saw an opportunity to wreak havoc on his life and then he turned up at your apartment. Pure coincidence, I'm sure."

Her eyes saw the back of her head as she pinched the bridge of her nose. "Whatever, I don't have time for this. I told your brother and I'll tell you: I'm not interested in starting any kind of Seer boarding school. Neither of you are welcome here again and I'm happy to make it impossible for you to go anywhere at all."

He held her gaze for several lengthy seconds, visible disdain dripping from the corners of his mouth. "I hope you're not so busy Seeing that you forget to watch your own back," he said in a low voice as he evaporated.

Charlie let out a cry of frustration, striking the doorframe where he had leant a moment before. This was neither a situation she wanted nor needed. If she continued earning at her current rate, she projected she would be able to leave the city in a little over two months. She didn't want to vacate sooner, but wouldn't risk her life for it if push came to shove.

A gentle knock on the door preceded her next client as he shuffled awkwardly into the room. Charlie left it unlocked before appointments and gave her visitors explicit instructions to show themselves in, lest they be seen standing in the hallway and subject to an unwanted line of questioning from an intrusive neighbour.

The sadness he brought in with him was palpable. Though he couldn't have been a day past thirty, his features sagged and bloodshot eyes were flanked by the shadows of what they had seen. He was a smartly dressed young man, albeit for the creases which ran through his black collared shirt, partially covered by a plaid sport coat. Grey trousers ran down to a pair of shiny two-tone Oxfords, which had just started to crease at the toe.

"Um, hi. I'm— I'm Diggory," he mumbled, casting a speculative glance at the waiting table.

Charlie wasn't one for theatrics. A simple white tablecloth was draped over her dining table with a long-stemmed white candle nursed in a silver cradle in its centre. She kept a lily growing in a ceramic pot on the nearby mantelpiece; the fireplace below it had long been boarded up. Wood was a luxury she could not, or rather, decided not to afford, and the open chimney had let in the biting winter chill.

"It's lovely to meet you, Diggory." She held out her hand for him, but he released it just as quickly as he accepted it. "Please, have a seat."

Settling in one of the dining chairs, his jacket bunched at the sides as he fumbled awkwardly with the buttons, a simple task made seemingly impossible with trembling fingers. Managing at last, he ran a hand over his mouth, a five o'clock shadow bristling audibly.

Charlie sat, arms on the table with hands facing upwards, ready to receive what needed to be told. It wasn't necessary to do this, but it saved her worrying about what to do with her hands.

"Is there someone you're hoping to talk to tonight, Diggory?" she asked, knowing the answer.

He nodded briefly, not meeting her eyes. He pursed his lips and swallowed, searching for words that seemed to elude him.

"He doesn't look good, does he?" a strong, clear woman's voice came from behind her. "I've never seen him like this."

"What's your name?" Charlie asked without turning around.

"Nadine. I was meant to be Nadine Lambert in a couple of weeks, but fate had other plans."

"Nadine is here," she told Diggory gently, with the tone of someone soothing a cowering animal. Even so, his face crumpled and his breathing hitched. "She says she was meant to be Nadine Lambert in a couple of weeks. Were you... engaged?"

He nodded, chin sinking into his collar.

"This wasn't the path I imagined for us either," confessed the voice. "There's so much I have to say that I can't find the beginning..."

"Is there anything you'd like to ask, Diggory? Any questions you had for Nadine?"

"Heck, I don't— I don't know." He ran his hands over his head and looked up for the first time, searching the room with watery eyes. "Where is she?"

A tall woman, skin the colour of Saharan sand, stepped out from behind Charlie to caress Diggory's cheek with the back of her fingers. Curls the same dark, rich tone of black coffee radiated out from her face, a baby blue gown clinging to her slender frame. "I'm here, my love."

"She's right beside you," Charlie said, inclining her head slightly to where the woman stood, looking down on him with longing.

He started slightly and turned, searching the air for a sign of her presence. She lowered herself so they were eye to eye, her face a few millimetres from his, but all he saw was the peeling wallpaper. So close, and yet worlds apart.

"Did it hurt?" he asked finally, still staring at the empty space. "Was she in pain when she..."

"No, actually. It was the strangest thing. I saw the car— the headlights, actually, coming towards me in the dark. They were moving too quickly and I just knew I couldn't move in time. As soon as I had that thought, I was overcome with this surreal peace. Like a blanket of bliss had been draped over me.

"I felt the force on my body as it was separated from me. It was like my vessel was taken and I was still standing there, just as I had been."

Charlie relayed the monologue as she spoke, years of practice allowing her to speak while listening.

"I'm not sure what I was expecting. A tunnel of light, a chorus of angels, a golden bridge with pearly gates, even the River Styx. What I wasn't expecting was..." She frowned. "Nothing. I could still hear the traffic roaring past, the driver screaming for someone to call an ambulance. I could still feel the road under my feet, smell the food wafting from a nearby takeaway.

"The difference was, I no longer felt like it was gravity keeping me on earth. I had a new anchor, a rope running from my heart to his. From where I was, I could see him pressing a stethoscope to his patient's chest and asking if the pain was sharp or dull. I could feel his exhaustion and his weary feet. And I knew he couldn't wait to finish work and come home to me." The sadness rolled off her voice in waves as she ran a hand he couldn't feel tenderly over his head.

"That was the worst night of my life," she uttered softly. "I suppose I can't say that. The worst of my existence. I could feel his pain and knew I couldn't do anything to stop it. I had to watch him sob without being able to hold him. I had to listen to him call my mother without consoling him. I had to witness his nightmares take hold without being able to wake him."

Charlie did her best to relay her words, but this was a struggle even for her. The amount of pain in the room was growing like a heavy storm cloud and she was having trouble centring herself.

"There was so much we had to do," he murmured wetly. "She had so much life. She was the kind of person who walked into a room..."

"And all eyes turned to her," Charlie finished gently. Nadine looked at her for the first time, sad eyes softening in appreciation.

Diggory nodded. "She was beautiful, but also fiercely intelligent. I knew better than to argue with her because she could reduce me to a blubbering child." Charlie wasn't sure if he was really talking to her, or simply needing someone to hear his words. Either way, it didn't matter, her attention was his.

"I didn't deserve her. Neither did the world, though. The day that I met her, she came into the hospital with her mother. She wouldn't leave her side. She physically stood between us until I explained exactly what we were doing and why." He gave a wry smile. "It should have driven me mad. It made my job so much harder, but I couldn't even be annoyed with her. She had fire in her eyes and a bear in her chest. What hope did I have?"

Nadine tilted her head affectionately. "I didn't know what to make of him at first. I've never trusted doctors, but he was so patient with me. And he took such good care of Mum. In the end, I knew if I could trust him with her life then I could trust him with anything."

Charlie relayed the sentiment and added, "This person you're talking about, Diggory, still very much exists. She is still beautiful, if not more so, still intelligent, and she has more fire in her eyes when she looks at you than I've ever seen. Our bodies might die, but our souls never do."

The couple were silent for a few seconds, Nadine's hands resting on his.

"I wish I could talk to her, just one more time. Hold her. Hear her laugh. Tell her I'll— tell her I'll see her soon," Diggory whispered.

"You have no idea, my love, how hard it is seeing you but knowing you're beyond my reach," Nadine whispered in return.

Charlie's heart ached, blurring her judgement. She had an idea, one she knew she would spend the next few days paying dearly for, but in that moment, it didn't matter.

"Hudson," she called suddenly. "Hudson, could you come here for a moment, please."

They looked at her in indignation, assuming she was calling a stranger into their last goodbye.

"I'm sorry, I need some help with something. But I think you will appreciate it," Charlie reassured them as Hudson materialised.

"My lady?" He looked in surprise from her to them before comprehension dawned on his face. "I see."

Though she didn't expect Nadine to take advantage of her gesture, Hudson would make sure no such situation eventuated.

"Nadine," Charlie addressed her, voice clear. "I am going to step back from my body and allow you to take the steering wheel, as it were. I won't be able to sustain us both for longer than ten minutes at the most. Hudson is here just in case you... forget the time."

Nadine and Diggory looked at her with expressions of disbelief. "Are you— are you sure?" Nadine asked finally, casting a glance over the elderly ghost by her side.

"I do not do this often," Charlie confessed. "But I know a good reason when I see one."

With that, she settled back in her chair, clearing her mind and drawing into focus a white ocean she had come to know well.

Breathe in, 2, 3, 4, breathe out, 2, 3, 4, breathe in, 2, 3, 4, breathe out, 2, 3, 4.

A warm tingling spread first through her feet, moving its way up her torso and into her arms, before enveloping her head. Her eyes opened without her bidding, but she now looked up at Diggory as though she were at the bottom of a pool. She moved around the table and raised a hand to tenderly brush the side of his face. Charlie felt a rush of emotion that wasn't hers, and knew Nadine was revelling in being able to touch him.

"Nadine?" he asked timidly, hands twitching, desperate to hold his fiancé, even though she looked like a stranger.

"Yes, love."

He all but fell out of the chair as he flung his arms around her middle, the side of his face pressed into her stomach. All Charlie felt was a faint pressure, or perhaps she just knew what she should be feeling.

Nadine sank to her knees so they were face to face, her forehead and nose meeting his. Somehow, it still wasn't close enough. "It's been torture watching you but not being able to touch you or talk to you."

"I would gladly exchange all my other senses for the ability to see you again," he choked. "I miss you. I miss you so much I can't bear it."

"I know. I feel it too. But please believe I haven't left your side." She cradled his face in her hands. "The idea of leaving you isn't— I can't."

"I don't know how to be without you." His chin crinkled. "Nothing seems worth it anymore. I can't see the point. And the world has just carried on as though one of its brightest lights hasn't gone out. How does life just keep moving?"

She hushed him gently. "Everyone knows loss, my love. If they haven't met her yet, then they will. And if they don't, then that means they never knew love like we did. Mother told me once, 'grief is the price we pay for love'. And I know I am in debt for the love I shared with you."

Hudson cleared his throat, interrupting the emotional exchange. "I do apologise, but I believe it's now time for a final goodbye."

Watching from the bottom of her pool, Charlie was glad for Hudson's presence of mind. In spite of herself, she had become lost in the lovers' plight. The water suddenly seemed much denser than before, like a lake on a rainy day, and it was losing clarity rapidly.

"I'm sorry," Nadine said. Charlie knew this was addressed to her.

"Will you visit?" Diggory asked, pulling himself back to search a stranger's eyes for the woman he loved.

"All the time." She smiled, running both thumbs across his cheeks to clear the tears. She paused. "May I?"

Again, Charlie knew she was speaking to her. She closed her eyes in consent, though she could barely see the man before her as she sank steadily deeper into the misty abyss.

Nadine pulled Diggory's face to hers and held him in a chaste kiss, neither breathing, nor daring to move lest the moment end.

"I love you," he said at long last, holding her hand to his chest.

"I love you more," she said, cradling his head in her hand one last time, before stepping back and allowing Charlie to emerge, gasping for air.

Five

THE AGREEMENT

The following day passed in a blur of bedsheets, uncomfortable dreams of drowning and a thundering headache. Charlie emerged from her chrysalis periodically, only to force feed herself bread and butter at the insistence of Hudson.

While dying was relatively easy, being brought back was hard work – and that was exactly what had happened. By stepping back and allowing Nadine to take control, her soul had slipped into a waiting room. Any longer, and she may not have been able to re-enter her body at all.

While Nadine hadn't tried to suppress any of her vitals and her body remained in relatively good health, the tax on the mind and soul was incomparable to any hangover or bout of flu she'd encountered. As long as she sat comatose, she delayed her escape. Charlie knew quite well what she had been in for when she offered Nadine the driving seat, but she justified her temporary discomfort by knowing she'd provided two heartbroken souls with a few minutes to say goodbye.

The following evening, she had finally mustered the energy to make herself a cup of coffee, to which she added a liberal dash of milk and sugar to coax her body back to its former glory, when there was a tentative knock at the door.

She looked up at Hudson, who had been pensively considering the rooftops from her window, but he only raised his eyebrows. "Do you have an appointment?"

"Oh yes, I booked one while I was unconscious." She was taken aback by her own sarcasm as she moved to the door. It turned out she wasn't a 'morning' person, even when she woke at 5 o'clock in the evening.

Opening the door, she took one look at who was waiting on the other side, abruptly shut it again and returned to her chair.

"No, that's not a problem I'm dealing with today," she declared, raising her steaming cup.

Hudson stared at her. "Who is—" He was interrupted by another knock at the door. "Do you not think someone will notice him banging on your door?"

"I will say he is my nephew from out of town. No one has asked if I have— hold on, how do you know it's a 'he'?" Her eyes narrowed.

"Well, I— I, uh, looked," he spluttered.

"A second ago you said you didn't know." She rounded on him. Hudson wasn't telling her something and she felt a flare of irritation. What was he playing at?

"Would you like to tell me why my brother is, once again, at your apartment?" The familiar smell of grease wafted over her. *Heavens to Betsy.*

"I wouldn't have a clue why that child is at my door or how he knew where I lived. Do you, Hudson?" She turned her back on the grubby young man to look at his elderly, refined counterpart.

Hudson removed his hat and began turning it distractedly, his face falling like a puppy who had been scolded.

"You told him?" she asked, her pitch rising. "Hudson, why would you do that? How could you go behind my back like that? Did you think about the danger you're putting me in? Putting *him* in? Just, why? Why did you do it?"

"Who's the old man?"

She turned to the greasy intruder. "Don't be disrespectful. And what about you? Why didn't you tell the kid to stay the bloody hell away?"

He swayed slightly as she pinned him with a stare. She blinked, the room was swaying with him. This was all too much in her current state and she leaned back against the countertop.

"I tried," he said through gritted teeth. "He didn't listen to me in life and he definitely doesn't listen to me in death. What's the matter, are we boring you?" he asked sardonically as her head slipped back.

"No," she said, blinking away the darkness which was rapidly threatening to engulf her. "No, I'm just— I'm fine."

"I think that's a bit of an overstatement," he muttered under his breath.

"Charlie, you cannot leave the child standing in the hallway any longer," Hudson cut in. "I believe it wise that you speak to Wynn yourself."

"Oh, you even know his name," she mumbled, pushing herself from the counter and making for the front door. Her vision swam and suddenly the floor was rising to catch her.

"Why did you even let her do it in the first place?"

"Young man, she is hardly mine to control."

"It's not about being controlling, it's about looking after her."

"If you had any inkling of what this young lady has already experienced in her short life, you would know she needs no looking after."

"Clearly."

Charlie lay still, wondering why her head was pounding and there were men bickering around her. With an internal groan of humiliation, she remembered; she had fainted.

Dimly recollecting where she had fallen, she was aware her face should have been pressed into the worn floorboards with her limbs unceremoniously splayed around her. Rather, she was nestled somewhere quite comfortable with a warm cloth across her forehead.

Despite her stirring, her would-be knights were too preoccupied to notice.

"You're just lucky we were here."

"In fact, sir, you being here is the very reason she took ill."

She considered continuing to pretend she was out cold, but the thought of listening to them for much longer was more than she could handle.

"And I daresay it's not the first time you've heard that," she quipped, blinking against the weight of her heavy eyelids.

Hudson, Wynn and the young man in stained overalls looked down at her in surprise. The view, she realised, was not dissimilar to the one she would have from her coffin – a notion that was a little more than disconcerting.

"Oh, look at that. She's alive and still has that delightful sense of humour," the greasy man commented.

"Do you have a name? I'm sure I can give you one that's rather apt," she asked, gingerly hoisting herself up on her forearms to lean back on the bony arm of the lounge.

He smirked. "Call me Rhett."

"Rhett? Like the noise a cat makes before it throws up?" She couldn't help herself.

"Actually, it's Welsh, you uncultured—"

"Must we continue with this frivolous to and fro?" Hudson interjected before Rhett could finish his sentence.

Though Hudson entertained Charlie's well-meaning banter now and again, he was an old fashioned ghost who removed himself from unnecessary conflict and believed the discourse between a man and a woman should be polite and chivalrous. Neither of which could be said about the conversation between Charlie and Rhett thus far.

Reluctantly, Rhett closed his mouth and folded his arms over his broad chest, looking at Hudson expectantly.

"Thank you." The wise, elderly man sighed deeply. "Charlie, are you alright?"

"Yes," she said, rubbing her head at the point it had evidently collided with the floor. "It seems my body has a convenient off-switch when it senses bull—," Hudson cleared his throat and she bit her tongue.

Instead, she eyed Wynn who, although tall for his age, had the muscle tone of a stick insect. "Who lifted me onto the lounge?"

Both Wynn and Rhett lifted a hand to point at Hudson who bowed his head, eyes fixed on the floor.

"I didn't know ghosts could move people," Wynn said excitedly. "I've seen some of them move little things, like a pen or a book, but not a whole person!"

"Hudson is a very old spirit." Charlie eyed the old man with respect. "The longer ghosts spend on earth, the stronger they become. But ghosts can wear themselves out, too, and would do well to remember that."

"What do you mean? How do they wear themselves out? Aren't they immortal?" Wynn's eyes were almost bulging out of his head.

Charlie sighed wearily. "Yes and no. Ghosts have an energy supply, like a lightbulb, in a way. They need to rest after expending themselves. If they exhaust themselves completely, their time is up."

"Indeed." The elderly gentleman shuffled his feet uncomfortably. "Well, it needed to be done. However, Wynn was also of great help and has been tending to you." He motioned to the damp cloth she was now wiping her eyes with.

"Thank you, Hudson. And thank you, Wynn," she added, somewhat reticently. "So, can someone please explain to me why Wynn is here?"

"That is because of me," Hudson confessed. "I was on my daily stroll, passing the downstairs cafe, when I saw you walking on the opposite pavement. Perhaps 'walking' is the wrong word, it was more of a stomp," he added humorously, but quickly continued when he glanced at her indignant expression.

"I was on the verge of approaching you to see what concerned you when I noticed you were being followed. Granted, it was only by this young chap," he gestured to Wynn, "but I decided on a closer inspection and was most surprised when he asked who I was.

"After introducing myself, inconspicuously, of course, he told me what happened in the cemetery. And I must say, I believe you acted too hastily," he said with the fatherly tone he adopted when he thought Charlie had made an error of judgement.

Strong, independent, fearless woman though she was, her eyes fell to the floor under his austere disapproval.

"It was not too long ago that you found yourself alone and fending for yourself in a dangerous city. You were fortunate you were taught the fundamentals. You knew how to navigate a world where your gift was considered a liability. Even so, you lost your way. Need I remind you, you have not needed to resort to picking pockets since you started receiving guidance." He peered at her with sparkling eyes.

She flushed, glancing at Wynn and Rhett who appeared simultaneously surprised and impressed.

"My point is, Wynn is quite like how you were then, ill-equipped to survive this world on his own. It will also be tremendously beneficial for you to mentor another Seer. You will hone your craft in ways you did not expect possible. When I have experienced doubt regarding which way to guide you, I have asked myself what your mother would have wished. And I think you know what she would have to say on this matter."

His words lodged in Charlie's brain like pins in a seamstress's cushion. She emulated her mother in more ways than one, with a fire in her soul, a sword for a tongue and an iron-clad will. Both Charlie's mother and grandmother had believed in protecting their own kind – not Seers specifically, but those who believed death wasn't the end, that there was a larger purpose than to serve the State. Those people offered pinpricks of light and hope in an otherwise grey and hostile world.

She sighed, realising there was really no choice to be made.

"Fine," Charlie agreed grudgingly, but before she had a chance to continue, Wynn had thrown himself at her, wrapping his scrawny arms around as much of her as the lounge allowed. Awkwardly, she patted the back of his head.

"Do I get a say in any of this?" Rhett's tone was petulant. Wynn disentangled himself and the three of them turned to stare at him.

"I mean, okay. Fine. But you bloody well better keep him safe. And you'll be seeing a hell of a lot more of me than you'd like to. I'm watching you." He obviously intended his tone to be menacing, but Charlie was more intimidated by the mildew in her bathroom.

She rolled her eyes. "Well, I must beg your pardon but this evening's festivities have been quite enough for now. Boy— Wynn, I mean, I'll see you here after school tomorrow. If anyone asks who you are, you're my nephew from out of town. Do you understand?"

Wynn nodded excitedly. "Yes! I won't tell anyone. What are you going to teach me? Can you show me how to let one possess me? What about banishing? Have you ever made a ghost really angry?"

Charlie raised an eyebrow at Hudson who smiled down at her with genial charm. *Jerk.*

Having made sure the hallway was clear, Charlie ushered Wynn out her door and bid Hudson a good evening. She turned to see Rhett still standing in her living room. "Oh, why are you still here?"

He pinned her with a discerning stare. "Is what the old man said true?"

"His name is Hudson," she chastised, "and what exactly did he say?"

His eyes flicked around the room as though he were looking for the words. "About you stepping back so the young couple could... say goodbye."

"Oh, erm.. Yes," she mumbled self-consciously.

He looked at her appraisingly for a few seconds and Charlie caught herself admitting that he was better looking without a dour frown rumpling his features. Stubble trickled across a strong jawline and meandered into his dark tousled hair. His blue eyes, now they were fixed on her, made her oddly uncomfortable.

"You might be a better person than I thought," he admitted, evaporating before she had a chance to reply.

Wynn dropped his school bag to the floor with as much noise as a small explosion. He was the picture of a dishevelled schoolboy, cheeks pink and hair windblown. His tie had blown over his shoulder and one side of his shirt had become untucked from his trousers. He had obviously run there.

"Did you see anyone on your way up here?" Charlie smoothed the tablecloth under her palms.

He shook his head, a little bit too enthusiastically, like a water-logged dog. "No. I ran really fast, just in case."

"Perfect," she rolled her eyes. "I'm sure that won't arouse suspicion. Come, sit." She gestured to the chair at the other side of the table.

"Is this where you See?" he asked, the chair squealing on the floor-boards as he took a seat.

"Yes, I choose not to partake in unnecessary showmanship. I feel it demeans my— I mean, *our* abilities. What kind of Seer would I be if I needed crystals and tarot cards?" she asked, and then nodded towards her lily. "She's the only thing I choose to keep. Lilies are a symbol of hope and rebirth – the spiritual continuum."

Wynn looked on in wonder. "Does it do anything? Can you use it to bring people back to life or something?"

"I wish." Charlie looked at the plant fondly. "She just helps keep me centred. And she's good company."

He frowned. "But she doesn't say anything?"

"Exactly. Now, what do you think our job as a Seer is?" She quickly steered them back on topic.

"Umm... to help people talk to the people they've lost?" he answered without conviction.

"Yes, but there's more to it than that." She stared at her hands pensively for a few seconds, fiddling with the silver band she wore on her pinky. "It can be disheartening to be a Seer; to know that there is more to life but to live in a world which refuses to believe in it."

She detected a familiar whiff of engine oil and knew Rhett was listening in.

"We are candles in the dark. It often feels like we are the only sources of light in the world and that continuing to burn is pointless. People try to snuff us out in fear and ignorance; we could cast light on something they want to remain hidden in darkness.

"All walks of people are drawn to light, some are hopeful, others inspired, but not all of them are well-intentioned. It can be terrifying," she told Wynn honestly. Charlie saw little point in sheltering the boy from the truths of the life that had chosen him.

"But while there is darkness, it is your responsibility to shine, lest the world fall into darkness completely. Fire creates fire, and candles light other candles. Once you create light, it is your duty to keep it burning for as long as you can."

Wynn's face was slack and, though his eyes were trained on her, she felt like he wasn't seeing her anymore. "Have I scared you?"

He swallowed and the hint of an Adam's apple bobbed in his throat. "No, I just hadn't thought of it that way."

"Seeing is much more than talking to the dead to find out where Aunt Marge hid the inheritance," she quipped, recalling the countless widows who had come to her asking if there were any hidden fortunes. "It's about hope, and the idea that our existence doesn't end in servitude of the State. It's about love, and ties so strong you can't be separated by different states of being.

"Some people will come to you for the wrong reasons, looking for money, revenge, and some may vilify you. You must remember it is an indication of their standing as a person and not yours. Be clear in your purpose and you'll find nothing can shake you. Questions?"

"What's the hardest part for you? Do you ever get scared?" Wynn asked with the glorious innocence of youth.

"All the time," Charlie answered truthfully. "This is the scariest thing you will ever do. You see both sides of humanity; the beautiful and the awful. You saw me yesterday," she cringed internally at the memory she'd rather repress, "and that was after one of the beautiful."

Wynn's already fair skin paled a shade and Charlie couldn't help but chuckle. "You will not need to do anything like that for a long time. You don't ever need to, if you don't want to. Recognise your boundaries and respect yourself enough to stick to them."

He nodded slowly. "I wanna help people, though. If I can. Losing someone is the worst feeling in the world." His age showed in that moment, a heartbroken little boy who had lost his big brother, and couldn't turn to his parents for comfort, or even acceptance.

"I'm sorry," she said gently. "It's a rough hand you've been dealt. I don't think many kids your age would have handled it nearly as well as you have."

"Yeah, well, what else am I gonna do?" he shifted in his chair, clearly uncomfortable with the attention. "I'm kinda lucky though, still being able to see him and talk to him. For however long he decides to hang around, anyway."

"He clearly cares for you very much." Her voice was sincere.

"Yeah." Wynn's face split into a grin. "The two of us together were a nightmare. As soon as I could walk, I'd do just about anything he told me to. Got into so much trouble because of him. But he was always on my side when I needed him to be. Always knew what I needed before I did."

"How long ago did he pass?" she asked carefully, not sure of the response she would receive.

"Just over a year, year and a bit. It's weird 'cause I'll be upset and miss him, and then I'll look up and he's there. But he's also still not really there, you know." He pulled the tennis ball out of his pocket and began turning it like an oracle's orb. "It's hard knowing what to feel."

"I know what you mean." She wasn't terribly good at this, in spite of the countless people she had sat opposite while they poured their hearts out. Charlie was the voice of the dead and was perfectly capable of relaying messages. But going off script and speaking from her own heart, that was a different skill set.

"I know I'm old and bitter, but I lost my mother when I was young. My grandmother raised me after that and I lost her a few years ago, too. They were my whole family. I guess I just want you to know that I understand your pain, and if you want to talk about it I'm here."

Even though she'd spoken quickly and gruffly, she knew the sentiment wasn't lost on Wynn. She glanced up from her fiddling hands and saw it in his eyes.

"Thank you," he said and meant it.

"Right," Charlie said loudly, abruptly fracturing the emotion which permeated the air like thick smoke. "I think that's enough for today. Where have you told your parents you are?"

"I told them I started taking after school Enlightenment studies," he said with a smirk.

"A good excuse, but do you know enough about the Enlightenment to talk about it if they ask you?"

He produced a red cloth-bound book from his bag. It bore gold imperial lettering across its front; '1850 to 1950: Humanity's Journey to Life's True Purpose'. "I've been reading this during lunch. It's kind of interesting, how there used to be churches and mosques and people used to pray out in the open, like a different world."

"It was," Charlie agreed. Her grandmother had often told her what it was like before the Enlightenment. She had lived through the decision of the world's powers to outlaw religion or worship of any kind, with the view it caused disharmony, distracted the masses from contributing to the global community, and that so called scientists had conclusively disproved the existence of an afterlife or deities.

Free will had been taken from millions, hope had been stolen from all, and lives of thousands had been lost. To hear it described as 'kind of interesting' was a grave injustice.

"I'll see you tomorrow, Wynn."

Six

THE GENTLEMAN

"In light of recent reports of incendiary activity, the State will be conducting random inspections over the coming weeks. Chief Enforcer Gerard Barron has assured law-abiding citizens there is no cause for concern. The inspections will be conducted by trained enforcement personnel to maintain safety and order in the city. Enforcement urges anyone with information regarding incendiary religious activity to call the informant hotline..."

Charlie's feet were glued to the sidewalk outside Polk Brothers, watching as the news anchor signed off and cut to an advertisement for Sugar Smacks. A small crowd had gathered alongside her to watch the announcement and she held her face carefully to conceal the jolts of panic shooting through her abdomen like electricity.

"It's about time," said a burly woman to her moustached husband. "They never should have stopped doing inspections. You only have to turn a blind eye for a moment and they're swarming like rats."

There were similar murmurings as the group dispersed, leaving Charlie staring back at her own reflection in the shop window beneath a large red and white banner declaring 'COOL INSIDE, IT'S AIR CONDITIONED'.

I don't look like an incendiary, she attempted to calm herself. *How stupid – what does an incendiary even look like?*

Without conscious thought, her legs began to walk as her thoughts spiralled. The client book and her savings were safely hidden, her dining table was just a dining table. She didn't own a telephone, in part because she couldn't afford one, but also so unexpected callers wouldn't unwittingly incriminate her. She was far too careful to be caught.

But Charlie also knew she wouldn't be able to teach Wynn at her apartment anymore. She would have to tell him that day. She prayed he would remember that he was her nephew from out of town and actually deliver the line convincingly if the need arose.

She wouldn't be able to See anymore – not in her apartment, and there was nowhere else as safe. How would she make money? Despite being tantalisingly close to leaving and starting her new life, she may have to dip into her savings if she couldn't take clients. This could set her plans back months, perhaps longer, depending on how long the inspections continued.

A huge object was suddenly blocking her path and she stumbled in an effort to prevent herself from colliding with it. Fred? She blinked in surprise, casting a furtive glance around to discover she had ended up in the stairwell of her building.

"Are you daft, girl?" He smoothed down his shirt over an extended belly. "You'd do well to watch where you're going. Or maybe you were trying to run into me, eh?"

Charlie fought her facial muscles to prevent them from contorting in revulsion. When Fred wasn't drunk, he thought himself a charismatic Casanova. At least, that's what the *filles de joie* on Parlour Street probably told him.

"Sorry, Fred." She forced a smile. "I really should watch where I'm going. You're obviously off somewhere, so I won't hold you up."

"Oh actually, I've been meaning to ask you." He put a meaty hand on her shoulder as she made to move past him. "Have you seen that boy that's been hanging around lately? Little scrawny kid, looks like he's from a yuppy, uptown family. Probably some private school larrikin looking for trouble. I reckon I'll report him. Don't want any of his friends turning up with him."

"No, no, there's no need for that," Charlie blurted. "I'm so sorry. I didn't realise he was bothering anyone. He's actually my nephew from out of town."

"Your nephew?" Fred's beady eyes narrowed. "I didn't know you had a nephew."

"Yes, it's the first time he's staying with me." Charlie's aptitude for deception rose quickly to the fore, inflecting her voice with as much conviction as she could muster. "My sister lives in the country, but she thought some city schooling would do him good." She also didn't have a sister, and her apartment was barely big enough for herself and Hudson. And Hudson didn't exactly have much luggage.

"I see," Fred drew out the word slowly, sounding like a keening donkey. "You don't look much alike. You're much easier on the eye. I'll bet he's not complaining about staying with his comely aunt."

Charlie swallowed the bile. "You're too kind, Fred. Now, I must go and start dinner as he'll be home from school soon."

"Ey, are you still doing that laundromat service?" He blocked her path again.

"Yes, I am," she replied curtly.

Charlie's standard anecdote when asked about her occupation was that she offered a specialty laundry service for expensive garments. The care that was required in cleaning such items warranted a hefty price, which explained why she only had a person or two a day visiting her apartment.

"I'll bring up a few things for you later, then. I like my trousers pressed well and my jackets crisp. I have to uphold my visage, afterall." He gestured towards his body, as if his gut wasn't threatening to burst through the last hole on his belt. "Dot just doesn't do the same job she used to. I guess I've been too kind to her, she's let her duties slip. Maybe I need to remind her where she'd be without me." His bulbous face produced an ingratiating smile.

"Thank you for thinking of me. I do have a few garments which need my attention at the moment so I may not have time for a little while," she mumbled vaguely.

He guffawed and pinched her cheek. "I know you'll make time for me, sweet cheeks."

With that, he finally took his leave – Charlie quietly simmering with anger and revulsion behind him.

She knew better than to cause a scene. Women had only recently received the right to vote and the world was still very much in the pocket of men.

Fred was no one of any societal significance, an accountant at a small brokerage firm. But his words held more weight than those of a single twenty-one-year-old laundry wench. Unwed, parentless and, for the most part, friendless, she knew she was easy prey.

Dot may have lost sight of her 'duties', but she probably hadn't lost sight of why she married the man; security, to be cared for in a society where she otherwise would be ignored. Although she had never spoken more than a few words to Dot when passing in the stairwell, Charlie's heart bled for the woman and the half-life she endured.

Charlie was an incendiary floating under the radar of a totalitarian regime. Slapping Fred in the face would provide temporary satisfaction, but likely also sabotage any hope of her slipping out of the city like a stealthy fox from the chicken coop.

"You can't come here anymore," Charlie informed Wynn abruptly as he once again dropped his school bag unceremoniously inside the front door.

To her surprise, he nodded. "I know. But there must be somewhere else we can go, isn't there?"

"I have to find somewhere, but I don't have many options. I need somewhere I can continue Seeing that won't draw attention." She ran a hand through her hair. "Lucky the city isn't crawling with people who want me dead."

"You could use my shop." Charlie had become accustomed to people appearing behind her, but she still jumped internally at the male voice by her ear.

She turned slowly to give him a withering stare. "Must you?"

"Sorry." He gave her a half-smirk. Her heart palpitated strangely. "But my shop's just been sitting there since... well, I died. I don't think ma and pa know what to do with it."

"That's a great idea!" Wynn chimed in. "No one's ever going to come looking 'round there."

Charlie was nonplussed. "Your shop? As in a mechanic shop? What am I supposed to do, ask them to pull up a seat in the back of a Chevy?"

"No," Rhett answered sheepishly. "We definitely never worked on a Chevy..."

Charlie saw the back of her head.

"Hey, I'm trying to help you here," he countered. "Yes, there are parts everywhere and the place probably needs a good sweep at this point, but there's a lunchroom with a table. The doors lock and there's no foot traffic in that part of town. Which, come to think of it, is probably why business never really took off," he mused.

"So, who owns the place now?"

"Our parents, I guess. Everything in my name would have gone to them. It wasn't like I was old enough to think I needed a will."

"What are the neighbouring buildings?"

"A storage facility and an industrial laundromat."

At this, Charlie's ears perked up. If she was ever stopped or questioned, the laundromat would tie in perfectly with her cover business.

"Let's have a look at it then."

It was indeed the last place on earth anyone would willingly visit. A dilapidated structure, making no attempt to lift the low aesthetic standards set by its neighbours, sat like a sleeping toad at the very end of an industrial culdesac.

While it had only gone unused for a year or so, the building was already showing signs of decay. The front entrance and garage door were the same shade of forget-me-not blue, the paint peeling in places like skin after a bad sunburn.

Bold red lettering spelled the word 'AUTO' across the building's face and a bird had evidently made its nest in the U's hospitable curve. Even in the fading light, Charlie could still make out a trail of ancient oil stains spilling over the driveway and out onto the bitumen.

To its left was another hulking monstrosity, with doors that looked like they could only be coaxed open with a bulldozer. On the right was a complex not much smaller than the garage, though much cleaner and well kept. The turquoise green sign on its front read 'CHEMICAL CLEANING' in red lettering, with a smaller sign below it advertising a job vacancy.

"Well, this is it," Rhett announced unnecessarily. Charlie noticed a tremor in his voice. She wasn't sure if he expected her immediate rejection, or perhaps he was maudlin, confronted with the remnants of a lost dream.

They approached the front door, Wynn bringing up the rear, and the handle yielded under Charlie's grip. The building woke from its slumber with a gentle creak. A makeshift counter of corrugated iron and a bumper bar stood immediately in front of them, the space behind large enough to have comfortably housed four cars at a time. She turned, looking for a light switch.

"Here," Rhett volunteered, knowing what she was after. Long, low-hanging fluorescent beams begrudgingly flickered to life.

The inner walls were a naked timber framework with mismatched shelves drilled in without any discernible pattern. Car parts littered the perimeter and a gantry hoist stood in the centre, soft with cobwebs but waiting dutifully for when it would again be needed.

Signs adorned the wall to her right, advertising 'PREMIUM MOTOR TUNE-UPS' and 'LET US RESTORE NEW CAR PERFORMANCE FOR YOU'.

Charlie's footsteps echoed as the garage swallowed her whole. There was still paperwork strewn across the front desk. She thought she could make out Rhett's name among the signatures. An awareness dawned on her that Rhett had spent the final years of his life here. He had not only worked here, but owned and run this place. At one point in time, he had taken a leap of faith and invested his life's savings into this unassuming little shop.

Images flickered through her mind; Rhett lifting the heavy garage door at first light, brewing a morning coffee and surveying the cars in his care for the day. His customers would have respected his commitment and recognised his passion, handing over their keys with the sure knowledge their automobile would be returned to them in better condition than when they left it. How satisfied he must have felt when they shook his hand for a job well done, grease stains be damned.

What else could she feel other than humble gratitude for him offering to share it with her?

"I know it's not pretty, but it's a safe place. Just needs a sweep and a bit of a dust," Rhett admitted, swatting at a cobweb and nodding with satisfaction when it came away with his energy.

"The kitchen is out the back."

The three of them made their way to a door at the back of the shop, labelled 'EMPLOYEES ONLY'. This one was more reluctant to grant her entrance and Charlie put her shoulder into the wood. She'd worn an old burgundy sweater that day and wasn't overly attached to it.

With a protesting scrape, the door grudgingly complied, giving way to a small but cosy lunch area. The floor was a checkered pattern of weary red and white linoleum. A small kitchenette complete with a fridge and duck-egg green microwave oven huddled in the corner. A few cups and plates still leaned precariously on the drying rack, a family of arachnids now calling them home. An unvarnished circular table took ownership of the room with a few plastic lawn chairs scattered around it.

The place had evidently remained untouched since Rhett's death, and Charlie wondered what it was like for him seeing the remnants of his former life exactly as he'd left it. She glanced sideways at him and watched as his eyes wandered over the abandoned space. Whatever emotions he felt, he was keeping carefully guarded behind a blank expression.

"This is weird," Wynn commented, opening the fridge and promptly retching in revulsion when he found a few items had been forgotten.

"Is my baloney sandwich still good?" Rhett asked playfully.

"Yeah, dare you to eat it," Wynn replied, holding his nose.

"Nah, might kill me." The two chortled.

"So, what do you think, Charlie?" Wynn looked up at her with bright eyes.

Charlie bit her lip. The place needed a thorough clean, there was no doubt about that, but the task wasn't beneath her. It was quiet and the windows still wore their drapes, shielding them from prying eyes. The table would give you splinters just by looking at it, but a tablecloth would fix that.

The tram line's last stop was an easy two streets away, so it wouldn't be difficult for her to get here. And, she reminded herself, the cleaning business next door was an excellent decoy if ever the need arose.

"I think this will do nicely," she announced finally and couldn't help but smile too when the brothers grinned at each other.

A sickle moon was hanging in the night sky as Charlie fumbled for her keys at her apartment door. An eerie, insipid light leaked in from the one small window at the end of the hall. The light had been out for months.

Home sweet home, she thought bitterly, kicking off her boots inside the front door and shrugging out of her sweater. Being on the top floor of the complex, it was often unforgivingly stuffy, even during the colder months.

Kitchen window open, a cool breeze swept her hair back from her face. Her would-be escape route from the city was laid out before her. She could drop her bag out of the window onto the neighbouring roof and use a sheet to shimmy herself down – or perhaps two, to be safe. From there it would be an easy jump from rooftop to rooftop until, finally, she would be free of the city's confines.

The plan was to stay in farmhouses on her journey from the city. Once she was far enough away and found a house that felt like it might be home, she would offer the owner cash in hand to part with his property. He would probably say no and she would move on, until she found one that said yes. And there would be no need to involve real estate agents or legal services.

A deed would be signed, her new life would be hers, and not a soul would know. There would be no neighbours leering at her, no paranoia that someone would notice her talking to the air, no old, grungy apartment which she couldn't even decorate because it belonged to someone else; just freedom.

"Thinking about doing a runner?" a voice from behind her asked.

Again, she squashed her internal jump but didn't need to turn to find out who it was; she knew the voice well enough by now.

"Did you miss me already?"

"Terribly," Rhett chided, coming to stand at the window beside her. "I just wanted to make sure you got home safely."

"How chivalrous," she remarked, but the gesture sent a ripple of nerves through her stomach. That was unwarranted, she admonished herself.

Yet she was painfully aware of their proximity as they stood there together, looking out at a city that had disappointed them both. He still smelled like grease, but there was an undertone of something else, was it coffee? Her head only came up to his muscle-bound shoulder, and she knew he must have been a strong, imposing man in life.

Though her head knew it was ridiculous, in her heart she felt safer being there with him than she had in years. She started when she felt his skin prickle against hers. "I didn't know if I'd be able to do that," he said with a sheepish smile.

"Do what?"

"Touch you."

Against her will, their eyes locked for a few seconds, his expression still frustratingly guarded. His skin still looked dewy, perhaps from the work he had been doing when he died. Most girls would have killed to have his unfairly thick eyelashes. His tongue darted out to wet his full lips.

She cleared her throat abruptly, turning back to the kitchen and breaking the rapidly escalating tension. What was going on?

"Wynn's very lucky to have a brother like you," she blurted out. It was the first thing that came to her mind.

Rhett blinked, apparently centring himself as well. "I reckon we're lucky to have each other. It's a tough world, tougher for some," he said, seeming to acknowledge the hands they had both been dealt. "Our parents are pretty strict, not really the type of people who tell you to follow your dreams when they tuck you in at night. I guess most of the time it only felt like we had each other."

"That must have made dying so much harder," she commented, before realising how stupid she sounded. "I mean, it's unfair enough to die so young, let alone when a child sees you as their world."

"Yeah, I guess that's why I was grateful for his gift. After all the years I spent resenting the world for giving it to him. I always told him to keep it quiet. He could have his ghostly friends but no one else could know about them. He tried to tell Pa once," his voice lowered in pitch, "gave him a bigger backhand than he'd ever given me. That's including the time I tried to take his car for a drive when I was twelve."

"I'm sorry," she whispered. She had often lamented having grown up without a father, wondering what sage advice she hadn't been privy to or if she would have learnt how to stop the dripping tap in her bathroom. But stories like that reminded her that having a whole family was not the same as having a happy family.

"Not your fault," he said lightly, now leaning against the windowsill with the night air licking at his hair.

"No, but sometimes being sorry is more than an apology. It's an acknowledgement that something bad happened to someone that didn't deserve it. I wish I had known you earlier." A flush rose to her cheeks when she heard herself babbling. "I mean, just so you wouldn't have had to go through that alone."

He surveyed her for a few seconds and she fought to retain her composure under his gaze. "You're very unexpected, Charlie."

"How so?"

"People usually say that they wish something hadn't happened to you, that they could erase the incident and your pain with it. But I've never wished it hadn't happened. It did, and that's that. It's made my little brother stronger, and the bad is as much a part of life as the good. Funnily enough, all I wanted at the time was someone I could talk to, someone I could trust without burdening Wynn."

Ordinarily, these types of conversations made Charlie uncomfortable at best, but talking to the man before her was easier than breathing.

"I know what you mean," she replied softly. A few seconds of silence stretched before them, but it wasn't the tense, uncomfortable silence someone was expected to fill. She found she enjoyed him just being there, and got the impression he felt the same way.

Seven

THE GARAGE

Dear Sir/Madam,

As one of our valued clients, we are writing to inform you that our laundromat service has relocated to 11, 63rd Street.

We feel the new premises will allow us to better meet your needs and continueproviding an exceptional level of service.

While there is ample road parking available, it is also close to the Western Ave tram stop, should you prefer to take advantage of public transport.

You may continue making bookings as per usual.

Kind regards,

C.H.

Charlie folded the last of the letters and addressed the envelope to the final name on her list, Mrs A. Durrigan.

She couldn't afford a home telephone, a luxury only enjoyed by wealthier families. A telephone, while convenient, could also be used as evidence against her if anyone else was present when a client called. Should clients wish to make a booking, they were to leave a note with their abbreviated name and preferred date and time in her mailbox. Notes had to be hand delivered, and the inclusion of Charlie's details would prevent them from using her services again. The notes were then to be burned at the soonest possibility.

Bookings were made at least one week in advance, and, should their booking conflict with another, Charlie would leave a new proposed time in their mailbox. If they heard nothing, the booking was confirmed. Clients were usually referred through word of mouth and were familiar with the procedure before their first appointment, but Charlie reminded them regularly regardless.

Her letterbox route through the city would take a few hours, but it was a blue-skyed morning and she was happy to be able to allow her coat a day of reprieve.

Charlie quietly relished the opportunity to visit the city's nicer suburbs and pretend, albeit briefly, that she too lived in one of the perfect pastel homesteads with manicured lawns and a coupe in the driveway.

Passing a couple of women in well-pressed frocks and sunhats, she smiled pleasantly at them as they glanced from her worn loafers to the dated brown satchel she clutched protectively to her midsection. Prompt whispering began as soon as they were behind her, but she didn't waste energy wondering what they had said. A 'penny pincher' was hardly the worst thing she could be called.

Having left mid-morning, the pathways were pleasantly empty of school children and workers. Out of habit, she listened to the sound of her own footsteps through the symmetrical streets, altering her pace slightly now and then to listen for anyone who might be following her. A poster plastered on a bus stop leered at her; 'DEFEND OUR FREEDOM' it read, with an Abraham Lincoln look-alike straightening his red and white hat. The irony didn't escape her.

As she made her last delivery to the letterbox of an unassuming townhouse, perspiration was gathering on her brow and her feet were complaining loudly. Still, there was more work to be done.

Hands planted on her hips, she surveyed the dusty interior of Rhett's shop. The longer she looked, the more she found; mice droppings sprinkled among car parts like chocolate treats, the remnants of a bird that had found its way in but never out, an impressive spider's web which stretched from the corner of the ceiling to the hoist in the middle of the room.

This was fine, she assured herself, not believing it. She had three hours until Wynn was due to meet her there after school and she was determined to at least have somewhere they could sit.

In the kitchen closet she found her weaponry; a broom, torn rags, and a bucket. They would have to suffice. She dimly remembered having relished cleaning as a child, the idea she was saving her mother some hard labour. Dustpan in one hand and broom in the other, she had scuttled along the floor looking for dust and dirt, proudly presenting her findings to her mother once she was sure every corner was clear.

"What a fine job you've done, Charlie," she'd once said. "You'd make someone a fine wife – but you can be a lot more than that, if you want to."

Memories of those days were foggy at best, but her mother had always walked with a surreal kind of grace. When Charlie was much closer to the floor, she had watched her feet carefully, trying to determine if they actually touched the ground when she moved. She had a voice like running water and a way of gently commanding the attention of anyone in her presence.

Charlie rarely let herself entertain 'what ifs', but today she let herself imagine what might have been. Perhaps, together, they would have started a new life in the countryside, with a cow for milk they'd let die from old age, and chickens who would have the run of the yard. It was a far cry from where life had taken Charlie, sweeping bits of dead bird, mice droppings and who knows what else from her makeshift 'office'.

Running a broom over the gantry hoist in an effort to dislodge the reluctant arachnid residents, a broken chain clanged. It hung, pointing at an old stain on the floor which was not like the others. It had an ochre tinge and seemed to have been inhaled deeply by the concrete.

Perhaps a rug was in order.

The kitchen was its own beast. The taps seemed to scream in protest but, mercifully, they still gave water. Even after having wiped the table and chairs three times, the water in her bucket still ran black. Without gloves, a bin bag or a match and gasoline, she decided to ignore the looming presence of the fridge.

Muffled footsteps in the garage told her she was not alone and she waited cautiously for the kitchen door to swing.

"Wow, it looks so much better already!" Wynn's enthusiasm was infectious and, although Charlie would never admit it, it pleased her to have impressed him.

"It will do for now," she said, taking a seat on one of the kitchen chairs which had miraculously changed colour from a dark grey to a bottle green.

Rhett stepped in behind the boy, quietly surveying the freshened space with his usual guarded expression which gave nothing away.

"I guess you can clean," he commented in mock amazement. "Would never have guessed it from the state of your place."

She threw a sodden rag at his head, expecting it to pass through, but was taken off guard when he raised a hand and caught it. Rhett was clearly just as surprised, staring at the rag in awe before it finally fell through his fingers. He looked from his little brother to Charlie, seeking confirmation of what he had just done.

"Oh my gosh, that was so cool!" Wynn jumped in excitement.

"Impressive," Charlie concurred as she met his eyes. *Was that a blush?* "But if you're done showing off, we have work to do."

He nodded absently, looking down at his hands as though he'd just manifested gold, and evaporated quietly into the ether.

While Wynn was clearly familiar with communicating with spirits, he also needed to understand the rules by which they were bound. They may not abide by the laws of physics, but they were governed by another set of laws regulating their ghostly existence.

Charlie held up a woody twig she had procured on her walk. It had scaly overlapping leaves, which took on the appearance of the braids she'd worn in her hair as a schoolgirl. "What is this?" she asked Wynn.

He stared at her blankly. "Umm, a branch?"

"This is from a cypress tree," she said, handing it to him for closer inspection. "Cypress has long been used for its spiritual properties. The Egyptians made coffins out of its wood. A Persian legend says it was the first tree grown in paradise. To the ancient Greeks, cypress was the tree of mourning and sacred to the god Hades. Today's scholars believe its aromatic branches were used to mask the smell of death."

Wynn held the leaves to his nose. "It just smells like tree."

"Yes, fresh and sweet. Like a walk in the park on the first day of spring. Even ancient cultures knew it was a powerful plant, and it is the most important tool I can give you. I always keep a twig or two by the bed, just in case.

"Cypress presents a barrier to ghosts, a line that can't be crossed. Keeping some on your person will ensure you are safe. Placing some on their grave will prevent them from wandering at all. But," she asserted firmly, "you must never do so lightly. It's not a prank you should play on a ghost; none will ever find it funny. It should only be used when absolutely necessary, when attempts to help the spirit crossover have been unsuccessful, and when they are a danger to yourself or others. Do you understand?"

Wynn nodded, eyes wide. "Have you – have you ever had to use it?"

"No, and I hope never to have to do so."

"What happens?" he pressed.

"I might tell you one day, but it's not today." The look on her face told him further questioning would result in the cypress being lodged in his person, so he lapsed reluctantly back into silence.

"It's a common myth that spirits are trapped here due to unfinished business. That's not always the case. It's down to choice, actually. Obviously, if they have unfinished business, they're likely to want to hang around until it's resolved, but a ghost can choose to remain here for all kinds of reasons. Fear of the Otherside, wanting to be with their family, enjoying their new-found freedom." She paused. "We choose to move around in this world and they have just as much free will, if not more than we do. Once a spirit crosses over, though, it is almost impossible for them to come back."

"Did your mum and grandma stay?" Wynn interrupted.

Charlie stiffened. "No, they didn't."

"Why not?"

"I don't know," she answered bluntly.

"Oh." He pondered his hands for a few seconds. "They must have thought you didn't need their help anymore."

She knew he intended this as a compliment, or at least something kind to say. She appreciated the effort but he had no idea how it felt to be the last one left breathing in a family.

"I guess so," she tried to end the conversation. "I think that's enough for today, Wynn. It's been a long one for me."

"I can help you, you know," he said as he scooped his backpack onto his shoulders. "Ma always gets me to sweep and to polish the silverware at home. She says I'm really good at it."

Wynn's unconditional enthusiasm once again forced a smile to Charlie's face. "Thanks, Wynn. See you tomorrow."

The boy offered to wait while she closed up, but she insisted he make it home before dusk. It was also best no one saw them together, so she stuck her head out the front door, casting a furtive look down the street to make sure it was empty, before shooing him out.

In no hurry to return to her empty apartment, she let her eyes roll over the empty workshop. Charlie had only disturbed what was absolutely necessary; dead leaves no longer carpeted the floor, spider webs had been removed from the beams of the ceiling, and she had managed not to gag while bagging and disposing of the remnants of some small animal.

But she hadn't touched the memories, the things that still made it Rhett's. Her hand trailed over the book on the counter, a log of customers and the work to be done. The list came to an abrupt end halfway down the page. There was a boyish charm to the scrawl and, with one finger, she traced Rhett's writing.

"Thanks but we're not looking for a bookkeeper right now." Rhett appeared behind her and she quickly withdrew her hand like a child caught touching something they shouldn't be.

"Sorry, I shouldn't have-"

He laughed good naturedly at her bashful expression. "It's fine, I don't mind. Just don't pick on my spelling. I was never much interested in school."

Charlie shrugged. "Books can only teach you so much."

"Yeah, well, street smarts didn't get me far, did they?" He paced the room slowly, pausing to contemplate the broken hoist.

Her eyes flickered to the ochre stain beneath it when she had an awful realisation. "Is that how you...?"

He nodded, running a hand up one of the metal legs. "Yeah. I guess I should have been checking it more often. Had a car up here and I was underneath, checking the fuel line. I sat up to come out and the chain snapped clean in half. Broke my neck, messed my head up a bit, too. If I'd still been lying down, I probably would have been okay."

"I'm sorry." Unconsciously, Charlie had taken a few steps closer as he spoke.

He met her eyes, his face apathetic. "Just one of those things, isn't it? Was just my time."

"I don't think I could handle it as well as you have."

He waved a dismissive hand. "I didn't, not at first. You wake up thinking you have your whole life ahead of you. You've got plans to build your business, buy a house, find a nice girl, settle down." His eyes flickered to hers and she looked away shyly. "And the next thing you know, you're looking at your own mangled body."

"What did you do?"

"I'm glad no one could see the way I carried on. Tried to get back in a few times, but it didn't feel like my body anymore. It just felt like this meat glove. I spent a good couple of hours feeling sorry for myself, but then I realised I needed to tell Wynn before anyone else did. I thought he'd take it better if he knew I was still here. Maybe it messed him up more, the shock of seeing my ghost without warning. I don't know, there's no rule book for this stuff."

He was rambling but Charlie hung on every word, painfully aware he'd only had his little brother to talk to since he died. While she knew he loved Wynn dearly, there was only so much burden you could place on one person. She knew, because that was how she felt about Hudson.

"I still think you handled it as well as anyone could have."

He faced her again, his features softening under her gaze. "Thanks. You do what you gotta do."

There was a pregnant pause as they took each other in. Charlie thought she saw a twitch as he made to move forward and she broke the spell, sweeping a hand through her hair as she stepped away. "I'd better close up."

She glanced back, noting the disappointment in the set of his jaw. "Yeah, okay."

Turning for the kitchen, she hesitated for a moment before looking back at him. "But, if you're not busy I wouldn't mind some company walking home?"

His features lifted into a sly smile. "I guess I can fit you in."

Charlie wasn't used to walking the streets with a male companion — or any companion, for that matter. She noticed he walked purposefully on her left, between her and the road, as gentlemen should, to protect her from the dust and dirt of passing cars. Not that he would offer much shelter, of course, but she found the small gesture endearing.

For a little while, there was only the steady march of their shoes on the pavement as they made their way towards the bustle of the inner city. Charlie searched desperately for a topic of conversation and had the impression he was doing the same thing.

"Why do-"

"Who did-"

They spoke at the same time before laughing awkwardly. "Ladies first," he offered.

"I was just wondering, did you have any friends? I mean, of course you had friends." She blushed as he snorted. "But who were the main people in your life, besides Wynn?"

"I had a couple of friends I hung onto from school. Never really been a big friendship group sort of person, you know. No girlfriend," he added. Charlie stared determinedly at the ground.

"No one good enough for you?" she jibed.

"I did have an endless line of women throwing themselves at me." He ran a hand through his hair and grinned as Charlie laughed. "I don't know, I guess I just wasn't interested. Having Wynn for a brother, I had different priorities, you know? The girls were always worried about their dresses and who was taking who to the drive-in. And I was worried about keeping my little brother alive."

"I know what you mean. I was always jealous of the girls at school. Their lives seemed so easy. Look pretty, find a husband and have children. Just didn't feel like we were part of the same world."

"Have you ever... had someone?"

"Like a boyfriend? No. I think he'd notice my habit of talking to the walls soon enough. What would I say to them? '*I'm an instrument for connecting with the dead and, by the way, there is an afterlife and everything you've been told is a lie. What would you like for dinner, honey?*'"

"It doesn't roll off the tongue, does it?" He mused. "Why do you do it? See for people when it's so dangerous?"

"What other options do I have? We've already established I can't marry, which means I could scrub toilets for 25 cents an hour. Besides, it's rewarding. Being able to connect people with their loved ones, seeing the looks on their faces when they realise that they're there, it's worth the risk. The world needs more hope."

She felt his gaze on her face and she shot him a glance, tucking her hair behind her ear.

"That's very... brave."

"Yes, well, like I said, what options do I have?"

"Well, we don't get to choose what we're born. People can be born into anything, but what we do with it makes us who we are. If you were born with this incredible gift and wasted it playing housewife to some guy who doesn't deserve you, I'd tell you you were a wimp. But you risk your own life every day to change the world."

"I wish that were true," she admitted as they passed a parking garage and she performed a quick scan for onlookers. "But as soon as I have enough money, I'm leaving the city and finding a place of my own. A little private farmhouse, somewhere far away in the countryside where I won't have to spend my life looking over my shoulder or pretending I'm someone I'm not."

"Won't you be lonely?"

Charlie shrugged. "No lonelier than I am now. I'm surrounded by people everyday, yet I can't have an honest conversation with anyone. I have Hudson. He's the only person I need."

"What about me?"

"What about you?"

"Could I visit?"

"I can't exactly stop you, can I?" She stuck her tongue out at him.

They fell into an easy silence as they reached the corner of the main street. A few cars trundled by, presumably businessmen who were running late for dinner again. The wall beside the corner store bore a poster of a man grinning at her, his feet up and a cigarette in hand, declaring 'I'd walk a mile for a Camel'. The shop keeper, still in a white apron, was sweeping the pavement in front of his wares. He glanced up at her and Charlie reflexively ducked her head in a bid to avoid attention.

"I'd better make sure Wynn got home safely. I'll see you later, farmgirl."

Rhett disappeared, leaving Charlie smiling idiotically on the sidewalk.

A wave of disappointment washed over Charlie as she shoved her way into her apartment and found the only person waiting there for her was Hudson.

"I can see you are beside yourself with excitement to see me," he teased, but Charlie detected an undertone of rejection. "Someone has certainly been busy lately."

She fell into her couch, springs protesting violently beneath her. "I'm sorry, Hudson. Today has been long."

While he already knew about the random inspections, she explained Rhett's mechanic shop which offered both privacy and convenience.

"He's a bit prickly on the surface, but he's a good soul when he lets his guard down. He cares so much for his little brother and he's already learning how to channel his energy!" Noticing Hudson's growing smile, she clamped her mouth shut.

"It sounds like you have taken a liking to the boys." His eyes sparkled. "Perhaps one more than the other."

"Don't be absurd," she snapped. "He's not my type. And even if he was, it's not exactly going to end in a 'happily ever after', is it?"

"My dear, love and logic regrettably do not reside in the same house."

"Love?!" she scoffed. "I've only known the guy for a few days. Besides, it's not like we can— I'm not interested!" she insisted again, slamming her hand on the arm of the lounge as if to reprimand herself.

"Yes, obviously. Though it is amusing how you assumed which one I was alluding to." Hudson gave Charlie an infuriating smile, before mercifully changing the conversation. "How is Wynn as a student?"

"Eager." She ran a hand through her hair. "Very eager. I think it will be more of a challenge teaching him to rein it in rather than to use it."

Charlie had never been afforded the luxury of ignorance. She had become aware at a painfully young age what the consequences were if you were unable to conceal your abilities. When she looked at Wynn, she felt simultaneous jealousy and pity; jealousy of his rosy outlook on the world, pity that he would have to learn some harsh realities sooner rather than later.

"The young chap is lucky to have found you then," Hudson remarked, rising from his seat and straightening his coat. She wondered if he was aware he always completed this little leaving ritual, just before he was going to evaporate. Perhaps some of life's habits were harder to break than others.

"Lucky to have found you, you mean." She arched an eyebrow at him and he shuffled awkwardly.

"Ah, yes, I suppose so." He tipped his hat. "Good evening, my lady."

"Good evening, Hudson."

The hot shower was as welcome as rain after a long drought. She stood there for as long as she could justify the water bill, head down and hair hanging around her face in thick, dark tendrils. The heat stung but it was a kind of therapy, if not self-flagellation and a means of paying for her sins.

Thud, thud, thud.

Charlie started, snapped out of her reverie by heavy knocking. It was evening and she didn't have any clients. In any case, they should now know not to come to her apartment. Was it a random inspection?

Thud, thud, thud.

"Just a second," she called, quickly towelling herself off and throwing on the first clothes she came across; a light blouse and capris.

Breathing deeply, attempting to quell the growing anxiety in her stomach and relocate her heart from her throat to her chest, she opened the front door to find an unwelcome face smiling coyly back at her.

Eight

THE ACCIDENT

"Hello, doll." He gave her a wink which he obviously intended to be alluring.

She placed a hand involuntarily on her stomach, from surprise or nausea she wasn't sure. "Fred, what are you doing here?"

"I've got business for you," he said, stepping to the side to reveal a hefty bag of laundry.

Oh, God. "Oh, you do too! I do appreciate you thinking of me, but I am quite busy at the moment. I probably won't be able to get to them as quickly as you'd like. I can give you the details of another—"

He held up a swollen hand to silence her. "Nonsense, I'm sure you'll make time for me. Besides, neighbours are meant to look after each other, aren't they?" Charlie got the distinct impression that he was referring to more than the laundry.

"I guess so," she said meekly, helpless as he pushed past her with his bag and into her unit.

"Wow, I guess these places don't get any nicer the higher you go," he commented, spying the cracks in the ceiling and the peeling paint. "For how much work you claim to do, it seems like you could afford something a bit nicer than this."

"I'm saving up for a place of my own," she answered honestly. "I'd prefer not to rent anymore."

He snorted. "By yourself? Good luck with that, property isn't a woman's game. You're not a bad looking sort, you'd be better off spending that money on getting your hair done and some nice clothes. Any luck and you'll find a man to take care of you."

She did her best to keep her eyes trained on Fred, but as he spoke, a tall, broad figure materialised beside him.

"Who the hell is this guy?" Rhett asked with revulsion.

Thankfully Fred didn't seem to expect an answer and was showing himself around her living room, scrutinising the sagging couch and, arguably the only thing of beauty in the place, her lily. Charlie widened her eyes at Rhett and jerked her head towards the door.

If he saw her, he didn't acknowledge it. He followed the odious man step for step, coming to stand in front of him and peering into Fred's perpetually shiny, reddened face.

"You know what they say about lilies?" the frog-like man asked, raising a hand to violate a leaf. She stiffened. Was it possible he knew?

"Their scientific name is Lilium. The Greeks believed they were created from Hera, the wife of Zeus," he said slowly, as if speaking to a toddler. "She was a lesser deity, beautiful but inferior. Quite appropriate really." He looked at her as though he'd just paid her a compliment but she couldn't bring herself to smile.

"I don't like him," Rhett commented, sizing him up.

Although Fred was three times wider than Rhett, Rhett stood at least a head above him and was roped with more muscle than Fred could ever hope for. But of course, that meant nothing, with only one of them being alive.

"I didn't realise you were so well versed on horticulture. Very interesting." She hoped she sounded sincere. "Well, thank you for trusting me with your garments. You must be—"

"Say, where is your nephew this evening? Didn't you say he was staying with you?" he interrupted, pinning her with bulging eyeballs.

Charlie made a rapid assessment; Wynn wouldn't be coming here at all anymore, there was no need to carry on the lie. And there was a distinct absence of anything in the flat that might belong to an almost adolescent boy. Not to mention the question of where he was sleeping.

Rhett frowned. "Is he talking about Wynn?"

"He went home," she rushed to fill the silence. "He hated it here. I must have been a very poor host, but he missed his mother dearly. He wasn't sleeping, was wagging school and started getting into fights with the other boys. He just couldn't stay here any longer."

"That's a shame. You could've used the practice taking care of a man – even a miniature one." He guffawed, as if he'd told a grand joke.

She bristled. "Yes, well, Dot must be wondering where you've got to."

"Not likely," he sneered. "The woman barely speaks. To me, anyway. I left her with plenty to clean up after dinner, so she'll be busy for a while. I might have to buy her a new recipe book, her cooking is starting to taste like swill."

"It'd be a real shame if this guy tripped down the stairs." Rhett was seething.

Charlie wasn't opposed to the idea, but it wouldn't bode well for her, being the last person who had seen him alive. In the interest of self-preservation, she shook her head minutely.

"She's lucky I'm such a nice guy," Fred continued. "Anyone else would put her out on the street. I could probably be persuaded to, if a young, pretty thing came along..."

Charlie tried to bite her tongue, but he was putting more strain on her patience than his shirt buttons. "Have you tried talking to her? Maybe she's not very happy."

"Well she ruddy well should be!" he snapped suddenly, rounding on her so quickly she jumped. "She's got a roof over her head and a well-established husband. It's her own fault she's never had children, that had nothing to do with me."

"It's none of my business, Fred." Charlie tried to extinguish the flames she had ignited. "I'm just saying perhaps you should spend some quality time together."

He raised a pudgy finger at her, glowering. "You're damn right it's none of your business and you'd do well to remember it."

Charlie knew the exchange could only get worse so, reluctantly, she dipped her head in compliance. "I overstepped. I apologise."

"You women are all the same," he snarled, advancing on her.

"Charlie," Rhett's voice was a warning she didn't need. He watched on helplessly, fists clenched.

"You're like Chihuahuas." Fred was still walking towards her, slowly and deliberately. "All bark and attitude, but you run with your tail between your legs as soon as the Dobermans put you in your place."

"Goodness, you're a cynologist as well. You must learn a lot down at the bar." Her temper was crackling.

"I think you need to watch your mouth, you insolent little—" He was raising a hand when his face went slack, staring at something over her shoulder.

She turned and found Rhett looking more menacing and powerful than she had ever seen him. His edges still blurred, but waves of energy were rolling off him and distorting the air, like bitumen under a harsh sun.

Could Fred see him?

"Get out," Rhett's voice boomed as an icy breeze rippled through the apartment.

Fred stumbled backwards, a shoe snagged on an uneven floorboard and he fell with a resounding boom, eyes wide and trained on Rhett, who was still pulsing with energy.

He pushed himself off the floor like a newborn lamb learning to walk, seized his bag of clothes and ran for the door. He cursed as he fumbled with the doorknob and fell into the hallway, leaving the door gaping behind him.

Turning in open-mouthed shock to Rhett, Charlie realised in horror that he wasn't done. "Rhett, don't!" But he was already gone.

She stood, paralysed. Seconds passed. What was he going to do? More importantly, what was *she* going to do?

A heavy thud echoed up the stairwell, accompanied by Fred's anguished yell. Then, silence. Had he killed him? She couldn't go and check, being found standing over a man with a recently broken neck would not end well for her.

Instead, she gingerly closed and latched the door, and waited for Rhett's return.

She was falling, tumbling endlessly through a vortex of reaching arms. They grabbed at her limbs as she spiralled past them, her head snapping back as they ripped at her hair. Her clothes were reduced to shreds of fabric billowing around her body in the infinite maelstrom of hands.

This must be Hell, she realised.

"You deserve to be here." One of the hands opened like a mouth and spoke.

"You'll catch up to your mother soon," said another.

She heard a scream somewhere below her. Perhaps a hand had told Florence her daughter was trapped in the same endless torture.

Charlie jolted awake, panting as her brain scrambled desperately to reclaim reality.

Her clothes, damp with sweat, hung off her limply as she struggled to make sense of her surroundings. It was still dark, the only light from the glow of a street lamp outside. She had fallen asleep on the lounge waiting for Rhett to return.

And he was watching her from the corner of the room. "Bad dream?"

"No worse than being awake," she dismissed his question. Prying herself out of the cavern she had formed in the cushions, the night's events bubbled to the surface and, with them, fear. "What happened to Fred?"

Rhett's usually stoic face was downcast. "He's still alive. He tripped, with some gentle persuasion. Knocked himself out but not for long. Then he limped home."

Charlie's chest expanded with a deep breath, uncertain whether it would have been preferable for him to live or die. "What did he see? Could he see you?"

"Honestly, I'm not sure," Rhett confessed. "I just felt so helpless, standing there and not being able to help you. He was going to hurt you, I knew he was. And the things he was saying, I just got so angry."

Charlie's eyes dropped to his clenched fists. "Maybe your emotions were so powerful they expanded your energy. You've already started to control physical objects, maybe this is an extension?"

"I guess." He ran both hands through his tousled hair. "I'm sorry, Charlie. I really did just want to help, but now..."

"It's okay." She pushed herself off the lounge to stand in front of him, her hands twitching as they thought about wrapping him in a comforting hug – one she couldn't give him. "If you hadn't done whatever you did, I'm not sure what would have happened. You could well have saved my life, for all we know."

He looked down at her, searching her eyes and raising a hand to her cheek, leaving a trail of warm electricity across her skin. "I don't want anything to happen to you."

She fought the inclination to lean into his form, knowing she would fall through him like a bird through a cloud.

"He will come back," she tried to divert him. "Probably with Enforcers."

"He can't prove what he saw."

"No, he can't." She paused, contemplating. "Claiming to be able to see or speak to spirits is unlawful. If he claims to have seen something, that would make him—"

"A Seer," Rhett finished, his mind working. "But you didn't see anything."

"No, I was just minding my own business and Fred decided to drop some laundry in. He started acting strangely and then went white as milk, staring at something I couldn't see. I was becoming terribly frightened and then he ran off," she said in her mock damsel-in-distress voice.

"You don't feel comfortable living in a building with an incendiary," Rhett supplied.

"No, I don't," she agreed.

"You think he should be locked away so he can't cause alarm or harm to anyone else."

"Yes, I do."

"You think Rhett is the most handsome man you've ever seen."

Agreement had been on the tip of her tongue when she laughed and swatted at the air comprising his arm. "I think this might work."

It was a long wait for the Enforcers, but she knew they would come. The arms of the clock marched steadily forward, each second encroaching on the one in which her fate would be decided. It was almost noon when a heavy fist found her door.

"This is Enforcement. We are performing an inspection. Open up," a nasally voice ordered from the other side.

Obediently, she opened the door and stood to one side.

"Ma'am." The man with the blocked nose stepped forward. He was only slightly taller than her and had long, gangly limbs. She had no intention of running, but if she did she had the distinct impression she would be at a disadvantage.

"We are responding to reports of suspicious activity concerning this household. Under Section 7 of the Theological Abolition Act 1921, we have the right to search this apartment and question you as we deem necessary. Any resistance on your behalf will lead to your arrest. Do you understand?"

Even if she didn't, Charlie doubted it would matter. "Yes, of course, please come in. I'm so glad you're here, I barely got a wink of sleep last night after what happened."

The blocked-nose-man stood to the side for the rest of the men to swarm her apartment like angry hornets. They wore identical navy blue coats, a large badge with an engraved judge's gavel fastened to the vest worn beneath. Their deadpan eyes peered out from beneath black flat-brim fedoras but didn't acknowledge her as they passed.

She counted eight, including the one standing in front of her. She suppressed a dry laugh at the sight of the men collectively attempting to maneuver in the coffin-sized unit without stepping on one another's toes.

"Why do you say that?" Blocked-nose-man already had a notepad in hand, using his mouth to uncap his pen.

"I don't think I've ever been so frightened, Officer..."

"Officer Gordon," he supplied.

"I run a small laundry service and Fred," she shivered for effect, "visited with a bag of washing last night. Officer Gordon, he was acting very peculiarly, talking about the symbolism of plants and telling me more about his marriage than is proper for me to know. I assumed he was simply having a bad day so I listened, as a good neighbour does."

Officer Gordon was scribbling animatedly. "How long have you been neighbours with Mr Fred Barron?"

"I have only lived here for a little over a year. I believe Fred and his wife moved into the building about five or so years ago."

He nodded and motioned for her to continue. "Anyway, Fred became quite angry – why, I have no idea. And then he saw something over my shoulder and froze. I turned around but there was no one there, Officer. Whatever he thinks he saw must have terrified him. He fell over backwards and then ran – didn't say another word."

"Mr Barron didn't say what he saw?"

"No, Officer Gordon. But he was convinced something was there." She leaned in and lowered her voice, "I've often wondered if he believed in you-know-what. His wife, Dot, seems positively miserable. I can only imagine what living with an incendiary would do to a person."

"That seems like something you should know, Miss Hall. Our records indicate your mother was arrested for religious crimes." His eyes locked on hers, wearing an expression of 'I've got you now'.

He must have taken her for a fool if he thought she hadn't been prepared for that.

"My mother, may she rest in peace, was a very ill woman, particularly towards the end of her life. It's not something I talk about often so please, forgive me." Her chin crinkled on cue. "Her... beliefs caused so much heartache for our little family. I've worked so hard to build a life for myself, to forget my unfortunate family history. And now the idea of someone bringing those beliefs back into my home..."

She threw her head back towards the ceiling, face crumpling in manufactured anguish, and raised her hands to cover her mouth. Perfect.

"There, there, love, we're here to protect you." She felt the man's hand touch her shoulder lightly.

"You don't— you don't think I'm crazy?" She looked at him with wide blue eyes, snivelling for authenticity.

He pulled a white handkerchief from within his coat and she accepted it from him with a pathetic smile. "I really shouldn't say before the findings of the investigation have been formalised, but we have no prior records of suspicious activity on your behalf. Assuming we don't find anything today, you have my word you will be protected from Mr Barron."

There was nothing there for them to find, not a tarot card or oracle's crystal in sight. Her only tools of the trade were her eyes. She did not write receipts. Her client book and savings were stored safely behind the air vent. She had been preparing for this for years.

"Do you have a dog?" one of the officers asked suddenly, fishing out a tennis ball from underneath the couch.

Damn it, Wynn. Oh well, a tennis ball was hardly incriminating.

"No, but I do love them. Sometimes I go down to the park and play fetch with the local pups." She smiled benignly.

The officer tossed it in the air a couple of times before resting it beside her lily on the mantelpiece.

"Nice plant," he commented, half-heartedly.

"So Mr Barron was telling me," she raised her eyebrows at Officer Gordon, "something about them being Greek and created from Hera?" She furrowed her brow, playing her young, simple woman card.

"Sounds like a bit of a kook to me." The officer wiped the non-existent dog slobber on his trousers before addressing his senior. "Nothing here, sir. Young lady here keeps a very tidy household."

"Thank you, gentlemen. That'll be all."

The Enforcers spilled out into the hallway, several chatting jovially about their evening plans as if they hadn't been about to confiscate her life.

She breathed a deep sigh, letting the tension in her shoulders dissipate. The door began to creek shut of its own accord and she looked up with a start to find a smug-faced Rhett leaning casually in the corner.

He broke into a slow clap. "Bravo, bravo. That was quite the performance."

She waved a hand to quieten him. "Shush! They could still be listening." But she couldn't suppress a triumphant smile.

"I don't think I've ever been so frightened! Oh, Officer!" He adopted a high pitched whine.

"I don't sound like that!" But she laughed in spite of herself and twirled on the spot, letting the anxiety fly off her fingertips.

When she stopped, she one again found herself face to face with Rhett, a little closer than could be deemed appropriate.

He raised a hand to try to sweep her hair from her face, but it blew gently as if caught in a breeze. His face, as always, was unfathomable, but the dark pools of his eyes betrayed his intent.

Charlie leaned in ever so slightly, drinking in his scent and reveling in the electricity thrumming over her skin. Lips parted and eyelids heavy, he leaned in too.

Head lifted, Charlie closed her eyes and plunged forward. After a moment of finding only air, her lips felt the familiar thrum of his energy. Heat spread from her mouth, down her neck and into her chest. There was a warm pressure on her back and she knew his hands were on her. She pushed harder, wanting to deepen their connection, as her hands lifted to find where he began.

But as she tried to grip his arms, her fingers fell through his energy and closed on her own palms. Her heart sank as she realised this is the closest they would ever be.

She lowered her head, breaking the connection. "Rhett, this isn't right."

"What's not right?" He was still leaning in, his signature smell of grease and coffee enveloping her senses.

"You're dead," she said quietly, reminding herself as much as him.

"Opposites attract." He grinned sheepishly. "I like you, Charlie. You make me feel more alive now than I ever was."

"What do you think's going to happen?" she snapped. "We'll snog and date, you'll propose and I'll get married to the invisible man and we'll live happily ever after?"

He stepped back as if she'd physically pushed him. "You can't say you don't like me, Not after that," he argued softly.

"It's not about liking you, Rhett." Her feelings of elation were quickly dissipating. "Nothing good can come of this. The only way this can end is in heartache."

The pair were quiet for a moment before Rhett lifted his head. "Is that so different to life?"

She was fighting a lump in her throat so she just stared and waited for him to make his point.

"Everything ends in heartache. Even if I were alive and we were to grow old together, one of us would be left heartbroken. Or we could break up and tear each other's hearts apart. Grief and pain is the price we pay for caring about something." He spoke quietly but with the surety of someone wise beyond his years.

Charlie searched but no words came to her and Rhett evaporated, leaving her with a regret-filled pit in her stomach.

Nine

THE OTHER SEER

When Enforcers made an arrest, they liked to do so as publicly as possible. They would say it was to set an example and dissuade others from following in the misguided footsteps of the incendiaries. Charlie had always been of the opinion that they just liked an audience when they flexed their muscles.

So it shouldn't have surprised her when Fred was arrested in broad daylight on the street outside their apartment complex.

Exiting the apartment block to a dreary day, Charlie peered up at the sun glowing meekly from behind a heavy veil of grey clouds. She had an appointment that afternoon at Rhett's shop. After the friction of the previous evening, she hoped she wasn't now stretching the friendship to use it.

Her footsteps faltered when she spotted Fred ambling up the street towards her, walking stick in hand and head partially mummified. One could almost feel sorry for him, until he used the stick to smack a child out of the way.

Doubling back and opting for the long route along the block, she paused when a patrol van pulled up to the curb next to her. She froze, as did others nearby. There was promise of an entertaining show and Charlie had the sinking feeling she was the main act.

Six coat-clad Enforcers emerged in unison, straightening their fedoras and conferring with one another as they looked up at her apartment block. Charlie choked on her own tongue. *Oh God, they're here for me.*

Eyes closed, bracing herself for the unnecessarily violent display they seemed to revel in, she waited. Memories of her mother erupted from the depths; the day she was arrested and squashed into the living room carpet, the day she was transferred to the Enlightenment facility, the day Charlie knew she wouldn't see her again.

Seconds passed. Carefully prying an eye open, she expected to find the men surrounding her. A few people cast withering looks her way; she was evidently blocking foot traffic.

"It's not me, you ruddy idiots!" a man bellowed from behind her and she whirled around, scarcely daring to believe the unfolding scene.

Two Enforcers were wrestling Fred to the ground as he bellowed like a wounded buffalo, struggling in spite of his incapacitation. Another stood in front of him, assumably reciting his rights and refusing to acknowledge the howls of rage echoing down the street.

As if choreographed, the sidewalk traffic promptly formed a ring, casting knowing glances to each other and speaking to their neighbours behind raised hands. A father lifted his infant son to give him a better view of the spectacle.

Charlie knew she should probably take the opportunity to leave and thank whoever was watching over her. She knew how easily she could have been the main act in this performance – and that she still could be. But out of morbid curiosity or sheer stupidity, her feet carried her towards the growing circus, trusting Fred wouldn't be able to distinguish her face in the crowd.

On her tiptoes, she peered over shoulders and between hats to catch a glimpse of the man she had framed. Charlie wondered if she should have felt something – guilt, remorse, even relief, but she felt nothing. The man had beaten and suppressed his wife while taking advantage of who knows how many vulnerable women. The mob jeered at him for a crime he hadn't committed, but justice had found him for the ones he had.

This was quite possibly the only justified prosecution the Enforcers had made in years. While people were incarcerated for praying for help, for holding hope there was a life after death and a deeper meaning to their existence, the true monsters walked free. Except, now, for this one.

The crowd parted to grant the parade passage to the vehicle, and she found herself on the frontline of the channel. She tried to push back into the crowd but was met with a sharp jab in her back and an, "Oi, watch it!"

Fred was still bellowing like an enraged bull, aggressively professing his innocence, and then his eyes found her.

"Her!" he yelled, spit landing on his second chin. "She's the one you want! She tricked me, I know she did! She's a witch!"

The Enforcers pushed him sharply to continue moving, but people were already moving away from Charlie, eyeing her suspiciously. A child, who had been standing by her knee, was wrenched away by his mother, who looked at her as though she had tried to kidnap him.

Charlie kept her composure, eyeing down Fred with a dignified grace he could never hope to possess. Fear was bubbling in her chest and her nails were digging into her palms, but she wouldn't give him the satisfaction of visibly rattling her.

"You are the only monster I see here." Though she didn't yell, her voice came from deep within the chasm of her chest in a powerful, authoritative timbre she didn't know she had.

She turned, parting the crowd with a defiant stare, and made her exit with the weight of eyes on her back.

That evening's appointment was a welcome return to normalcy. Valerie was a referral from another client. Charlie mused at the glances the young woman sitting across from her was casting around the new venue. *She's just lucky I cleaned the place.*

She had fought the urge to reach out to Rhett and tell him that their plan had worked. Instead, she immersed herself in the temporary distraction.

The girl was pretty, with honey blonde hair skimming her shoulders and petite glasses perched on a sharp nose. Her hazel eyes were slightly wide-set over peaked cheekbones. She had the kind of classic beauty her grandmother had idealised.

"You don't want to be cute," she had told Charlie, who was struggling with teenage insecurities. "Little girls are cute. Puppies are cute. It's what we call things that are benign and harmless. You are strong, intelligent and beautiful. You will have your looks forever because they take root in the way you carry yourself and present to the world. Don't waste another second crying over not being considered 'cute'."

"This is an interesting place to do business," the girl commented, sweeping her hair behind her ear with long, slender fingers.

"I know, I apologise." Charlie dipped her head. "I'm sure you understand how risky it would be to use my own home at the moment."

The girl nodded slowly, still surveying the dilapidated surroundings. Charlie bristled at the thinly veiled judgement; she was a Seer, not a renovator.

"Who are you hoping to hear from today?" Charlie reclaimed her attention.

"Oh, my sister," Valerie replied. "My little sister, her name's Eileen. She died from pneumonia a few years ago." She spoke with unsettlingly little emotion, as though she was ordering from the chip shop.

"I'm sorry to hear that," Charlie sympathised, but Valerie's eyes were once again wandering the walls.

With a frown, Charlie closed her eyes and plunged confidently into the darkness. *Eileen,* she called, *Eileen, your sister Valerie would like to talk to you.*

The tingle of electricity warmed the back of her hand and she opened her eyes to find a girl standing next to her. Not a day older than thirteen, she wore a blue pinafore, her blonde hair pulled back into a tidy braid. There was something oddly familiar about her.

"Thank you for coming, Eileen."

"It's okay!" piped up the young girl. "I wasn't doing much."

"Your sister would like to talk to you, if that's okay."

A small smile played at the corners of her rosy lips as she nodded. "Mhm!"

Valerie was paying closer attention to Charlie now, eyeing her steadily as she conversed with her sibling. "You can see her?"

"Yes, she's standing right here." Charlie motioned to Eileen who was rocking back and forth on her heels.

"What does she look like?" Valerie asked abruptly.

Surely she knows what her sister looks like. Charlie paused before deciding the woman was making sure she wasn't a con artist.

"She's wearing a blue pinafore and has her blonde hair tied back into a braid. She looks about thirteen years old."

The woman nodded, eyes widening as though she was only just seeing her. "What's her favourite colour?"

More proof? Really?

Charlie raised her eyebrows at Eileen. "Green!" she exclaimed. "Like a rose-ringed parakeet!"

"Green... like a rose-ringed parakeet?" Charlie repeated awkwardly.

"You can actually see her," Valerie's voice escalated with excitement as she pushed herself forward in the chair.

"I told you so!" Eileen poked her tongue out at her sister.

Charlie looked between the two of them in bewilderment; they were talking to each other, therefore they could see each other.

"You can— you're a—" Charlie floundered, watching Valerie's already impossibly wide smile grow even wider.

"A Seer? Yes, and we've been looking for another one for such a long time!" Valerie clapped in delight.

"Such a long time!" Eileen mimicked.

"Okay..." Charlie drew a deep breath, beginning to wish she had never taken this client. "Someone referred you to me – who was it? How did you find me?"

"I've had my ear to the ground for the past year and I've been making appointments with as many so-called Seers as I could. You wouldn't believe how many fakes are out there, I mean why would anyone pretend to be something that could get them killed?" She didn't wait for Charlie to answer. "Anyway, Eileen was actually the one who found you. I think you know her friend, Wynn?"

The pieces clicked in Charlie's mind; the graveyard. The day she met Wynn he had been talking to a ghost, a girl about his age with blonde hair pulled back into a braid and a blue pinafore. This girl.

"Wynn told you about me," Charlie concluded, not impressed. She had gone years without a soul knowing about her abilities, and now it was like trying to keep water in a sieve.

Eileen nodded happily, unaware that she was playing a key role in Charlie's rapidly disintegrating life. Charlie pinched the bridge of her nose, the other hand cracking the knuckles of her fingers individually. After several seconds of silence, she looked up at the pair whose faces had lost their enthusiasm and fallen considerably upon seeing her reaction.

"What do you want from me?" she asked finally.

Valerie blinked at her. "Aren't you excited? To finally find someone like you?"

"No," she answered honestly. "The fewer people who know about what I do, the better. And that's a policy you should adopt, too." She eyeballed Valerie. "The last thing I want is to organise a bloody cult."

"We aren't going to tell anyone." Eileen looked offended.

"I obviously didn't think Wynn would tell anyone either." She ran a hand through her hair. "You still haven't told me what you want."

"There are more people like us," Valerie began, obviously put-off by Charlie's lack-lustre attitude. "Not just Seers, there are people who believe in a higher power. People who are praying and dreaming in fear. People who believe in freedom of belief. True freedom, not what we're being fed. They're everywhere, but they're isolated. But what if they were united?"

"You want to organise a rebellion," Charlie surmised flatly. "You must be joking."

"Is it really so ridiculous? What about last century's slave revolution? People segregated are powerless, but together the possibilities are limitless. That's exactly what the State wants – that's why gatherings and groups were banned so quickly, just as the Enlightenment was beginning. As soon as we were scattered, we could be controlled."

"And how many thousands will have to die in the process? This isn't a game, and any ignorant acolytes who join you on your quest will be thrown straight to the wolves. Mothers, fathers, children, whole families will be executed because of your foolish fantasy." Charlie was past the point of reasoning. "If you want that on your head, then please proceed, but I'll have no part in it."

She stood abruptly and slammed the chair under the table. "I believe your time is up."

Valerie stood uneasily; tall and willowy, she was at least a head taller than Charlie, and the honey-haired girl looked down her nose at her.

"I hope you realise we're the same, perhaps not in values and hunger for justice," there was contempt in Valerie's voice, "but we've both been given the same gift. Something in our blood is the same."

Eileen was fading in and out hesitantly, unsure whether she should leave or stay.

Heading for the door, Valerie looked over her shoulder and appraised Charlie as she stood there glowering. "I'll be back. There are more like us and I'll find them. Maybe you'll be willing when you can see for yourself."

Charlie listened for the heavy thud of the front door to make sure she was gone, and then crossed to the closest wall just to beat her head against it softly.

This was bad. The odds seemed to be stacking against her; Wynn, Fred, the inspections, now this. Her years of careful planning and calculated decisions could easily be undermined if any one of these bees became a hornet.

She had asked her mother once why she had only chosen to have one child, not realising at that age that even she was there by pure accident. But Florence had responded with her signature acuity, "One day you may understand the love a mother has for her child. I would give my life for you, and I would rather give my life for one child than have to choose."

While other children were playing hopscotch and swapping cigarette cards, Charlie was already beginning to understand that not all things in her world were guaranteed. The things she valued had to be given precedence.

Now she lived with one focus; survival.

"Hudson!"

"Yes, my lady?" He was never far away. "My, my, this place is... charming?"

Hudson, in his bowler hat and well-pressed suit, looked quite out of place in the shabby-sheek kitchen. Looking down, he stepped off the questionable stain on which he had been standing.

"The decor is the least of my worries, Hudson." She turned to her wisened friend, a warm comfort quelling her anxiety as her eyes fell on him. "How do they keep finding me?"

"Who has found you?" A small alarm bell rang in his tone.

Charlie relayed the events of the Seeing, Hudson listening intently, his well-rehearsed expression hiding any sign of concern. "And obviously she didn't pay me a single cent, so it was quite literally for nothing," she finished.

Hudson was the kind of man who liked to consider his words before he committed to them, however the silence that followed stretched to new limits. Charlie was fidgeting restlessly when he finally cleared his throat.

"Your safety is my utmost concern," he began diplomatically, "and I have always supported your endeavour to save as much money as you can before relocating to the country. There, I trust you will be truly safe. Without that anxiety, I wonder if I may finally be able to truly rest."

Surprised by this admission, Charlie fought the overwhelming urge to draw him into a tight hug. She had never known her grandfather, but she doubted he would have provided the same love and care Hudson had shown her.

Without recognising the gravitas of his last words, he continued, "On the other hand, all that is needed for evil to triumph is for good men to do nothing. Or women, that is," he added with an apologetic head tilt.

"Are you saying I should join an army of Seers to overthrow the

State's authoritarian powers? Lead some kind of uprising?" she asked incredulously. "What are we even going to do? *See* them to death?"

"I'm not telling you to do one thing or another." The old man raised a hand to calm her. "I always support your decisions and this is no exception. If anything were possible, I would have you hide away in the countryside while the vilified minorities rise up and herald a new age of democracy and freedom. However, they are also someone's daughter, father, brother, aunt. Surely their lives are of equal value."

Charlie stared at him blankly. "So you're encouraging me to join the rebellion?"

"No, my lady, I'm encouraging you to consider your choices." Hudson had a way of capturing his many years of hard-worn experience in the way he spoke. "That was quite a proposition to receive without forewarning. Valerie said she will be back, so carry on as you are. Continue saving and keeping your head low. Have faith and your path will find you."

"That's all very helpful, Hudson. But you know, we can trace this little chain of events back to you," she jibed. While he was the kindest soul she had ever met, in directing Wynn to her apartment, he had also pointed trouble her way.

"I'm just joking," she added hurriedly, seeing his face fall slightly. The last thing she wanted was for Hudson to stop talking to her. He was, once again, the only friend she had.

Ten

THE JAZZ BAR

Without cause for hurry, Charlie opted to make the journey home by foot and meandered slowly through the streets, relishing the way the crisp night breeze kissed her nose and played with her hair.

Elms lined the streets, their leaves dancing in the glow of post lights, queues of yellow taxis with checkered stripes eagerly awaiting their next intoxicated patron. The tram tracks running beside her pointed directly to the moon that breached the city's skyline. Charlie wasn't blind to the city's beauty, though she guessed it was much more appealing to those it wasn't trying to kill.

Even well away from State Street, the sidewalk was still littered with revellers enjoying the raucous nightlife. Men in sport coats with women on their arms in knee-grazing cocktail dresses and petticoats clicked along the pavement in pumps and oxfords. They emerged and disappeared from the glowing doors of aromatic restaurants, interspersed with the occasional dimly-lit lounge and piano bar.

She passed a jazz lounge, the seductive croon of a saxophone slithering onto the street to beckon passersby. A neon sign reading 'Flamingo Jazz' spilled a soft pink light onto the footpath. Laughter and chatter grew louder as the door opened for a couple of women leaving to be home at a respectable hour. It promised a temporary escape from life's mediocrity. In another life, she would have added her voice to the chorus.

Giggling, a young couple emerged from a neighbouring sunken stairway. Scarf dangling precariously from his shoulders, the boy was mumbling unfiltered promises into the petite blonde's ear as she smiled lasciviously and clung to his waist like she was worried he would slip into the night.

Driven perhaps by a subconscious desire for the same freedoms they enjoyed without second thought, she found herself passing beneath the neon sign and into a dimly lit space. The aroma of smoke and liquor flooded her senses but not quickly enough; she had already realised she was underdressed.

Women in knee-length frocks which flared at the waist smiled and blinked enticingly at the suited gentlemen they sat opposite. The sparkle of jewellery and expensive watches winked at her, standing in the doorway in her frayed coat and loafers.

A grand piano sat in the corner, tamed by a man with ebony skin. A saxophone and bass flanked him, each mastered by someone lost in the shadows.

She stepped backwards, attempting to extricate herself from a poor decision, when she collided with something solid.

"Oh, my apologies, Miss," the solid-something said.

She grimaced; an unnoticed exit had been too much to ask for.

Charlie turned slowly, trying to minimise the extent of her faux pas. But she wasn't prepared for the young man she came face to face with. Dark hazel eyes peered down at her from a foot above, trapping her where she stood. Polished to perfection, his skin was smoother than glass and his hair had been thoughtfully sculpted to dip enigmatically over his forehead. He smelled like spice and wood.

God help her, she couldn't stop staring.

"Are you okay?" he asked, ducking his head for a closer inspection.

"Fine," she croaked and cleared her throat, nervously tucking a few tendrils behind her ear. "I'm fine. I'm so sorry, I should watch where I'm going."

"Please don't apologise, you would never have spoken to me

otherwise." He smiled sheepishly, revealing a row of perfectly straight, whiter-than-paper teeth.

You're still staring, her brain informed her.

"I would offer to buy you a drink but it would seem I'm too late."

"Oh, I wasn't— I haven't— I mean, I was just looking for someone but they're not here, so I should really be going." She waited for her feet to move; they didn't.

"So perhaps my timing is perfect, less so for the unfortunate person who missed you. Would you share a drink with me?" Palm up, he offered her his hand, but the beaming gold cufflinks kicked her sharply in the shins.

"I'm afraid I'm not dressed nearly well enough..."

He gave her an appraising inspection, lingering where her hair curved around her cheek. "Yet you shine brighter than any girl in the room. They could stand to be reminded it's not trinkets and glitter that makes one beautiful."

Again, he offered her his hand and, in a state of befuddled shock, she tentatively accepted. He escorted her to an empty booth off to the side, private enough that she felt safe from ogling eyes but public enough that any fears she held of being abducted were quickly allayed.

He saw that she was comfortably seated before he settled on the opposite side of the mahogany table. "May I ask your name?"

"Charlie," she said simply, still waiting for the spectacle of a man sitting opposite her to remove his mask.

"Just Charlie?"

"It's short for Charlotte, but I've never felt like that's my name. It's much too gentle and dainty for me," she confessed, wondering why she was sharing this with a stranger.

"Are you not gentle and dainty?" he asked with another stunning smile. Was he flirting with her?

"Do I look gentle and dainty?" Was she flirting back?

He considered her for a moment, opening his perfect lips to reply before a leggy waitress interjected to ask for their drink order.

"I will have a whisky, neat, please. And the lovely lady would like..."

He waited for her to supply an answer. But Charlie's voice caught in her throat; she hadn't ordered a drink at a bar in- had she *ever* drunk at a bar? What did young women even drink?

Apparently he interpreted her silence as a challenge to choose something for her. "A White Russian," he told the waitress.

He looked to her for reassurance as the waitress left. "An interesting choice," she commented.

"Decadent and strong with a soft and subtle follow through." He scrutinised her. "Yes, I think it's quite appropriate."

"I would have preferred a Manhattan," she jibed.

"Ah, but you aren't dainty or sweet," he replied with a wink and she laughed.

"I'm afraid I can't argue with your logic, Mister..."

"James," he supplied. "Just James."

Charlie had the odd sensation of having stepped into someone else's life, a fantasy she'd nursed for some time. Not once had she been intercepted by a handsome stranger in a bar, been bought a drink and flattered. Then again, it was difficult for that to happen when she spent her evenings at home in the company of a sixty-something-year-old ghost.

"Well, Just James." She smiled at the server as their drinks appeared before them. "I find it quite hard to believe that a young man like yourself would come to such an establishment alone."

Having finally recovered her voice, Charlie had to establish she was not usually the quiet, subservient female. She leaned forward on the table and took a deep sip of her drink.

"Do I not seem like a lone wolf?" he asked in feigned offence. "Perhaps I was looking forward to brooding in solitude over my whisky."

"I'm afraid there's not a word in that sentence I believe."

James returned the chuckle, a deep baritone timbre which tickled her toes. "I guess I can't pull off the mysterious recluse. I was actually meant to be meeting some friends, but they can see I am otherwise engaged." He nodded to a few gentlemen sitting at the bar who were casting knowing looks over their shoulders and chortling.

"Oh, I'm sorry." Charlie's cheeks grew warm. "I promise I won't keep you from them for long."

"Please don't go making such hasty threats. Believe me, your company is much more enjoyable."

With the slow croon of Night Train soothing her soul and the cocktail pacifying the anxious knot in her stomach, the tension in her shoulders began to fall away. Much to her relief, the other patrons were distracted by booze, slow dancing and their own intimate conversations. Very few threw glances her way. If she were honest with herself, those that did were probably ogling her handsome drinking partner.

The conversation with James felt delightfully normal, a welcome reprieve from the cacophony of chaos which had come to permeate her days. He was polite and well-spoken, respectfully flattering her when the opportunity presented itself, just as a young man should.

They talked effortlessly about everything and nothing – from speculating about the intentions of their fellow patrons before it turned, to Charlie's chagrin, to their opinions on the world and what it had become.

"While I can see freedom of belief is preferable," he began diplomatically, "I also recognise we humans are too fallible to be trusted with it. Religion has been the source of so much conflict and bloodshed. Right now, we're unified under a central cause – the State – and making great strides. With a common focus, who can say what we will achieve?"

"I am afraid I must disagree with you," Charlie said with the confidence she had found at the bottom of her glass. "Progression and captivity cannot coexist. As humans, we have evolved this far because we have been allowed discourse; when we silence those who offer alternative views, we prevent the development of society.

"Life can be cruel. It leaves the best of us battered and broken. And all of us, at some point, will find ourselves left with nothing but a bleak void in which we may have held hope – but we were not allowed."

He stared at her, expression unfathomable. Her liquid courage waned and she had the distinct impression whatever spark he saw in her had sputtered out.

"My apologies, the drink went straight to my head. I think I should excuse myself." Without pausing, she collected herself and fled onto the street, head bowed in regret.

She should never have set foot in that lounge, she berated herself. She should never have entertained the attention of such a normal, well-intentioned man. Promising herself she would never be so stupid again, she drew her coat tight and pushed into the night.

"Charlie!" she was being called. Had she upset him? Maybe she had finally said enough to find herself prosecuted.

"Charlie!" She didn't turn around, hoping vaguely it was an alcohol-induced hallucination. That hope was lost as James appeared at her shoulder, his jog falling into a walk beside her.

"Why did you leave?"

"I assumed I offended you." She kept her eyes on the sidewalk. "It is probably for the best – people like us are not meant to consort."

"Consort?" He sounded amused. "Why would I be offended? You left me speechless which, my friends will tell you, is no easy feat. I'm quite the opposite of offended, I'm in awe."

She stopped on the street corner, her feet unsure of what to do and her mind not providing any clarity. The drink truly had gone to her head and she was an overflowing beaker of anxiety, embarrassment and desire.

Not necessarily desire for him, she realised as she stared at his unblemished face, half hidden in the shadow of a street sign. The desire was for the life he promised, the one he would assume was implicitly granted to everyone. Conversation with him was easy, but meaningless. He offered her an escape, but not protection. He could never know any more about her than she had already revealed. They both deserved more than that.

"Thank you for a lovely evening and for the drink, James. But I think it's best that tonight remains something I can look back on fondly. We are leading very different lives, and I am certain yours is not headed in the same direction as mine."

She held out her hand to shake his and was taken aback when he lowered his head to kiss it.

"You are a mysterious girl, Charlie." He considered her eyes carefully, looking for a hole in her resolve. "I will not pursue you if it is not what you wish, but you know where to find me if you reconsider." He went to turn away and then appeared to admonish himself. "At the very least, please allow me to walk you home. The streets are no place for a woman alone at night."

She considered telling him she had seen and dealt with far worse than anything the streets could throw at her, but she nodded in acceptance and their steps fell into an easy coalescence.

"It's not that I don't see the appeal of religion, you know," he said suddenly.

Charlie cast a furtive look over her shoulder to make sure no one was within earshot.

"I've lost people. People I would very much like to see again. While I do believe they're gone, returned to the earth from which they were born, I wouldn't be upset if I was wrong. I hope I am, in fact."

"Who have you lost?" While tempting to call them by name and prove her case, she knew better than to reveal her secret to a man she had just met.

"Grandparents, as you would expect, but the one I dwell on was a friend. We had grown up together, more or less, and he was just at the beginning of life when it was taken from him. It seems a terrible injustice for a deity, if there is one, to let that happen to someone so young, doesn't it?

"He questioned everything, too. He would have liked you, actually." He chuckled. "He probably would have beaten me to the punch in buying you a drink."

"I hope you do get to see him again, one day." Charlie gave him a sad smile which he returned.

"You saved me some of my dignity tonight, you know," he confessed as they passed the heavy wooden doors of the State Bank. "My friends... Well, I always find myself footing the bill. I don't mind; I was lucky enough to be born into privilege and I enjoy sharing it. But sometimes it feels like that's the only reason I'm there."

Charlie felt a pang of sympathy. It was not a situation she understood, nor probably ever would. But she knew sadness when she saw it.

"I wasn't looking for anyone in the bar," she confessed in turn. "I was walking home and I heard the music and the laughter. I wondered what it would be like to be one of the voices. But as soon as I stepped inside, I realised I didn't belong there."

"Perhaps we are two sides of the same coin." James cast a sideways glance at her.

"Perhaps we are."

The rest of the walk past in a companionable silence, their footsteps providing a rhythm for her mind to pace to. James stepped aside often to make way for other women and the elderly so they did not have to step out onto the street. She quietly enjoyed being seen with a gentleman, however short-lived it would be.

Stopping at the front door to her apartment block, she shuffled her feet in embarrassment as he took in the weary, sagging facade. As if on cue, a rat scurried between them and into a nearby drainhole.

"Thank you for your company and seeing me home safely." She looked up at him cautiously, anticipating a look of judgement or disgust. She found neither in his eyes, nothing except perhaps concern.

"Thank you for allowing me." Once more, he collected her gloveless hand, kissed it gently and returned it to her side. "Until next time."

Knowing there would be no next time, she gave him a small smile and, being as ladylike as possible, shouldered her way through the heavy door.

The ascent was painfully longer than usual, each echoing step in the stairwell confirming her solitude.

A distant wail roused her from her self pity, a muffled echo of pain or grief. Was it an animal? No, it sounded too human. Had someone in the building died? A slamming door reverberated through the walls, followed by the sounds of a blubbering woman.

"Please, you have to give me more time. He left me with nothing and I've got no family to speak of! I will find the money, please don't turn me out!"

"Law's the law," a man's curt reply came. "If you can't pay rent by Friday, you'll have to find somewhere that accepts 'thank yous' as payment."

The woman's cries retreated and then silenced after the click of a door. But the man's footsteps were fast approaching the stairwell where Charlie was still standing. She darted up to the next landing, peering down over the banister to confirm her suspicions.

Building manager, Patrick Burrows, clad in a mud-brown pinstripe suit, emerged below her. He tightened his tie and dusted off his sleeves as if to purge himself of the unpleasant situation. His whistle floating behind him, he disappeared down the stairs.

Charlie's stomach clenched; she hadn't considered what would happen to Dot. She had assumed Fred's wife would simply be glad to be rid of the adulterous scumbag. Of course he had gambled their savings away or spent it on other means of pleasure, with no thought of what would become of her if something happened to him. Although, he was probably not expecting to be arrested for crimes against the State.

Married women had no place in the workforce, and Dot had played the homemaker as expected. For a woman to seek employment at her age was unheard of, but in any case, her husband's crimes would tarnish her. Even if she were a spritely twenty-year-old, not even a downtown cleaning service would consider taking her on given Fred's incarceration.

Unconsciously having reached her apartment, the sagging couch enveloped Charlie, and she inhaled deeply. There was a smell in the air that she recognised.

"He looked like a nice guy." Rhett was leaning against the kitchen door frame, looking nonplussed.

"I didn't think you were talking to me," she replied coyly, quelling the small burst of excitement she felt at seeing him again.

He shrugged. "Just making sure you got home safe." His tone was short.

"Oh." It would have been one of the nicest things anyone had done for her in a while, had James not just extended the same courtesy. "Thank you."

He nodded awkwardly, eyes on the frayed rug. His usually broad shoulders sagged inward, reducing his height considerably. He looked vulnerable, almost as much so as she felt.

"So, who was he?" He brought them back to the topic.

She pinched the bridge of her nose. "That was Mr Burrows, he's the building manager. I'm going to have to do something about Dot because he's threatening to turn her out and—"

"You were out drinking with the building manager?" he repeated.

"Oh." She realised her mistake. Of course he had seen her with James. "Just someone I met in the Pink Flamingo," she admitted, knowing the conclusions he would jump to.

To her surprise, he let out a bark of laughter. "The Pink Flamingo? You? Dressed like that?"

She drew herself up indignantly. "Why couldn't I be a patron at the Pink Flamingo?"

He snorted. "I know the type that go there. More money than sense. They live on daddy's dollar and haven't worked a day in their lives. That's why they look like that – all they do is preen themselves and then flap about on the town."

She fought back a smile. "Yes, well, I realised that as soon as I walked in. I've never felt so out of place in my life, which is saying something. I tried to back out and literally ran into James. He insisted on buying me a drink and then walking me home. That's all."

While fully aware she was not obliged to explain herself to Rhett, nor did she owe him anything, Charlie had nothing to hide and maintained honesty was the best policy. With Rhett, anyway.

Rhett fidgeted with something in his pocket. "Well, James was always a decent guy."

"He seemed like he was - wait, how do you know his name?" Charlie's eyes narrowed. "Were you following me?"

Rhett snorted. "That's what you think of me, is it? That I just follow you around like a lost puppy?"

"Answer my question."

He was squeezing the windowsill behind him, knuckles white. His level of control was impressive, and more than a little off-putting.

"He was my friend," he answered quietly, turning his back to her to stare out the window.

"Oh." Of all the men in the city who she could have run into. But why was Rhett so upset? "Did you want to talk to him?"

"No, I don't want to talk to him!" He struck the windowsill with his fist and a loose piece of wood fell from the outside. "How do you think it feels? Seeing you with one of my friends, watching him walk you home at night and kiss your hand. Knowing he can give you things I never can."

Stunned, Charlie quietly closed her gaping mouth. "Rhett, it wasn't like that..."

"That's not the point." He turned to her, jaw clenched. "The point is that it could be. With him. With anyone. Anyone but me."

A tense silence loomed. Charlie fumbled, searching for words that wouldn't come.

"Anyway." Rhett straightened his grease-stained overalls. "Now that I know you're home safe, I won't impose any longer."

"Rhett, stop being like-"

"Like what?"

"Like this! What do you want me to do?"

He sighed deeply, appearing to contemplate his words before something within him snapped. "I want you to go out with me. And come with me to the movie theatre where we won't watch the film. I want you to be there when I get home from work and for you to tell me about your day. I want you to tell the sleazy guys who hit on you that you're already spoken for. I want you to be with me."

Charlie stared, mouth falling back open as she blinked. While she knew he liked her, she hadn't expected such an admission. She felt it too, the connection they had in spite of their separation across planes of being.

"I'm sorry." He brought his hands up to rub his temple. "That was a lot. I haven't been in this position before, you know? That's no excuse, though."

"Rhett." Charlie chewed her lip, scared of the emotions that were bubbling up inside her chest. "You already know I have never had a boyfriend. I have never been on a date, either. This evening was probably the closest I've come."

His eyes fell again and she quickly continued. "I have never felt that anyone could truly understand me. No matter who I chose, there would always be an invisible wall preventing me from experiencing love as it should be. A relationship should only be for two people who are able to commit themselves entirely. And I never can. Tonight was a glimpse of the normal life I will never have. It was a reminder that I will face life alone. Flesh and blood though I may be, I don't belong in this world.

"So, you see, we are sort of in the same boat. You are the only person I've ever been able to speak so candidly to. If we had met in this life, I would have gladly *not* watched a film with you." A smile flickered across his face, which she returned.

"Rhett, I don't want this to—"

"Don't." He held up a hand. "You don't need to say anything. I'm sorry I haven't acted the perfect gentleman. Being dead is no excuse for being an arse." He paused, appearing to struggle with something internally. "I'm grateful you're there for Wynn, and you deserve better than some overgrown sulking toddler."

She smirked. "Are you comparing yourself to a toddler?"

"I'll never admit to it."

A laugh pealed from her weary chest. "Thanks, Rhett. I'm glad to have you back."

"You look like you need a cup of tea." He wasn't wrong.

"Are you offering?"

"I've been practising. Just tell me which cup you like the least."

His bashful smile told her she would shortly be cleaning up broken porcelain, but she didn't have it in her to rebuff him.

"The brown one with a crack through the handle."

He busied himself in the kitchen while she retreated for shower. Now feeling as emotionally spent as her body did, she let the hot water cascade over her for far too long. It was comforting to hear background noise in the apartment that wasn't the disconcerting sound of scurrying rats or argumentative neighbours. It wasn't until Rhett knocked timidly on the door to inform her the tea was getting cold that she grudgingly turned off the water and climbed into her nightclothes.

To her disbelief, she returned to the kitchen to find a cooling cup of tea waiting for her on the bench. Granted, he hadn't added the sugar, but the level of control Rhett had mastered so quickly was impressive.

He was slumped against the windowsill, looking smug but exhausted, his edges having frayed a little. Still in his work clothes, she could almost pretend he had returned home from a long day at the shop, weary and satisfied from his efforts. She tried not to let her eyes linker on the way his shoulders rounded nicely under his shirt.

Could Charlie have been his wife? Even if she had allowed herself to fall into a relationship, she doubted her ability to play the doting, caring housewife he would have wanted. That wasn't what she was made of. Regardless, life had made the choice for them. His blurred edges made it hard to distinguish where he ended and the night sky behind him began. There was still a lingering tension which Charlie made a point of ignoring.

"Did you really make this?" She brought the cup to her lips and sipped.

He nodded, pride rolling off him in waves.

"I am impressed." She cradled the cup in both hands, enjoying the warmth, and leant back against the counter. "How often do you practice?"

He shrugged with a smirk. "I'm just a quick study."

She quirked an eyebrow and he relented. "All the time."

Charlie had never encountered a ghost so intent on mastering the physical world. If Rhett was a malevolent spirit, there may be cause for concern. Surely he would never try to harm anyone.

Wouldn't he? Her mind replayed the audio of Fred plummeting to the bottom of the stairs. He had been protecting her, but the last thing she needed was a self-appointed guardian who took it upon himself to deliver justice. Is that what would become of their complicated relationship?

"Why?" she asked, doing her best to keep a light tone.

He shrugged again. "You don't have siblings." Charlie knew it was both a statement and a question, so she shook her head. "I hated the idea of not being able to protect him. You know, I took the hard ones from Pa. I pushed bullies back into line. A big brother is always meant to be there to keep you safe. When I realised I wouldn't be, I knew I had to figure this ghost thing out."

His intentions were pure, but this wasn't the natural order. Then again, there was nothing natural about the world they lived in, so perhaps it was not up to Charlie to judge.

"Does your father still..." She trailed off, not knowing how to phrase the sensitive question.

He shook his head. "No, he's been really busy with work lately, as I'm sure you can imagine. The inspections and investigations mean he's working pretty long days."

Charlie's heart dropped. "What— what does he do?"

His eyes widened. "Didn't Wynn tell you?"

"Tell me what?"

He swallowed, eyes darting across the floor and then up the walls, unable to look at her. "He's the Chief Enforcer."

Eleven

THE COUNTRY

Gerard Barron was a national hero. Under his command spanning three short years, 57 religious congregations had been discovered and disbanded, 138 rebels had been incarcerated and/or 'rehabilitated', and 34 incendiaries had been executed.

The Chief Enforcer was the legal backbone of the Enlightenment. Without him, the legislation was a threatening but meaningless document. Reporting directly to the President, he oversaw the operations of the Enforcement Division and was praised for its ongoing success.

Though it wasn't required of him, he often took part in investigations. He said it was important he remained close to the frontline, that his men needed a fearless leader, not an observer who gave orders from behind a desk. Charlie knew, though, it was because he revelled in the trauma left in his wake.

The man never missed a public execution.

Charlie had come to simultaneously hate, pity and fear the Chief Enforcer, and now she discovered he was the father of the boy she had been mentoring to develop his abilities as a Seer.

Rhett had done his best to calm her. "I thought you knew," he said repeatedly, followed by assurances that she was safe and Wynn would never breathe a word.

Realising his promises were as effective as a jug of water on a bushfire, he evaporated with a murmured apology, leaving Charlie with the messy mosaic of shattered porcelain and tea she had just made for herself.

It was not a matter of if, but when she would be discovered. Every second she remained in the city was a second closer to her arrest and subsequent execution – a certainty considering she had been acting against the State with the son of the Chief Enforcer.

On her knees, she began sweeping the broken cup into a dustpan, tea seeping through her pants.

While her blood boiled at having had the truth concealed from her, she was livid with herself for having been so trusting and naive. Her mother hadn't died for Charlie to behave so foolishly. She knew better.

Nine thousand, two hundred and seventy dollars. That was all the money she had in the world. Most Americans would gawk at having that much cash in their bank account, let alone stored in an air vent.

The average house went for $7-8,000, but who knew how much a farmer would want for his established homestead. Who knew what he would say when asked to part with his livelihood. She had hoped to have a little leftover for basic furniture and provisions, but it was entirely unknown.

Her goal had been twelve thousand, but she had run out of time.

Feeling like she had aged years in just a few days, she looked around the dilapidated flat with new eyes. Though she resented its confinement, it had kept her safe. She hated its smallness, but she had survived in its cosy embrace. As people age, wrinkle and sag, buildings grow old and weary. It had served its purpose admirably and, for that, she was grateful.

The clock had been leering at her for the past several minutes and, finally, she made eye contact with it; 11:30 pm. The chances of an inspection between now and dawn were slim; there would be no public spectacle with everyone in bed.

Charlie's bones ached and there was no certainty of when she would again enjoy the luxury of a bed. It could take weeks, she prayed not months, of travelling through the countryside before she might find someone willing to part with their lifeblood.

She collected and disposed of the ceramic shards scattered around the kitchen, climbing reluctantly into bed. It creaked and protested. The warm blankets usually brought her comfort and security. Tonight they offered no relief as she quietly mourned the oppressive apartment she had loathed since stepping foot in it.

Her eyelids had barely closed when the bells of the city clock signalled daybreak.

Having mentally rehearsed this morning for years, she packed with precise minimalism. There was no room for luxury when one had to carry it on their back. The only pair of shoes she took were the ones on her feet.

Prising the money from its hiding place behind the vent, an eerie sense of finality settled over her in a dense cloud. Life as she knew it had come to an end, and another she couldn't fathom was beginning. Alone, once again.

Separating the money into smaller bundles, she hid some in the bag's separate compartments, more in her shoes and coat pockets. If she was mugged, she was determined not to have everything taken from her at once.

Her lily watched mournfully from the mantelpiece, drooping sadly over the side of its pot. Illogically, it was the one thing she longed to take with her but couldn't.

"My lady?"

The sound of Hudson's voice almost brought Charlie to tears. He was, once again, the only person she had left in the world, dead or not.

"It's time, Hudson," she informed him, still looking at her photosynthetic child. "Wynn and Rhett's father is the Chief Enforcer, Gerard Barron. It's too dangerous for me to stay here any longer."

She felt his energy shift in shock, it rippled through the room like disturbed water. "Charlie, you must forgive me. I had no idea..."

"I know." She turned and gave him a small, warm smile. "Maybe this was the push I needed. I don't know if I ever would have felt ready to leave. Yes, I hate this place, but it's familiar. I've always known what would happen when I left in the morning and I always had somewhere safe to call home. Now, I have no idea where I'm going and I'm terrified."

"Perfectly normal," he murmured, still grappling with the revelation. "Once again, you demonstrate wisdom beyond your years. I feel you will not need me much longer."

She blanched. "You won't leave me too soon, will you?" She was being selfish, asking him to hover between worlds, belonging in neither. But as the rest of her world fell away, she couldn't bear to consider losing her only enduring friend. "I don't know how I'll make it through this without you."

He placed his hands on her shoulders in a fatherly embrace, warm electricity thrumming down her arms and around her collarbone. "I'm not going anywhere until I know you're safe and happy."

Charlie had never been a crier, but she fought to keep her composure. It had been a hell of a week.

Backpack filled to the brim, she cast a final look over her former home and placed her key beside her beloved lily. It had been a companion through dark hours and a non-judgemental observer when it felt like the world might swallow her up and no one would notice.

Her head cocked; she had an idea.

Knock, knock, knock.

Charlie placed the lily tenderly by the door and made a swift departure, hovering at the corner of the stairwell. It was oddly reminiscent of a child's game of knock and run.

Several seconds later, Dot emerged bleary-eyed, clad in a canary yellow nightgown. She was a thin, fragile woman with skin stretched too tightly over her bones. Even fresh out of bed, her greying hair was pulled back in a neat bun. Dot was the kind of woman you knew had been beautiful in her youth and still carried herself with poise, in spite of the man who had done his best to demean and belittle her for years.

She searched the hallway in confusion, looking for her inappropriately early caller. With a frown, Dot began to retreat before spotting the plant at her feet. Picking it up, she turned it gingerly, looking for an indicator of whom it might be from. Spotting the envelope taped to its base, she edged tentatively backwards and let the door drift shut behind her.

Charlie needed only to wait a few seconds for the small scream. Satisfied smile in place, she descended those horrid stairs for the final time.

The first rays of a watery sun were beginning to filter through a heavy grey blanket. It was a morning only fit for hot coffee and a book, neither of which she had the luxury of.

Shrugging her bag higher so it sat on her shoulder blades, she took to the streets, gloriously desolate, save for a few early risers and paperboys atop their bicycles. With pedestrians still shaking off the persistent tendrils of sleep, no one cast an eye her way as she made a bee-line for the city's edge and the promise of unhindered freedom and fresh, clean country air.

Once she was there, she would contact Rhett. He would have to understand. So would Wynn.

The young boy had grown on her with his bright eyes and eager persistence. Surely his father would grant him some level of security; he wouldn't prosecute his own son. Charlie shook the thought from her head, it was absurd.

The compact city high-rises soon gave way to the sprawl of suburbia. As she hurried down the streets, she walked below the path of rooftops she had always imagined leaping across to her escape. Well-dressed businessmen and the occasional pleat-skirted woman emerged from their modest pastel houses and climbed into their Crosley station wagons, Roadmasters and coupes. No one spared a glance at the girl in grey cigarette pants and brown surcoat jacket as she scampered past.

The last of the houses dripped past her and a vast expanse of empty fields lay sprawled out before her. She readied herself for an alarm, for someone to grab her from behind or yell, 'Stop her!' But nothing came.

The only sounds on the fresh breeze were those of birds hunting their morning meal and the distant calls of the city lost somewhere behind her. She was free.

Delirious laughter ripped from her chest as she broke into a skip, pirouetting as she'd once done in her long-forgotten youth. Inhaling deeply, the scent of soil and grass invaded her senses, gloriously absent of petrol or cigarette smoke. No one gawked at her childish display. No one murmured about her sanity. There was only the blissful whispering of the wind in the tall grass.

Freedom.

She walked without concern that day, passing a few farmhouses with plump cows and thick-coated sheep, but it was still too close to the city. The further away, the better.

Real estate window shopping had always been a guilty pleasure; perusing house listings and choosing her favourite to mentally decorate with her own personal flair. Today felt a little like that; she liked the way apple trees softened the frontage of one property, and the rustic barn attached to another.

A herd of cows lowed gently to her as she meandered along the dirt road, no other person in sight. The noon sun was peeking through the dense layer of cloud when she decided to stop for a bite to eat.

She'd packed rations to last her for a couple of weeks if she ate sparingly; a few bananas and apples which she would need to eat first, and tins of tuna and spam with crackers to see her through the second week. There would surely be fruit and vegetables which she could purchase on her travels, but would the farmer really notice a couple of absent ears of corn?

Against the thick trunk of a weeping tree she dropped to her knees and sank her teeth into an apple with a satisfying crunch. The sharp sound in the otherwise quiet countryside was disconcerting, and she looked around to make sure no one had heard her. She was being absurd, of course; there wasn't another building for miles.

Charlie had been putting off reaching out to Rhett but, unable to further justify her procrastination, she closed her eyes and called his name into the darkness. No one answered.

Frowning, she called his name again, louder now, but still, he didn't come. That was odd. Perhaps he was angry with her for abandoning his brother.

Charlie shrugged, trying to cast off the anxiety creeping into her shoulders. Rhett was mad, but he would get over it, she told herself.

Trying to drown out the doubt which had begun to swirl in her head, she chewed loudly and likened herself to a farm animal. She didn't need to worry about what was considered ladylike anymore – there was no one out here to care.

Wanting to be as far away from the city by nightfall as possible, she clambered back to her feet and hoisted her belongings back into position. While not complaining just yet, the tense muscles in her feet informed her they would be later.

Her trudging footsteps in the pebble-speckled dirt again put an end to the blissful silence. Perhaps, she fantasised, tomorrow would bring some blue sky and sunshine. She walked until the final tendrils of light began to slip away and she shivered into her jacket. Finding a place to sleep was something she had been dreading for most of the day. A farmhouse had appeared further down the road which she eyed with trepidation; she hated asking for favours.

Life as a Seer taught one to walk with caution. No one could be trusted and most people would sacrifice their neighbour as soon as offer them eggs.

The house loomed larger as she approached. A greying roof with too many peaks sat on a white exterior which, on closer inspection, was awash with dirt and water stains. A dim light glowed from within, shining through musk pink curtains. With any luck, a woman would be inside.

A simple wooden fence fringed the property, corralling a few sheep bleating nervously as they huddled together for the night. The distant cluck of hens came from somewhere behind the house. A stone well stood to one side of the path leading up to the house, but it was covered in sheets of wood, evidently untouched for some time.

The front porch groaned under her weight and, hesitantly, she raised her hand to a blue wooden door, sun bleached to periwinkle where the awning hadn't protected it.

Knock, knock, knock.

She had mentally rehearsed a small speech as she approached but now, hearing someone unlatching the door, it vacated her.

As the door creaked open, the barrel of a shotgun peered through.

Twelve

THE FARMSTEAD

"Who is it?" It was a croaky masculine voice that could only belong to a man who had smoked for most of his life.

"I... uh..." she fumbled, searching for words. The gun pointed at her face made it difficult to think of anything else.

"You've got five seconds to tell me who you are and what you want or you can get the hell off my property." The gun tapped twice against the doorframe.

"I'm— I'm sorry." Her palms were wet. "I'm just passing through and was hoping you might have a room, or even a shed, where I could spend the night. I have money, I can pay."

The door swung open with a screech, revealing a balding man in a stained singlet, half-smoked cigarette hanging from his lips.

His eyes travelled over her slowly as she stood there, feeling oddly exposed. She was on the verge of telling him not to worry when he stood back from the door and gestured for her to walk inside with a grunt.

"Thank you," she mumbled. Charlie stepped by him, brushing against the wall to give the man as wide a berth as possible.

Photo frames and mounted plates were scattered haphazardly across the walls. Furniture was packed into every corner; shelving units, odd armchairs and side tables. She shuffled along awkwardly, not knowing where to stand that wouldn't be in the way.

The smell of something delicious was wafting down the hallway, accompanied by the clattering sounds of someone cooking.

"Who is it, Darryl?" a woman's voice called over the racket.

"A drifter," he called back, motioning for her to continue shuffling towards the kitchen.

She obliged, hoping his wife was the hospitable one.

Pots and pans hung from the ceiling above wooden benchtops, packed front to back with utensils, saucepans and cans of food; Van Camp's Pork Beans, Vacu-Dry Peach Slices and Dixie Blend Coffee.

On the verge of apologising for arriving at a bad time, she quickly realised the couple were accustomed to their cluttered home and this was perfectly ordinary. A plump woman was moving easily about the kitchen, stirring this and turning that. To each their own, but she was privately quite glad she only needed to stay the night.

"Hello, dear. You're looking a bit peaky," the portly woman commented, now furiously mashing potatoes with a hefty arm. "How far have you come?"

"I only left the city this morning. I'm afraid this is just my face." She gave a feeble attempt at humour.

The lady smiled at her good naturedly. "Well, we're willing to share what we have, but if you expect to eat then you'd best put your things down and make yourself useful."

Only too happy to pull her weight, Charlie slung off her backpack and stood awkwardly for a moment, looking for a surface that wasn't covered in knick-knacks. Finally, she stowed it beneath one of the counters where it couldn't be tripped over.

The woman motioned to some carrots wedged between a stack of bowls and a bread bin. "They need to be peeled and chopped."

Rolling up her sleeves, Charlie busied herself with preparing the vegetables, trying to surreptitiously take in her surroundings as she worked. To her relief, Darryl had disappeared.

The space was cramped, to be polite, but not dirty. It was full of all the things that were evidently of value to them; tokens from life and objects that might be useful at some point. But the floors were as clean as the plates and the woman wiped down her workspace as she went. Intruding flies would be hard-pressed to find a crumb.

"Thank you very much for your hospitality. My name is Florence, by the way." Charlie thought it best not to give her real name to anyone on her journey, though being pursued across the countryside was unlikely.

"Lovely to meet you, dear. You can call me Betsy." Charlie detected a subtle southern twang.

Betsy had a halo of thick, bouncing chestnut curls which bobbed as she worked. She was fuller-figured and obviously quite strong. Charlie watched as she pummelled dough into a layer of flour scattered across the counter; the woman's fists were like mallets.

"So, where are you travelling to, dear?" Betsy had the no-nonsense air of a woman who asked what she wanted to, social etiquette be damned.

"To be honest, I'm not sure, but I'll know when I get there." Charlie was focusing intently on dicing the carrots without also serving up her finger. She imagined it was probably quite frustrating for Betsy to watch.

"That's a new one, never heard that. Not wise for a pretty young thing like you to be wandering about on her own, much less without a plan. My giddy aunt!"

"I think today was the safest I've felt in years," Charlie confessed. "You are the first people I've seen since I left the city. I think you're on to a good thing, living out here," she added, attempting to soften her host.

Betsy hummed in approval. "You're quite right there. I can count our visits to the city on one hand, usually to see an execution," she added with the same off-handedness with which one speaks about the weather. "And I can't stand all the people milling about like cattle. It's so dreadfully noisy, goodness."

"That is something I'm enjoying out here," Charlie agreed, "the peace and quiet."

Charlie couldn't recall ever having eaten shepherd's pie. Neither her grandmother nor her mother were ones to spend longer than they had to in the kitchen, so meals were usually simple; vegetables and potatoes with a protein like beef or fish a couple of times a week. She didn't mind, she was full and happy.

"Can you work, girl?" Darryl rasped across the table before coughing a lung into his food. Charlie grimaced; he hadn't covered his mouth.

"I beg your pardon?" Her fork was halfway to her mouth, laden with possibly the most complex meal she had ever eaten. She wasn't sure if she liked it.

"Are you deaf? I asked if you can work. Or are you one of those uppity office types who thinks they're too good for labour?" A few pieces of mince stuck to his unkempt stubble like maggots. At least, she hoped it was mince.

"No, no, I can work." She fixed her eyes on her plate to avoid nausea. "Is there something I can help with?"

Darryl barked a harsh laugh which Betsy joined with a giggle, too high pitched for her size.

"There's always something, kid. Do you have any idea how much work a farm is?" His tone was condescending and she didn't appreciate it.

"I imagine a great deal," she replied curtly.

"Too bloody right. In the morning you'll help me disc the field. It'll be spring in a minute, we oughta ready for seeding," he explained as if she were a five year old.

She realised her annoyance was probably misplaced; she had no idea what he was talking about. She had assumed life on a farm would be easy to figure out, it didn't require an education, after all. Perhaps there was more to it than she had estimated.

"I'm happy to help," she replied before complimenting Betsy on her shepherd's pie. Internally, she didn't think it had been worth the effort.

Charlie helped Betsy clean up after dinner while Darryl listened to the wireless, an ever-present cigarette hanging from his mouth. On today's broadcast of American Farmer, Layne R. Beaty was reporting on the nation's corn crop. She looked around anxiously for where the plates belonged, before realising there was already a stack of them sitting on the benchtop next to the stove.

Well that's... convenient?

"You're a good little helper," Betsy commented, bustling back into the kitchen. "Why don't you grab your things and I'll show you to your room?"

Practically giddy at the thought of resting her weary feet, she retrieved her backpack and followed Betsy through a rabbit's warren of corridors and rooms. The house had looked deceptively small from the front, but the building was longer than it was wide. Each room was filled with bits and pieces of its own. Charlie wondered vaguely if there was any organisation system and, if not, how they ever found anything.

Finally, Betsy stood to the side of an open door. "Here we are."

Peering cautiously inside, Charlie was met with what was obviously a little girl's room; a soft pink four-poster bed took pride of place, a two-storey doll's house sat beneath the window which was clad in pink tulle curtains laced with white ribbon, and a cacophony of toys spilled over a basket nearby.

"Will this do, dear?"

Charlie had only one question she wanted to ask: where was their daughter? Judging from the room's decor, the girl must only be eight or nine at the most, hardly old enough to have moved away. Perhaps she went to a boarding school.

Not wanting to be intrusive, she smiled and nodded. "This is lovely, thank you." She had definitely expected to be spending the night somewhere far worse.

Betsy clapped her hands together. "Wonderful! The washroom is the second door down the hall, then you'd best get some rest. Darryl will be up at the crack of dawn looking for you."

Charlie had a sneaking suspicion Darryl would be up well before the sun, but she murmured her thanks and dropped her bag at the foot of the bed. There was a nightgown buried somewhere in there, along with her toothbrush.

The hair on her neck prickled and she glanced up at the door; Betsy was still standing there watching her.

"Is there anything the matter, Betsy?" she asked, midway through rummaging.

Betsy started, as if woken from a dream. "Oh, goodness no. Sorry, dear. I was a million miles away. That's what happens when you get to my age." She laughed noncommittally, wringing her hands. "Well, goodnight dear."

Charlie was left standing by the young girl's bed, a little seed of discomfort growing in her stomach. She shook her head to dislodge the unease and gathered her toiletries. Fishing the wads of cash from her pockets and shoes, she buried them in the depths of her bag.

The bathroom, which was only slightly bigger than the one in Charlie's apartment- *old* apartment, was a clash of pale blue and maroon. Blue birds on roses adorned every third tile on the vanity, which was cross-thatched with burgundy squares. A gaudy bouquet of red flowers adorned the toilet cistern. Closer inspection revealed they were made of plastic and probably older than she was.

A sea of ice blue linoleum stretched out beneath a once-white enameled bathtub. The years had not been kind and now a rust stain from where the water had dripped for years was hard to miss. Betsy had begun to draw her a bath and steam was already creeping up the mirror.

Their hospitality was beginning to make her nervous; surely not all country folk would be so eager to welcome a complete stranger into their home? Charlie had offered Darryl money and he hadn't mentioned it again. She was expected to work, she reminded herself, but so far this didn't appear a fair trade.

The bathwater was gloriously hot and Charlie let it purge one foot at a time and then slowly immersed the rest of her weary bones. Not wanting to leave the couple without hot water, she turned off the tap and let her eyes close with a sigh.

The silence was deafening, so impenetrable that she was left with only the sound of the sporadically dripping tap and her own heartbeat. There was no city traffic, no drunkards yelling on the streets, no one moving furniture in an adjacent apartment; only silence. While it was peaceful at first, the quietness amplified her own thoughts and gave her worries room to stretch.

She wondered how long it would take Mr Burrows to knock on the apartment door, demanding the rent payment that he would never receive. How many times would he knock before forcefully entering the unit and discovering she wasn't there? Would he call the police or simply re-advertise the flat as being fully furnished for a higher rate?

Perhaps Rhett would answer her tonight. Charlie had thought *she* was the one who should be angry with *him* given the omission of his father's occupation. Perhaps he felt guilty, even ashamed.

With more anticipation at the thought of seeing Rhett than she would like to admit, she hurriedly finished her bath and brushed her teeth, grimacing at how the fluorescent bathroom bleached the colour from her skin.

Sitting on the pale pink patchwork quilt adorning her bed for the evening, she closed her eyes and reached into the darkness. *Rhett.*

She waited for the smell of grease and coffee which she had grown to appreciate, or the tingling sensation of his fingers on her arm. But she opened her eyes to find she was still quite alone. A thought she had been refusing to acknowledge finally forced its way to the front of her mind; something was wrong.

Hudson! she called into the darkness of her eyelids.

"My lady," her elderly friend was there almost instantly and he cast an approving eye over her surroundings. "I must say, I did not expect to find you anywhere so pleasant this evening."

"I guess I got lucky, but they're a bit strange." She didn't waste her time elaborating; they hadn't actually done anything after all. "Sorry, Hudson, I actually have a favour to ask of you. I haven't been able to contact Rhett since I left. I thought he may have been angry at first, but something doesn't feel right..."

She trailed off, aware she probably sounded like a girl with a crush on a boy who wasn't returning her interest. If only life was that simple.

If Hudson thought the same, he didn't show it. "I will see if I can find him, but I think it more likely he simply needs some time. As do we all on occasion."

"Thanks, Hudson."

The room felt oddly claustrophobic after her elderly friend left. With only the faintest moonlight trickling through the curtains, framed woodland creatures leered down at her, a tall standing mirror in the corner reflected the coats hanging behind the door and gave the impression someone was standing there.

After tossing and turning for an age, an uneasy sleep finally took her. She had only just begun to dream – once again of infinite falling – when she was awoken by a light scratching sound. She listened for a few seconds, trying to orient herself and wondering if it was a mouse in the rafters. No, it was coming from just a few feet away from her – inside the room.

She turned her head slowly with an eyelid cracked open, trying to maintain the illusion of sleep. Someone was sitting on the floor beside the bed. Charlie could only just make out the form of someone hunched over and facing away from her, working at something on the floor in front of them. Becoming painfully aware that she was dressed only in a nightgown in a stranger's house and without anything to defend herself, she watched for several seconds. The person showed no interest in her, just the task before them.

Hesitantly, she extended a hand toward the beaded lamp and, with a click, revealed a small girl with long, golden hair trailing down to the floor. She didn't turn around or flinch, just continued to scratch.

Blinking away the clouds of sleep, Charlie realised her edges were blurry. As much as she wished she could simply roll over and pretend she wasn't there, experience had taught her that ignoring a fire usually didn't put it out.

"Hello," she whispered. "My name's Charlie. What's yours?"

"Why are you in my bed?" she asked in a childishly angelic voice without bothering to turn around.

"I'm sorry, I'm only borrowing it for the night. I'm on a really long journey and your mum and dad were kind enough to let me stay here."

Silence followed, filled only with the girl's unnerving scratching at the floor. "It's a lovely room. What's your name?" Charlie asked again, compelled to break the uncomfortable hush.

"Jennifer," the girl replied this time, still not looking at the stranger occupying her bed.

"It's nice to meet you, Jennifer. How are you?"

"Good."

"How long have you lived here?"

"Always."

"What are you doing down there?"

"Drawing." That was a relief.

"May I see?"

Charlie heard a pencil drop and the rustle of paper as the little girl clambered to her feet and faced her.

She was small, petite and perfect, with a prominent birthmark stretching down one side of her face. It curled around one of her dark, wide-set eyes and tapered off at her jaw. It made Jennifer more beautiful still, but she kept her face turned slightly away in a meagre attempt to hide the blemish in shadow.

Her dainty fingers clutched a charcoal drawing – what looked to be a farmhouse with a few sparse trees and hundreds of black water droplets covering the page.

"You're very good at drawing," Charlie complimented, maintaining her whisper. "Is that this house?"

"It's the day I died," Jennifer replied simply.

At least she knew she had passed. Charlie gave an internal sigh of relief. She'd only had to have that conversation and was in no hurry to do so again.

"Would you like to tell me what happened?"

"I fell down the well," she said in the same lilting voice. Charlie's stomach turned as she recalled the boarded-up well at the property's entrance. It was little wonder they had never wanted to look into its watery depths again.

"That must have been very scary," she replied carefully, not wanting to upset the girl. But Jennifer continued to stare at her, expressionless and unreadable. Charlie was becoming very self-conscious about being in the young girl's bed.

"Do you mind that I'm staying in your room?"

Jennifer shook her head twice. "No."

"Thank you, that's very nice of you."

"I have to go now."

"Where are you going?" But Jennifer was already evaporating before her, the drawing floating gently to the ground.

Charlie ran a hand through her bed hair; of all the houses. Not wanting Darryl or Betsy to find the drawing in the morning, she fetched it and folded it neatly, reaching under the bed for her bag to hide it in its depths, but she clawed at empty air.

Perhaps she had pushed it further under than she thought. She lifted the blanket hanging over the bedside; her bag was gone. Frowning, she walked the perimeter of the bed but found nothing.

Had Jennifer hidden it from her? The bag was almost the same size as the small girl, the only place in the room big enough to conceal it was the shoulder-high white closet. But it only held Jennifer's clothes, waiting for her to come back and fill them.

"Jennifer," she whispered. "Jennifer!" But the little girl didn't return.

Panic was setting in; her life's savings were in that bag. Everything she had worked for, the foundations of her new existence. Clad only in her nightgown and bed socks, she could hardly go rifling through the house. With no other option, she climbed reluctantly back into bed.

"Jennifer, I really need my things. Please bring them back by the morning or I will be very upset." But there was no sign she had heard her.

Thirteen

THE PLOUGH

In spite of the anxiety bubbling in her stomach, Charlie must have fallen asleep again because, the next thing she knew, Betsy was marching unannounced into her room.

As she predicted, they were up before the sun and she strained to see the clothes Betsy was laying out for her at the foot of the bed.

"Good morning dear, did you sleep well?" She didn't wait for an answer. "You'd best wear these today so you don't ruin your things. They should fit you, I was about your size back in the day. Now, pop these on and Darryl will meet you outside."

While Charlie was still rubbing her eyes and mourning her lost sleep, Betsy seemed to vanish as quickly as she'd appeared.

Her grandmother had often said allowing yourself to lie in bed after waking creates a spoiled mind. It was the subject of more than one disagreement they had had during her teenage years.

She felt like her grandmother might appear at the end of her bed then and there, rousing on her for her reluctance to start the day. Silently wishing she was back in her city apartment where she allowed herself to rise well after the sun, she swung her legs over the bed and threw on the clothes she'd been given with only a cursory inspection.

They were generously loose but the hardy material scratched against her skin. Again, she ducked her head under the bed and scanned the room but her bag still wasn't anywhere to be seen. At least she wouldn't have to have that conversation with them until later; 'excuse me, I have to be going now but your deceased daughter has stolen my things'.

Praying that Jennifer would tire of her game soon, she pulled on the workboots Betsy had left for her by the door, which fit surprisingly well, and made her way to the kitchen where she had noticed the back door leading out to the rear verandah.

Cold morning air slapped her face as she drew her collar up for the imaginary benefit it provided. Darryl was already standing there waiting for her, hoe in hand and the red glow of a cigarette hovering like a firefly in front of his face. The chickens were flapping happily around Betsy's feet as she scattered vegetable scraps and told them to show some manners.

Charlie stood awkwardly before Darryl, feeling the heavy boots sink into the soil. He was wearing the same stained singlet as yesterday, now partially covered with a long-sleeved jacket with patches on the elbows.

"Know how to use one of these?" he asked gruffly, without morning pleasantries.

She understood the basic concept and had seen it once or twice on the television, but in practice she had no idea. "Not really."

He snorted in disgust, triggering a deep, phlegmy cough. Charlie looked away to hide her revulsion when he spat at the ground behind him.

"You're gonna learn today," and with that, he turned and walked purposefully away from the house. Assuming this was her lead to follow, she walked like a faithful dog on his heels.

They reached a wooden gate at the rear of the property, where she assumed their property ended, but he kicked it open and continued through it to stand authoritatively at the edge of a field. Uneven mounds of dirt stretched for at least a mile in either direction.

"Spring's coming and we need to get this soil ready." Darryl kicked at a rock before handing her the hoe, which she accepted hesitantly. "This will loosen the dirt so we can seed properly."

"You can see here the rows are already marked out." He raised both arms in front of him, pointing out lines she had to squint to distinguish.

She stood there awkwardly, hoe in hand and a far cry from her city apartment – which suddenly didn't seem so bad, after all.

"Well? What are you waiting for?" He gestured one hand aggressively towards the hoe.

Resigned, she gritted her teeth and raised the hoe in front of her, letting it fall into the dirt with a dull thud.

"Not like that!" He snatched the tool out of her hands.

He held it so the metal protrusion skimmed the front of his shoulder and stepped forward with his left foot, dipping into a lunge as he drove the hoe down in front of him, as though he were striking a rat with a club.

Without another word, he handed the hoe back to her and waited.

While she couldn't care less about this man or his crop, she had her self-esteem to consider and would rather not be consigned to the category of imbecile.

She mimicked his movements to the best of her ability, like a dancer learning a new step. After the third or fourth thud of the hoe in the soil, Darryl must have been satisfied with her performance because he stalked off towards the house.

It was slow work, and she was sure they had machinery for such menial labour now, but she took it as a lesson in life; knowing how to work the land could do her no harm. Inwardly, she begrudged not having been offered so much as a coffee before being relegated to the yard. The lack of caffeine, compounded with the anxiety of her life's savings being missing, were provoking a throbbing headache.

The rising sun soon christened the freshly turned soil and warmed the air so it no longer stung as she sucked it into her lungs. Meadowlarks danced above her head in beautiful flashes of charcoal and crimson, inspecting the newly churned dirt for an easy breakfast.

As the sun climbed higher, it didn't take long for her gratitude to dissipate. The back of her neck was prickling in the heat, and, as she began to sweat, the long-sleeved shirt and trousers she had been given to wear trapped a layer of humidity against her skin.

Hours past and beads of sweat were rolling off the tip of her nose, mingling with the dirt which rose in clouds and clung to the moisture. She stood to stretch her back which ached from the incessant bending. Surely Betsy would appear soon with a cold pitcher of homemade lemonade; she seemed like the type.

As if on cue, Charlie detected movement in her peripheral vision and looked eagerly towards the house. Her stomach flipped; Jennifer was playing among the chickens. They seemed to be aware of her presence and flapped beyond her reach each time she extended her little fingers.

"Jennifer!" she whispered as loudly as she could, still bent over to maintain the pretence she was working. "Jennifer!"

The girl looked toward her with the same deadpan expression she had worn the previous night. She wore dark blue overalls with a pink collared shirt protruding from her neckline; the picture of the farmer's daughter.

"Come here!" Charlie gestured with one hand while she swung the hoe again with the other. "Please," she added, somewhat desperately.

Seeming to consider her request for a moment, Jennifer pranced towards her slowly, taking time to twirl midway, without a care in the world.

"It's good to see you again, Jennifer. Do you like playing with the chickens?" She hoped building a rapport with the girl would increase the likelihood of her things being returned.

Jennifer nodded, swinging her arms in small circles. "I used to help mother feed them."

"Did you? Wow, I wish I'd had some pets when I was younger." Realising the little girl was not going to willingly partake in conversation, she blundered on.

"Say, Jennifer, do you think you could return my things to my— I mean, your room today please? I will have to get going very soon and I won't be able to leave without them." She was finding it difficult to both hoe and hold a conversation with the pain that was now shooting up the right side of her back.

"I didn't take them," she answered in her light, lilting voice.

"You didn't?" Charlie stared at her blankly, the anxiety in her stomach now bubbling in earnest. "Then who did?"

Jennifer shrugged before turning to skip back towards the chickens, Charlie's instincts told her she was telling the truth. But if Jennifer hadn't taken them, that only left one alternative.

Betsy emerged onto the back verandah, glass of what looked to be lemonade in hand, but Charlie wasn't flooded with the relief she'd expected.

Fourteen

THE TRAP

Homemade lemonade had always seemed like something of a delicacy to Charlie. Her mother had never made it, nor had her grandmother. Neither subscribed to the idea of a woman spending any longer in the kitchen than she had to.

The drinks menu of her childhood had been water, tea or coffee, but if you asked for either of the latter you were to take it black to save the fuss. By the time she was fifteen, Charlie was sure she had the hardened palette of a fifty-year-old Italian barista.

So the homemade lemonade, as she gulped it down, tasted like the sweetest nectar life had to offer. She was drinking the lemon sherbets she had saved her pocket money for as a child. She was swallowing the spring sunshine and could nearly feel it coursing through her veins. It was almost enough to make her forget that the thief who had her money was likely standing in front of her.

"My goodness, dear, you must have been thirsty," Betsy commented as Charlie drained the glass.

"It's hot work," she responded with some resentment. She would have preferred to pay for her stay rather than be resigned to stoop labour. "I really must be going soon, half the day has already slipped away."

"Exactly, that's why you should stay here another night. There's no sense leaving now, you're going to be looking for another place to sleep as soon as you start walking."

The clock on the wall supported her argument; it was half-past noon.

"Stay another night and you can leave bright and early tomorrow morning. How does that sound?"

Betsy had a point. She wouldn't cover nearly enough ground if she left now and was already well outside the grasping claws of the city. It also gave her more time to find her things. She wasn't stepping a foot off the property without all the money she had worked so hard for.

"Okay, only if you're sure I'm not imposing."

"Marvellous!" Betsy clapped her hands together. Charlie had come to realise this happened when she was excited. But the sturdy woman then dabbed the perspiration from Charlie's brow with a handkerchief and smoothed some of the unruly strands back into her ponytail.

Was she fussing over her? The actions felt like she was doting; almost motherly.

"Well, now that you're staying another night, you'll be able to finish hoeing the rest of the field! Darryl will be pleased."

Charlie stifled a groan. *Marvellous.*

With a pickle and cheese sandwich now sitting on her stomach, she retrieved her hoe from where she had left it propped against the splintering fence and set back to work, wondering bitterly how many cigarettes Darryl had gone through while she'd been toiling.

And if he was counting the notes as she worked.

The sun was just dipping behind the peaked roof of the house when Betsy called her in for the day. Dripping with sweat, hair clinging to her face and neck, she retreated gladly into the cool shade and kicked off her dirt-caked boots at the door.

"Good job I put those clothes out for you! I would have hated for you to ruin your own. I've left some nice comfy capris and a matching shirt on your bed. They haven't fit me in years and there's no sense in them going unworn. I'll wager they're comfier than anything you've brought with you."

More clothes? Betsy's sentiment could have been genuine, but Charlie was growing steadily more suspicious of the pleasant-faced woman. But why would the woman take her things and give her her own clothes to wear? It didn't make any sense.

She had at least been honest about the clothes being comfy; the capris and top were a matching set of light cotton in pale pink, dotted with small white flowers. Having scrubbed herself clean in the bath, the material felt like it was floating over her skin.

The mirror told a different tale; she winced in horror at the state of her sunburnt face, which looked like it had aged years in just a couple of days. A bright red flush was deepening on her cheeks and forehead and her hair was nothing but an untidy tangle of charcoal brambles.

You wanted a farm life, she reminded herself grimly. And she still did. Surely it would be more rewarding working for your own dream as opposed to keeping someone else's alive.

Dinner that evening was chicken stew, and it was difficult not to picture the spritely hens who were clucking about outside. This one died of natural causes, Charlie told herself, not believing it.

"So, don't your parents have something to say about you just packing your bags and leaving town?" Betsy nosed, hacking at a chicken wing to separate it from the body.

Charlie paused, reaching a protective arm around her past and holding it close to her chest. "My parents aren't around anymore," she answered simply, not mentioning that she had never known her father. Such an omission usually garnered scandalous expressions and mortified gasps.

"Oh, I'm sorry to hear that, dear." Betsy squeezed one of her shoulders and Charlie had to glance back surreptitiously to make sure she wasn't covered in chicken juice.

"It was a long time ago," she said dismissively. "If you don't mind me asking, in whose room am I staying?" She could be nosey too.

To her horror, Betsy's knife slipped as she sawed into the chicken, and sliced a neat cut through her left index finger. "Oh, my word!"

"Are you alright?" Reflexively, Charlie crossed to her, taking her hand and forcing it under the running tap to clean out some of the bacteria.

"How clumsy of me," Betsy muttered bashfully. "You'd think I hadn't spent most of my life in the kitchen."

"Do you have some iodine?"

"Below the bathroom sink, thank you, dear."

She passed Darryl who was smoking in the living room. He undoubtedly would have heard the commotion in spite of his wireless, but apparently he didn't care to ask.

Once again in the maroon and blue bathroom, she opened the cabinet and found the iodine with some cotton wool and bandages. It was only a cut so she opted for the smallest one.

As she made to return to the kitchen, she noticed a neighbouring door was ajar. Casting a furtive look over her shoulder to make sure neither of the couple had followed her, she pushed gently and, thankfully, it gave without a squeak.

A queen-sized four-poster bed stood in the middle of the room, not dissimilar to Jennifer's but much bigger, covered in a patchwork quilt of miscellaneous orange fabrics. It matched a tapestry of a sunrise over farmland that hung to her right.

She wasn't sure what she was looking for when she bent down to scan under the bed and saw the protruding handle of a bag. Was that—?

"Did you find it, dear?"

"Yes, I've got it," she called back, righting herself quickly and making her way back through the cramped hallway.

That had looked like the handle of her bag, the brown leather strap had been almost identical. But was she sure enough to accuse Betsy of having stolen her things? Or perhaps the right question was *why* would she steal her things?

"Here," she poured some iodine on a cotton wool ball and dabbed at Betsy's cut, noticing that the woman clenched down on her jaw but didn't flinch.

"Thank you, dear. It's so nice having someone around to help."

Charlie was unravelling the small bandage when she paused; had she found a motive? Was Betsy so fed up being confined to a house with Darryl, a man with the personality of a hungry toddler, that she felt the need to trap Charlie there with her for company?

Finger bandaged, Betsy tried to flex it before realising her new compromised range of motion. "Oh, but how am I going to finish dinner?"

"Don't worry, I'll see to it. I think you've done all the hard work anyway." She gestured towards the chicken which had been hacked apart like a – well, chicken.

Placing the bowl of steaming chicken stew on the dining table was a surreal experience. Any fantasies Charlie held of being a mother disappeared when she was old enough to comprehend that she would be resigning another human to the same half-life she was leading.

On the odd occasion she did allow herself to pretend she might meet a nice man and create smaller versions of themselves, she was always out playing in the dirt with their children, or returning home from a day at work she found fulfilling. Never had she seen herself in an apron serving chicken stew.

"This looks wonderful, dear!" Betsy clapped her hands together, and Charlie couldn't help noticing how her arms jiggled as she did so. "It's so wonderful having a girl around again."

Betsy's face fell slack, pulling her hand to her chest as she tried to retract her last words, but they were already floating in the air.

"I mean, since I was young, that is..."

"God damn it, Betsy, you always do this." Darryl thumped a fist on the table, still clasping a cigarette between two knuckles.

"I misspoke," Betsy said quietly, taking Darryl's bowl gingerly to fill it with stew.

"That's for damn sure. I got you another one, Elizabeth, and you're gonna lose that one too if you're not careful."

Betsy's lip quivered. "No, no, please, I'll be careful."

The exchange baffled Charlie, who sat with wide eyes, too bewildered to feign polite interest in her food.

Jennifer suddenly stepped by her mother's side and Charlie wondered how long she'd been there. The little girl wore the same deadpan expression she always seemed to, but her eyes were fixed on her father.

Betsy turned her watery eyes on Charlie. "I'm sorry, dear, we don't mean to make you uncomfortable."

"No, you just have a talent for it." Darryl raised his glass for a hefty sip of amber liquid; was that whisky?

"Darryl, please..."

"Darryl please what?" He rose from his chair abruptly, sending it screeching back over the wooden floors. "I've given you everything you could ever want and you're still asking for more, nagging bitch."

"That is completely unnecessary," Charlie's voice erupted from her.

"Are you talking to me?" Darryl turned on her and Jennifer was suddenly by her side.

"I don't see anyone else here in need of reprimand." Charlie's tongue was too fast for her brain, which advised her she was quickly getting herself into trouble.

"You watch yourself, girl." Darryl stood over her and Charlie rose from her chair to come nose-to-nose with the glowering man. "I will not have a woman speak to me that way."

"Then perhaps you should find yourself a man."

Charlie knew the hand was coming before she saw it and the sting coincided with Betsy's scream.

"Don't hurt her! Please, Darryl!"

"Shut up!" A vein throbbed in his temple and Charlie had the overwhelming urge to see if it would explode if she struck him back, but she was clear-minded enough to know the ending of that scenario would not fall in her favour.

"I own you now," he snarled, "and you'd best not bite the hand that feeds you. Now get out of my sight."

Betsy's hands were suddenly around her shoulders, pulling Charlie back from Darryl's livid gaze and down the hallway.

"Let me go," Charlie demanded, shaking off Betsy's hands and escorting herself to Jennifer's bedroom where she stood, panicking, with her hands in her hair.

"There, there, dear, it's alright." Betsy followed her in, closing the door behind them, and began stroking the back of Charlie's cheek like a mother calming a distressed infant.

"Darryl gets a little riled up when he's had a drink, but he'll be right as rain tomorrow. You can just apologise and that will be that."

"Apologise?" Charlie repeated incredulously. "Betsy, that is no man, and you deserve much better. You should leave with me tomorrow."

She knew she may as well have been talking to air before she even finished speaking, but she couldn't allow herself to say nothing.

Betsy laughed as though she'd been told a childish joke. "Nonsense. And where would I go? I have my chickens, a roof over my head, and food on the table every night. You could do much worse than this, you know. You'll be safe here, we'll take care of you."

Was Betsy trying to convince her to stay?

"Betsy, I appreciate the offer, I truly do. But I have spent my life living under the conditions imposed by other people. I do not want anyone to take care of, nor do I want anyone to take care of me. I am finally claiming life on my own terms. You should consider doing the same."

Betsy's hand returned to her cheek and the woman peered at her with something that looked like pity. "My dear girl, you have no idea what horrors this world holds. You might chase your dreams but all you will find is nightmares. Please, sleep on my offer. There is no hurry to decide."

Fifteen

THE DEAL

Sleep was no more obliging than usual and Charlie's fervent attempts to imagine she was back in her city apartment were hindered by the occasional snore coming from down the hallway. Darryl had presumably fallen asleep on the couch in his whisky-fuelled stupor.

The faint rustle of clothing came from somewhere near the door and she started, launching herself out of the bed, hands raised in defence.

To her surprise, Hudson was at the end of the bed, wearing an expression of bewilderment.

"Oh, hello," she said with relief, lowering her hands and settling herself back on the bed as her heart rate returned to normal.

"Is everything quite alright, my lady?" Hudson's concern was so genuine, she almost couldn't bring herself to tell him the truth.

"It depends how you define 'alright'."

He arched an eyebrow at her.

"I wish I'd never come here, Hudson. These people are crazy. The man is an abusive drunk, the woman is in denial and their daughter is dead. She says she fell down the well but I wouldn't be surprised if he had something to do with it. I was in the heat all day doing hoeing, my back is killing me, and my life's savings are missing!"

She took a deep breath, feeling some relief that some of her bottled resentment had been uncorked.

"Stoop work is no work for a lady." Hudson's voice was dripping with disapproval.

"Well, I can hardly expect to be given something for nothing. I'm just paying my way." She didn't like to worry Hudson so she tried to lighten her voice.

"I suppose that is reasonable. But I'm afraid this is not a social visit," his voice deepened, and she glanced up at him, watching as his brow furrowed and his feet began to shuffle.

"I found Rhett, and I do not bear good news." His tone was sombre, but she forced her face to remain calm in spite of her growing panic. "Young Wynn has been arrested for religious affiliation and organisation."

"What?!" she yelled a whisper. "He hasn't organised anything! His own father did this to him? Are you sure?"

"Quite sure, my lady. Rhett has, understandably, not wanted to leave his side while he awaits trial. Wynn has been offered a more lenient sentence should he name those he has consorted with, which he has refused to do."

She had obviously fallen off the bed because she felt her knees hit the floor, her head coming to rest against the bed quilt. She didn't care if Darryl or Betsy heard her; what could they do that was worse than this?

Her dreams of a quiet farmhouse with chickens who would come when she called and a cow who would munch happily on the grass as she milked her, an idyllic life of freedom, fell away from under her feet.

"I have to go back." There was no other option. She could not leave Wynn, a defenceless child, alone to bear the brunt of an unjust punishment. He had trusted her, and where was she now he needed her?

"He's only a child! How could he be prosecuted for organising anything?"

"I do not know the details, I do apologise. I came here to alert you as soon as I found out."

She had been so careful. They had been so careful. But in a city full of eyes and ears, even the quietest can be heard, and the smallest can be seen.

"When is his trial?"

There was a prolonged pause. "In two days."

"Two days?!" She blanched. "What time is it?"

"Just after 2 o'clock, my lady."

"I have to leave." Charlie's head whirled. "If I don't escape now, who knows when I'll get another chance?"

"What will you do about your savings?"

She chewed her lip. The time was now.

Less than a minute later, Charlie crept into the hallway, gently rolling over her toes so that, with the added cacophony of Darryl in the lounge room, she was as quiet as death.

Their bedroom door had been left ajar and Charlie placed her ear at the gap, listening intently. Deep breathing came from within, followed by the contented snort of someone in a heavy slumber.

Gently, she pushed against the wood so it swung open millimetre by millimetre, and made a gap just big enough for her to slip through. Listening again and feeling sure that Betsy was still asleep, Charlie side stepped into the room, the cotton clothes brushing silently against the frame.

It was darker here than in the hallway and she silently begged her eyes to adjust to the impenetrable black. Squatting so she couldn't be seen if Betsy opened her eyes, she ambled awkwardly towards the bed and froze when she hit her head on the frame with a dull thud.

Berating herself, she waited for the switch of the light and the shriek of horror when Betsy discovered her crouched at the end of her bed like a waiting animal. But her breathing remained deep and measured and Charlie thanked whoever was looking after her.

She reached an arm under the bed and felt around blindly, falling short of where she had seen the strap lying earlier that day.

Praying Betsy hadn't moved it, she lowered herself gingerly to the floor and shuffled herself beneath the bed like an inept spider. Face pressed into the rug, which smelled like dust and shoes, she reached forward again, praying silently, as her fingers skimmed something in the dark.

Shuffling herself further into the black cave, she wrapped her fingers around the leather strap and tugged gently. It was slow, painstaking work, and she begged Betsy not to let the muffled dragging rouse her. It felt lighter than it had on her back.

Whole minutes passed as Charlie alternated between shuffling herself back in small increments and pulling the bag towards her. At last she was again crouching by the end of the bed and hoisted the bag onto one shoulder to prevent the straps from tickling the floor.

As she did so, the material flapped against her back. The bag was empty. Fighting the urge to let out a cry of frustration, she grit her teeth and glared at the woman on the bed.

But Betsy was already sitting up, her beady eyes glaring right back at her.

Charlie froze, one hand on the bag strap, the other ready to make a grab for the door handle.

The woman's eyes glinted in the dark as she stared at Charlie, seeming to consider what she would do with her. Charlie swallowed, weighing her options. She could run now, but she didn't have her money. This couple wouldn't claim everything she had worked for.

Finally, Betsy raised a finger to her lips, telling Charlie to be quiet as she peeled back the covers and slid out of the bed, being careful not to wake her snoring husband. Taking Charlie by the arm, the woman's fingernails buried themselves in her skin. Betsy said nothing, but the expression on her face told Charlie everything she needed to know; stay quiet and do as she was told.

Escorting Charlie forcefully back to Jennifer's bedroom, it was only after the door was firmly closed that Betsy rounded on her in disgust.

"This is how you repay us?" she whispered furiously. "Skulking off in the middle of the night without so much as a thank you?"

"Where are my things?" Charlie asked levelly, not dignifying the notion the couple deserved a morsel of gratitude.

For a second, Charlie thought the woman might slap her. "They are safe," she hissed. "As are you. A lot safer than you would be anywhere else. We're helping you. You'll see that soon enough."

"You are not helping me, you have imprisoned me!" Charlie seethed, keeping her bubbling anger in check, lest she woke Darryl and his gun.

"You don't know what a prison is, girl." Betsy was in her face now. Charlie could smell her halitosis. "You're just a spoiled city brat and you've been sent to us to set the natural order right."

"Betsy, please." Charlie wasn't above begging. "Please, just give me my things and I'll be on my way. I won't breathe a word of this to anyone."

"And what would you tell them? That we force fed you, gave you clean clothes, a warm bed, a bath?" Betsy snorted. "Do let us know when to expect the police."

With that she turned and rested a hand on the door handle. "Darryl will have a fit if he hears of this. I won't tell him, but if you try anything so stupid again, my dear, I won't be able to stop him."

The door closed softly behind her. There was the click of a solid lock falling into place and Charlie was left in silence. An unfamiliar sensation began gnawing at her lower intestine, one she soon recognised as fear. The last time she had been truly afraid was when she was left alone in the world, after the death of her grandmother. It was a feeling of helplessness, a lack of control over your own fate.

Her bag had been empty. They could have burnt her belongings and the money along with them for all she knew. Without any evidence of her former life, she could be passed off as their crazed daughter claiming to be someone she was not.

She tasted blood and drew a hand to her lip; she'd bitten through the skin. Although she wanted more than anything to call Hudson for the reassurance that everything would be all right, she decided there was no sense in worrying him. Not without a plan.

Charlie lay back on the bed, not bothering to remove her clothes or peel back the sheets. There was a way out of this mess and she would find it.

Morning light blinded Charlie as Betsy bustled in to throw open the curtains.

"Good morning, sleepyhead!" She was absurdly chipper. "You'd best be up and dressed; the day's already slipping away. You're lucky Darryl had a bit of a lie in this morning himself."

Apparently Betsy was acting under the pretence that the events of the previous night had never happened. So, too, did she ignore the fact Charlie was still lying atop the bedsheets in the clothes she had attempted to make her escape in.

She left the room briefly, humming. Charlie eyed the open door, but the woman wasn't gone for a second. "Here now, there's some more clothes." She set a neatly folded pile at the end of the bed. "Pop those on and I'll see you in the kitchen."

Her humming retreated down the hallway. Perhaps the woman had truly forgotten, or thought she'd had a very realistic dream.

Charlie considered staying in bed like a defiant teenager before, reluctantly, deciding it was better to play their game. The clothes were a pair of faded blue overalls with a checkered shirt to wear underneath. She looked every part the farm hand she'd hoped to be, just not under these circumstances.

Boots on, she trudged out to the kitchen where there was a cup of black coffee waiting for her. Betsy must have forgotten, she decided. That was a stroke in Charlie's favour.

There was a sharp intermittent thud floating in through the back door.

"Once you've got that in your belly, Darryl's out the back waiting for you. Got something different planned for you today, which is nice!" The woman continued talking asininely, not seeming to notice Charlie was yet to utter a word.

The liquid scalded her tongue but she downed it as quickly as she could, not wanting to spend more time alone with either of them than was absolutely necessary. "Thanks," she muttered, leaving the empty cup in the sink before emerging onto the back verandah.

Back to the door, shirt already dark with perspiration, Darryl swung an axe over his head and brought it down with a sharp thwack, splitting the small log clean in half. He tugged the toe of the axe free from the wooden base and fetched another log from the pile.

Sensing someone behind him, he turned and gave Charlie a look of disdain, like he couldn't have cared if she'd died in the night. Cigarette dangling from his mouth, he turned back to the log and repeated the motion. Maybe he was trying to instil fear in her.

Axe hanging by his side, he jerked his head for her to follow and stalked off towards a large corrugated iron shed at the back of the property. Years of weather had left the steel grey with a tinge of rust and stubborn weeds had wound around its frame.

He swung open its two large doors which creaked and protested bitterly, revealing something that could have passed as a torture device. It had three wheels; two large ones at the back and a small third one at the front. A large blade hung down in the middle, connected to a steering device and a lever. The ochre tinge was still discernible through the blanket of cobwebs.

"You know what this is?" Darryl kicked one of the wheels with the toe of his boot.

Charlie shook her head.

"This here is a plough, and a better one than you."

She blinked, controlling her fury. Her hours of labour the previous day hadn't been necessary, it had just been for his entertainment.

"You're to get her up to workin' again. Oil, everything you need is over there." He swung the axe towards some sagging shelves. "I don't want to see you until it's done."

Charlie fought the urge to tell his retreating back how much she would miss him. Grateful for the temporary solitude, she took in the house from where she stood, combing the perimeter for anything that might hint at the location of her things. Accepting that she probably wouldn't find one of her dresses flapping on the roof, she turned reluctantly back to the task at hand. A long-handled broom was propped up against the wall. She used it to work away the dense spider webs, swiping it at the floor when the bristles became too clogged with the sticky silk to be effective.

Satisfied in spite of herself, she reached a hand toward the lever, squeezing it gently. The blade twitched but didn't retract from the ground, rendered immobile with rust. She had oiled a door handle once, surely this wasn't so dissimilar.

The shelves were laden with dust-layered bottles; vermin poison, fertiliser, glue, many of them she couldn't make out the labels. A green and yellow can stood out and she lifted it gingerly; *Genuine John Deere Special-Purpose Oil.*

She plucked gingerly at a bundle of rags, ready to run should something with more than two legs have decided to make them its home.

Not having much idea what she was doing, she doused the rusted monster where its joins met, the centre bores of the wheels and the mouth of the lever. Sure she had used too much, she dabbed at the liquid, which was running thick and fast down its body.

Grasping the handles, she began alternating between rocking it back and forth and applying pressure to the lever. More oil. Rocking again. Squeeze the lever. Oil. Rock. Lever.

"That's my dad's," a small voice came from behind her. Jennifer had been watching her work.

"Yes." Charlie gave a sharp push and noticed a few bolts were coming loose. "He's asked me to clean this up for him."

"I could never help him with things like that," she said sadly.

Charlie scanned the shelves for a spanner, finding one behind a box of nails. "Of course you couldn't, you're only a little girl."

"I'm older than you think."

"How old are you?"

"Twelve."

Charlie turned to look at her again. The girl couldn't have been any older than five. "Do you mean that's how old you would be if you were still alive?"

"No. That's how old I was when I died." She tip-toed around the shed slowly, being careful to leave a wide berth around the well-oiled monstrosity, even though it couldn't blemish her overalls, until she was standing in front of Charlie. "I'm not like the other kids."

This was the longest exchange she'd had with the girl and, she had to admit, she was more articulate than the average five-year-old. "What do you mean?"

The girl shrugged. "I didn't get bigger like I should have. Mama tried to find a doctor who could help. They said something was wrong with me."

"Oh." Words failed Charlie as she took the girl in, all four feet of her. "I'm sorry to hear that."

Jennifer shrugged again, reaching a dainty hand up to play with her strawberry blonde hair. "My dad was upset. He said I wasn't good for anything."

Charlie had no trouble believing that. "What did he do?"

Jennifer looked towards the front of the property, her expression of sad contemplation quickly giving way to one of fear.

Charlie looked up and made eye contact with Betsy, standing at the door of the shed. The bowl of fruit and glass of water she had been carrying crashed to the ground as she raised her hands to her face.

"Darryl! Darryl!" Betsy had hold of Charlie's elbow, dragging her around the yard with surprising strength for an older woman. "Darryl!"

"I was just talking to myself," Charlie pleaded again. They could turn her over to the Enforcers, or they might have done something much worse.

"Oh no you weren't. You can see my Jenny! I know you can. You're a Seer. Darryl!"

The man emerged from the house, hoisted a suspender over his shoulder and took a long drag of his cigarette. "Quit your screaming, woman. What's she done?"

"I found her talking to Jenny." Betsy placed her hands on Charlie's shoulders, squeezing her like a prize pig. "She's a Seer, Darryl, a Seer! Do you know what this means?"

Tendrils of smoke curled out of Darryl's nose. "That she's going straight to the Enforcers."

"No!" Betsy shrieked, clutching at Charlie possessively. "She was meant to come to us! Darryl, we can talk to Jenny again! It was meant to be. Our little girl's still here and we can talk to her!"

"And what do you think she's going to say, Bets?" His tone was patronising. "Tell us to plant some magic beans and how to bring her back to life? She's gone. Get it through your head."

He disappeared back into the house, letting the door slam behind him. Charlie watched the scene unfold, aware her value to Betsy had just gone up.

Betsy looked at her with wet eyes, seeming to see her properly for the first time since her arrival. "Come with me." She tugged Charlie's arm and led her away from the house.

A dozen or so cows were grazing over the crest of a small hill. A few of them looked up at the women with mild interest before returning their mouths to the grass. Standing in the middle of their paddock, the hill was just high enough to block their view of the house. Betsy carefully chose a spot clear of manure and sat on her knees, gesturing for Charlie to do the same.

"Don't listen to him, he was more upset about losing her than he'll ever admit. He's a strong man and this is how he copes."

There were many other words Charlie would have used to describe Darryl, but strong wasn't one of them. Deciding silence was the best policy, she watched Betsy expectantly.

"Is she here now? Can you see her?"

Mind ticking methodically, Charlie was aware they had reached a juncture in their relationship. She had something Betsy wanted, and it wasn't something that could be prised out of her dead fingers. It couldn't be taken by force, which meant Charlie now had a bargaining chip.

"Darryl scared her away," she told Betsy slowly, watching the woman's face crinkle in dismay.

"Can you call her back?" Betsy clutched at her hand. "Can you tell her Mama wants to talk to her?"

"I could," Charlie withdrew her hand and interlaced her fingers. "I can help you talk to her and get whatever closure you need. But in return, you have to give me back my belongings and let me go on my way."

Betsy pursed her lips, expression unfathomable and Charlie held her gaze. For a few seconds, there was only the sound of a contented moo and grass being ground into paste.

"Fine," she agreed finally, rocking back on her feet and squinting at Charlie with disappointment. "Once I have finished speaking with her, you are free to go."

Charlie searched her eyes for any sign of misintention, but she only found resignation. "Where are my things?"

"You won't be able to get there on your own." Betsy waved a hand in dismissal. "You'll need help. But first you will let me speak to my daughter."

Sighing reluctantly, Charlie looked over her shoulder to see if Jennifer had been listening. The girl was gently stroking the head of a calf and the creature appeared to be enjoying it. Animals often seemed more perceptive than humans.

Charlie raised a hand to beckon her closer and the girl sauntered over slowly, floating hazily over the long grass.

"Your mother would like to talk to you." She watched Jennifer's face, not wanting to make her do anything she didn't want to. "Is that okay?" The girl nodded.

"Betsy, what would you like to say to Jennifer?"

The woman's eyes were weeping again. "Are you really there, Jenny? Mama misses you, I miss you so much!" Her face fell into tears and Jennifer reached up to place a hand on her shoulder.

"I'm right here, Mama. You don't have to miss me."

"She's touching your shoulder." Charlie watched Betsy search the space next to her, looking for her lost daughter. "And she says you don't have to miss her, that she's right here."

The woman smiled wetly. "Has she changed at all? What a stupid question, you wouldn't know. How does she look?"

Her earlier conversation with the little girl still fresh in her mind, Charlie answered carefully, "She's a pretty little thing. She has long blonde hair and a birthmark on her face. I'd say she's about five years old."

Betsy exhaled sharply. "Yes, you would, because of her condition. I prayed every day – in secret, of course – for the Lord to make her better. I thought for a little girl to be given such an affliction there must be a Devil, so it's only logical that there's a God, too."

Jennifer listened sadly, trying to brush her mother's hair with her tiny fingers.

"If there is, He never listened," Betsy continued, oblivious. "But I guess I was right about one thing; about there being something else. What's it like, Jenny? How is it over there?"

Jennifer shrugged, forgetting her invisibility. "I don't know, Mama. I've never left."

"She's never crossed over. She's been with you since she died," Charlie relayed. The divide between worlds wasn't one that could be crossed like a bridge. Once one left earth, it was almost impossible to come back.

"You're a good girl, Jenny. You always knew not to go far from home." Betsy drew a deep, shuddering breath."I'm sorry I let you down, Jenny. I'll never forgive myself. I never should've left you out there on your own."

"I wasn't alone, Mama. Papa was out there with me."

An awful feeling crept into Charlie's chest. "She said Darryl was out there with her."

Betsy froze, blinking at the ground. "Are you sure, Jenny? Your father was out here," she gestured to the cows, "spreading hay. He didn't find you until—" She trailed off, biting her lip.

But Jennifer shook her head. "No, Mama. He was playing with me at the well."

Charlie sensed an escalating tension and was beginning to wish she wasn't the translator of this particular conversation. "She says he was playing with her at the well."

Betsy was still staring at a patch of dirt in front of her, lines on her forehead deepening. "That can't be right. She must have forgotten."

The little girl pouted but Charlie held her tongue. A seed had been planted and, if there was a truth to be found, Betsy would uncover it on her own.

"She was a clever little thing, you know, in her own way." Betsy seemed to be talking to Charlie now. "Had this way of knowing whatever I was thinking. I could never hide anything from her. But in this world, you know, who knows what would have become of her. Maybe what happened was a mercy."

"Why do you say that?"

Betsy pinned her with a stare. "Imagine you gave birth to a beautiful baby girl. Those first cries were like music because she was everything you'd hoped for. You hold her in your arms and she's this perfect little thing. The world hasn't ruined her yet, and she doesn't know to be scared of it.

"As the months go on, you start to feel like something's not quite right. She doesn't seem interested in moving or talking, and she's not putting on weight like she should. At six months old, she's still the weight of a newborn. And so you find a doctor and they tell you your little girl will always stay a little girl. She'll probably never get bigger than a ten-year-old and, even if she does, she'll never think like an adult.

"Everything you ever wanted for her, the dreams you had of your perfect young lady finding her place in the world and, one day, having a family of her own, gone in an instant. Her short life will be a struggle of looking for acceptance, love she'll never get from anyone but you. And she'll never understand why.

"Tell me, is that something you'd wish on her?"

Charlie couldn't imagine how Betsy had felt and she wouldn't pretend to. There wasn't a simple answer to such a heavily weighted question. It seemed rhetorical in any event, so she allowed it to hang unanswered between them.

"Nightmares, child," Betsy whispered. "This world only holds nightmares."

Jennifer was still hovering by her mother's side. The monologue didn't seem to have perturbed her. It was evidently everything she already knew.

"Is there anything else you'd like to say to Jennifer?"

Betsy smiled. "Not for now."

For now? "It's time for you to give me back my things, then."

"Oh, I'm not done talking to my daughter," Betsy answered lightly. "There's much more still to talk about, just not now."

"But you said—" Charlie's nostrils flared, remembering her choice of words.

"I said when I was done speaking with her." Betsy pushed herself up, hands on her knees. "And I'm not finished yet."

Charlie grit her teeth. "And when will you be finished?"

The woman raised her hands. "Perhaps tonight, perhaps tomorrow. We will see. You'd best get back to what you were doing. Talk to you soon, Jenny! Mama loves you."

"Love you, Mama," Jennifer called, but Charlie didn't repeat her.

Sixteen

THE BANG

Betsy left Charlie sitting in the paddock, staring after her with contempt. Charlie now knew she had no intention of returning her bag. If she had been reluctant to allow her to leave before, she would never let the Seer slip away now she had a connection to her daughter.

Quietly seething, she pulled up a fistful of grass from the roots.

"What's wrong?" Charlie looked up and jumped, finding Jennifer leaning down and well inside her personal space.

She swallowed, not knowing how to tell the girl her parents were psychopaths. "How long ago did you die, Jennifer?"

The girl shrugged. "I don't know. A really long time."

"And why have you stayed here for so long?"

She looked towards the crest of the hill where her mother had disappeared. "Because it's home."

"Right," Charlie concurred. "You feel safe here, don't you? Your parents are here, your room is here, all your memories are here. You're comfortable here."

She waited for Jennifer to nod in agreement before continuing. "I had a family, too. They're gone now and I miss them very much. I had a home as well, but without them it didn't feel like one anymore. So I saved up all my money and decided to try to find a home of my own, somewhere I could make new memories and be comfortable – just like you.

"But now, someone has taken all my money and your parents don't want me to leave. This isn't my home, Jennifer, it's yours. I don't belong here and being here makes me sad."

Jennifer bit her lip. "Mama would be mad at me for telling you."

"I won't tell her that you told me, I promise." Charlie extended a pinky but the little girl eyed it curiously. Apparently she had never heard of a pinky swear.

"But then I wouldn't be able to talk to them."

"No," Charlie conceded. "But do you think it's fair for me to be trapped here?"

Jennifer blinked at her before wavering and dissipated where she stood. Charlie dropped her head. It had all been too much for Jennifer to handle.

Collecting herself, she dusted the loose grass off her legs and stalked back towards the shed. The house stood a few feet off the ground, supported by strong pillars and lattice skirting around the base. Much of it had deteriorated, leaving gaping holes to the impenetrable blackness beneath. One hole towards the rear corner was particularly large and Charlie considered climbing within to hide.

The thought made her stop; a hiding place. Casting furtive glances towards the windows and seeing there were no faces peering out at her, she scurried towards the opening.

The lack of spider webs made her wary, as if they had recently been cleared by someone else climbing in. She extended one leg inside, found her footing and crouched, easing the rest of her body through the opening. Her overalls snagged on a rogue nail protruding from the lattice. She unhooked herself before turning to the dark and waiting for her eyes to adjust.

It had evidently served as a home to more than a few creatures, with droppings littering the floor and an accompanying dank smell. She shuffled herself further inside, trying not to let her knees touch the ground. While she wasn't particularly worried about ruining Betsy's clothes, she'd rather not be covered in vermin excrement for the rest of the day.

She bumped her head on a low hanging beam and muffled a curse, cradling her forehead and waiting for the throbbing to subside. Something moved above her head and she flinched, waiting for whatever it was to fall on her. But the weight shifted again. Footsteps were pacing above her, and she realised she must be beneath the living room.

"How would she know that, Darryl? She couldn't have." Betsy's voice floated down through the floorboards.

"You're only getting more gullible the older you become," Darryl retorted. "She hasn't told you nothing. This is what their kind does. They find some sad, gullible sack like you and use 'em for what they're worth."

"Jennifer said you were out there with her."

"What?"

"Jennifer said you were out there with her when she— when she fell."

"I was in the shed, you know that!"

"Why would she lie?"

"For Pete's sake!" The sound of something being slammed shook a little bit of dust into Charlie's eyes. "I will not be questioned by some city psycho trying to scare us into doing what she wants!"

"Why would our daughter say that?"

"Our daughter isn't saying anything! She's dead!"

"You should talk to her."

"What?"

"You should talk to her. Through Charlie. See for yourself."

"I don't need to see nothing for myself. You've lost your marbles, that's all I can see."

"Don't you miss her?" Betsy had kept a surprisingly cool voice to this point but it now began to break.

"We both know what happened was a kindness. It was the best thing that could've happened."

"How can you be so cold?"

"Don't gimme that, you know it too. She couldn't work and she couldn't wed, so what was the point?"

Betsy was choking on her tears now. "She was ours."

Darryl gave an exasperated sigh. "You're too emotional. It was the right thing to do."

"Right thing to do?"

"Right thing to happen! You know what I mean, stop harassing me."

There was silence and Charlie imagined Betsy staring at him in disbelief. Eventually her footsteps shuffled away. Though she hardly considered Betsy her friend, she prayed she would have the sense to keep questioning.

The cobwebs must have been cleared by an animal because there was nothing beneath the house except dust and dirt. Clambering back out into the daylight, she squinted against the glaring sun and made her way back to the shed. But she had no intention of working on the plough.

"Jennifer," she called. "Jennifer?"

"Mhm?" The little girl was already by her side.

Charlie pondered how to approach this conversation. She had never been particularly good with children. "Are you alright?"

"Yes. Why wouldn't I be?"

"Well, that might have been a hard conversation for you. And even though you're obviously brave and handled it very well, I want to make sure you're not upset."

"Oh." From her expression, she still didn't see what there was to be upset about. "I'm fine."

"That's good." Charlie hesitated. "Would you mind if I asked you more about the day you died?"

She scuffed her tiny boot on the dirt floor. "I don't really like to talk about that."

"I don't blame you and I'm sorry to ask, but it's important I know what happened."

"Why?"

"Because you matter."

Jennifer chewed her lip thoughtfully. "I don't really. Papa said I was never good for anything."

"Do you believe that?" The girl shrugged and Charlie's heart wilted, realising that she did.

"Jennifer, no two people are born the same. We're all made from a different recipe, whether it's blonde or brown hair, blue or green eyes, dark or light skin, two legs or six." The little girl giggled.

"Some of us grow to be big, hulking beasts." She held her arms out to her sides and puffed out her cheeks in her best impression of a puffer fish. "And some of us stay small." She shrank, crouching down. "And those are the most powerful people of all, because they're under-estimated. No one suspects them until it's too late!" Charlie lurched forward as if to grab Jennifer and the girl dodged, giggling madly.

"You matter because only you can be you. And the world wanted you here, because here you are." Charlie sat cross-legged, hoping Jennifer heard her.

"You're funny." Something about Jennifer's energy shifted. "We were playing in the yard. Papa was teaching me how to play hacky sack. I think he called it a hit-stop, where I dropped the sack and tried to hit it back into my hand with my knee."

"That sounds hard." Jennifer nodded. "Where was your mother?"

"Cooking."

"What was she cooking?"

"Dinner. We were having green bean casserole."

"And what happened?"

"I wasn't very good at it. I kicked it so far that I didn't know where it went. I was looking for it and looking for it, and then Papa said it had gone down the well. So I climbed up on the edge to look down and I... fell."

"Just like that?"

Jennifer chewed her lip before shaking her head. "It was probably an accident. Papa wouldn't have meant it."

"Did he push you?"

"He was probably trying to pull me back."

Charlie sighed, knowing Jennifer would never be able to accept her own father had killed her. And it was probably better that way. A rage-fuelled fire for the man, if he could so be called, had been lit in her chest.

"Thank you for telling me." They sat in silence for a few moments before Jennifer rose and climbed into Charlie's lap. The tingle of her energy thrummed through her legs and Charlie wrapped her arms around her awkwardly, guessing from the warmth of the air where her body was.

Charlie had never considered herself maternal, but in that moment, she would have given her life in an instant for this innocent girl to know a life with love. They stayed like that for a while, Charlie wasn't sure how long. She had no intention of working any more than she had. It was sickening that she had done anything for him at all.

It wasn't until Jennifer gave her a fond pat on the head and evaporated that she staggered to her feet, shaking them to redistribute the blood. She searched the shelves; she would need something to defend herself. A spanner? Too light. A sledgehammer? Too heavy. A screwdriver? Probably the best option she had. It was light in her pocket and she kept the handle facing up where it was within easy reach of her fingertips.

There were some spray bottles she would have liked to take as well, but none would fit easily in her clothes. With her meagre weapon and defiant resolution, she stalked back to the house, the late afternoon sun giving birth to shadows as it waned.

It was an unpleasant silence that descended over dinner. There were only the irksome sounds of mastication and teeth grinding the chicken and vegetables. Charlie picked at it, trying not to wonder which of the flock they were eating.

Betsy hadn't asked for her help preparing dinner. Charlie assumed she had wanted to be alone with her thoughts. Darryl hadn't come to check on the state of the plough. It seemed he also had other things on his mind. Charlie had closed herself in Jennifer's room, jamming a children's book beneath the door should either of them have tried to pay her a visit. But they didn't.

Hudson had listened to her plan and agreed to help her, albeit with the caution one would expect from a grandparent. He would only step in if he felt he was needed; Charlie didn't want him draining his energy unless absolutely necessary. Although, by this point, it would take a lot for the seasoned spirit to come close to diminishing his reserves.

He stood in the corner of the dining room, watching with quiet intent. He hadn't voiced his opinion of Darryl, nor did he need to from the way his mouth curled in revolt when he looked at him.

Heart hammering, Charlie tried to calm herself. "So how do you pass the time out here?"

Both Darryl and Betsy stopped chewing for a second, obviously wondering if she had lost the plot.

"There's a lot of work to be done on a farm," Betsy answered politely. "We don't often find ourselves with spare time."

"It's so nice out here. It's a shame you don't get a chance to enjoy it. Especially with all this space. Did Jennifer play any sport?"

Darryl was glowering at his food. "She couldn't, not with her condition," Betsy supplied again.

"Oh, really? So it was just the once you played hacky sack with her, then?" Charlie turned to Darryl.

He choked on his food, his already red face turning crimson as he hacked.

"You played hacky sack with Jenny?" Betsy's brow knitted.

"I don't know what you're talking about," Darryl spluttered, regaining control over his lungs.

Charlie eyed his shotgun leaning against the doorframe. He would only have to lean over to grab it. "You don't remember? I suppose it was a long time ago. Jennifer said she wasn't very good at it, either. You were doing the 'hit-stop drill', I think she called it."

At this, Darryl's face went slack. His eyes were pinned on Charlie, seeing her for the first time, as his brain scrambled desperately behind them. If he hadn't thought she was genuine before, he knew she was now.

Betsy's fork was still hovering halfway to her mouth. "Were you truly teaching her? You haven't played in years."

"I wasn't and I haven't." His scowl snapped back into place.

"Was it too hard to play again? You know, after what happened."

"What happened?" Betsy lowered her fork.

His nostrils flared. "Shut up."

"Apparently the sack fell down the well—"

"Shut up!"

"That's what Darryl said anyway."

"Shut up!"

"So poor Jennifer leant over to look for it."

"I said shut up, you lying whore!" Darryl slammed his fists on the table. Betsy's eyes were wide, mouth slightly ajar as the scene unfolded. Hudson stepped in closer.

"I've definitely never sold that particular service," Charlie replied curtly.

"That's it, I've had enough of you!" His left arm reached for the gun, his right still splayed on the table.

Without thinking, Charlie grabbed the screwdriver from her pocket and, before Betsy had a chance to scream, she brought it down on Darryl's hand, driving the metal between the bones and lodging the point in the table.

He let out an anguished yell, knocking the gun from where it had been leaning. Blood was streaming from the wound, pooling on the wood. Betsy and Charlie were on their feet now. Betsy's face was contorted in horror, but not from her husband's mutilated hand.

"What happened when she looked down the well, Darryl?"

He was still reaching for the gun but it was just beyond his fingertips. In desperation, he closed his fist around the handle of the screwdriver, grimacing in pain as he pulled it free. He stood slowly, pointing it at Charlie with a maniacal expression as he advanced around the table.

Charlie swallowed, sliding her knife from the table and balling her fist around it. It was only a butter knife but it was all she had.

Hudson stepped forward, ready to protect her, but Betsy had found her senses. She jumped forward, seized the gun and raised it, trembling, towards her husband.

He froze. "What do you think you're doing?"

"Y-y-you tell m-me what h-happened." Betsy was trying valiantly to be fierce but her facade failed her.

"Or what?" he spat, holding his hand as blood coursed down his arm. "You don't know how to use that thing."

Betsy pulled the fore-end towards her before sliding it away, the menacing click of the firing pin draining the blood from his face.

"Tell me what happened." She was more confident now.

He swallowed, eyes on the barrel. "It was an accident."

"Liar," Charlie hissed.

"Shut up!" he yelled again.

"What happened?" Betsy pressed.

He grit his teeth and cracked his neck, a vein throbbing above his collar. "You're gonna believe this lunatic over your own husband? Where's the proof?"

Betsy didn't look away from him. "Charlie, what was I doing?"

Charlie blinked. "What?"

"What was I doing?" she asked again. "When Jenny died, what was I doing?"

Charlie's brain scrambled, she knew this. "Cooking!"

Darryl snorted. "When aren't you cooking?"

"You were cooking dinner. Green bean casserole." Charlie stared defiantly at Darryl, as he visibly wilted under the force of her determination.

That was all Betsy needed. She levelled the barrel with her eye. "Last chance."

"I did you a favour!" he screamed, his chair crashing against the wall as he put his heel into it. "I did us all a favour. She was a burden, and that's all she ever would be. She never woulda worked and she never woulda married. I showed her mercy."

Face contorting with emotion Charlie could never have imagined, Betsy took a step towards him. "You— " she choked, "monster! How dare you. Your own daughter. I trusted you. She trusted you. All these years I believed you."

"Come on, Bets. You're always so emotional. Think logically for once."

"I am thinking logically for once and I think you should leave."

He guffawed. "You think you can kick me outta my own house? Not bloody likely."

Sensing his cue, Hudson gave him a firm push in on Darryl's chest and he stumbled backwards. He blinked, searching for where the blow had come from. "What the hell was that?"

"I think Jennifer wants you to leave, too." Charlie nodded towards Hudson who pushed him again.

Visibly scared for the first time, Darryl backed into the living room. "How are you doing that?"

"I'm not doing anything. Jennifer's stronger than you gave her credit for. Stronger in death than you ever could be in life."

"You bastard!" Betsy cried. There was a deafening bang and Charlie raised her hands to her ringing ears, but she still heard Darryl bellow in pain.

"Dammit!" He dropped to the floor, hands on his thigh, writhing in anguish.

"You're going to need someone to look at that," Betsy acknowledged. "Best start walking."

"You crazy bitch!" he spat. She pumped the fore-end, empty shell clattering to the floor as a new one took its place.

Not needing to be told again, he scrambled towards the door, leg dragging behind him and leaving a trail of blood in his wake.

Betsy followed him, gun pointed at his back, as she watched him fall down the front steps and onto the lawn.

"You'll pay for this, whore!" he yelled into the night, stumbling away. "You're just like her. Useless."

Bang. Darryl dropped like a sack of rocks. Hands over her ears, Charlie waited for movement or a cry of pain, but none came.

Shoulder to shoulder, Betsy, Hudson and Charlie stood on the porch, looking out at Darryl's lifeless body. A grim finality hung in the air.

"He's dead." Betsy's voice was small. "I killed him."

Charlie just stared in disbelief.

"I had to." Betsy turned to her. "He would've come back, he would've— "

"I know," Charlie found her voice. "He deserved it."

Betsy would never have to worry about his shadow emerging from the night to exact his revenge. For the first time in years she was free of his shackles. She never had to listen to his abuse again.

Unfortunately, Charlie still did.

A dark form was clambering up from where his body had fallen, stretching its limbs like a tarantula emerging from an egg. "Shit."

Betsy turned to her, eyes wide. "Oh, dear!"

Charlie grimaced. Oh dear, indeed.

Seventeen

THE BURIAL

Darryl's dark figure examined himself, extending his arms and flexing his fingers. Realising he was standing on his own back, he jumped away in horror. Charlie could see the cogs ticking as he moved in for closer inspection. She could almost pinpoint the moment the realisation struck him; he was dead.

"You bitch!" he bellowed, eyeing Betsy with contempt. But Betsy was still staring at Charlie, waiting for an indication of what her dead husband was doing.

"I don't think he's particularly happy," Charlie commented, deadpan.

"He can't— " Betsy's voice tremored.

"No, he can't hurt us. He's not strong enough. Not yet, anyway."

Darryl was storming towards them and Charlie found a small pleasure in the fact that he could no longer intimidate his wife. She stared right through him.

"I'll make you pay!" he hissed, striking at her and falling forward as his fist passed clean through.

"You're about as threatening as a blowfly," Charlie observed. "Somewhat annoying but that's all."

He advanced on her, face thunderous. "I will make your life a living hell."

"You probably could but you're not going to get that chance." She turned to Betsy. "We have to bury him. You get the shovel, I'll get the cypress. I'll explain soon," she added, in response to the bewildered expression on Betsy's face.

Charlie had never realised how large graves really were. Most people, she lamented, didn't appreciate the effort involved in digging them. Inspecting her blistered fingers, she reluctantly gripped the shovel handle and resumed her attack on the ground. To be fair, she conceded, most people never had to dig one.

She had passed a number of cypress trees on her journey. It was second nature by now that she noted each one she saw. The last one had only been about a mile down the road, so she jogged there and back to collect as much as she could carry. Darryl yelling constant abuse at her back was all the motivation she needed.

Time was also encroaching on Wynn's trial. With a bit of haste and a lot of luck, she could have Darryl trapped in the ground and be back in the city by the next afternoon.

Hudson had vanished quickly, taking Jennifer with him at Charlie's request. She didn't know where earth-bound ghosts went to rest, but Hudson would keep the girl safe. He was the only person Charlie could trust. Dead or alive.

"You do have an option, you know," she said conversationally between Darryl's stream of profanities. "I don't have to trap you here. An eternity of staring at the dirt sounds awful to me, personally."

"And what's my choice? Crossing over to who-knows-where? Meeting my maker?" He snorted. "A bit of twig isn't going to stop me, you daft—"

"That's enough," Charlie cut him off.

"I'm sorry you still have to listen to him, dear." Betsy was leaning against a nearby tree, sleeves rolled up to her elbows and dirt smeared on her frock. Sweat glistened on her brow as Charlie took her turn on the shovel.

"Not for much longer."

With Darryl's limbs dangling over the sides of an old wheelbarrow, they had pushed him a few miles away from the house. It made no difference to Charlie where he was buried, but she understood Betsy didn't want to look out the window every morning to the freshly turned mound of dirt containing her dead husband.

His limbs had bounced with a life of their own as the wheelbarrow trundled over the uneven terrain. Betsy didn't seem concerned about his demise, or even her part in it. She spoke only of her daughter and repeated that she had never known. Jennifer was safe, Charlie assured her. Mercifully, she hadn't been present for the evening's events.

When the amber glow of the house's lights hovered like fireflies in the distance, they had started to dig near a weeping willow tree to mark the grave. It was the only thing, though, that would ever weep there.

"Do you think this is deep enough?" Looking up at Betsy from the depths of the hole, Charlie shivered. Betsy nodded her approval but Charlie was already hoisting herself out of the pit.

"Would you like to do the honours?" Charlie motioned towards the wheelbarrow.

Betsy straightened, grasping the handles and moving the wheelbarrow into position. "I hope you rot, you bastard." She upended it with a grunt of effort, her husband's body dropping with a heavy thud to the bottom of the pit.

"Till death do us part, sweet 'art," he mumbled bitterly.

Wanting to be thorough, Charlie had dragged a veritable cypress tree behind them and she set about snapping it into smaller sections. Starting at his feet she worked her way steadily up to his head, making sure he was smothered in leafy branches.

"Hang on." Darryl was moving closer against his will. His legs and arms were working furiously to move himself away but he was being dragged backwards towards his body. "Fucking stop!"

"No chance." Charlie continued her work purposefully, ensuring he was completely covered in the leaves.

He clawed at the side of the grave as he was slowly drawn into the void. A scream of terror escaping, as his own body slowly enveloped him like a large predatory snake. Charlie only lamented that Betsy couldn't watch the man who had murdered her daughter be sentenced to the eternal damnation he deserved.

His arms flailed madly, face contorting in terror until he was completely entrapped and the screaming finally stopped. There was an eerie silence, only the night's gentle breeze whispering secrets into the willow tree above them.

"Is it done?" Betsy looked down at the body.

"It's done."

They observed him for a few seconds longer, as if making sure he was truly dead. Charlie kicked at a lump of dirt, sending it scattering across his back. Betsy retrieved the shovel and began covering her husband's remains and his trapped, tortured soul.

"You know I have to go now, Betsy." The woman stiffened, shovel pausing mid air. "There's a boy who needs my help. A boy who trusted me to do the right thing and I didn't. He's about Jennifer's age and now he's going to take the fall on my behalf, unless I can get back to help him in time."

For a few seconds there was only the regular crunch of the shifting soil. "And what am I meant to do? Here all alone. No husband, a daughter trapped here and I can't even talk to her."

"Souls are never trapped here, it's a choice. Except, of course, for this one." She eyed the portion of Darryl's back which hadn't yet been immersed in dirt. "Usually it's because they feel there's something left undone or they feel responsible for something. I think Jennifer's here because she's worried about you. I can only imagine how hard it was losing her, and how hard it would be letting her go again, but there's somewhere she would be much happier. I think, with your permission, she might go."

If there were tears in Betsy's eyes she didn't lift her head. There was only the rhythmic crunch, splatter, crunch, splatter of the dirt.

"It would be selfish of me, wouldn't it?"

"I think it's normal to try to hold onto what we've lost. Jennifer lived her life aware of the restrictions of her body, and I'm sure you don't want her to feel that same entrapment in death."

"Will you let me say goodbye?"

"Of course."

They worked in silence for another hour or so, taking turns when their arms started to burn. The process of replacing the dirt was easier than removing it but still tiresome. Charlie's stomach emanated a hollow growl and she realised she hadn't eaten properly since the day before.

When the dirt was once again level with the grass, they smoothed it over with the back of the shovel and stood back, taking stock of their work. There was a gap in the air as they wondered if they should say something or mark the grave in some way. Silently agreeing there was no need, their weary feet took them back to the house, empty wheelbarrow trundling in front, minus its gruesome burden.

It was surreal walking back through the door in which Darryl had first brandished his gun at her, tapping the barrel on the doorframe menacingly. Why had she not run then?

Betsy just stood, arms by her sides, in the middle of the living room, staring at the remnants of the chaos. A smashed plate with food on the floor, the upended chair against the wall, a spatter of blood where a bullet had found his leg.

"I'll help you clean up." Charlie started heading for the kitchen to look for a dustpan.

"No, please don't." Betsy stopped her. "I don't know what I'll do with myself now. It will be good to... be busy. For a little while at least. And there are more important matters you can help me with."

Nodding, Charlie closed her eyes and probed the darkness. Hudson, Jennifer.

There was a high pitched giggle as they appeared in the room. Hudson was leaning over her, looking every bit like a grandfather finishing a story as Jennifer squealed in delight. Charlie smiled. "You look like you've had fun."

Hudson's warm eyes smiled at her and she knew he had enjoyed having the girl in his care, if only for a few hours. Jennifer nodded happily.

"You're a very strong girl, Jennifer. To have gone through what you have and stayed here to make sure your mother is alright." She licked her lips. "Your father isn't going to be here anymore. He left, and he won't be back."

"Where did he go?" Jennifer was clinging to Hudson's hand.

He crouched down beside her, groaning out of habit because his weary bones surely could no longer be bothering him. "We all make choices in life, my child, and sometimes those choices require careful reflection. Some choices need to be thought about for a long time, indeed.

"None of us are born bad but some of us lose our way. Your father lost his way and harmed the people he should have cared for. Now he is like us, but somewhere he will be made to think about what he has done."

Her little face looked thoughtful as she tried to make sense of what she'd just heard. "You mean Papa's in a time out?"

Charlie stifled a laugh. "Something like that."

Betsy was staring at her blankly, oblivious to the conversation.When Charlie relayed the dialogue, Betsy wasn't in the frame of mind to see the humour but the corners of her mouth twitched reflexively. "What would you like to say to Jennifer?"

Looking haggard and worn beyond her years, Betsy lowered herself gently onto the lounge. She fumbled with her hands in her lap, dirt pushed into the wrinkles and lines of her fingers.

"Your Papa's gone away, Jenny. He won't bother either of us anymore. I'm sorry I didn't know. I'm sorry I didn't protect you." She choked but swallowed her tears, ploughing on determinedly. "I know you've stayed here to take care of me, to make sure I'm okay. Well I'm okay now, Jenny. And I don't want you to spend any more time trapped here."

"She's sitting in front of you," Charlie told her gently.

Betsy looked up at the space in which Jennifer was kneeling, hands on her mother's knees. "I love you, Jenny. And I will love you every day of this life and into the next. But it's not fair of me to ask you to stay here anymore. There's a place for you somewhere. And wherever that is, I know you'll be happy and loved until I get there myself."

Jennifer's face sank. "I don't want to go, Mama. I'm scared."

"You don't have to be scared, Jennifer." Charlie took a seat beside Betsy. "You know that feeling of being tucked into bed at night and being warm and cosy while your mother sang you a lullaby? Do you remember how safe and loved you were?" Jennifer's eyes were wide; she knew. "That's what it's like."

"You'll see your grandma and grandpa, Jenny. They'll be so excited to meet you. I know they'll take good care of you, too." Betsy sniffled.

Jennifer looked around for Hudson who nodded at her reassuringly. "There is nothing to be frightened of, child."

"How long will I have to wait for Mama?"

"Oh, you don't have to worry about that. Years might pass here on earth, but to you it will feel like a blink of an eye before your mother is with you again." She glanced at Betsy who, to her surprise, was holding her own.

She nodded. "I'll be there soon, Jenny. Don't you worry."

Hudson extended his hand. "Come, Jennifer. I can take you part of the way."

Jennifer took his hand softly and rose to her feet before throwing her arms around her mother who jumped in surprise.

Betsy gasped. "I feel this warmth."

"That's her." Charlie was fighting her own tears now.

Betsy dropped her head and leant into the warmth. "I love you so much, Jenny. Thank you for being my daughter. I'll see you soon, baby."

"Love you, Mama," Jennifer whispered, taking Hudson's hand again and letting him lead her towards the door.

Charlie repeated what she'd said, and Betsy clutched her hands to her mouth.

As Hudson and Jennifer approached, the door fell away to a glowing tunnel. A warm breeze came from within, accompanied by a gentle hum which could only be described as the sound of peace. Whatever

Jennifer saw down that tunnel made her smile and, with one last look at her mother, she blew a kiss and stepped into the warm glow. Hudson released her hand as the door sealed behind her. "Goodbye, little one."

Trudging the road back towards the city, Charlie wasn't the same person who had left only a few days ago. Her optimism had been replaced by determination, her hope by acceptance, and her triumph by guilt. The uneven ground tripped her occasionally and the odd mosquito nipped at her exposed neck, which she slapped at half-heartedly.

She hunched forward under the weight of her bag, now heavy with its rightful cargo.

"We may need your friend to help," Betsy had admitted contritely when Charlie asked, for the final time, where her things were.

Peering down into the blackness of the well, the depths were impenetrable. Had Betsy not told her, Charlie never would have found them. Throwing a disdainful glare at Betsy, she bit her tongue. The woman had been punished enough.

"It's dry as a bone down there, your things will be just fine." Charlie arched an eyebrow at Betsy's choice of analogy, as that was without a doubt where Jennifer's bones still lay.

They fastened a bucket to a long stretch of rope and lowered it down, further and further still until there was an echoing clunk as it found the stony bottom.

"Hudson?" Charlie didn't want to ask him to plunge himself down that horrific hole, but there was little choice. He nodded without complaint and evaporated. She couldn't see him down in the abyss, but his voice soon rang out.

"Charlie?"

"Yes?"

"Let's make two journeys. Betsy should not watch the first."

Hesitantly, she made eye contact with Betsy. "I'm sure you agree your daughter deserves a proper resting place." Betsy's tears seemed to have run dry. All she could do was close her eyes and nod her head. "I think it would be best if you wait inside."

The woman seemed inclined to argue, opening her mouth and closing it several times before thinking better of it and retreating into the house.

"Okay, Hudson."

He called when the bones were safely inside the bucket. Charlie pulled it up slowly, not wanting the bucket to snag on a rock and have the bones unceremoniously dumped back to the bottom of the well. Seeing remains was one thing, but having spoken to the young girl to whom they belonged only minutes prior was another.

Steeling herself, the sight still caused her head to reel and she instinctively squeezed the rope tighter to ensure she didn't lose her grip.

The yard was relatively barren, save for a few tenacious trees and an untended garden bed. So Charlie, with Hudson by her side, carried the bones to the crest of the small hill behind the house and laid the bones out as best she could, in the shape they should have been. Spotting some butterfly weed meandering along the dilapidated fence, she picked it in handfuls and scattered the orange flowers across Jennifer's skeleton.

"Let's get my things, and then we'll ask where she'd like her buried."

Hudson nodded. He had seen much in his many years on earth, more than any one person should have to. Yet plucking the bones from the bottom of the well had affected him deeply and he opted for silence over open maudlin lamentation.

They repeated the process and Charlie hauled her things up, relieved to see the wads of cash were among her clothes. Betsy, or Darryl, evidently hadn't bothered searching her things. They had only wanted to dispose of them in order to keep her there as long as possible.

Betsy reacted to the sight of her daughter's remains with surprising grace. She sat with them and wept until Charlie pulled her into a hug. She couldn't hate the woman; not now her world had been taken from her. Her shoulder grew wet as she held her there, aware it may be the last physical comfort Betsy would have for some time.

As the minutes ticked on, the thought of Wynn facing the courtroom alone appeared unwelcome in her mind's eye. She drew away from Betsy gently, holding her by the shoulders to ensure she didn't keel over where she sat.

"No, I'll do it myself," Betsy replied when asked if she would like help burying her daughter. "She's my Jenny. I brought her into this world and I will lay her to rest."

It was an unsettling thing to walk away from a grieving mother, knowing no amount of time would heal the wounds her soul bore. She could have stayed and kept her company through those first few desolate days, but it would be at the expense of another child; a child Charlie could ensure had the chance at life Jennifer had never received.

It seemed a fitting punishment to have to return as soon as she had left, tail between her legs and suitably chastened by what she had found. She had fled, not thinking about the boy who had placed his faith in her. The boy who had biological parents but not loving ones, who had spent every year of his short life pretending he was one of the wolves he ran with rather than a sheep. She had left him surrounded by them. Of course it was only a matter of time until they'd sniffed him out.

Dreams of a farmhouse of her own were firmly behind her now and trying to recall them was like trying to grasp fog. Evidently her subconscious knew any more rumination would only serve as torture. In her heart of hearts, Charlie had known she'd never escape the city's claws. Life just wasn't that kind.

Eighteen

THE COURTHOUSE

The courthouse was a building Charlie had always made a point of avoiding. Large and imposing with statues of the forefathers guarding the stone steps, it loomed over passersby as a grim reminder that they lived by its law.

Its foundations, however, did not run into the earth. It had been built on a prison which now held the condemned until they were called for trial. That's where Wynn was.

Exhaustion had packed the bags her bloodshot eyes were holding and her brain was an addled mess of anxiety, determination and fatigue. She looked distinctly out of place in her boots, wrinkled trousers and grubby blouse, and probably a face that belonged on a corpse. She did not look like she belonged in the city and the steady stream of foot traffic wasn't slow to remind her of this with furtive glances.

Drawing a deep breath she wished was a stiff drink, she planted her boots firmly on the steps – but the illusion of confidence didn't stretch past her knees.

Uniform-clad security guards waited just inside the door and Charlie half expected them to take an arm each and haul her straight to a cell. They would soon enough.

"Can we see inside your bag please, Miss?" The guard was polite but she knew it wasn't a question.

She held it open, wondering what he made of the girl carrying a week's worth of clothes and food on her back. But he reserved comment and, satisfied she wasn't concealing a weapon, he nodded for her to proceed.

An ornate ceiling hung at least three stories above her, with more detail in the intricate patterns than had gone into her whole apartment building. Two large mahogany doors stood with imposing grandeur at either end of the wall facing her. Three booths sat between them with prim secretaries filing paperwork and registering spectators as they arrived. The court was not limited to religious crime, however those cases inevitably drew the largest crowds.

On either side hung blackboards with a series of names, indicating which courtroom they were to be trialled in. Daphne Smith, Reginald Harper, Gregory Fisher. Her stomach churned as she found Wynn Barron listed on the board to the left. There were no times beside the names, just the order in which they were to be sentenced.

She joined the short queue to be registered behind a tall man wearing a fedora and grey suit with a long-strapped camera slung over one shoulder. He must have been from the local paper.

Her stomach twisting itself in knots, each step towards the counter sent palpitations rippling through her heart. Too soon, the journalist was called forward and she watched as he fished his identification out of his inner pocket.

A secretary with auburn hair plastered back into a bun and heavy eyeshadow glanced up at her. "Next."

She could still turn around and leave but, knowing any life she built would be coloured with guilt, she proceeded to the booth.

"Name please." The woman sounded bored.

"Charlotte Hall."

"Date of birth?"

"August 1st, 1935."

"Trial of interest?"

She paused, there was no point lying. "Wynn Barron."

The secretary arched a plucked eyebrow but said nothing as she scribbled in the book before her.

"Do you have a form of identification?"

"Oh, yes. One moment, I'm sorry." She dropped her bag to the floor and plunged an arm inside, feeling around for the small book she had packed at the bottom for safe keeping.

"Here it is." She produced her identity card, emblazoned with the coat of arms; a large eagle with its wings outstretched.

The lady inspected it closely and looked up at her shrewdly, determining that she was in fact the girl in the photograph. Charlie couldn't blame her; life had not been kind since it was taken.

Eventually she must have been satisfied. "Courtroom one," she said, handing it back to her. "Next, please."

Charlie blinked, that was it? She retrieved her bag and stepped aside. "Would you mind me asking what time—" But the lady was already asking the next waiting spectator for their name and showed no interest in helping Charlie further.

Gathering herself, she proceeded to the impressive doors on the left which dwarfed her in size. A guard stood to the side, looking at her expectantly.

She smiled meekly. "May I go in?"

He nodded. "Take a seat down the back and please don't disrupt the proceedings." He grasped an ornate gold handle and pulled the door open with surprising ease.

She nodded her thanks and stepped inside.

"...than to believe you would fall victim to the D.A.'s courtroom melodrama. What the prosecution has presented is pure speculation and nothing more. The facts of the matter are that Mr Fisher did what was necessary to protect his small but growing family."

A well-dressed, slick-haired lawyer finished his address to a dozen suit-clad men and highly polished women sitting in the gallery. Behind him, the judge sat high on the bench, listening to the monologue with mild interest. A pair of silver spectacles sat on a large hooked nose which curved over a silver moustache. His receding hair had been sculpted forward, obviously determined to extend the limited coverage it was able to provide.

A step down and to his right, a red-faced man was wringing his fedora in his hands. His tie was cutting into his fleshy neck and the suit jacket didn't quite sit properly on his wide frame. Charlie quickly ascertained this must be Mr Fisher.

To the judge's other side, a tall, surly bailiff was glaring at her and Charlie quickly slid into a seat by the door. An elderly woman in the neighbouring chair looked at her reproachfully and shuffled sideways in her seat to put more distance between them.

"Mr Jones was guilty of trespassing and, whatever the man's intentions that night, he broke the law and paid the price. I ask each of you to consider what you would have done if you stood in Mr Fisher's shoes."

"Ha! Probably shoulda done a better job of keeping his missus satisfied, amiright?" Startled, Charlie looked around for the offender, but the gallery remained straight-faced and focused on the witness stand.

Oblivious to the heckler, the lawyer took the time to make eye contact with each member of the jury in turn. Some met his gaze while others shuffled uncomfortably in their seats. After a few seconds, he gave a nod to his client and sat without fanfare.

The judge cleared his throat. "Members of the jury, the defendant in this case is charged with a criminal offence. Under our legal system, a person is innocent until proven guilty beyond a reasonable doubt. This means that the State must place before you enough evidence to convince you, to the satisfaction of your good sense, that such a crime was committed by Mr Fisher."

"Let's 'ope you've all got better sense than him, that's all I can say." Again, Charlie's eyes flicked from person to person, searching for the silhouette that didn't match. There was something different about a man in a bowler hat in the front row and, as she tried to focus on him, his edges refused to oblige. *Was that Mr Jones?*

"First-degree murder is, needless to say, a grave and serious offence. In order to prove first-degree murder, you, ladies and gentlemen of the jury, must believe beyond a reasonable doubt that the defendant killed an individual without lawful justification and either: intended to kill or do great bodily harm; or knew that the act created a strong probability of causing death or great bodily harm; or was attempting or committed a forcible felony other than second-degree murder. Bailiff, please show the jury to their chambers."

The bailiff led the procession from the room, fronted by men with their chests out, exuding self-importance, while a few whispering women, already deliberating on the verdict, brought up the rear. The man in the bowler hat, who Charlie assumed to be Mr Jones, trailed behind them, arms swinging freely as he whistled. He was evidently looking forward to the show.

Mr Fisher was escorted quietly from the room, eyes fixed on the ground, a guard clutching each arm. The judge rose from his seat, exiting through a door behind the bench and the room broke into a noisy chatter. Stretching his lanky arms towards the ceiling and distending his potbelly, one lawyer approached his slick-haired adversary, extending a pudgy hand.

Charlie had never been privy to a court case and she had the awful feeling she had just intruded on someone's personal business. For a few glorious minutes, she had quite forgotten why she was here and what she was about to do.

How long would the jury take? What if they couldn't reach a decision? Would Wynn's case be delayed for another day? How long would she have to endure this state of anticipatory dread?

As it turned out, the answer was two hours.

All ten of her nails now bitten down to the skin, Charlie had begun cracking each individual joint in her hands. The elderly woman next to her had found another seat eight fingers ago, but forming friendships was not of concern today.

The lawyers were the first to return to their seats. One cast a sideways glance at the other, who was staring determinedly at the bench, apparently willing the judge to appear and call an end to the drawn-out rigmarole.

Again accompanied by two guards, Mr Fisher was returned to his roost. A light sheen covered his face and his handcuffs clinked in time with the wringing of his hands.

A stream of jurors soon snaked its way into the room, but it was not the triumphant procession she had expected. Their expressions were dour and several faces were still flushed from argument. When they sat, it was with arms crossed and lips pursed.

"What a load of absolute bullshit!" Mr Jones stormed in behind them and leaned over the stand to stare directly into the eyes of one of the red-faced men. "That bastard killed me, do you not understand? It wasn't bloody trespassing if his wife wanted me there — which she definitely damn well did!"

The man frowned, almost as though he was aware something was too close to his face, but he shook his head, dismissing the strange sensation as a draft of air or some such thing.

"All rise," a voice commanded, and the room obeyed.

The judge reappeared, adjusting his spectacles and smoothing his robes before taking his seat. The room followed suit.

"Will the jury foreman please stand?"

The red-faced man stood. He was stockily built and his arms hung unnaturally far from his body as if he were trying to accentuate his size.

"Who made this one king of the rats?" Mr Jones tried to spit at the foreman's feet, visibility disappointed when he couldn't manifest the saliva.

"Has the jury reached a unanimous verdict?"

"Yes, Your Honour, we have."

Mr Fisher exhaled sharply and looked up at the ceiling. In another life, the spectators might have thought he was praying.

"Please hand your decision to the bailiff who will read the judgement."

The paper shook slightly as the red-faced man extended it towards the bailiff, who considered it carefully for several seconds before speaking.

"The jury finds the defendant, Mr Fisher, not guilty."

"This is an outrage!" Mr Jones bellowed, features contorted in anger.

Fisher's face melted in shock. Eyes wide, he looked to his attorney for confirmation that he had heard correctly. When the defence gave him a triumphant smile and a decisive nod, his face broke into an open-mouthed sob of relief.

"Mr Fisher, you are free to go. The jury is thanked for its service and is now excused. Court is adjourned."

The room that had been so still moments ago was suddenly bustling with bodies. Charlie glanced around for Mr Jones but his blurry silhouette was nowhere to be found. Evidently he couldn't bring himself to watch his murderer set free.

A large clock above the bench read 3:36 pm. The dreadful anticipation which had been lurking in her fingertips and toes now surged up her limbs towards her heart. She both desperately wanted Wynn's trial to be done and simultaneously wanted it to be postponed indefinitely.

"Don't put off till tomorrow what you can get done today," her grandmother's voice echoed between her ears. Charlie doubted this is what she'd meant.

In the sudden cacophony, Fisher had disappeared from his seat. She wondered idly if he had been taken out the way he came in, or simply allowed to waltz out the door a free man.

The witness stand now waited expectantly for its next case. It had probably been host to thousands. It had witnessed exoneration, anguish, persecution, and had cradled many souls as they were sentenced to death. The chair did not discriminate.

Charlie waited, expecting some of the crowd to dissipate between trials. The bodies, however, seemed to double by the second. A crowd had been growing in the lobby and, with word the Fisher trial was over, they spilled into the room like vermin to scraps. A few journalists pushed ruthlessly through the throng, fighting for positions from which they would be able to document the spectacle. Their large cameras rested on their laps, lenses already extended and at the ready.

The air grew heavier with the thrum of shuffling footsteps and hushed whispers. The walls themselves seemed to lean in, eager for the next spectacle. Charlie quickly found herself sandwiched between two polished spectators, both of whom looked at her reprehensibly before reluctantly accepting the only remaining seats. There must have been well over a hundred people crammed into the space that was ill-equipped for such an audience.

"I don't see the Chief," a gentleman murmured to his associate in front of her. "Reckon he couldn't stand the shame?"

The other man snorted. "Rotten egg in every family. Don't blame him for wanting to disown the delinquent."

Charlie grit her jaw, trying to block out the commentary. Soon enough, their judgement would be placed on her. She was still picking anxiously at her nails when a sudden frenzy erupted, journalists leaping to their feet and snapping flashes of the boy being led through the door.

Nineteen

THE HEARING

Although she knew why she was there, Charlie found no amount of foresight could have prepared her for seeing Wynn in handcuffs. Her stomach plummeted as the guards led him through the back door. There was a sudden frenzy as the journalists stood and snapped flashes of the impotent child. Wynn tried to raise his hands to shield his eyes from the assault, but the guards wrenched them back down to his sides.

The overalls had never been intended for someone so small and hung on him like a homemade parachute. He jumped when a guard told him to sit but hurried to obey the order, squirming back on the unyielding wood until his back was pressed against the rear of the chair.

Had anyone else been able to see Rhett, they would have thought both of them were on trial. The older brother stuck dutifully to the side of his small sibling, murmuring words of comfort he couldn't possibly believe.

While she knew it was possible for ghosts to weary, she had never seen it in person. Rhett's edges seemed to have frayed. Small wisps of his energy trailed off into nothing like tentacles from his body. If there was ever proof that spirits too needed rest, Rhett was it.

Neither looked in Charlie's direction. The pair were focused on a point on the floor. Charlie supposed Rhett had told him to keep his head down, as he should.

If Charlie had felt shock at the sight of Wynn, it was nothing to the wave of nausea that rolled through her as his father followed through the door.

As quickly as the cacophony had exploded, it was silenced by the Chief Enforcer's black expression. A thick walrus moustache couldn't hide the downturn of his mouth. Dark, deep set eyes settled on one face at a time, challenging the room to disrespect his presence. His jacket breast bore a dozen badges which glinted in the courtroom's artificial light, each a testimony of his service to the country.

The petite shadow of a woman hovered behind him, black veil concealing her face as she raised a tissue to her nose with a lace-gloved hand. Barron paused at the doorway, taking in the scene, before striding purposefully towards the front row of the gallery, his wife trailing behind him. The journalists who had fought for those seats only minutes earlier quickly scrambled, vacating the bench for the dictator and his meagre consort.

Neither looked at their handcuffed son, who seemed to shrink in fear as they passed. In that moment, Charlie wanted nothing more than to shield him from the judgemental eyes and speculative whispers. She wanted to steal him away from the prison he had been born into and give him a life where he was coddled and doted on; as every child should be.

She almost didn't notice the slim pair of high heels slink past her. With a sweetly whispered "excuse me" and a flutter of her eyelashes, a chair was quickly vacated and her prim legs folded one over the other as she took the seat demurely. They lead up to a pencil skirt which was a size too small and bunched at the thigh. She wouldn't have noticed her at all, had it not been for the young, blonde-haired girl in a blue pinafore who seemed to be glued to her side.

In her court attire, Valerie was almost unrecognisable from the audacious woman who had sat across from her in the garage. With a delicate finger on the bridge of her petite glasses, she pushed them up her nose and drew a notebook from her bag, seeming to look over a list.

Why was she there? Something felt off about the way she sat back in her chair, as though she was there to watch a show. Charlie tried to withhold the conclusions her mind was jumping to; perhaps she was there to support Wynn.

"All rise." Hundreds of shoes striking the floor echoed like thunder through the room.

A new judge emerged from his chambers, back stooped and feet shuffling frantically to remain under his body as it moved. His bones audibly creaked as he sat.

"The Honorable Judge Wickham presiding, this court is now in session," the bailiff announced. "Please be seated. We are here for the trial of the State v. Wynn Barron."

Judge Wickham considered the papers in front of him, his nose very nearly touching the words. "Will the defendant please stand?"

Charlie stretched a hand beneath the pew and felt for an opening; there was a strip of wood running the full length of the seat against which people could press the backs of their heels. But there was a gap below the seat itself, where her calves sat.

Slowly and quietly, she lifted her bag into the opening and pressed it back against the wall, ensuring the straps were safely tucked out of sight. One of the men by her side gave her a sideways glance and she feigned addressing an itch on her leg.

Sliding from his chair, Wynn stood, looking every bit the child he was. Rhett was still murmuring in his ear, resting a hand on the boy's shoulder so he could feel something, anything, beyond the terror running through him.

"Mr Barron." The judge summoned a deep breath which whistled as it passed through his ventricles. "You are charged with first-degree religious organisation and affiliation, attempt to organise religious worship and incite rebellion towards the State. This is a class A felony. If convicted, you will face a sentence of up to twenty years in prison, in addition to a period of Enlightenment as determined by the institution. The State charges that you engaged in religious activities knowingly and willingly. How do you plead?"

Now visibly shaking, Wynn seemed to be trying to steady himself, but the tears had already sprung to his eyes as his throat constricted. Reflexively, his brother tried to pull him into a hug and his face crumpled too, when he realised he couldn't hold him.

"You can do this," she now heard Rhett say, his forehead almost touching Wynn's temple. "You are bigger than them. You are more than they will ever be."

Wynn gulped, opening his mouth to speak.

"Those charges are mine, Your Honour."

The gallery reeled around, searching for the source of the voice. Charlie stood to claim ownership, hiding her shaking fists in her pockets. "Wynn is innocent and I am pleading guilty."

The entire court looked at her with open-mouthed shock. Heads swivelled from Wynn to Charlie in confusion. Trying desperately not to look towards the boy for fear she would dissolve into tears, she stared down the judge defiantly. She was surrendering on her own terms.

"Charlie, no, you can't!" Wynn's tears may have been halted by shock, but they were back in full force now, streaming down the boy's face as he realised what she was doing.

Whispers and exclamations of shock were beginning to bubble as the audience took in the scene. Charlie was aware of Barron staring at her from the front of the room and she pointedly avoided eye contact.

"Your Honour, I fear the court is making a grave mistake," she called over the growing commotion." I am a practising Seer and have been for many years. I allow people to speak to the dead, to talk to their loved ones one last time." Gasps rippled through the crowd, accompanied by a few hollow laughs and noises of disbelief.

"That's quite enough, Miss," Judge Wickham sputtered, hand searching for his gavel.

"I give them hope that there is more to our existence than this." She gestured to their overbearingly authoritarian surroundings.

"That's enough!" The gavel smacked, having no effect on the growing clamour.

"I believed Wynn to have a similar gift, and I persuaded him to join me. I believed we could achieve much more together. He is a smart boy and, of course, refused. Until I threatened to tell his father he was preaching to me."

"You what?" The room hushed as the Chief Enforcer stood. He and Charlie stared at each other across the heads of the crowd, Charlie doing her best not to wilt unter his penetrating stare. He turned to address his son. "Do you know this lunatic, boy?"

Wynn's eyes were wide as he tried to take in the unfolding scene. His mouth gaped, looking from his father to Charlie as he struggled to find the right answer.

Charlie hadn't known what to expect when she confessed her crimes (albeit partially fabricated) to the face of justice. A massive outcry, to be tackled to the ground, to be dragged around the streets by her ear, shamed and spat at, but it wasn't this; disbelief.

She was, at least, being stared at, but it was not with the contempt she had imagined. Wherever she looked, she was met with expressions of incredulity and, in some cases, pity.

"It's true," she added testily, hoping to prompt the crowd from their shock-induced stupor.

Judge Wickham shook himself. "Well, I say Miss..."

"Hall," she supplied. "Miss Charlotte Hall."

"Miss Hall, do you understand the severity of the crimes to which you claim ownership?" He clearly thought her an imbecile. "Mr Barron is being tried as a child. Your punishment, if you were to be convicted, would be death."

"I am aware," she answered flatly. "But I refuse to allow a child to take the punishment for my actions."

Judge Wickham leaned back in his seat, as much as his skeletal hunch would allow, and sighed a deep wheeze. "Miss Hall, I do not know the relationship you have with Mr Barron and nor do I wish to. You are clearly attempting to distract the court and invoke leniency on Mr Barron. As you are hindering court proceedings, I must ask you to leave."

Now Charlie's mouth was the one to fall open. "I have to – what?!"

"If you will not leave voluntarily, you will be escorted from the building."

Even the Chief Enforcer seemed to have dismissed her, having given her a last wuthering glare before turning his back on her and reclaiming his seat.

The gallery was whispering again. A few words floated to her as she stood there in disbelief; "attention seeker", "trouble maker", "unruly woman".

"You think I'm lying?" A short burst of maniacal laughter escaped her which, she had to admit, did nothing to support the case that she was not, in fact, delusional. "Why would I lie?"

"It is of no concern to me. Guard!" He waved his hand in the direction of the door where a burly, uniformed man had appeared. "Please see this woman out."

Face still plastered with disbelief, she looked to Wynn and Rhett, hoping to find guidance in their faces. But their faces mirrored hers. Wynn's upper lip still glistened from the tears he'd shed a mere minute ago. It wasn't direction she found in his face, but courage.

Before the guard could touch her, she sprung from the chair and dashed for the door, elbowing through the bodies with tactless grace. Most of them moved out of her way, not wanting her to touch them. The thundering of her boots echoed through the cavernous foyer as she sprinted for the street.

Breathless, she stood before the courthouse, foot traffic weaving around her and muttering curses for barging through so rudely. But this was of no consequence compared to their reactions when she opened her arms and began to scream.

Twenty

THE CONFESSION

"They're lying to you!" Charlie belted at the top of her lungs, causing a nearby woman to shriek and drop her handbag.

"They tell you there is nothing more than this – that we live and die for the State. That the ones you've loved and lost are gone forever. That there is no hope."

A circle started to form around her, of people both wanting to put as much distance between themselves and this delirious woman and wanting to watch the spectacle.

"I know these are lies because I see your dead. I talk to them." She searched the milling crowd for a blurry outline.

"You!" She singled out a man in a blue work uniform – he had an elderly gentleman standing beside him. "You look just like your father. He still wears his navy uniform and service medal. He holds himself like a hero." The man stared at her, stunned, while his father tipped his hat to her.

"You!" She found a young woman in a vibrant yellow A-line skirt, with another young woman flanking her. "I don't know if she's your sister or your friend, but she is beautiful. Her ponytail comes down to her waist and she doesn't need the high heels she's wearing, she's as tall and slender as a fashion model."

"Tell her I can breathe easy now!" the young, blurry-edged lady called to her, patting her chest with a smile.

"And she says she can breathe easy now," Charlie repeated, watching as the girl clasped a hand to her mouth, swaying, and a nearby gentleman steadied her.

"You have the right to believe," she yelled to the crowd as the doors to the court burst open behind her. "You have the right to hope!"

Rough hands seized both her arms and pulled her back towards the stairs, where she fell on the first and was held, dangling like a puppet, with her arms above her head.

"Get up," a male voice ordered.

She tried to comply, her feet slipping out from under her as she attempted to gain purchase on the stairs but she was ripped up them, mercilessly. The crowd was still watching and she felt a flicker of shame for being seen without her bearings.

"I am not a preacher," she yelled and the grip on one of her arms twisted painfully. "I do not know if God is real, I do not know if there is Heaven or Hell, but I know there is hope."

A sharp jab struck her between the shoulder blades; one of the men had planted his knee in her spine and her legs gave out completely. She allowed herself to be dragged up the remainder of the stairs like a rag doll, watching the crowd watch her. For a moment, Charlie could have sworn she saw the face of her mother somewhere in the commotion, but then she was in the foyer and the doors swung shut behind her with a resounding thud.

Her legs trailed listlessly in front of her as she was dragged backwards to a side room she hadn't noticed before. There was another set of stairs leading downwards this time and she squirmed uncomfortably as her legs were lifted higher than her head.

"Quit moving," the voice said. "You chose not to walk."

"I don't recall being asked," she quipped and the heel of a boot found her lower back.

The dull screech of a heavy door told her she had been brought to one of the court's holding cells. Not bothering to lift her onto the bench or help her to her feet, the guards dropped her on the cement floor and slammed the barred-gate shut behind them.

"Enforcement has been called," one of them said as he locked her cage with a large key. "They will be here soon to formally charge you."

He shook the gate to ensure it was locked and then struck it with the palm of his hand so the bars surrounding her reverberated for dramatic effect.

"Looking forward to it," she answered flatly, not bothering to lift her head from the floor to see what he looked like.

She wondered if Wynn's trial had been stalled. If not, she would convince them to overrule whatever punishment had been assigned to him. Her status as societal menace had just been well and truly established, and surely the Chief Enforcer would welcome the opportunity to blame his son's actions on a scapegoat. Charlie would decline the right to an attorney, making it all too easy for him. There was little point in accepting help when she would be pleading guilty.

The familiar smell of grease and coffee wafted over her. "I can't believe you just did that." Rhett stood over her, peering down into her face.

"Neither can I, to be honest." She pushed herself up on her elbows and scanned the dungeon she'd been dragged to. There were three other cells in the grungy, dimly lit basement. She assumed the accused were brought here from the prison on the morning they were to be tried. The other cells now stood empty and waiting for a new day. It didn't matter, she reflected, if anyone heard her talking to the air, but the paranoia was hard to shake.

"What happened to Wynn? Did they finish the trial?"

Rhett shook his head. "Adjourned to a later date. Apparently they were concerned for the judge's safety." A small smile crept onto his face.

She chuckled bitterly. "Where is he now?"

"On the way back to Ingbridge Correctional Centre. He's being held at the women's prison because of his age."

"I don't see how he can be imprisoned at all. He's a child."

Rhett shrugged with defeat, looking like he'd had the same conversation with himself a dozen times. "They said he knew what he was doing, especially given Father's position. He couldn't exactly claim ignorance."

Charlie sat up and crossed her legs. The cold from the cement was creeping through the seat of her pants but she didn't care much. "I'm sorry, Rhett. I should never have left him here. I thought he'd be safe. I never thought his own father would..." She trailed off, unsure how much was proper to say when the man was Rhett's father as well.

Rhett dropped to his knees in front of her, leaning down to look into her face. "You think this was your fault? It had nothing to do with you."

"Of course it did. Someone obviously noticed he was spending too much time with the strange young woman on the top floor. Or maybe they overheard something, saw something..."

"It was Valerie. She's an informant."

"What?" Charlie looked up at him in shock. "But she's a Seer, too. Her sister—"

"Helps her," he finished bitterly.

She blinked at him. "I don't understand."

He sighed, pushing himself back to his feet, he began to pace the small cage. "If it's anyone's fault, it's mine. Wynn started playing with her little sister, Eileen. My only stipulation was that he not do it in front of Father. I told him to go to the graveyard, somewhere people wouldn't notice him. I didn't even think..."

Rhett took a deep, centring breath. "Valerie was caught practising a few years ago, but she struck a deal. She agreed to assist Enforcement with finding as many Seers and believers as possible. It must have been after Eileen died because she uses her as bait, her own dead little sister."

Charlie's stomach churned. "She came after me. She knew I was a Seer and tried to convince me to join her in finding others. Why wouldn't she just report me?"

"That was the same thing she said to Wynn." Rhett kicked at one of the bars but his foot passed clean through; his energy was depleted. "Intent to organise religion is a greater crime than simply believing. She told him to meet her somewhere, waited until he asked about finding others, and that was all the proof they needed. They were ready and waiting."

It wasn't enough that the world wanted people like her dead, now they were turning on their own kind. "What now?" she asked blankly.

The answer hung in the air as Rhett sank down beside her and leaned in so his energy warmed her side; they would wait for whatever came next.

"You don't have to stay," she whispered softly after a few minutes. "You look exhausted."

"I didn't even know I could feel tired anymore, but I guess I can," he replied without opening his eyes. "But I'm not going anywhere. The last time I left you, you disappeared."

She swallowed the guilt and glanced at the bars. "I think I'll have a hard time going anywhere now."

For a few seconds there was only the distant sound of rumbling traffic and a tap dripping in a nearby room. "I'm not leaving him again," she promised quietly. "Either of you."

The energy thrumming down her side grew warmer. "I know."

Several hours had passed before the door to the stairwell clanged open and heavy footsteps descended the stairs. Charlie supposed they had been in no rush considering she was already safely behind bars. Not to mention, they had been denied the thrill of public arrest.

"Charlotte Hall?"

"Unfortunately."

"We are here to place you under arrest for disturbance of the peace and attempting to initiate public rebellion. You will be held in remand at Ingbridge Correctional Centre until the date of your trial which is yet to be determined. Do you understand?"

"What if I say no?"

The bearded Enforcer glared at her from beneath his hat; apparently the only answer to that question she would receive.

She rose to her feet and brought herself to stand face to face with her jailor, albeit through iron bars.

"I came here to set the record straight. I coerced Wynn Barron and blackmailed him into joining my mission. The child should go free."

"That will be decided at the trial," came the blunt response.

"Mine or his?"

"Question time is over. Count your blessings the Chief Enforcer had other business to attend to."

"You'd be hailed a hero, you know. If you were the one to prove the Barron boy's innocence. I'm sure the Chief would thank you personally."

The Enforcer had busied himself with a set of keys and chose not to acknowledge her attempt at persuasion, but Charlie was sure she heard an echo as the cogs in his head started to turn.

She felt more shame in being placed in handcuffs than she had imagined. The Enforcer squeezed them shut a little tighter than was probably necessary and the cold steel cut into the sensitive underside of her wrists. Having convinced Rhett to check on Wynn, she was quietly relieved he wasn't here to see her helpless and manacled.

With a firm and unnecessary jab in the back, she was pushed onto a small unmarked bus and found herself surrounded by several other female prisoners. She was guided to an unforgivingly hard seat and her handcuffs were attached to the seat between her legs and locked in place. Wire mesh separated the inmates from the driver. The floor beneath her was stained with something she tried not to think about.

"So you're who we've been waiting for," a voice behind her remarked with annoyed contempt. Charlie glanced over her shoulder; she was a stocky brunette with hair above her shoulders that looked like it had been hacked off with a knife.

"Sorry," Charlie muttered.

She could feel the inmates eyes roaming over her clothes which contrasted starkly with the uniform grey linen dresses the others wore, with hemlines down to their calves.

"You're not in Kansas anymore, Dorothy."

Charlie glanced back in spite of herself. The woman gave her a malevolent grin and an unsettling giggle.

"This is Unit 19, this is Unit 19." A guard at the steering wheel held a two-way radio to his mouth. "We are departing the courthouse and are en route to Ingbridge. Over."

A female voice muffled with static replied, "Thank you, Unit 19, message received. Your status is confirmed."

It had been several years since Charlie had been a passenger on a bus; the tram was the more affordable and convenient option. She may have enjoyed the experience, had it not been delivering her to incarceration.

The other passengers showed no inclination to talk to her, so she embraced the silence punctuated by the rumbling engine and tyres stroking the bitumen.

"Charlie!" someone was whispering her name. Unsure whether the voice belonged to someone classified in the living or departed category, she slowly scanned the interior of the bus for the source.

A pair of eyes were peering at her over the back of a seat from the front of the bus, and Charlie immediately recognised the wide blue orbs as belonging to Wynn. She gave him a small smile and tried to raise her hand to wave, only to hear the chain clink in protest. Her eyes flicked to his travel partner who was looking back at her too. Her smile widened when she saw it was Rhett.

It was all she could do not to burst into laughter at the concept of the three of them being on a bus together, headed for prison. The situation was anything but funny and she was vaguely aware her senses must have abandoned her. She tried to stifle the laughter, but it escaped as a strangled choke. A few of the women cast sideways looks at her.

"What's so funny, spaz?" the stocky woman behind her probed.

Charlie shook her head. "Life."

The woman snorted and Charlie heard her mutter to her neighbour, "Told you she was crazy."

The prison was well outside the city's borders. Staring forlornly out the window, she recognised some of the houses she had passed only two days ago. In all likelihood, very little had changed for the residents of the pastel-perfect dwellings. It was time for the wives to be serving dinner while the husbands regaled the family with events from their day. The children would be hiding peas beneath their plates in an effort to avoid eating their vegetables.

The city soon fell behind them and Charlie once again found herself travelling through vast fields and knee-high crops. They must have been travelling for an hour before someone kicked the back of her seat and she jumped. "Welcome to the Land of Oz, Dorothy."

Twenty-One

THE PRISON

In the distance, Ingbridge looked like it could have been a small farming community. Surrounded by a sprawling patchwork quilt of fields dotted with trees and the occasional farm animal, it was only as they drew nearer that she could discern the two-storey wire fence enclosing the facility. Several shed-like buildings were spread with symmetrical precision around the oval, some linked with enclosed passageways.

The sun was beginning its descent towards the distant horizon and the building's windows reflected the burnt orange rays like watchful eyes.

Waiting guards pulled open the gates as the bus approached and began to close them again before they had even passed through. The next time Charlie saw the other side of those gates would be the date of her trial.

The bus drew to a stop and there was tentative movement amongst her companions as they tried to stretch their legs and a few shuffled their feet impatiently. The door groaned open and one of the guards boarded while her partner waited outside.

"Welcome back, ladies," the guard crooned as she unlocked their restraints one by one.

"Thank you, ma'am," each recited in turn, but none moved.

"Hello there." The guard stopped in front of Charlie, looking down at her with the bemused expression of a child having just found a new toy. "You must be Miss Hall."

Unsure if this was a statement or a question, Charlie nodded minutely.

"Speak up, I can't hear you."

"Yes, ma'am."

"Oh good, you're not a mute idiot."

The girls around her giggled quietly. Charlie raised her eyes to meet hers. "No, ma'am."

"We should get along just fine then." She gave her a patronising smile. "Ladies, single file, off the bus. Mr Andrews will take you to be searched before you're returned to your cells. Miss Hall, follow me for induction."

Induction sounded like she was attending her first day of college, but she doubted her grand tour would be followed by a 'meet the Professors' session.

Wynn was obviously included in 'ladies' because he joined the line of women queuing past Andrews who used a mechanical counter to keep track of the number as he called them. She wasn't sure why he needed it, considering there were only eight inmates in total.

Disembarking the bus, a large, cement two-storey building loomed over her, looking about as inviting as, well, a prison. A few cars were scattered along the front, evidently belonging to the guards. As Rhett wandered off with Wynn, she saw him double back to admire a gleaming red truck. Evidently new from the dealership, it seemed to glow in the evening light and its trayback didn't look like it had ever held an ounce of dirt.

"Chevy coupe utility," she heard him remark to his little brother. "Would've liked me one of them."

She was led away from the line of women towards the front door, a cold uninviting combination of metal and glass. Retrieving a hefty set of keys from her pocket, the guard unlocked the heavy door and motioned for her to step past.

Inside felt colder than out. The linoleum floor was a speckled grey, the walls an impenetrable white. Fluorescent lights buzzed on the ceiling, casting everything in a colour-bleaching glow. The receptionist's desk was protected by a glass screen with a few perforations through which to speak. It was unmanned; evidently it was after business hours.

"Follow me." The guard stepped in front of Charlie again and led her down a deserted corridor. The eerie quiet and the way their footsteps bounced off the empty walls reminded her of an abandoned hospital.

The illusion continued when she was shown to a small room, reminiscent of a doctor's office. A height chart had been pinned to the wall beside a set of scales. There was a simple brown desk with seats facing each other. A large camera with an even larger bulb sat waiting at the side.

"You may sit." The guard sounded like she was offering her a kindness rather than a basic human right.

Charlie sat.

The guard retrieved a heavy book from the desk drawer and thumbed it open to the page marked with a thick leather strap.

"Your full name please."

"Charlotte Malbon Hall."

"Date of birth?"

"August 1st, 1935."

"Next of kin?"

"No one."

The guard glanced up at her to assess whether or not she was being truthful. Apparently she was satisfied because she didn't push the matter further.

"Medical conditions?"

"No."

"Are you pregnant?"

"No."

The line of questioning continued until Charlie felt her whole being was summarised on that single page. Without anyone to notice she was gone, it could be torn up and she would simply disappear from the world.

Finally she was asked to weigh herself and stand in front of the height chart. The guard thrust a plaque at her with a number scribbled in chalk; 1721967. She was a number now, nothing more.

When the camera was raised to take her photo, Charlie was not asked to smile or tilt her head the way she had seen some girls pose for photos with friends and family. She stared down the barrel blankly and felt some of her soul fall away with the flash. Both sides of her profile were then immortalised as well. Charlie had perhaps only had a handful taken in her life. Her grandmother would likely not have treasured these as she did the others.

From there, she was led to a small changing room, complete with a lone shower in the corner without a privacy screen. A solitary bench stood in the middle of the room. The guard pulled out a tub from beneath the seat and let it fall with an empty clunk.

"Place your belongings in the tub."

She held her arms away from her body. "I don't have any."

The guard shot her a bemused expression. "You're wearing them."

Her face burned as she realised she would have to strip. Waiting for the guard to turn around, she played awkwardly with the hem of her shirt for a second, before realising privacy was a luxury she would no longer enjoy.

She turned away slightly in an effort to preserve what dignity she could and divested herself of her old life. Clothes in the tub, she shivered, holding her arms across herself.

"Face me."

Reluctantly, she turned towards the guard, hands desperately trying to preserve her modesty. A flashlight blinded her and her eyes squeezed shut in protest.

"Open your mouth."

She complied, half expecting a gag to be inserted to prevent her from screaming.

"Lift up your tongue."

The tip of her tongue touched the roof of her mouth.

"Hold your arms out to your sides." The guard held her arms out like a plane to demonstrate.

Gnawing at her lip, Charlie replicated the movement, feeling the last of her dignity expunged like a swatted fly.

"Turn around."

She faced the opposite wall, arms still extended.

"You can lower your arms. Now squat and cough."

Charlie blanched; surely she wasn't serious.

"Is there a problem, inmate?"

Inmate. That word had been swirling somewhere in her subconscious, but to have it wrenched from her mind and branded on her forehead was nauseating. She gritted her teeth as one does before immersing oneself in icy water and squatted with as much bashful propriety as possible.

Cough, cough.

"You can take a shower now. Make the most of it, you won't have as much privacy from now on."

This was privacy?

The water pressure was a little more than a weak trickle and she waited several seconds for the heat she relished, but the most it could muster was a feeble tepid warmth. She dragged her fingernails through her hair at the roots, scrubbing at the sins of the day. A single bar of soap was tethered to the showerhead and, as she slathered her skin, she banished thoughts from her mind of how many people had done the same before her.

Wondering how long she could prolong delivery to her cell, she stood with the water cascading over her until the guard became impatient. Which, as it turned out, was not very long.

"That's enough, inmate."

I have a name, she thought acidly, but begrudgingly shut off the tap. A thin brown towel had been left on the bench beside a neatly pressed grey uniform. Her clothes had disappeared, probably to be used for rags in the kitchen.

The guard was still watching and she dried herself hastily. The rough fabric of the uniform caught on her still damp skin as she hurriedly tried to reclaim some dignity. The material hung loosely around her torso, as though the last wearer had been heavily pregnant. Her hair hung in a dripping tangled mass at the back of her head, but it seemed a hairbrush was an unnecessary extravagance.

Black slip-on shoes with buckle straps sat on the floor beside a pair of plain white socks. She slid her feet into both, her toes wiggling in search of some comfort in the thin canvas sole but not finding any.

"Will I get my things back?" Charlie stood back up to her full height.

The guard smirked. "If you ever get out of here, yes."

Charlie nodded, knowing well enough it was improbable she would ever walk as a free woman again.

"In the meantime," she crossed to a row of lockers and opened one at a time, filling a tub like the one Charlie had placed her belongings in, "these are the only things you need to worry about."

Thrusting the tub towards her, Charlie found what looked like folded bed sheets, grey and white pyjamas, another grey uniform, white underwear, socks, a toothbrush, a hair comb, sanitary napkins and a roll of toilet paper.

"You can purchase anything else you need from the inmate commissary." Charlie stared at her blankly. "The prison store," she added.

"Oh," was all she could muster as she stared into the tiny tub which now held everything she owned in the world.

"Right, time to see your cell."

The night sky had claimed the last vestiges of daylight while they had been inside and a chill wind caressed her legs. Emerging from the rear of the building, she found herself in a round courtyard with concrete pathways connecting the structures around the outskirts like join-the-dots.

"Welcome to Ingbridge Correctional Centre, the State's only level one maximum-security female facility." The guard didn't look at her as she walked and spoke, as though she was hoping to be done with this exchange as quickly as possible.

"During your time here, you must abide by the prison rules. They are designed to keep you safe. When you break one of these rules, it is called an offence. An offence will lead to punishment."

The guard kept a brisk pace and addressed the night air, as Charlie half-jogged behind her, carrying the tub awkwardly in front of her.

"You will not behave in a way that could offend, threaten or hurt another inmate and especially not a guard. This includes physical and verbal assault.

"You will not prevent the staff from doing their jobs. You will not consume drugs or alcohol or assist others in obtaining drugs, alcohol or any type of contraband. You will not cause damage to the prison. You will do as you are instructed by prison staff.

"And finally, you will not plan or attempt to escape. We are miles away from the closest township and we can drive a lot faster than your legs can move."

She spoke as though she were reciting the menu items on offer at a local restaurant, not bothering to confirm whether or not Charlie had heard her.

"This is the exercise yard." She nodded vaguely in the direction of the quadrangle they were walking beside, enclosed by a mesh fence iced with swirls of concertina wire. It was partly cemented, with a tennis net stretching across one corner. "You will be granted an hour of rec daily, so long as you uphold the rules.

"The shower block is to your right. Your unit has an allocated showering time, it is up to you to negotiate your order. As you're a freshie, get used to waiting."

They were walking towards one of the ugly three-storey cell blocks located at the back of the property. It was lifeless, sinister, flat grey with bars over the dimly lit windows and stains creeping down from the roof. It was oddly quiet considering the hundreds of women who she knew were housed within its walls.

The guard lifted a ring laden with keys from her pocket and unlocked a heavy mint-green door. The walls were lined with three rows of cells and a network of cross-thatched bars. Metal walkways stretched the length of the floors, the space otherwise open to allow an unobstructed view of even the topmost cells. A corrugated iron roof perched high above it all.

A gentle murmuring filled the space, like the relentless hum of a beehive. As the guard led her past the other cells, Charlie kept her head down, ignoring the odd *psst* and giggle as she filed passed.

Their footsteps sent resounding tremors through the metal stairs as they climbed to the second floor and bypassed a row of cells. Charlie could feel the weight of hundreds of eyes on her diminutive frame, not built to withstand such a substantial load. She actually found herself eager to shut herself within her cell, away from the whispers and curious eyes of the women she would be sharing every moment of her new life with.

At last, the guard stopped in front of a cell just as unremarkable as the others.

"McKinsey, you've got a new cellmate," she addressed someone already waiting within and lifted her bulky set of keys again to permit Charlie entry.

Twenty-Two

THE CELLMATE

Hesitantly, she stepped past the iron barricade and looked for the woman she would be sharing quarters with. A bunk bed stood to her left, a figure huddled beneath the covers.

Her cellmate didn't move as she walked over carefully and placed the tub of her belongings on the lower bunk. Nor did she move as the leaden door slammed shut and sealed them both within, nothing to distract them but the other's company.

"Hello," she broke the silence gingerly. "I'm Charlie."

The lump beneath the blankets showed no sign the woman had heard her.

Not entirely sure what could be classed as a normal reception in prison, she supposed she should be happy with the fact that she wasn't being pushed up against the bars with a hand at her throat.

Her cell mate obviously wanted the top bunk, and Charlie had no desire to ask her for it.

The room had only two other pieces of furniture; a metal sink featuring a steadily dripping tap and a stainless steel toilet without a seat or lid. *Charming.* The cell had one window, the glass of which had been covered with a film to blur the outside world. Even if one were able to break the glass, the bars bolted to the brickwork wouldn't grant you any more freedom than a breath of fresh air.

The windowsill was already decorated with a toothbrush, hairbrush, a few magazines and what looked like a box of cookies. Not wanting to encroach on her cellmate's space, Charlie slid her own belongings beneath the bed and sat with a sigh. She could feel the springs through the flimsy, inch-thick mattress, the coarse orange blanket covering it adding little in the way of comfort.

With resignation, she swung her legs onto the bed and, for the first time, lay in the grave she had dug. Above her, the mattress's underside was stained and discoloured with bodily fluids. The wall beside her had been inscribed with the names of previous tenants, along with a few suggestions of how she could pass her time. 'I luv Charlie' had been etched into the brickwork. 'Sorry, but I'm not looking for a relationship right now,' she thought miserably.

Not having eaten since she escaped the farmhouse, an emptiness had settled inside her, but it wasn't a void she craved food to fill. The thought of eating seemed redundant; what good was there in feeding a cow before it was sent to slaughter? And she would be, Charlie knew. There was no doubt her public execution would be arranged within the month, owing to her corruption of a minor – namely, the Chief Enforcer's son.

Wynn could be in a neighbouring building or in the cell directly above her for all she knew. The chances of her being able to talk to him were minimal, but she would try reaching out to Rhett when she was alone.

Charlie scoffed at herself; she wouldn't even have solitude in the shower from now on. But she supposed it didn't matter if the other women saw her talking to herself; they would all know what she was in for soon enough.

The mattress above her creaked as her cellmate changed position. Perhaps she had finally awoken.

"Hi, sorry for waking you," Charlie said meagerly.

But still, the silence continued.

"Hey, new girl."

Charlie propped her head up, the voice hadn't come from above her but there was no one else in the room.

"Hello?"

"It's your neighbour."

"Oh." Charlie scanned the brickwork and found a crevice which seemed to lead through to the next cell. "Uh, hello."

"Your friend in there ain't gon say anything to you, so leave her be." Her tone was more direct than harsh, but it startled Charlie nonetheless.

"I didn't mean any offence." She didn't know how she could have already managed to offend her cellmate but she hoped the woman huddled above her hadn't taken it as such.

"Good," her neighbour whispered through the crack. "Then, you'll keep it down before a guard gets on both of you."

"Oh, right. Sorry."

"That's the first rule you need to know, new girl. Keep your head low, and your voice lower. You'll be okay."

"Right, err, thanks..." Charlie accepted the warning as an olive branch. Who was her new neighbour? What did she look like? How long had she been there? What had she done? The questions whirred inside her head, but she didn't dare ask them.

There would be time to find out. Too much time.

Charlie sighed and curled up on her side. While she yearned to see a familiar face, she didn't want Hudson to step ghostly foot in a place like this. She wouldn't call him, but he would find her eventually. A person usually needed to be in one place long enough for a spirit to be able to detect their energy. And she wasn't going anywhere anytime soon.

Once the guards had performed their final headcount for the night and their cell lights were switched off, she silently allowed the tears to fall.

It was still dark when a loud voice announced the morning count, and Charlie momentarily panicked as her mind grappled with where she was. As her bearings slowly returned, the panic subsided into a resigned acceptance of her changed circumstances.

The frame of the bed swayed as her cellmate lowered herself to the floor for the first time. A short girl with cropped dark hair, she glanced at Charlie, showing no sign of the sleep inertia Charlie was struggling to wipe away.

Groggily, Charlie rolled out of the bed, her back stiff from the unforgiving mattress. The atrium lights had remained on throughout the night and now their cell lights flickered to life. Awkwardly, she tugged at the hem of her pyjamas and combed her fingers through her matted hair in a futile attempt to restore some semblance of orderliness. She could hear the heavy impact of boots as they drew closer along the metal walkway.

Her cellmate waved her hands towards the bed, then motioned dismissively towards her hair. Still blinking stupidly through the remnants of sleep, Charlie looked from the girl to her bed and back again.

Exasperated, the woman threw down her hands and hurriedly made Charlie's bed, tucking the sheet, smoothing the blanket and adjusting the pillow. In a matter of seconds, she was again standing by the bars and pointed to a spot next to her. Charlie quickly stepped onto it. "Thank you," she whispered to the girl, who nodded back and again faced the bars.

The corners of Charlies's mouth twitched into half a smile. Maybe life with her cellmate wouldn't be so tense after all.

"...144, 145, 146..." the guard was pressing a counter as he passed their cell and scanned the room briefly, including a quick appraisal that they were both still alive.

As he moved out of sight, Charlie glanced to her cellmate for guidance. She shook her head minutely and remained in position. Another minute passed before the final numbers were called, followed by a "Thank you, ladies".

Her cellmate's eyes were fixed on the women across the void and, seeing them relax and slouch back to their beds, she turned to the windowsill and busied herself with her things.

Fumbling around beneath the bed, Charlie grasped the hair comb and began hacking at her mop. The gentle murmur of voices was building again, like traffic steadily growing heavier as the morning peak approached. Exaggerated yawns could be heard from the neighbouring blocks as the women performed their morning ablutions. The combing continued long after it was knot-free, simply because she wasn't sure what she was supposed to do next.

There was the sound of shuffling behind her and Charlie turned to find the dark-haired girl standing by the sink, the windowsill partially cleared to hold some of her things.

"Oh, thank you." The sincerity in Charlie's voice was genuine. She had half expected to be woken in the middle of the night with a sheet around her neck, so the girl's gesture was deeply appreciated. "My name's Charlie, what's yours?"

But the girl had already turned away from her and begun to change, stripping out of her pyjamas and pulling on a pair of grey sweatpants and matching long-sleeved shirt.

Her refusal to speak to Charlie didn't align with her hospitality, so she tried again. "My name's Charlie," she said a bit louder. "What's yours?"

The woman was applying a carefully measured dab of toothpaste to her sparsely bristled brush when she threw an awkward sideways glance at Charlie, as if she was wondering why she was still staring at her. Suddenly her mouth formed an 'o' and her hand flew to her face. Touching a finger to her cheek near her ear, she moved it in a small arch that ended near her mouth.

Watching Charlie blink, the woman gave a little disappointed sigh. She pointed to her ear and shook her head.

"Oh!" Charlie's cheeks grew warmer with embarrassment. No wonder she hadn't been replying to her. "I'm so sorry!" Realising she was still talking to a deaf woman, she held her hands up in apology and mouthed the word "sorry".

The girl smiled and raised a hand in dismissal. Reaching over her shoulder, she fumbled with the tag of her shirt and turned for Charlie to inspect it.

In faded, capital lettering was the name 'Anna'.

"Anna." Charlie placed a hand on her shoulder to indicate she had read it. "It's nice to meet you." She exaggerated the movements of her mouth and Anna nodded.

Scanning the small cell for something with which she could write her name, a memory resurfaced and she jumped back onto her bed to point eagerly at the inscribed declaration of love for Charlie.

"Charlie," she mouthed, pointing from the inscription on the wall to herself.

Anna eyed the inscription, then pointed from it to Charlie, who clapped. "Yes!"

The girls beamed at each other for a second, seemingly delighted at having simply managed to exchange names. Charlie was oddly fond of her already, this girl she had just met – and in a prison, no less. She was inexplicably grateful to have been housed with her.

Anna motioned to her clothes and jogged on the spot. Interpreting this as being time for exercise, Charlie rummaged through her meagre tub, extracting a pair of pants and a shirt that matched hers. Not yet used to the lack of privacy, Charlie turned shyly into the corner as she changed clothes hurriedly. The nip in the morning air only fuelled her urgency.

The clatter of keys reverberating off metal bars and the distinctive clicks of locks falling open melded with quiet chatter as women emerged from their cells.

Their cell door open, Anna waited patiently as Charlie pulled on her shoes and, together, they joined the stream of women clad in uniform grey filtering along the metal walkways and down the staircases. A watchful guard stood at either end of the building, issuing an occasional "keep it down" and "watch your space".

Charlie kept her eyes on the ground in front of her, consciously pulling her arms tight to her body and being careful not to step on the back of anyone's heel. No one seemed to notice her as they chatted about expecting visitors and their hopes for release in the not too distant future.

"Do you think he'll come?" one petite blonde asked her gaggle of friends. "It's been months, another broad has to have caught his eye by now."

"Your brain's in your girdle. He's brought you flowers every week for three months," replied one.

"Even if he doesn't, who cares?" asked a lanky brunette. "Men are like lipstick. If they reach their use-by date, there's always a new one waiting to be picked up."

The group giggled before switching the conversation to complain about the state of their skin.

Like a stream of water, the women coursed along the pathway and into the exercise yard, where some began to walk while others stretched half-heartedly in their own interpretation of exercise.

Anna pointed to the track which had been worn in the grass and Charlie nodded, falling into step beside her. Feet still tender and blistered from her trek across the countryside, their quiet cries of protest were drowned out by the euphoria of the sun's gentle warmth and the fickle early morning breeze teasing her hair.

Charlie caught herself before attempting to start a conversation with her partner. Perhaps there was a library and a book on sign language from which she could learn some basic phrases. Not that she expected to be her roommate for long, but Anna seemed the sort of person worth getting to know.

"Oh look, the defect found a friend."

A trio had stopped walking in front of them, crossing their arms as they planted their feet in the middle of the path.

"Isn't that sweet," one of them crooned. With broad shoulders and a pale face, she looked like she'd spent the better half of her life working in a factory.

"You don't have to walk with that, you know," the petite blonde she had heard talking earlier flicked a disdainful glance towards Anna, who kept her eyes fixed on the path. She couldn't hear their taunts, but it wasn't hard to divine their meaning.

"I dunno, I heard she's a loony. They heard her talking to herself," the third member, who looked like she could be related to the broad-shouldered factory worker, chimed in.

"That makes sense." The blonde smirked. "Birds of a feather and all that. At least they've contained the gimps in one cell."

Her cronies let out a riotous laugh as Charlie and Anna stepped around them, refusing to give them the satisfaction of even a flicker of emotion.

Again, Charlie felt compelled to offer a few words of reassurance. Instead, she tried to convey her support through her unwavering presence at Anna's shoulder. Anna said nothing, but also seemed content with Charlie's company.

Charlie found her eyes probing the fences of the facility, despite having no intention to run from her fate. Even if she had the inclination, the concertina-topped fence was imposingly high and unclimbable, and the concrete path which ran around the perimeter prevented even the most determined from digging beneath it.

Guards were stationed at either end of the yard, no movement went unseen.

The facility was much larger than the hundred-or-so girls ambling around the yard; perhaps exercise times were staggered with other blocks to prevent overcrowding and unnecessary socialisation.

Wynn had to be in one of the buildings standing over them; frustratingly close but impossibly far away. She may not have the chance to speak with him again – ever.

Scanning the groups of women scattered across the yard, she spotted a few blurry-edged figures amongst them. Initially surprised that anyone would willingly continue their sentence in death, she soon realised they had likely not been inmates at all. Mothers, fathers and grandparents watched over their loved ones with expressions of sad acceptance. While they couldn't remove their daughters and granddaughters from this awful place, they were evidently committed to staying with them through the ordeal.

A couple of picnic tables had been claimed by groups of Black and

Hispanic women. Most were engaged in conversation and soaking in the morning sun, but Charlie felt one look up at her as they passed.

"Hey, new girl!"

Charlie recognised the voice and paused.

"I'm your neighbour." She swung her legs over the seat and pushed herself upright with an uncanny grace as her long black braids swayed around her shoulders. "You can call me Denise."

"Charlie." She held out a hand, wishing she knew more about prison etiquette.

Denise looked at her hand and let out a throaty, boisterous laugh. She gave the hand a sideways slap and pulled her into a one-armed hug.

"Welcome home, new girl. I know it's a bit hard to get used to, but after a while, you're gonna really hate it."

Charlie giggled in spite of herself.

"Hey, I'm Tani."

Charlie wasn't short, but she was suddenly dwarfed by a broad-shouldered woman."Hi," she replied meekly, extending her hand.

Tani grinned, motioning for her to close her hand, and gave her a gentle fistbump.

Denise raised her eyebrows at Anna, before jamming her right hand twice between the fingers of her left hand.

Anna laughed and signed something back, touching her thumb to her chest and pivoting her hand forward.

"You speak sign language, too?" Charlie watched the exchange.

"A little bit." Denise waved a hand dismissively. "Stick around Anna and you'll pick up a few signs. Especially if you're a lifer."

"Oh," was all that came out of Charlie. She quickly realised she still didn't know what crimes these women had committed. Not that she could cast judgement. She was a lifer, just as Denise had put it.

"Don't worry, new girl. I'm not asking for your life story." Denise bounced flat hands from one side to the next. "Take it easy."

Denise smiled knowingly at Tani before they turned back to the other women. Anna nudged Charlie and nodded back towards the walking track.

This day would be a long one, but at least there were people she knew a little better now. She wasn't alone.

Twenty-Three

THE SENTENCE

Charlie had long been under the illusion that prisoners spend the majority of their days dwelling on the ceiling, tennis ball in hand as they drummed a steady beat against the opposing wall. She had imagined boredom and a frustrating restlessness being confined to a metal and concrete box.

It was with surprise, then, that she pricked her finger for the fourth time on the needle as she attempted to navigate the grey fabric inexpertly through an uncooperative sewing machine.

"Don't worry about the blood," the guard had told her the first time, "it will come out in the wash."

Charlie glanced at her neighbour who had finished three shirts in the time it had taken her to butcher half of one.

Sewing was never a skill her mother or grandmother had imparted. Despite it being one of the important skills (as deemed by society) for a woman to have, they held it on par with cooking and household chores. Why should one spend any longer on those tasks than they absolutely had to?

Pushing gently on the pedal again, she succeeded in snagging the material and sewing an unfashionable hitch into the side of the dress. *Perfect.*

She raised the needle and began to pluck at her most recent disaster.

There was the odd whisper of conversation in the orderly rows, but most worked in compliant silence.

It made sense that their uniforms were manufactured in house. The prison was equipped with a workforce that was virtually free; bar the obligatory few cents an hour. Charlie didn't want anything from the commissary, not that she even knew what was on offer, but she might be able to afford a small 'thank you' for Anna and Denise before she left.

Charlie wasn't sure how long her new friends had been there, or how much longer they would stay, but she imagined that anyone would quickly grow tired of the meal rotation. Charlie couldn't stomach the idea of many more breakfasts as bland as the one she'd had that morning.

"We get this special treat on the weekends where they combine breakfast and lunch and call it brunch. Sounds fancy but it wasn't one of them fancy white lady kind of brunches. It's just 'cause it saves 'em money," Denise had explained to her as they stood waiting in the queue.

Charlie forwent the orange juice for a cup of black coffee which, while not having the same strong-bodied flavour provided by her local cafe, was enough to bring life to her lethargic bones. Although she didn't consciously feel hungry, her body accepted the bowl of shredded wheat with milk and a Mapleine roll. Never having found pleasure in smoking, she accepted the cigarette and handed it to Denise who sat at the table behind them.

Inmates seemed to gather strategically based on racial and social groups. Asian women claimed their own table, as did the Latinos and Hispanics. The majority of residents, though, were whites who organised themselves based on class. In spite of the uniform grey, the wealthy could still be distinguished by their well-kept hair and in the way they held themselves while refusing to acknowledge those they considered beneath them. The lower white class drew attention as they heckled passersby and grinned with gaps in their teeth.

Denise had shaken her head when Charlie gestured to the seat opposite Anna and herself and instead joined the same African-American women she had sat with in the exercise yard. There was an order to be preserved and the prison hierarchy took precedence over friendships, temporary or otherwise.

Surreptitiously, Charlie scanned the hall for Wynn's short brown hair but picking him out in such a diverse crowd was impossible. There was every possibility Wynn was being held separately and received his meals in his cell.

She hadn't seen Rhett since they disembarked the bus and hadn't received a moment of privacy to summon him. She was also sorely missing her elderly friend. Some reassuring words from Hudson were something she would have happily paid for.

Anna's non-judgemental company was something Charlie was grateful for, but she felt a pang of guilt for wanting someone she could speak candidly with. She was currently playing out her deepest fears, facing the sentence she had spent her life training to avoid. And for the first time since her grandmother's death, she felt truly alone. The chaotic thoughts were locked in her head with no release, like a pressure valve refusing to budge.

It was almost amusing to find herself sitting there, sewing machine before her, worrying over how badly she was butchering the dress she was supposed to be making. She snorted in derision, a few girls turning their heads to see what she found so amusing. Charlie just smiled and shook her head; she couldn't begin to explain.

Her block was permitted to shower at 4 o'clock and dinner was served at 5 o'clock, obviously with the intention of having all prisoners back in their cells before nightfall when an escapee would be harder to spot in the dark.

The line for the showers was at least seventy bodies long, growing longer as certain groups pulled in their members so they could skip the queue. Charlie was in no hurry but, even if she was, she knew better than to reprimand Denise's friends for their manners.

"They need to put separate showers in our rooms," a whiny voice said behind her. "It's 1956, this is positively medieval."

"Yeah, they didn't even have running water but this is definitely the same," someone else quipped.

Clinging to Anna's side as usual, the sounds emanating from the showers soon became difficult for Charlie to ignore. The prison's rule of silence didn't seem to be enforced here, as women cackled and yelled to their friends standing in the same room. It felt like Charlie was preparing to enter a men's locker room, but she squared her shoulders to hide her apprehension and stepped inside.

"Towel, soap," said the female guard unenthusiastically as she handed Charlie what she said.

To Charlie's horror, she found fifty women attempting to shower in a room with a capacity of thirty. Somehow, despite the soap and shampoo, it still smelled of damp and sweat. They disrobed and made their way to a row of shower heads with the least number of bodies under them, trying unsuccessfully to avoid stepping on discarded clothes as they went.

"It's alright, honey, I'm done." A woman old enough to be her mother stepped aside to allow Charlie room to wash.

"Thank you." Charlie smiled while trying to maintain eye contact. "I didn't think it would be so crowded."

The woman shrugged. "The guards usually just want the showers done quickly. The more of us they let in at once, the sooner they can park their rears somewhere."

The heat and humidity in the room was overwhelming. The water was near scalding but Charlie didn't have the courage to turn it down. The other women seemed to enjoy the burn, as if it were purging their sins.

Water sloshed around Charlie's feet, the drain holes were clogged with the mashed up remnants of partially used cakes of soap. She washed quickly, lathering herself copiously, and let the water carry away whatever dignity she had left.

Stepping aside for someone else to take her place, she looked for her towel, now lost somewhere in an indistinguishably tangled mess. Plucking one at random and hoping they were all the same, she towelled off but soon realised the humidity made it near impossible to pull her clothes on regardless.

Supper was a flavourless bowl of split pea soup with a side of beet and onion salad. Again, she accepted the cigarette and passed it to Denise who, again, sat with her group. The canteen area was like a patchwork quilt of colour and class and Anna and Charlie were the loose threads dangling from the edges.

Anna downed her fork and pointed to her food, then with her right hand touched her four fingers to her thumb and raised it to her mouth.

"Food," she mouthed.

Charlie replicated the movement. "Food." That would be an easy one to remember.

She then patted the table and held her forearms horizontally in front of her, tapping them together once.

"Table."

The labelling continued as they worked their way through their surroundings; chair, clothes, woman, group.

Anna and Charlie were beaming with delight when a sharp crack on the table ruptured their cocoon.

"What is this, a bloody magic show?"

The same guard who had been on shower duty was leaning over them, baton in hand.

"No, ma'am," Charlie answered quickly, pulling her arms back to her body. "Anna was teaching me some sign language."

"How wholesome," the guard sneered. "If I see you waving your hands around like monkeys again, you can go and practise your tricks in seg. Understand?"

"Yes, ma'am." Charlie nodded, but Anna evidently hadn't moved because the guard glowered at her. "Understand?" she asked again, lips barely moving, making it almost impossible for Anna to lip read.

To Charlie's relief, Anna seemed to work out what was expected and nodded.

"Cat got your tongue, inmate? Speak up."

Anna blinked at her.

"I'm waiting, inmate."

The surrounding tables had turned to watch the show. It must've been a welcomed diversion from the monotonous tedium. The murmurs and giggles said as much.

Charlie couldn't let the humiliation continue. "Please, ma'am, she's deaf."

"Right, deaf, not dumb. Or perhaps I was wrong?"

Anna kept silent, her stare steady despite tears pooling at the corners.

"Fine, have it your way. Off to seg!"

She struck the table again with the baton, causing Charlie to jump to her feet. A hush had fallen over the entire room.

"Start walking." The baton found a home in the hollow of her back and pushed her forward, forcing her feet to stumble forward. Behind her, Anna rose demurely to her feet, not seeming to notice the baton as it thwacked her arm.

She could feel eyes staring at her and Anna as they passed, but Charlie kept her gaze fixed on the door, doing her best to appear unfazed.

Her suspicions of what seg involved were confirmed when they were led to a small building at the back of the facility and thrown into separate cells smaller than a parking space.

"I'm sure some alone time is just what you each need." The guard smirked as she slammed the door, leaving Charlie alone in the dimly lit room. "We don't give baby killers any special treatment here."

Charlie froze; baby killer? She had only just met Anna but surely no one as pure and warm as her would be capable of such a thing. She pushed it out of her mind. Whatever she was here for, Anna would tell her when she was ready.

They had passed several doors identical to the one she was now locked behind, but with the thickness of the walls, Anna and their other neighbours may as well have been miles away. A thin mattress was wedged into a corner. No bed frame, it sat uninvitingly on the cold concrete. The ubiquitous toilet and sink sat side by side on the opposite wall. The only other fixture was a table bolted to the wall, measuring less than a square foot. The air reeked of mildew and depression.

By no means was Charlie ecstatic with her new quarters, but she was one of the few people in the world on whom solitary confinement was wasted.

"Hudson, Rhett!"

Almost instantly, the air shifted and the two men stood before her, expressions falling in distaste as they took in their surroundings.

"You didn't," Rhett said simply, shoulders slouching in exasperation.

"My word, where are we?" Hudson stepped away from the wall and dusted the sleeves of his coat, as though his ethereal form could be tarnished by the dank surroundings.

"She's gone and got herself in the SHU."

"Shoe?" Charlie and Hudson asked simultaneously.

"Special Housing... something or other. Isolation," he clarified.

Hudson turned to her, horrified. "My lady, what have you done?"

Charlie huffed at the implication that she was there because of some transgression on her part. "An awful guard was bullying my cellmate. I figured I'm leaving in a body bag either way, so I didn't see the harm in intervening."

An uncomfortable silence stretched between them, not even a distant chatter or hum of traffic to fill the void. It was an unearthly, all-consuming stillness. Hudson shuffled his feet anxiously while Rhett stared determinedly at the floor.

"There's no point pretending otherwise." Charlie leaned against the wall, quickly peeling herself back off when she felt moisture seep through her clothes. "With the charges I've confessed to, there's no other way this is going to end."

"We don't know that yet," Hudson murmured quietly. Charlie decided not to argue with him; perhaps he still needed to hold onto some slim fragment of hope.

Still refusing to make eye contact, Rhett evidently had not yet rested. His figure still seemed to waver, like a waning battery slowly losing power before it ran out of steam completely.

"You haven't been resting, have you?" She scrutinised him closely.

He sucked his teeth. "I've had things to do."

"What kind of things?"

He bristled. "Just... things. It doesn't matter."

Her nostrils flared but she decided against pushing him further. "How is Wynn?"

Rhett's broad shoulders lifted in ambivalence. "As well as can be expected, I guess. He's awful shook up about you – you know, being a martyr and all that." Charlie rolled her eyes at the jibe. "But they've got him in a quiet wing, just a couple of young ones in there with him. I think he quite likes the attention." He grinned.

The easy flowing conversation provided Charlie with some semblance of normalcy in her otherwise inverted world. Rhett's smile was a warm breeze in the snow, but even talking seemed to be draining him and he visibly flickered before them.

"Rhett, you need to rest," Charlie told him firmly. He opened his mouth to argue but she cut him off before he could speak. "I know you want to be there for your brother but if you don't take care of yourself, Wynn's going to have to get used to life without you being around at all."

Frowning, Rhett turned to Hudson. "Really? Can ghosts die?"

"Not in the same way humans do," Hudson began tactfully. "A ghost's energy source is not infinite. We are not designed to exist on this plane for extended periods of time. Should we wish to extend our time here, we must preserve our resources. You may have already noticed some things which were in your power before, are no longer."

Rhett's face fell. Hudson had evidently stumbled upon a truth. "And what if the resources have already been... expended?"

"That's not to say they are gone permanently. Charlie is right; you must rest. Wynn is a strong young chap. I will keep an eye on him for you," Hudson offered in the same warm-hearted manner a grandfather offers to watch his grandchild.

Looking like he was about to continue arguing, Rhett finally sighed in resignation. "Fine, but promise me you'll get me the second something happens."

Hudson nodded. "Of course."

Rhett held Charlie's gaze for a few seconds, his lips on the verge of saying something before he abruptly evaporated.

"You can go too, Hudson." Charlie dropped herself onto the bed, cringing as her tailbone hit the concrete through the thin padding. "There's no sense in us both suffering in this hole."

"My dear," he settled himself on the metal table, legs crossed at the ankles, "I could never allow you to spend the night alone in such a dreadful place."

True to his word, Hudson briefly left three times during the night to ensure Wynn was okay. He returned within minutes each time and Charlie kept her eyes closed to maintain the illusion of sleep, though she was sure he knew that's all it was.

As the morning light penetrated the dense darkness, the jangle of keys ruptured her depressive stupor. A different guard stood at the door, not the one who had thrown her in the previous night.

"You got lucky, inmate. Warden wants to see you."

"Me?" Charlie questioned unnecessarily, as though he could see Hudson still sitting dutifully beside her.

At the guard's withering glare, Charlie stumbled to her feet. The hard floor had been pressing uncomfortably into her lower back and her legs tingled as circulation returned.

"Hold out your hands."

Charlie obliged, rewarded with the cold steel of handcuffs cutting into her skin once again.

"Move it."

He led Charlie into the crisp morning air, the distant murmur of prisoners awakening permeating the quiet. She hoped Anna wouldn't be far behind her. Proceeding to the front building in which her humanity was first stripped from her, the guard held the door open and ushered her to the very back of the building and up a set of stairs.

He knocked twice on an unremarkable wooden door bearing a tarnished metal plaque which simply read, "Warden".

"Enter."

A shrew-faced woman with petite spectacles sat behind a thick-legged red wood desk, a leather top barely visible under a chaos of papers and folders.

"Warden, I have prisoner Charlotte Hall as you requested."

Her finger continued trailing down a list of appointments in a black diary. "She may sit," she said, not looking up.

The chair was a dark green leather, with cracks beginning to run through the seat from years of service. Though it was probably a perfectly ordinary chair, it felt like the most comfortable chair in the world as Charlie sank herself into it, bones groaning from the overnight torture.

The warden sighed and snapped the diary shut, leaning back in her chair and removing her spectacles as she surveyed Charlie for the first time. Her salt and pepper hair was pulled back into a tight bun which lifted the corners of her wilting eyes.

"The courts have processed your sentencing," she announced without emotion.

"My sentencing?" Charlie repeated, assuming there was a mistake. "I haven't had my trial yet."

"You pleaded guilty to crimes for which there is only one punishment. The courts saw a trial to be an unnecessary waste of their time."

Charlie stared in disbelief. "No trial?"

"Correct," she replied impatiently, lifting a few papers as she searched for something. "Your sentence was delivered yesterday evening." She produced an envelope which she threw unceremoniously on the desk before Charlie.

"Please read and confirm that you understand."

Miss Hall,

The court has thoroughly reviewed and considered the record concerning the defendant, including both the guilty and penalty proceedings as well as memorandum submitted by both the State and the defence.

The court has also considered the aggravating factors the jury has found to exist beyond a reasonable doubt and the mitigating factors established by the evidence. The court acknowledges that this is not a quantitative comparison, but instead requires a qualitative analysis of each aggravating factor and each mitigating circumstance.

The court has assigned appropriate weight to each and has found that the aggravating factors found to exist heavily outweigh the mitigating circumstances presented. The court finds the recommendation to impose a death sentence is consistent with its verdict and is based on the evidence presented regarding the aggravating and mitigating circumstances.

Therefore the court finds that the sentence of death is the appropriate penalty the court should impose for the act of initiating public rebellion through blackmail of a minor and the attempted kidnapping of that minor, as charged in Count 1 of the indictment.

Accordingly, as to Count 1, for the act of attempting to initiate public rebellion through blackmail of a minor and the attempted kidnapping of that minor, the defendant Charlotte Hall is hereby sentenced to death.

The defendant shall be delivered into the custody of the Illinois Department of Corrections where she shall be confined until the date selected by the Governor of the State and on that date, the defendant shall be executed in a method provided for by the laws of the State of Illinois.

Long live the State.

Signed,

Edward J. Hooper

Chief Judge of the Supreme Court

Twenty-Four

THE READING

"But I didn't even enter a plea! What mitigating circumstances? What jury? I haven't been allowed to speak!"

"The State has considered both of your public testimonials and saw no need to collect a third," she answered matter-of-factly.

"Both—" Charlie stopped herself, recalling her initial proclamation in the court itself before taking to the street. She stared at the letter for what could have been seconds or minutes, time had faded away. "This cannot be legal."

The warden leaned forward over the desk, smirking. "The State is the law."

Charlie had known this would be her sentence, but she expected she would have the basic human right of a trial, not to be thrown in the garbage awaiting the collection service. She had imagined being able to make her case, to look the judge in the eye as she told him who she was and what she stood for. But they had handed her a sentence worse than death alone; they had taken her voice. There was nothing more she could do; she was already dead.

"When?" Charlie felt like she should be crying but there was only the hollow resentment that had settled in her chest.

"Next Friday."

She didn't need to ask how. Now declared an enemy of the State, her neck would be broken as she hung from the gallows, surrounded by judgemental onlookers who came to witness supposed justice.

"Has Wynn been released?"

"That is no concern of yours."

"Like hell, it's not. The sole reason I came forward was because I did not want him persecuted for my actions. I am willingly exchanging my life for his and I have a right to know if he will go free."

"A right." The warden rolled her eyes and smirked. "You are a death row prisoner. Your rights are gone."

Seething hatred boiled in Charlie's stomach as she glared at the smug, haughty woman sitting opposite her.

"You will remain in your cell for the time being and be transferred to solitary confinement the evening prior to your execution," the warden said easily. "Ordinarily death row prisoners are immediately segregated from other inmates, however I see an opportunity to set an example for your fellow prisoners."

"And what example is that?" Charlie refused to address her as 'ma'am'.

The warden smiled broadly. "That service to the State comes before all else, and distractive fairy tales will not be tolerated."

Charlie lifted her chin. "I wish I could be there when you find out Hell is real."

Shrill laughter rang out as the warden threw her head back. "What a shame, I shall miss your comedy."

She looked over Charlie's head to the guard who must have still been standing behind her. "Take the prisoner back to her cell."

"Not to seg, ma'am?"

"No." The warden opened her diary again, perusing her day's appointments. "Let the other women get to know her. I want them to notice her absence next Friday."

Rolled oats, canned plums and a piece of stale bread. Charlie stared at her food without seeing it. Nor did she hear the quiet thrum of morning conversation as it floated around her.

As the guard had walked her back to her block, Hudson had confirmed Wynn was being set free. She should have felt relief, vindication, even, perhaps, peace. But the tired voice in her head had simply said 'good' and abandoned her with the clawing knowledge each step her feet marched, each breath that filled her chest, each time she blinked her eyes against the glaring sun, was now numbered.

She had refused to acknowledge Anna, who had bounced eagerly off the bed at her return. Instead, she had curled into the fetal position on the lower bunk and surrendered to morbid despondency. She hadn't heard the guards when they announced morning count until Anna, woken by the light, grabbed her arm and pulled her forcefully from the bed. She used the same force when Charlie didn't move for breakfast.

Anna pulled her up by the arm again, raising her hand to her mouth. "Eat", she mouthed.

But there's no point, Charlie answered silently, before her feet reluctantly complied as Anna put an arm around her and guided her from her bed all the way to where she now sat, staring at her food.

Anna elbowed her gently and again signed an order to eat. She was so caring, maternal. Not the makings of a child murderer.

The plum's juices spilled onto the oats as she stabbed at it with her fork, macabrely reminiscent of blood pouring from an open wound. She pushed the thought from her mind so she would be able to chew without gagging. Forcing the mouthful down her throat was painful enough.

The only faint silver lining was that she had no living family. There was no one to whom she had to break the news. There was no one to attempt to console over a time-restricted phone call. There was no one she was condemning to a bitter fate of loss and resentment, no one who would have to carry on without her. That, and she was at least certain her soul would continue elsewhere.

She wondered idly if the other prisoners would make claims for her things, not that she would be leaving much behind. Her prison earnings, meagre as they were, would be left to Anna. Perhaps she should be grateful she had so little, at least she would not have to experience what it was to be picked apart by vultures.

The day continued as normal, whatever normal was in a place like this. Life proceeded inexorably around her as hers neared its end.

If it were possible, the clothes she sewed became even worse and began to resemble what one would expect to remove from the victim of a shark attack. The guard threatened to send her to the SHU if the quality of her work didn't improve but, seeing the threat had little impact on Charlie, he instead turned to the other women, announcing that they would have to work twice as hard to compensate for her inability to do her fair share.

She sensed daggers being thrown at her, but they fell like pebbles against a brick wall. For the first time in her life, she was truly invincible. Without the capacity to feel, she couldn't be hurt. They had taken her life and her humanity with it.

Time passed in a blur of grey uniforms, unheard conversations and mindless marching from one place to another.

It wasn't until they had been interned for the evening and the cells were bathed in the glow of a single hanging dome light in the middle of the hall that her facade broke and the tears began. She didn't sob, lest the other women heard her. She didn't shake, lest Anna felt the bed move. In silence she lay morose and desolate, the pillow becoming wet behind her ears.

"Psst... hey, Charlie."

Denise was calling her. She swallowed but didn't respond, wishing the bed would simply envelop her and quietly remove her from the world.

"Are you okay, Char?"

She didn't know. No one would ask someone who had just been sentenced to execution if they were "okay".

"As okay as I can be." Charlie tried to pull herself together. "Just a bad day, you know? Bad month, actually."

"I hear ya. Is there anything I can do?" Denise sounded genuinely concerned, but what could she do from behind a foot of concrete?

"Thanks, but I don't think so. I appreciate what you've done already. You know, just being nice."

Denise snorted. "Ya know it's a messed up world when you gotta thank someone for being nice. My ma always said it cost nothing, but people are too worried about what they can take to see what they can give."

"She sounds like a good woman."

"Why thank you, hon. I try."

Charlie started, sitting bolt upright in bed when she realised a buxom middle aged woman was standing by her bed. Her eyes smiled and she tilted her head gently, apologising for small heart attack.

"She was." Denise's voice had lowered an octave. "Wish I was more like her, to be honest."

"What a load of self-pitying bullocks." The woman rolled her eyes.

"Denise," Charlie murmured. "What would you say to your mother if she was here?"

There was silence for a second and Charlie pictured Denise with her legs tucked to her chest, her chin resting on her knees. "Well she ain't, is she? No point thinking like that."

"Actually..." Charlie paused, not sure this was a good idea for her emotionally exhausted brain, but then threw caution to the wind. "She is here, Denise. She's standing right in front of me."

"What are you talking about, Char?"

"I'm a Seer, Denise. That's what I'm in for."

Charlie pictured Denise's mouth falling open. "Quit messing around, Char."

"Tell her it's just as well she ain't on kitchen duty here. You'd all be goners."

"She says you were never much help in the kitchen." There was silence and Charlie knew she was listening.

"I asked her to watch the onions one day. Came back to a pot of black, smoking goop. Watch em she did. Just watched em burn right up."

Charlie couldn't help but let out a giggle, repeating the story and earning a gasp through the crack.

"I didn't think Seers were real!" she whispered in shock.

"They don't want you to. We're out there. Hiding. But your mother's here, and I'm not messing. So what would you like to say?"

"Her name's Lanelle. I just want her to know it was an accident."

Lanelle snorted. "Even if it wasn't, I wouldn't have blamed her. That filth was bad news. I knew he was nothing but trouble from the second I saw him."

Charlie was often privy to very private conversations and the sense of coming into a story halfway through. She repeated Lanelle's words, not liking the direction the exchange was taking. A pregnant pause ensued as they processed what they'd just heard.

"Wait, she knew it was an accident?" Charlie fought the desire to ask what said accident was.

"Yes, child." Lanelle flapped her hands in exasperation. "You couldn't even kill a chicken for dinner. Did you forget who raised you?"

So Denise had been accused of murder, Charlie deduced with an uncomfortable shudder.

"But... why'd you do it?" Denise choked on her words, evidently on the verge of tears.

Lanelle sucked in a deep breath, chewing her lip as she tried to find the words. "I couldn't stand the thought of watching what they'll do to you."

Charlie's skin had thickened to the emotional conversations she had to relay so regularly but, as she repeated Lanelle's words, an awful pang went through her heart.

Thick, wet sobs broke through the wall, interrupted by Lanelle's ragged breaths. "I thought you were ashamed, Ma."

"Oh, God, child." Lanelle's commanding posture collapsed and she disappeared, likely now sitting beside Denise on the other side of the wall, cradling her face as she cried.

"The only shame I feel is for humanity. I fear we are beyond salvation."

The words were muffled, but Charlie could still distinguish them.

As she had trained herself, she continued to mechanically repeat

Lanelle's words, but there was something different about this conversation. There was an unspoken tragedy here which went beyond a car accident. She dared not ask; it was none of her business, she was simply the messenger.

"I'm sorry, Ma." Denise's voice was heavy and distorted. "I never meant for any of this to happen."

Charlie could hear Lanelle's gentle *ssshhh* from behind the wall, and felt guilty knowing how much Denise wanted to hear that sound.

"It's not your fault, I'm sorry I couldn't protect you. And not being able to be there with you when you needed me the most was too much for me to bear."

"I don't want you to watch, Ma. I don't want you there. I just wanna know you'll be waiting for me."

Lanelle's voice was strained now, cracking despite her fierce resolve. "I brought you into this world and I'll bring you into the next, child."

Muffled sobs continued well into the night. Charlie imagined Denise with a pillow clamped firmly over her face.

For the first time since she had been sentenced, she felt something stir in her hollow chest.

Breakfast was as unappetising as Charlie had come to expect, yet she helped herself to an apple and black coffee. Anna looked on approvingly.

Charlie had been watching Denise moving slowly along the line, eyes bloodshot and swollen from their night of torture. As she approached with her tray, Charlie held out the cigarette for her to take as she passed. To her surprise, Denise took the seat opposite and stared at her.

Whispers rustled like the leaves of trees behind her as Denise's group watched on in confusion.

"Uh... Denise?" one of them asked, but she didn't acknowledge them.

"He was twenty years older than me, a businessman from Detroit," she began, eyes fixed on Charlie's.

"I met him at the grocery store and he starts talking to me, this well dressed white man. He seems pleasant enough and he asks me what I do. I tell him I clean houses. He asks if I would clean his. I say yes. Our family sure needs the money."

The surrounding tables leaned in; Denise didn't seem to care.

"So twice a week I start cleaning his house. It's a nice house, one of the nicest I've seen. I know he's got money. He's interested in me, I know he is. I'm not interested in him, but I figure he might take care of me. Maybe I can even have an allowance to give to my family."

She was barely breathing between her sentences now, driven by some urgency to free her trapped story. "Then he asks if I'll stop cleaning other houses, he wants me to work for him and only him. Now I'm not sure at first, but he says he's gonna cover my weekly earnings plus some. So I agree.

"He tries to kiss me a couple times and I let him. It ain't so bad. But then one day he doesn't let me leave. I think he might be joking, but he ain't. He tells me there's nowhere else I need to be. I tell him I gotta go home to see my family, that my papa ain't well. It's a lie, but he's scaring me.

"I know where he keeps the keys but he blocks me. I try to push past him and he holds a gun to my neck. I don't even know what I'm doing, but I grab his hand and turn it away from me. He shoves me back into the table. I squeeze. And bang. He's dead."

A few quiet gasps rang out around them, which Denise ignored.

"I'm charged with murder, they don't listen. The whiter-than-cream jury sits there and judges me, and a few days later my ma kills herself. So now I'm here, with the weight of two souls on my shoulders, waiting for my day to die."

Blinking slowly, Charlie wasn't sure how to respond to such a heart-wrenching revelation and took a few moments to collect herself. Eventually, all she could manage was a simple question. "Why are you telling me this?"

The eye contact still hadn't broken. "I thought my ma killed herself cause of me. Cause of the shame. I've always kinda felt like I deserved my sentence. Not for *him*, but for her. I'm tired of living in the guilt and I ain't gonna pretend anymore. And neither should you."

The connections the other women were drawing could almost be seen above their heads; Charlie had helped Denise talk to her dead mother. Charlie was a Seer.

"Shhh," Charlie raised a hand, imploring Denise to be quiet. She dipped her head, as though she could hide from the dozens of eyes directed at her.

Denise considered her for a moment before lowering her voice gently. "You're already on death row. Why you still hiding?"

As Charlie left the breakfast table and dropped her plate and cutlery into the waiting tubs, she could feel that something had changed. Her name seemed to fall around her like rain but no one was calling her, they were talking about her.

She had always hid to protect herself, as her grandmother had instructed. "Don't get caught." Well, she already had been. What was the good in hiding now?

She could slink through the prison for her remaining days, neither confirming nor denying the accusations, and die a coward. Or she could step into her truth and own her identity as she had never previously allowed herself.

The choice was a daunting one, but she sensed it had already been made.

Giving up on any success as a seamstress, Charlie stared at her woeful attempt at sewing in an elastic to the waist of some track pants.

Suddenly, they were snatched from beneath her nose and replaced with a clean-lined, perfectly sewn pair she couldn't hope to emulate. Brow furrowed, she looked up at her neighbour who had already set to work unpicking her disaster.

"Is it true?"

Charlie didn't need to ask what. "Yes."

The woman wet her lips. "I was wondering if I could talk to my grandfather."

And so went Charlie's days. She was accosted in the exercise yard, at meals, even in the shower block where she politely asked if that was where they really wanted to summon their deceased family member.

In bizarre contrast to the outside world where people like her were vilified and God was spoken about behind closed doors, she suddenly found herself sought after, respected even. Not all of them, of course, were open to the idea, but those loyal to the State kept a wary distance from her and didn't dare voice their disapproval.

While she wasn't being paid as such, the other prisoners made a point of exchanging what they could for her service. It was quite a surprise the first time she was ushered forward in the queue for lunch, or given space to enjoy a showerhead to herself.

It was easy to become lost in the pretence that she had a place here, that she mattered.

The illusion was swiftly wrenched out from under her when a guard pulled her away from her sewing work. Not that she was the one sewing, of course.

"We need your measurements," he had said brusquely, and the implications shattered Charlie's manufactured bubble of safety.

She once again found herself in the makeshift doctor's office, told to strip down to her underwear, and stand on the scales. The numbers bounced chaotically before settling; she had lost a few pounds over the past week.

"1,260 divided by 138... 9 feet," the guard muttered to himself, scribbling.

Again, her height was measured for accuracy, but the tape was also stretched around her waist, hips and bust. He even recorded her shoe size, as though it mattered if they fit properly.

He was the farmer evaluating his livestock, and she was the lamb being sized up for slaughter.

Without any further discussion, she redressed and the guard led her back to continue working as if this were any normal day.

"You don't have long left, do you?" Denise asked her over dinner.

She had taken to sitting opposite Charlie every meal now. Her friends spread across the two tables, Charlie and Anna having been welcomed into the fold.

"Three days," Charlie replied, not asking how she knew. News travelled within the walls without even being announced.

The pea soup splashed thickly as Denise watched it fall from her spoon. "This ain't right."

Shrugging, Charlie tried to appear ambivalent. "Law's the law. You don't even know the full story."

"I know enough, and I know there's plenty of death and grief in this world. We need all the hope we can get."

She lifted her chin at a tall girl with muscular forearms. "Tani, do you still play the spoons?"

Tani grinned and nodded. Denise noticed Charlie's furrowed brow. "She don't actually play with them. She makes keys."

"Oh?" Charlie's eyebrows shot up hopefully.

"Yeah. If they work, well, that's a different story."

"They worked! Once." Tani's shoulders slouched, though she was still a full head taller than anyone else at the table.

"Then why are you still here?" Denise waited expectantly.

"Well, I was surprised." Tani turned the spoon over in her hands. "Wasn't really expecting it to work and I didn't know what to do next."

"So she closed the door, hid it under her pillow and got it confiscated," Denise summarised.

The group chuckled and Charlie did her best to join in, hiding her welling disappointment. She really wasn't going to get out of here.

Twenty-Five

THE PLAN

The newfound acceptance in a community was a welcome distraction, despite it being a community Charlie had never consciously wished to be a part of. There was a simple, human pleasure in the light-hearted banter that followed dinner, how Anna sat on her bed and continued teaching her to sign, and how Denise said goodnight through the wall.

It was only in the absence of these distractions that the voice in the back of Charlie's mind came to the forefront and she heard it properly for the first time all day; three days left.

She had never been afraid of the dark; she relished the reprieve nighttime brought. It had been a blanket to comfort her between long days of anxiety and lies. Now, she hated its silence and the way it amplified her thoughts. She hated its darkness and the way it encouraged her vivid imagination.

So it was with quiet relief that she heard a throat clear and found Rhett standing beside her bed.

"Oh, Rhett!" She swung her legs off the bed and stood in front of him, unsure of whether she was eager for the distraction or for the other reasons which she pushed from her mind.

But Rhett didn't mirror her enthusiasm. "Hudson just told me..." He sucked on his lip, eyes glassy. "I'm sorry, Charlie. I should've been here with you the whole time. But I didn't know they'd already..."

Oh, he wanted to talk about her death anyway.

"It's okay, Rhett." Charlie slumped her shoulders, stopping herself from raising a hand to brush the hair away from his face. He still looked worn and on the edge of collapse. She wondered how close he had come to dissolving into nothing, and how dangerously close he still was to that edge. "There's nothing to be done."

"Wynn needs to know," he said heavily.

She sighed and nodded, knowing it wouldn't be an easy conversation. "I'm sorry."

"You didn't need to do this, you know." He ran a hand through his hair. "They weren't going to kill him. He could've gotten out in—"

"In how long?" Charlie asked sharply, in no mood to entertain fictitious scenarios. "I saw what they did to my mother. They took her away to one of their Enlightenment facilities. Within a few years, she was a husk of the person she was. The last time I saw her, she couldn't tell me my name. All she could do was praise our glorious leader and hail the state.

"If you think I was going to allow Wynn to meet that same fate, you don't know me at all."

There was silence as Rhett took her in. "I didn't know that."

She bristled, uncomfortable with the way he was now looking at her. "It doesn't matter."

"It matters to me," he said softly. "What happened?"

Charlie chewed her lip, reluctant to unbottle the memories she had kept contained for so long. With a resigned sigh, she sat back on the bed and looked at her hands while she found the right starting point.

"An undercover Enforcer had been watching our house. He pretended to be a mourner wanting to communicate with his sister. My mother was trusting. Too trusting. She took him to her Seeing room where he arrested her. The court proceedings were for the sake of formality; she wasn't offered a lawyer or the opportunity to enter a plea. The judge quickly decided that her 'sanity was not intact' and the kindest thing for the State to do was house her indefinitely in an Enlightenment facility.

"The irony is that those four white walls, the daily Enlightenment sessions and isolation meant my mother's sanity really did slip away.

"My grandmother received a letter one day, granting family visitation because of my mother's 'remarkable progress'. But the woman we found wasn't my mother.

"She was just a skeleton, a shell of a person with her eyes fixed on that awful white linoleum. We asked her how she was, if she could hear us. All she could say were things like, 'This is the only life we live', 'Long live the State', 'There is no life after death, only life as we know it'.

"I started crying. I was still just a kid. That woman looked like she could have been my mother, but her soul was long gone. The staff turned us out because I was disrupting her recovery. The next we heard of my mother was a formal letter saying she had died after a violent episode with an Enlightenment Officer. We never got her body back.

"My grandma raised me from then on, teaching me to stay hidden and to see my 'gift' for what it is: a liability. When she left, Hudson found me. And it's been him and I ever since."

Charlie kept her eyes firmly focused on the backs of her hands, not wanting to see Rhett's expression.

He didn't let the silence linger for long. "And neither of them... stayed?"

She cracked her fingers, not knowing how to answer the question that would come next. The one that had tortured her for years. The one that she had yelled at the ceiling on more than one tear-stained night. *Why* hadn't they stayed?

"The night my grandma passed, I was walking down the hallway when I swear I saw a flash of my mother's spirit disappearing into the bedroom. She was this glowing, white, ethereal thing. I only saw her for a second but she looked young. Healthy. I ran down the hall and flung the door open just in time to see them disappear."

"And-"

"I don't know," she snapped, unnecessarily harsh. "I don't know why they didn't stay. I guess they didn't think I needed them."

Quietly, Rhett lowered himself beside her onto the bed. "Can I tell you something?"

She nodded, not wanting to speak and betray the lump that had grown in her throat.

"When I died, I didn't get a choice. One minute, I was working in the shop, the next I was standing next to my own body. Was pretty weird, tell you the truth. But there was no angel standing there to give me an ultimatum. There was no light for me to walk towards or a tunnel to investigate. I was just here and didn't get to have a say in the matter.

"What I'm saying is, maybe they didn't have a choice, either."

She nodded, angling her face away from the light in an effort to hide the shine of her eyes. He knew, it seemed, because she felt the warmth of his energy spread across her shoulders as he wrapped an arm around her.

"Not everything makes sense. Actually, a lot of stuff doesn't. But how boring would life be if it did?"

She exhaled a chuckle, allowing herself to lean into the calming thrum of his electricity. For several seconds they sat like that in the silence, finding comfort in the closest thing they had to touch.

"I don't know if I want to stay or go," she admitted, knowing he would understand her meaning.

He exhaled deeply and she was sure she felt his breath graze her arms. "If you stay, it's going to be much harder to get rid of me."

She chuckled. "You're not so bad."

"You're kind of lucky, you know." He ignored her derisive snort. "Whether you stay here or go there, there are people waiting who l-care about you."

She tried not to focus on what he might have been about to say. Her heart burst into a gallop. Maybe she was lucky. "And, either way, you'll end up there too, right?"

"I guess I will, some day."

The idea of having the people she cared for in one place brought Charlie some comfort. She was surprised to feel a very real, deep longing for that place. But there was someone she needed to take care of here, first.

"Rhett, there's something I need you to do. Not for me, but for Wynn."

"What's that?"

Reluctantly, she shuffled away from him so she could be sure he was following. "At the very back of the courtroom, on the left-hand side, there's a gap between the back of the seat and the wall. It has a wooden plank in front of it but there's space to reach inside."

He nodded slowly.

"That's where I hid my bag. It's probably not still there but, if it is, I want Wynn to have it. Will you make sure he gets it *safely*?" She emphasised the last word, aware they probably had different definitions of the concept.

"Sure," he answered, confused. "But I don't think your skirts are going to look any good on him."

She rolled her eyes. "It's got nothing to do with clothes, Rhett. He's the closest thing I have to family. There's something important in there and I want him to have it."

He sat back to look at her intently. "There has to be a way to get you out of here."

She snorted. "And how is that? Sorry to break it to you, Rhett, but I think your days of negotiation are behind you."

She could see an idea forming in his blurry-edged head and he looked at her, eyes sparkling. "What if you were dead, too?"

Charlie blinked. "I feel like you might be missing the goal here."

Rhett shook his head and reached out to place his hands on top of hers. Her heart thudded.

"What happens to you when you step back and let a spirit in?"

"Well, I feel like I'm looking up from the bottom of a pool. I can make out what's happening but I can't control myself. If I stay down there too long, I'll die." She raised one eyebrow, beginning to see the string he was following.

"So your heart rate drops, your breathing slows. When they come to take you, if you let me step in and we time it right, they might just think you're already dead."

The idea was a flimsy one but, for someone on death row, even the remote possibility of escape was tempting. If it failed, she was dead. If she didn't try, she was dead anyway.

"And then what?"

"I guess you'll be taken to the morgue. And I'd say they don't have as much security there. Usually those folks don't run very fast."

Too focused on the sudden possibility of freedom, Charlie didn't even roll her eyes at the pitiful joke. "It probably won't work. But it might."

Rhett nodded, eyes gleaming. "It might."

"My only caveat is is," she hesitated, knowing she was probably about to offend him, "it might have to be Hudson."

As expected, he recoiled in indignation. "Why?"

The frayed tendrils of energy still hovered around his form like broken tentacles. She raised a hand to his arm and he looked down at it too, as though he hoped to feel her touch.

"You're not ready yet, Rhett," she said gently. "Look, you're still too spent. If I asked you to do that for me, it would probably be the last thing you did."

He bristled. "I know myself, Charlie."

"I know you do, but I would never forgive myself if something happened. And Hudson will be able to do it easily. You can save my life next time," she added with a smile.

His face dropped down to his chest but he nodded reluctantly. "Yeah, okay. But the coupon's going to expire soon so you'd better use it."

"You'll be transported to the Death House on Thursday evening," the warden informed her casually. She was once again leafing through her diary, obviously knowing the macabre information she was reeling off so well that she needed no reference.

Could they not have thought of a more appealing name? Charlie thought dully.

"Once at the Death House, a guard will take your request for your last meal. You will be taken to a cell where you will sleep or reflect on your choices. How you choose to spend the time is of no consequence. At 4.30 am, you will awaken to allow sufficient time for a possible stay of execution." Her lips quirked as if the idea of someone coming to Charlie's aid was amusing to her.

"Until 8 am, you will be permitted to spend time with your family." She seemed to place unnecessary emphasis on the word, as if she knew Charlie had none.

"You will have lunch at 10.30 am and, in the afternoon, you will be dressed for your execution. At 3 pm you will receive your final meal. Witnesses will arrive at approximately 4 pm and, finally, you will be executed at 5 pm. Do you have any questions?"

The warden looked up at her for the first time since she sat down and it occurred to Charlie how little she knew about the woman who had just handed her her death notice. Not even her name.

In her heart of hearts, Charlie knew the events would probably unfold just as the warden had listed them. Rhett and Charlie's plan would fail, she would be hoisted onto a bus like an animal bound for the abattoir and, before a live audience, her life would end.

But there was a chance, the faintest glimmer of hope fighting against the creeping darkness in her soul. She had told the other girls that she didn't want to escape and it was true; she didn't want to escape at the expense of someone else's life.

This was a way she might just be able to slip away, no blood in her wake.

"What do you think happens when we die?" she asked the warden pointedly, watching her eyebrows twitch in surprise.

Evidently, that had not been the question she was anticipating.

"We are dead," she replied bluntly. "What happens when a lightbulb burns out? Or a battery is exhausted? Without electricity it's dead, gone, useless."

Charlie smiled slightly. "But we're more than metal and wires. We aren't powered by batteries, so what do you think makes us run?"

The warden sighed irritably and snapped her diary shut. "If you are quite done wasting my time, the guard will escort you back to your cell."

"Nothing further, ma'am."

She nodded curtly at the guard who took Charlie by the arm and steered her towards the door. "You better stay away from water," she called over her shoulder, grinning at the look of irritation she had earned.

"You have to let us do something, Char!"

"We have to figure something out now, you've only got two more days."

"I'm working on a new spoon."

"She doesn't want anyone to get hurt!"

"We could hoist her over the fence?"

"Yeah, I'm sure no one will notice us playing human pyramid."

"Guys, please!" Charlie held her hands up to the group who had formed around her in the exercise yard. The chatter was overwhelming. "None of you have to do anything. This isn't your fight."

She had come to appreciate that hour of semi-normalcy in the morning. The freedom to walk without a guard by her side or manhandling her was a welcome liberty. Her definition of freedom had changed dramatically in the time she'd been within these walls, and she noted how she now used it to describe even the most trivial privileges. Being able to choose her own brand of coffee, for instance, was a freedom she missed.

The past few mornings had brought a newfound sense of freedom; the ability to practise her gift and help a few women communicate with those they had loved and lost. Unintentionally, Charlie had earned the trust and respect of most of the prisoners on her block, and they were more invested than ever in trying to circumvent her nearing execution date.

"Well it's not like you're still fighting for yourself." Denise put a hand on her hip, staring Charlie down as though she had personally offended her.

Anna pointed one finger at her head before pointing both index fingers towards Denise and nodded.

Charlie gnawed on her lip as she contemplated how much to share. If they all knew what she expected to do, the reaction wouldn't be authentic. The guards weren't stupid, and if the whole block was in on the plot, they would quickly smell a rat.

"I have an idea," she said slowly, eyeing the group as they leaned in. "But I can't say what it is. If it's going to work, it's important that it seems like a surprise."

Denise narrowed her eyes, scanning Charlie's face as though she was trying to extract the thoughts from her brain.

"And you don't need no help?"

Charlie shook her head. "No."

"You ain't worried about us blabbing, are ya?" Tani seemed surprised.

"No, no, of course not." Charlie hated the idea of the women she had come to not only like, but respect as people, second-guessing how she saw them. "I trust you, all of you." She looked around at the little protective circle which had formed around her. "This is the only way I can make sure none of you are hurt at my expense."

Tani shared a look with Denise but said nothing.

Denise sighed and pinned Charlie with another impenetrable stare. "It better be good, Char."

Charlie grimaced noncommittally. It wasn't, but it was all she had.

Tani let out a low whistle. "Baby, would ya look at that body."

Confused, Charlie looked around; no one in this place had hips or a waistline in their regulation grey uniforms. But Tani was staring past the exercise yard towards the front of the facility where a cherry red truck was pulling into the front gates. It was the same car Rhett had admired when they arrived.

"It ain't hard to hotwire a car, you know." Tani didn't seem to be talking to anyone in particular, ogling the car as it disappeared from view behind the square block-like administration building. "Just take off the cover, cut the power wires and hook 'em up."

Charlie kept her expression in check. So that's why Tani was here.

"Don't go jumping to conclusions." She had noticed something in Charlie's face anyway. "My daddy was a tow truck driver. Used to take me out on jobs. Did himself outta work, though. He was too good with cars and a lot of the time he could get em to start. Taught me, too."

"I wasn't — he sounds like a good man." Charlie admonished herself for her undeserved assumption.

Tani nodded, seeming not to hold it against her.

Charlie felt eyes boring into her back and cast a glance over her shoulder. The trio who had formed her welcoming committee were skulking past. The petite blonde and her cronies had kept their distance since Charlie's acceptance by the block.

As always, Anna and Charlie stood side by side, watching the conversation unfold. Eyeing them both disdainfully, the blonde muttered something under her breath and her friends laughed. Feeling empowered by the group surrounding her, Charlie looked the little ringleader in the eye, silently challenging her to share her comment.

After a moment of indecision, the blonde's lips turned up into a sneer before gesturing to Anna. "She ever tell you what she did?"

Charlie felt Anna stiffen beside her, aware she was the topic of conversation. "Doesn't matter," Charlie replied coolly. "Whatever it is, she's a better person than the three of you put together."

With raised eyebrows, the blonde turned to her chums before bursting into laughter. "Goodness, you are funny, aren't you? Why don't you ask her and see if you still think so? If she's even game to tell you, of course."

Charlie narrowed her eyes, holding her gaze until the blonde gave a final grin and motioned for the others to continue following her around the track.

Placing a gentle hand on Anna's shoulder, Charlie gave her a small smile as they turned back to the group. It didn't matter what she had done, Charlie had already resolved. She was the first person who had shown her kindness in this awful place. Whatever it was, she was paying her dues and Charlie was in no position to pass judgement.

Breakfast. Sewing. Lunch. Cleaning. Showers. Supper.

Time had never moved so quickly and attempting to hold onto the precious seconds slipping by was akin to nursing water in her hands.

The clocks leered at her. Only a matter of hours left now, they snickered, ticking on. The sun, too, seemed to be in on the joke and fell in a hurry once it had reached its noon peak.

Only seconds ago she had been standing in the courtyard talking to her newfound friends, now she found herself staring at her bed, wondering where the day had gone. She remembered the nights she had climbed into bed before her life imploded and asked the same question. 'Where has the time gone?' she had muttered sleepily, content that tomorrow brought a new day. Time had seemed infinite and whatever wasn't achieved one day could be done the next.

Now, on the evening of her last day in prison, the last night she would sleep in the bed she had reviled so vehemently, she again asked where the time had gone, knowing hers had all but run out.

Anna's eyes peered over the Vogue magazine she had been reading, the cover promising the reader to help 'make an asset of your shortcomings'.

"Are you okay?" she asked, pointing at Charlie with her index finger before turning her hand and opening her middle and forefinger like scissors.

Charlie was quietly proud she had understood the question.

She nodded, trying to appear unfazed. "One more day," she mouthed, extending her index finger.

Dropping the magazine to her lap, Anna looked at her thoughtfully. What do you say to someone who is about to die? She obviously didn't know any more than Charlie did.

"What do you like to do?" Charlie asked, raising her hand to her chest and pulling it away, as if pulling at a thread. The sign for 'like' was the only word in that question she knew.

Anna raised the magazine. "Reading," she mouthed.

"Magazines?" Charlie pointed.

"Anything." She smiled shyly.

"May I sit?" Charlie pointed to the space next to her on the coarse orange blanket.

Nodding eagerly, Anna patted the bed in invitation.

Charlie promptly hoisted herself onto the top bunk and settled herself beside Anna, reading over her shoulder. For a moment they contemplated the beautiful dresses they would never wear before Anna gently closed the magazine and gave Charlie a sideways look.

"I need to tell you something," she partially mouthed, partially signed.

Charlie knew she was referring to the incident in the yard. She shook her head. "You don't need to."

"I want to," Anna signed defiantly, before reaching behind Charlie to produce a small notebook from beneath her pillow. She flipped to the back page where a pencil was wedged and began to write.

"I was a mother," she scribbled. "His father left before he was born, so it was just me and Dylan. He was perfect. He slept beside me so I could feel when he woke or started crying. He never slept well but I didn't mind. He was perfect and I loved him." She smiled at Charlie, eyes shining, as she waited for her to read.

"But one day, he didn't wake me up. I woke up to the morning light. I knew something was wrong. He was lying the same way as when I'd kissed him goodnight. I touched him and he was cold. He wasn't breathing. He had died right beside me." The courage with which she had lifted her head was fading now and she just stared at the words.

"They couldn't find the cause of death. They said I wasn't fit to be a mother, that I wouldn't have known if something was wrong with him. That he was probably smothered during the night."

She looked up at Charlie now, eyes wide and desperate. When she returned her pencil to the page, it was haphazard and frantic. "I don't know what happened but he wasn't smothered. And I wasn't a perfect mother, but I did my best."

"You're here because they- because they think you killed your son?" Charlie whispered, the words too awful to say any louder.

Anna nodded, her chin breaking as she brought her left hand to her face. "No one believes me." She underlined the last words before dropping the pencil and crumpling where she sat.

Charlie promptly wrapped an arm around her trembling shoulders. "I believe you," she said, before gently tugging Anna's hands away from her face so she could see her. "I believe you," she repeated.

Tears streaked down Anna's face as Charlie pulled her into a tight hug and held her there until the shudders stopped and her breathing became less ragged.

It was a weight no parent should have to bear to lose their child, let alone be blamed for it. Charlie would never say she knew her pain, but she knew a little of what it was like to be condemned based on ability.

Anna pulled herself away with an apologetic smile and opened the magazine where they had left off, as though nothing had happened.

Charlie slept fitfully and was awake before daybreak to witness the beginning of her last full day on earth. *Perhaps* her last full day on earth, she forced herself to acknowledge the little spark of hope still faintly burning like embers in a forgotten fireplace.

She begged that day not to go so quickly, for time to show some compassion and slow its relentless march. But it didn't listen.

Her newly found friends gathered around her in the yard, but all looked at a loss for words. They stood awkwardly, not sure where to look, air pregnant with the inconvenient certainty that she would die tomorrow. Finally, Charlie had had enough of the uncomfortable quiet and began to walk the track.

Denise and Anna walked beside her in companionable, non-judgemental silence. It simultaneously warmed and broke her heart to have found such pure souls in such an unpleasant place, only to have to leave them there.

Again, she silently promised herself that she would help free them if she was able to free herself.

"Are you scared?" Denise asked so quietly Charlie looked at her to make sure it hadn't been the wind.

She didn't need to ask what she was talking about. "Yes and no. I've seen enough of death to know it's the easiest thing we'll ever do, just like being born. It happens without us trying. And from what I know of the Otherside, it's not somewhere anyone wants to come back from.

"What I am scared of is that I won't be the last. People are going to keep dying. Seers like me, others whose only crime whose hope. How many more people have to lose their lives before the masses wake up?"

Denise stopped abruptly, forcing Charlie to turn and look at her. "Can you see all these people following us?"

To Charlie's surprise, most of the block was following in a slow procession behind them.

"Bad things become permanent when good people stop believing anything else is possible. We see what we expect to see, until something forces us to see it differently. And all these people," she waved her hand at the group, "are seeing it differently now.

"You can't change the whole world at once. You gotta change the world for one person at a time. Some of us ain't had anything to be grateful for, haven't had hope, in years. But we do now. So I think you gotta practice what you preach, Char. Have hope that the other Seers and believers out there are doin' exactly what you've done here. Maybe one day it'll be enough."

And with that, Denise continued walking, leaving Charlie to contemplate the dirt before falling into step behind her.

Charlie hadn't previously bothered with the prison store, which was really a glorified hole in the wall.

A surly-faced woman sat flicking her pen behind a reinforced window with shelves stocked with various goods behind her. The lower shelves held snacks like canned Spam, Oreos, Almond Joys and Twinkies. An assortment of goods were stacked above them, from handkerchiefs and handheld mirrors, to magnified reading glasses and notebooks. At the very top were hygiene products, toothbrushes, soap, even some Halo shampoo.

"What do you want?"

"Ummm..." Charlie scanned the shelves behind her, not finding what she was looking for. "Do you have any reading material?"

"Reading material?" the lady repeated unpleasantly. "Like what?"

"Magazines or books?"

The woman sighed. "So do you want a magazine or a book?"

"Err... it depends what you have."

It seemed what the lady did not have was patience, because she rolled her eyes and fetched something from beside her which she more or less slammed onto the counter.

"Here, a book. That'll be $1.99."

The abstract face of *Invisible Man* leered up at her, already worn around the edges by its previous owner. Well, Anna had said she liked to read everything.

"I'll take it, thank you."

"Prisoner number?"

Charlie searched the recesses of her brain. "1721967."

"There you go."

"How much money do I have left?"

"Do I look like a bank?" she muttered, consulting her records. "Two dollars."

"Do you have any cook books?"

The woman threw her head back and sighed as though she'd been asked to recite pi to the 100th decimal point, before reaching behind her and smacking the first thing she grabbed on the counter.

'*Cooking with the Experts*'. She hoped Denise would see the humour in it.

"I'll take that too, please."

The woman slid them below the window towards her.

"Thank you." Charlie tried to elicit a smile from her but only earned a glower before scurrying away.

There was a narrow window in the afternoons of 'free time' between supper and showers – an ironic term given their distinct lack of freedom. Charlie wasn't one for emotional goodbyes and so, when she returned to the cell and Anna wasn't there, she tore two small pieces of paper from Anna's diary. 'For you' she wrote on one, 'for Denise' on the other, before slipping the books beneath Anna's pillow.

Dress clinging to her back and hair a mop of unruly wet curls, Charlie returned to her cell before dinner, pondering what her last prison supper would be. Combing at the knotted mess with her fingers, she stopped short when she found Rhett already there waiting for her.

"They're early."

"What?" Her heart dropped. "I thought they were taking me tonight?"

"Well, they're here. And you'll be in handcuffs any minute."

She tried to steady her breathing. "Will you check how long we have? Too early or too late and this won't work. Where's Hudson?"

"I'll find him." He evaporated before her.

Panic surged; she wasn't ready. Did she need her toothbrush? Her hair comb? Did those things even matter anymore?

"It's time." Rhett reappeared in front of her, hands clenched in fists by his sides, as though he was preparing to run a marathon.

"Where's Hudson?" she asked again.

"I don't know, but if we don't do this now, we won't get another chance."

"But—"

"Charlie." He brought his face to within an inch of hers. "I will be okay. We both will be."

Charlie breathed deeply and steadied herself, filling her lungs with as much air as they could take. She quietly willed her beating heart to continue, knowing it would soon be a struggle. Finally, she nodded.

"Ready." He visibly steeled himself.

As they had planned, she began pacing the cell, expressing quiet gratitude that Anna was still in the shower block. Back and forth, her feet struck the cement with a textured crunch as she circled in clear view of the cells opposite.

Mimicking the instances of fainting she had witnessed, she brought a hand to her head before allowing herself to collapse, landing artfully on her side while being careful not to strike her head on the way down.

Somewhere, someone screamed.

Twenty-Six

THE TRANSFER

Eyes closed, she allowed herself to fall into the impenetrable blackness of the darkest recesses of her mind. Soon, she was floating in a vast lake of water and, ever so slowly, sinking to the bottom.

A commotion grew in the surrounding cells.

"She's collapsed!" someone yelled.

"Do you think she's dead?" asked another.

Hurried footsteps reverberated on the metal stairs as the guards neared, finally hastening to a jog as the screams grew louder and more frantic.

"Faster, useless cads!"

A new consciousness moved into the space she'd made at the front of her mind. She recognised the calm, reassuring presence as Rhett's. Being present in a body must have been a strange sensation for him and she prayed he would be able to fight the urge to flex her fingers and wiggle her toes.

Her body jerked slightly as if someone had nudged her with a boot to encourage her to come to. People were standing over her. The soft thud of her heart was slow and becoming slower. In a few minutes, it would be undetectable to the average person. A few minutes after that, it would stop completely. But Rhett wouldn't let her get to that point.

Thud, thud, thud.

"What do we do?" a distant voice asked.

Her body jerked again, more violently this time. Rhett had taken those kicks for her – the first physical sensations he'd felt in years. If it bothered him, he didn't say.

There was a sigh of irritation. "Get her to the infirmary."

"How? I don't think she's walking."

"Get the stretcher, you idiot."

A distant rumble was growing as prisoners yelled to each other for information; a chaotic whirlwind of questions and half-answers.

"Is she dead?"

"She's not moving."

"Isn't that the Seer?"

"She just dropped!"

There was concern in some of the voices, as though they cared whether she lived or died. The thought sparked a gentle warmth in the water. It had been a long time since anyone had cared about her. Anyone living, that was.

Thud. Thud. Thud.

Charlie swayed as her body was hoisted onto the stretcher. Still sinking downward, she became less connected to the world around her the deeper she went. As the noise moved further away, she lost connection with what her body was doing. Her skin was probably quite pale by this point, the picture of death.

"Are you okay?" Rhett's voice was clearer than she had ever heard it, the gravelly texture palpable. For the first time she wasn't hearing it with her ears, his soul was talking to hers.

"Mhmm," she mumbled sleepily, enjoying the blissful way the water rocked her body as it was carried down the stairs and corridors. She was seaweed at the mercy of the ocean currents, rolling with the relentless waves.

"I won't let anything happen to you, Charlie." She felt the promise more than she heard it. A protective warmth swirled around her, like a refreshing, summery breeze flowing in to carry her somewhere nicer than this.

"I know," she answered simply, not trying to keep track of where she was or what was happening to her body. She trusted Rhett and that he would do what needed to be done.

"You're even more beautiful in here, you know. Your container doesn't do you justice."

She smiled at the word 'container', knowing that was all it was. A temporary vessel that one day she would have no need for. Even now, the weary pains in her feet had disappeared and her aching back was a memory.

"What have you done to her?"

"We didn't do nothin'! This is how we found her."

"1... 2... 3... lift."

The voices sounded like they were on the other side of a thick glass window. The water rocked again as her body was moved.

Thud... Thud...

"Is she alive?"

"There's a pulse but it's weak."

"Does it matter? She's dead tomorrow, anyway."

"The warden will have a fit if she dies. The Chief Enforcer is attending tomorrow's ceremony in person and she's awful keen to be the one to hand her over to him."

It wasn't working. They weren't going to let her go so easily. "Don't listen to them, Charlie. Just relax."

But Charlie was already at the bottom of the pool looking up at the dancing light, not able to descend any further lest the darkness close over her completely. "It's not going to work," she told him groggily.

"Yes, it will." Filled with such fierce determination, his voice frightened her and she felt the water grow heavier as if he was pushing down on her.

The light shrank to a faint dancing circle and the voices became increasingly distant and muted until they were completely indistinguishable. She lost all sense of space and time – she was floating, suspended in an endless, senseless void.

"Rhett... I can't..."

Thud...

She should have felt... something. There should have been panic as the world floated away. There should have been anger at her journey ending here, without reason or purpose. But there was only a growing calm rolling through her like waves lapping at the shore. No longer contained by flesh, her lifeforce spread its wings and relished the freedom it had forgotten.

The darkness was changing. Shapes began to emerge from the black, each a colour she had no name for, practising a dance she had never seen. The colours grew closer until they mingled with her energy, cleansing her of the dirt and decay time on earth had left her with. Their embrace was methodical, loving, doting. Through their ministrations, it became clear they were preparing her for something.

Someone was calling her but not by her name. It was with a tug that ran through her as if she had a rope lassoed around her waist. There was an energy, a soul, multiple souls rushing forward to welcome her as hers plunged forward as well. There were no words, but there was joy – purer than any she had felt on earth. She could almost see them – silhouettes of light against a backdrop of celestial colour.

The problems she had been so intent on solving just moments ago had been left in a bad dream. At once, all of it made sense because none of it mattered.

A sudden current ran through the space, like that caused by a small earthquake. The shapes moved back reflexively and the pulling sensation weakened. The silhouettes halted, watching. There was another jolt, and another. A chasm was opening above her. She reached out for the shapes, trying to anchor herself. She wouldn't go back, this was where she belonged.

"It's not time." The voice came from all around her, a powerful, inhuman baritone. She reeled around, searching for the source. She wanted to see if it was a man or woman who could speak with all the energy of the universe. But she was already being pulled up, reborn into the lake she had submerged herself in.

Panicked voices broke through the silence and suddenly she was rushing through water, being pulled up against her will, limbs dragging behind her like those of a helpless rag doll.

She was jolted back into her body by a final harsh compression on her chest and her lungs expanded in a desperate gasp for air. The man who had been bent over her stepped backwards, straightening his coat and adjusting his glasses.

Her head spun, eyes darting as she struggled to find her bearings. She didn't know this place. The swirling colours and familiar shapes were gone – replaced by the cold, clinical surrounds of a medical surgery. She didn't know these people. Those she knew and loved were nowhere to be found – her mother, grandmother, Hudson, Rhett – Rhett!

Awareness pierced her mind like a hot needle. Searching the room wildly for Rhett, she attempted to push herself onto her elbows but hands on both shoulders held her firmly to the gurney. A throbbing ache clapped through her skull so forcefully she thought she might be ill. Don't faint. Don't faint.

"There now, easy does it, Miss Hall."

A painful flashlight invaded her eyes as a doctor inspected them first and then her mouth, which she opened reticently in response to probing fingers. The cold metal of a stethoscope impinged on her chest as he listened to her breathe. She barely noticed. Rhett was gone.

"Well? What's wrong with her?"

The doctor shook his head in confusion, scanning her from head to toe, searching for an explanation. "She appears to be in fine physical health. Did you fall and hit your head?" he asked her loudly, as though he thought she was incapacitated.

"I don't remember," she answered, giving into her drooping eyelids and letting them rest. They had failed. They had failed and Rhett was gone. She had completely drained his energy and he had disappeared. Fighting the welling tears, she swallowed and begged her face not to break in front of the men who cared only that she lived long enough to die on their terms.

"Is she good to go, then?"

The doctor huffed, lighting a cigarette. "It seems so. Make sure she's kept under observation tonight."

"Don't worry, Doc, she won't be left alone for a second."

Charlie had begun to shake with silent sobs as she accepted the awful certainty that her last flicker of hope had finally been extinguished. These were the last twenty-four hours she would spend alive.

Gruff hands hauled her upright and cuffed her hands behind her back, as though she were in any state to pose the smallest threat.

"Are you sure, Doc? She's shaking pretty bad."

A waft of second hand smoke infiltrated her senses as the doctor drew his face close to hers. She kept her wet eyelids pointed to the floor, refusing to make eye contact with him.

"She's fine, just a scared little girl. Should be an easy one for you."

The guard snorted derisively. "Right then, let's go, sweetheart."

Pulled rather than led from the infirmary, her shoes caught on the linoleum as her legs refused to cooperate. Dragged up a flight of stairs, she found herself on the ground level of the main building at the front of the facility.

Emerging into a cool afternoon breeze, there was the distant sound of a riot from one of the blocks. She would be naive to think it wasn't a result of her performance.

One of the guards cursed. "What's all that about?"

"Don't worry, they'll be fine." The other opened the door of a Ford with a black bonnet and white doors. "If they can't handle a girls' slumber party, they shouldn't be in Enforcement."

There was coarse laughter as she was thrust onto the beige leather seat and the door slammed behind her.

The engine thrummed to life and they pulled away, travelling swiftly through the gates opened for them by a waiting guard. She didn't look at his face, it didn't matter who he was.

She was going to die. It was a certainty now, though it always had been. As a newfound dread spread through her like poison, she realised how desperately she had been clinging to that ill-conceived, mockery of a plan. Not only had it failed in extricating her, but it had taken away one of the few people she truly cared for. Even tears abandoned her as she sat there in a stupor, struggling to comprehend his loss, as well as that of her own life.

Leaving the glowing lights of the prison behind them, framed in a bleak landscape of laurel green and copper brown, she contemplated twisting herself so she could open the door behind her and roll out of the moving car. It was an idea she didn't entertain for long. They were in the middle of nowhere and, on foot, she didn't stand a chance. Especially not in her current state; exhausted and depleted from sharing her body with another soul.

Charlie had a vague idea where the public execution stadium was and had always made the effort to avoid that part of town. On the outskirts of the city, it was far enough from suburbia that people didn't feel tainted by the acts carried out there. They could watch the show and revel in the knowledge justice was being served before coming home to their children, thankful they hadn't given birth to such blights on humanity.

Charlie had expected them to take the most direct route through the heart of the city but they gave the perimeter a wide berth, perhaps with the intention of dissuading anyone with the disloyal intention of intercepting their precious cargo.

And all too soon there it was; a hulking indictment on the vanity of humanity. The otherwise featureless landscape was afflicted by an ugly monstrosity made all the more incongruous by the absence of a neighbouring building within a five-mile radius.

A grandstand large enough to seat a thousand adult men formed a semi-circle around a levelled pitch. As they drew closer, she could make out a small platform at its centre, dominated by a standing wooden frame.

That was where she would die. An involuntary gasp escaped her and the guards, who had been discussing their weekend plans, glanced over their shoulders at her.

"Not what you were expecting?" asked one.

"I'll bet she's wishing she made some different choices," the other commented.

There were no barricades through which spectators had to pass to watch the spectacle, it was a free-for-all. A dirt track had been worn from the road around a wire fence which maintained a wide, circular space around the gallows.

A comparatively small building sat behind the grandstand, enclosed by a familiar razor wire-topped fence. It was a weathered grey brick building with a boisterous yellow front door and window frames to match. The gate was open and waiting for their arrival. The enclosure was just big enough for their vehicle to pull into the parking bay. As they ground to a halt, a uniformed woman emerged from within the building, licking her fingers and adjusting her straining belt as she locked the gate behind them.

"You're early," she barked as the guards opened their doors.

"I've got dinner plans," replied the driver.

"We nearly didn't make it at all with the stunt this one pulled." The conversation was muffled briefly as they closed their doors and resumed as they opened hers. "...said she might've hit her head but she seems fine. As long as she can walk a hundred metres tomorrow, eh."

"Wouldn't be the first to try and kill themselves rather than let us do it for them. Defeats the point, if you ask me."

There was an acrid sterility to the smell of the place. A pervasive odour of disinfectant clung to her hair and clothes as she exited the car. It only grew stronger as she was marched directly to her cell, as if the room had been scrubbed ceiling to floor with peroxide.

But there was an undertone of another scent still lurking in the corners, one which couldn't be erased with all the bleach and baking soda in the world; death. The clean white of the walls couldn't mask the echoes of sorrow the room had witnessed time and time again.

A bed, a toilet, a sink, a stool and a bench; by now she expected nothing more. All were bolted to the floor to prevent the prisoner from weaponising them against others, or possibly themselves. The rising moon peered through one small window, its eerily morbid glow framed by narrow bars.

"Right, I'll give you the grand tour," one of them scoffed. "This is your room. The end."

The three guffawed heartily as her handcuffs were unlocked and she was pushed into the room with a sharp blow to her back.

"Oh, and I need to take your last meal request. What'll it be?"

In truth, Charlie didn't care. Of all of life's pleasures, food was one which now seemed ridiculously trivial.

Casting her mind back to one of the fonder memories of her childhood, she found a younger version of herself giggling as her mother and grandmother debated how long roast beef needed to be cooked for. Whatever their answer, it wasn't the right one. It was as hard and chewy as old leather but still they ate it, throwing jibes back and forth about how neither of them had managed to keep a husband and laughing hysterically together.

"Roast beef, please. With mustard."

The guard withdrew his notebook. "Roast beef..."

"And a White Russian."

The guard stopped; they looked at each other. "Can she do that?" One shrugged and turned to the woman.

"I don't think there's any rule against it?" Her answer sounded like a question.

"Erm... Alright then," the guard continued scribbling.

"Leave her with you, Maddock?"

"All's well. You go on now, boys. Wouldn't want you to miss your dinner plans," she mocked.

"Hey, it's early days with the Missus. I've gotta be on good behaviour for a little while."

"What's the point? She's gonna find out sooner or later..."

The conversation trailed off as they wandered outside.

There were two doors to her cell: one led directly outside and was the one which she had been brought through, the other consisted only of narrow iron bars and led to an office space complete with a small kitchenette.

Charlie watched as Maddock returned to the desk, resuming her consumption of something that ran down her fingers as she bit into it. A radio was squawking in the background, partway through the evening news.

With little else to do, Charlie perched on the stool, which dug into her coccyx uncomfortably. She couldn't bring herself to settle on the same bed so many condemned others had just yet.

Charlie had never feared death. It was impossible when one was surrounded by ghosts and the certainty that life would go on, in some form or another. But what she now realised, sitting in the last room she would ever see alive, was that she had always thought she was above it, somehow. She broke the so-called laws of nature to speak to the dead and console the living, never pausing to imagine the day she would be beyond the veil.

Her brief glimpse into the Otherside should have brought some comfort. There was the knowledge that all her earthly woes would die with her body, releasing her for a new kind of existence her mortal mind couldn't begin to comprehend.

Why, then, did it not bring her comfort? Why, then, was she not looking forward to tomorrow when her battle to survive would finally be over and she would *hopefully* be reunited with her mother and grandmother?

It wasn't her fate that mattered, she realised. What happened to her now was irrelevant. Her fear came from the knowledge that life for everyone else would continue. Believers would continue to live in the shadows, vilified and hunted, tortured into compliance or killed where they were too strong willed.

Wynn would be left to face the world alone, Charlie gone and his big brother with her - *because* of her. Her brief interlude with death had led her to believe Rhett was right — souls didn't get to choose whether they stayed or moved on. And Wynn would think she had left him intentionally, abandoned by those he had trusted, just as she had been.

Knowing solitude was a forlorn hope for the night, she seized the ambient noise of the radio as an opportunity.

Hudson.

Somehow, his face aged as he took her in. Looking back at the sorrowful, elderly man framed in death's door, she felt a pang of guilt for calling him here. This was a place he never deserved to be summoned.

"He's gone, Hudson," she whispered, unsure if her falling tears were new or if they hadn't stopped. "Rhett's gone."

Expecting the wizened man's mouth to drop in shock, she watched in surprise as he sighed deeply.

"No, he's not."

She blinked. "But he— he has to be?"

Removing his hat and turning it over in his fingers, he took a seat on the table beside her.

"Rhett realises he made an error of judgement. Although he has been profoundly weakened, that is not what is troubling him. He is deeply ashamed of the position he put you in."

"He was just trying to save me. He couldn't find you and— I don't understand."

"My lady, I was never informed of this plan."

The pieces began to fall into place. "Oh."

"He wanted to prove he could save you on his own."

"Oh."

"He had no intention of involving me in this plan and, when it became apparent it would not transpire as desired, he became desperate. He pushed you back far further than he should have. You were dead, Charlie.'

"Oh," still seemed to be the most intelligible answer she could produce and Hudson allowed her a minute to collect her thoughts.

"Well, what he did was surely stupid, but I'm still alive. He didn't mean to kill me." The voice in her head acknowledged the absurdity of Rhett having accidentally murdered her. "And the plan would have carried out exactly the same way had you been in his place."

"I have spoken with him at length to impress the same sentiment.

He is, as you know, frustratingly stubborn." He grimaced and Charlie couldn't help but smirk. "As I said, he is weak, but I am certain he will find the strength to materialise before—" He trailed off, not wanting to voice Charlie's imminent fate.

Letting out a sigh of relief, she slumped forward, elbows on her knees, and cradled her head in her hands.

"Thank you, Hudson." She leaned back to look at him. "You know, for everything."

He continued to fumble with the brim of his hat, mouth opening but not finding the words.

"I know this isn't the ending either of us imagined, but I am beginning to think it's for the best. I don't understand this world, and it doesn't understand me. All my life I wanted nothing more than to escape the crowds of the city and have a private sanctuary to call my own. Well, now I really am gaining my freedom."

"As always, my lady, you continue to astound me with a wisdom that transcends your years. My greatest joy has been as your companion for the past few years, and I will be eternally grateful to your grandmother for asking me to watch over you."

Charlie's brain short-circuited. Hudson knew her grandmother? He couldn't have, her mother was the one with the gift.

"You mean my mother?"

His eyes twinkled. "No, my lady. I knew your grandmother."

"You mean after she passed?"

"Oh no, I was a good friend of your grandmother's in life and in death. You must forgive me, my lady, but she asked that I never share this knowledge with you. Given current circumstances, however, I feel that such promises are expunged."

Charlie's earliest memories had been of strangers coming to the house to speak with their lost loved ones, but they had been coming to talk to her mother, had they not? She was imprisoned for it, they took her life for it.

"But my mother—"

"Made the greatest sacrifice a mother can make. She never inherited the gift. As you know, it tends to skip generations. But when the Enforcers came she made the only decision she could. She knew she could not raise you to manage your gift and navigate the ways of the world. Not in the way your grandmother could."

The ground had been removed from beneath her and Charlie was falling. "My mother wasn't a Seer, but she took the fall just the same."

"Indeed, in a most profound gesture of love."

"But then my grandma didn't practise?"

"She taught you the theory, did she not? After what happened to your mother, she removed herself from Seeing altogether. She could not risk exposing either of you."

"But you knew her?"

A small smile lifted his heavy face. "I knew her well. Rose was as beautiful as her namesake. Her mother and I were overjoyed to have a child after so many years of believing we couldn't. She was our gift."

It was too much, Charlie rose from the stool and began pacing in a frantic circle. "No, no, no, no, that would mean— that would mean you're my great grandfather."

He shifted uncertainly. "Yes, it does."

Twenty-Seven

THE LAST DAY

She bit down on a manic laugh, pulling at her hair. "I'm not sure how you expected me to react to this, Hudson. If I even still call you that anymore. Why drop this on me now?"

He shrugged. "It seemed appropriate. I didn't want you leaving this life under any false pretences."

Collapsing on the bed, she buried her face in her knees. Her grandmother had been a Seer all along and her mother had sacrificed her own life to give Charlie the best chance of survival she could. And look how she had repaid her debt.

"So you came back? From the Otherside?"

"Oh, no. It is very rare for a spirit to come back once they've passed over. I have never left, simply because I never felt that my duty was done as a father or grandfather. Then you arrived and your grandmother and I agreed that, should anything happen to her, we couldn't leave you alone. And so I stayed."

He became sombre, looking at his hands on his hat. "Parents are not meant to watch their children die, let alone their grandchildren. Seeing what happened to your mother was unspeakable. It broke my heart that I could not do so much as keep her company while she suffered in that place."

"And here you are, about to watch your great-granddaughter die."

When the old man looked up at her, his eyes shone. "Yes."

The gravity of the heartbreak this man had lived through pierced a hole in Charlie's soul and buried itself. No one should be asked to live through what he had - although 'live' was a term she used loosely.

"You don't have to be there, you know," Charlie told him softly, bringing her bubbling emotions down to a gentle simmer.

"My dear, how could I watch your life play out and not be there for your final bow?" The tender kindness with which he looked at her, had always looked at her, now made sense. She had always thought him a sweet soul, which he was, but she was also his own flesh and blood.

She pulled herself up to sit on the stool again, leaning into him until she could feel the prickly warmth of his energy. "I'm glad mother and grandma don't have to see."

"As am I, my lady. But I will be there every step of the way."

Supper that evening was not dissimilar to what had been served in the prison; sausages, peas and a boiled potato. She picked at the meal and pushed most of it around her plate until she couldn't look at it anymore and slid it back under her door.

Snores from the adjoining room told her that Maddock had fallen asleep. She stretched out on her own bed, opting for the end which gave her a partial view of the night sky. Having long abandoned any hope of sleeping, she chatted sporadically to Hudson, asking him the questions about her family she had never had anyone to ask.

It was as easy to talk with him then as it had been before and she quickly realised any fears she held about their relationship changing were unfounded. She had loved him as a grandfather, and now she knew it to be true.

It was before the sun had risen that an alarm sounded, along with Maddock's unimpressed groaning at being awoken. Charlie stared at the ceiling through the cacophony of noises from the next room; footsteps stumbling to the washroom, the whir of a kettle being boiled, the clink of coffee being stirred.

Maddock peered in through the bars, ensuring Charlie had survived the night.

"Morning, Hall," she grunted, blowing on her steaming coffee.

"Morning," she replied, supposing there was nothing good about it.

"You got any visitors coming this morning?"

"No." *Well, None that you can see.*

She tutted. "Shame." And with that, she meandered back to her desk.

A short time later there was the sound of her breakfast being slid into her cell but she had no inclination to see what she'd been served. Though half expecting Hudson to prompt her to eat, he maintained his companionable silence.

Finally, out of an inability to remain still any longer, she pushed herself from the bed and surveyed the now cold bowl porridge, uninterested. "Excuse me, may I have a coffee, please?"

Maddock had apparently been relieved from her post as a different uniformed guard now sat at the desk, newspaper spread in front of him.

Peering up at her from beneath a thick head of silver hair, he seemed to weigh up whether he wanted to oblige. Evidently deciding she at least deserved a coffee on her last day alive, he nodded and rose to put the kettle on.

"How do you take it?" he asked over his shoulder.

Somewhat surprised he hadn't just thrust a bitter cup of black muck at her, she replied, "One sugar, please."

Stirring as he walked to her, he handed her the paper cup carefully. Taking it gingerly between the bars, she noted he had used two cups so it wasn't too hot for her to hold.

"Thank you."

He nodded but continued to watch her, searching for something he couldn't place in her appearance.

"You're not the sort we usually see in here."

Not knowing how to respond, she raised her eyebrows and blew on her coffee, relishing the way the tendrils of steam tickled her nose.

"What did you do?"

She bit her lip, not sure this was a conversation she wanted to have today, before deciding there was little else to do.

"I'm a Seer."

Expecting a snort of derision or a pointed comment about how stupid she had been, he simply nodded. "Well, I hope death brings you whatever you're looking for."

Quietly surprised at his decency, they surveyed each other, sharing a second of mutual respect. "Thank you."

Returning to her stool, she settled herself beside Hudson who, true to his word, had remained by her side throughout the night. It was a subdued silence that followed as the sun reclaimed the sky and her cell was bathed in a warm, orange glow.

"Come on now, boy, what are you doing here?"

Charlie keened her ears. There had been no sound of a car pulling up to the building announcing anyone's arrival.

"She's my friend, Michael. Can I see her, please?"

Hudson and Charlie looked at each other in disbelief; they knew that voice.

"Does your father know you're here?"

There was an awkward pause. "Not really, no."

"You're going to get me fired, kid."

"I won't tell, I promise. But I can't not say— I can't not say—" There was a sniffle followed by Michael's hasty attempts to pacify him.

"Hey now, there's no need for that. I'll tell you what, I can do five minutes but that's all, okay? And this stays between us."

Another sniffle. "Okay."

There was a knock on the bars of her cell. "Hall, you have a visitor. Face to the wall and hands behind your back, please."

Obligingly, she rested her forehead against the cool concrete of the wall and interlaced her fingers behind her back. Keys clattered against the bars, a lock clicked and the door creaked dully as it drifted open.

Michael was considerably more gentle placing her in handcuffs than his predecessors and she felt him wiggle them to make sure there was room around her wrists.

"Alright, Hall, have a seat."

She sat and watched as he fetched a wooden stool and held the door open. "Five minutes," he repeated as Wynn stepped, blotchy faced, into the cell.

"Wynn!" The blood rushed from her face. Though she was glad to see him, he could be putting himself right back in the trouble she had gotten him out of.

His upper lip glistened with snot which he wiped at with the back sleeve of his jacket. "I had to come see you."

"What if your father finds out?" she hissed unnecessarily, as Michael was evidently on the same page.

"He won't. And Michael is a friend, he won't tell."

"I'd like to believe that, but I really thought you would have learned by now that not everyone can be trusted."

She hadn't intended to wound with her words, but the boy's bottom lip quivered and he dissolved into sobs. "I know it's my fault, I know it is. This is all because of me and I can't— I can't fix it!" His hands were in fists on either side of his head.

"Wynn, that's not what I meant." She lifted herself off the stool with the intention of giving him an armless hug but the sound of a throat clearing stopped her.

Michael was still standing at the door and an arched eyebrow told her she wasn't allowed to approach him.

"If anyone is at fault, Wynn, it's me. I should have taken care of you and I didn't, but I'm trying to make it right now."

"No one is at fault here," Hudson interjected calmly. "Some events unfold with very little encouragement on our part. It is not a matter of whether or not we can change the tides, but how we choose to captain the ship."

"But you're going to be gone and I'm going to be alone..."

"You won't be alone." Charlie leaned forward, hoping he could read the sincerity in her eyes. "Your parents love you, and you have an older brother who not only loves you but can help you with your gift."

"But I don't know where he is either!" he wailed.

Charlie grimaced. "I'm afraid that's my fault too. He will be back, I promise. He just needs a rest."

"So he just needs to sleep?"

"We do not sleep in the way we do in life," Hudson interjected.

"Everything we do earthside takes energy and, every now and then, we need to recharge. I have spoken to him myself and he is quite well."

Some of the tension in Wynn's shoulders visibly released. "I thought he'd left."

"He wouldn't leave you, Wynn. Not for a long time and not until you're ready. He did a very selfless thing and tried to help me. Whether it worked or not, I think I will owe him when I get over there." She forced a small smile, intentionally leaving out the part where he had almost killed her.

"Will you stay, too?" The hope now shining through Wynn's face was heart wrenching and Charlie realised she shouldn't make promises she couldn't keep.

"If I can," she replied tentatively. "To tell you the truth, Wynn, I don't know what will happen when I die. I thought my mother and grandma would have stayed but they didn't."

Although she tried to be soft with her words, his face still fell before peering up at the gentleman beside her. "What happens, Hudson?"

"I imagine it is different for everyone," he replied diplomatically. "However, my desire to stay was so strong that it seems I was not so much as given the option to leave. I simply slipped out of my body."

Remembering Michael was still standing guard at the gate, Charlie cast a nervous eye at him but he was staring determinedly at the wall, pretending not to hear them both talking to thin air.

"Wynn, I don't want you there today, okay?" Charlie set her mouth into a hard line. "I don't want you to see it, you're far too young to have to see something like this."

The boy dropped his eyes to the floor. "Dad wants me there."

Fury rose like bile in the back of Charlie's throat at the thought of that man forcing his young son to watch her execution. He likely saw it as an opportunity to teach him a lesson.

"Hudson, will you stay with him?"

The bowler hat tipped as he nodded.

"Alright, Wynn, we're well over five minutes now."

Charlie and the boy looked at each other, more emotion in a look than could be put in words. Suddenly the boy flung himself at her and wrapped his arms tight around her neck.

"Wynn, you can't—" Michael tried to interject before sighing.

"You'll be okay, Wynn," she mumbled into his shoulder. "You're a good kid and you're going to be okay."

"I'll miss you," he replied wetly. "You're my best friend."

She shut her eyes against the tears as Michael put a hand on the boy's back. "Alright, time to go now."

Reluctantly, Wynn pulled his arms from her as he was led from the room, taking one last forlorn look back at her before disappearing through the door.

"Dear me." She hung her head as she listened to Michael comforting Wynn in the next room, offering to call him a taxi before finally a door closed and silence resumed.

"Face to the wall, please."

Just as careful removing the handcuffs, Michael gave her a gentle pat on the shoulder before removing himself and locking her within once more.

"You handled that with grace, my lady."

"It runs in the family," she replied.

As the day progressed, the building grew busier. Though she did her best not to listen to the conversations as people came and went, she knew her uniform was ready and that they had finished testing the gallows.

She unequivocally refused to touch her lunch and Michael simply nodded apologetically, returning the tray to the kitchenette's small fridge.

A short while later, Charlie was on her toes peering out the window as the sun passed its midday peak when she heard a bag being slid beneath the door.

"You'll need to put these on when you're ready. No rush, but they'll be here in about an hour."

She didn't reply and Michael's footsteps retreated.

It was not a dissimilar uniform to the one she was wearing; a calf-length linen dress but in a confronting shade of orange.

"I don't think this will suit my complexion," she mused to Hudson, but the elderly gentleman seemed to have lost his sense of humour. Quietly, he moved to the adjoining room as she changed.

It was an awful feeling, to step into the clothes you knew you would die in. And to not, at the very least, be able to die in your own clothes. It was another way of removing her identity, just another miscreant whose absence would make the world a better place.

How terrible it must have been for the others who had gone before her and those yet to follow. Those who didn't share Charlie's gift, those that were forbidden from believing in something else. To live this last day and take those dreaded steps to the gallows believing their existence was about to snuffed out like a candle was more than anyone should have to bear.

Even with the knowledge her existence was far from over, Charlie found this looming deadline nauseating. Though her life hadn't been a happy one, she knew how to navigate its certainties. Rather, she *had* known. Don't make friends, don't draw attention, and don't talk to ghosts in public. Those simple rules had kept her alive, and she had broken all of them.

After the noose tightened around her neck, there was no knowing where she would be thrown. She could be forced to watch as the crowd jeered her swinging corpse and try to placate a traumatised Wynn. Or she could be relegated to the Otherside, at peace and surrounded by love, but without being able to reassure the boy she so cared for.

Too anxious now to sit, she began pacing. On his return to the room, Hudson sat again, observing her.

"I apologise if I am speaking out of turn, but you have nothing to fear, my lady. Dying was the easiest thing I have ever done. You may experience brief discomfort, if that, but it will be over before you're aware of what's happening."

Charlie sighed, scuffing the obscenely polished shoes at the ground. "I'm not scared of the pain, Hudson. It's the not knowing."

Hudson frowned. "But surely you of all people do know what happens next?"

"Do I? Where will I go? Do I have a choice? You don't seem to think so, and neither does Rhett."

"Is there a particular place you would prefer to go?"

"I should want to be with mum and grandma, shouldn't I? But I just... I don't feel like I'm finished. What about Wynn? Who will take care of him? And Rhett will think I didn't want to stay." She raised a hand to the wall, tracing the grit between the bricks like she was solving a maze.

"My dear, I will protect that child with my life. Or my soul, as it were. I assure you I will remain with him after-" he cut himself off, not wanting to say 'your death'. "As for Rhett, well, I think you would know by now that the universe has a way of making sure we end up exactly where we're meant to."

His eyes twinkled and, though he had done little to pacify her trepidation, Charlie lapsed into an uneasy silence.

True to Michael's word, several vehicles arrived an hour later. They parked at the perimeter, the facility not big enough to accommodate the convoy.

"Oh look, my entourage is here," she muttered, dimly aware she seemed to have lost her last thread of sanity.

Casual hellos and good afternoons followed as they do when colleagues greet each other on a mundane day in the office. How often did they do this, she wondered, and how little did her death affect them?

Rhett was yet to make an appearance and, as the day marched on, she hoped he would not leave it too late. Perhaps he could stay with her throughout the 'process'. With Hudson taking care of Wynn, she could use a friend on that dreadful platform.

"Face to the wall, please."

Again she complied, and as she listened to the increasingly familiar scrape of the lock, a new scent wafted into the cell. It was almost deliciously fragrant enough to overpower the clinical smell of bleach and ammonia.

"Your roast beef, madam." She twitched a smile as she watched, from the corner of her eye, Michael place a steaming plate of roast beef and gravy with a side of mashed potato on her table.

"Thank you," she said to the wall before adding, "Not just for that, but for being so kind."

"Kindness is free," he said lightly. "Don't move just yet, I believe there's something else..."

He disappeared briefly before re-emerging with a large plastic cup. "I must say this is one of the more unusual requests I've seen, but it is a Friday, so there'll be no judgement from me."

They had actually agreed to the White Russian. Charlie grinned into the wall. She thanked Michael again as the lock scraped shut behind him.

"That looks lovely," Hudson commented as Charlie attempted to scoot her stool closer before realising it was bolted to the floor.

"You're lucky you were never subjected to mother's cooking." Her knife and fork slid easily through the tender meat, nothing like the one from her childhood.

"I imagine she inherited her skills from Rose who, believe me, was never terribly interested in being a housewife." He smiled benignly.

Although her stomach took an adamant stance on not being hungry, it was the tastiest meal she'd had in what felt like years. Putting the knowledge that it was the last thing she would taste to the back of her mind, she relished the juices baptising her tongue and the satisfying softness of potatoes which had been mashed to just the right consistency.

Somehow she cleaned the plate, losing herself in the rich flavours and sensory experience. Disappointment washed over her as she looked down at the streaks of gravy spread sadly across the plate.

"Can you still eat when you're dead, Hudson?"

"Oh yes, it's just not a necessity. And one doesn't have to be concerned with becoming portly." He tapped his tummy.

The cocktail, while not holding quite the same appeal without an elegant glass, was the perfect dessert – one she wished she'd indulged in more often. The bitter taste of vodka and coffee melded pleasantly with the thick cream which she scooped from her top lip with her tongue.

Hudson sighed. "I do wish you hadn't waited until now to start living."

She nodded, so did she.

Soon the noise began to grow outside and she wished she could have another shot. The distant rumble of cars melded with the chatter of a growing crowd who, Charlie realised with a nauseating twinge, was there to watch her die.

Trembling and not knowing what to do with herself anymore, she alternated between pacing anxiously and throwing her arms in a hysterical sort of warm up exercise. Almost on the verge of tears, she halted as she recognised a familiar smell.

"Well, it's taken you long enough." Turning, she came face to face with Rhett, a literal ghost of his former self. No longer just blurry around his edges, he was translucent enough for her to see Hudson's concerned grimace through his chest.

"Yeah, sorry." He ran a hand through his unruly hair and shuffled awkwardly. "I guess you could say I've been a bit out of it."

"I'm just impressed you managed to make this day about you," she jibed, attempting to break the tension which had descended on the room.

He smirked at her attempt at humour and his drawn expression seemed to relax a little. "I'm real sorry, Charlie, about what happened. About what I did, I mean. It was stupid and I was just trying to—"

"Forget it," she cut him off. "It's not like I have to worry about you doing it again. Besides, pretty soon we're going to be on the same plane and I'm going to be able to kick your butt."

The smirk widened to a grin. "I wouldn't count on that. Should see the last Seer who thought she could take me."

Charlie's eyebrows knitted. "What are you talking about?"

Looking unabashedly proud of himself, he smiled. "Remember our friend Valerie?"

"The woman who turned on her own kind and scouts the city looking for fresh victims to feed the Enforcers in exchange for her own skin? Vaguely."

He nodded. "She's got her own room in Dunning now. Poor thing was having trouble sleeping, maybe haunted by a guilty conscience. She lost the plot at Dominick's one day and they hauled her up for public safety."

The name Dunning had struck fear into the hearts of many for decades. A place for those classed as insane and beyond help to be locked away from the public eye in some of the most inhumane conditions imaginable. Charlie shivered involuntarily, grateful in part that Valerie could do no more harm, but wondering if anyone really deserved to live and die in that place.

"Well, that explains why you're looking so well these days," she quipped.

"Thanks, I've been working out." He flexed a bicep that might have been impressive once, but suddenly his eyes fixed over Charlie's head, face falling slack.

Charlie turned to find a face staring at her through the bars, one she had last seen glaring at her with the same contempt in the courtroom.

The Chief Enforcer himself, Gerard Barron, wore an expression of utter disdain as he took her in. She swallowed, squaring her shoulders and lifting her chin defiantly as she planted her stance.

Without looking away from her, he turned the key in its lock and let the door swing open slowly, the dull screech raising the tiny hairs on her arms. He did not ask her to sit or face the wall as the guards had done, but walked slowly, purposefully towards her until his face hovered over hers. She was the worm he had found in his apple, the muck on his shoe, and his expression said he was eager to be rid of such an annoying inconvenience.

Anyone else might have stepped backwards, dropped down onto

the floor to wail and beg for forgiveness, for another chance at life. But she stared back into his icy, grey eyes, not finding a soul or shred of humanity. The silence was as thick as an arctic snow storm and both refused to break it. Not a sound came from the adjoining room either, as those within listened for what he would do.

Without breaking eye contact, Barron reached into his coat pocket and Charlie vaguely hoped it was a gun so the ordeal could be done with. Instead, he pulled out a cigar and an ornate silver lighter. *Click, click.* The cigar foot glowed to life and he drew a long, deep breath before allowing the smoke to wash over Charlie's face and hair.

Please, I grew up in downtown Blanford, she thought, still refusing to blink.

His eyes began to study her, from the messy tendrils of her black hair, to her crystal blue eyes, the defiant line of her lip and down her slim frame, the girl he had dismissed in the courtroom as a troublemaking time-waster. She felt oddly exposed, as though he were committing her every detail to memory, so he could clearly recall the girl he killed when the mood struck.

Finally, he cracked his neck before speaking in a deep gravelly voice, "It will be a pleasure to watch you die."

Fighting the urge to punch him in his distended gut, she opted for the most infuriating act she could think of and instead spread her mouth into an arrogant smile.

An anger seemed to ignite behind his cold eyes and he puffed briefly on his cigar before turning on his heel and allowing the door to slam behind him.

"Make her suffer," she heard him say.

Still in shock, she stood in place for a few seconds before her feet agreed to move and the air returned to her lungs.

"I have to say," she looked at Rhett who wore an expression of torment, "I don't think your dad likes me."

But it seemed Rhett's sense of humour had finally found its limit and he simply stared back at her, eyes full of quiet sorrow.

"Prisoner, face to the wall. It's time."

Twenty-Eight

THE EXECUTION

The palm of a hand between her shoulder blades pushed her face against the cold concrete of the wall as another set of hands worked to secure hers in handcuffs. Dimly, Charlie realised that's where they would stay until the end.

She was patted down, head to toe, in a final check for concealed weapons. Neither of the men behind her could be Michael, they were not nearly as gentle or respectful.

Her heart thudded against the wall of her chest, the beat to which her final minutes would be lived. It was no longer dread or anxiety that flooded her stomach, it was an awful final acceptance. Like the feeling one must have the split second after jumping off a bridge.

People were talking around her but she couldn't hear them. Focused solely on the presence of Hudson and Rhett by her side, she was vaguely aware of someone fussing over her, straightening her uniform and tying her hair back into a tight ponytail.

When the wind whipped the wisps of hair left around her face and her shoes crunched in the dirt, she realised she had been led outside. There was an awful monotonous drone like that of an almighty wasps' nest. It was the sound of hundreds of eager spectators waiting in the grandstand to see her brought to justice.

A guard on either arm, she was forced forward at a pace she couldn't alter. Hudson walked in front of her, as though he were trying to shield her from what was to come.

As she neared the oval, there were shrieks from the crowd and exclamations of "there she is!"

Blood rushed to her ears.

She wondered if there was anyone in the crowd she had crossed paths with at some point. Perhaps even the barista who poured her favourite coffee was now eagerly informing her companion that she always knew something was "off about her".

Blackness threatened to engulf her vision. Charlie's legs buckled, but she was reefed back to her feet with a sharp blow to her side for good measure. The noise grew louder the closer she got. It seemed her impending demise was working the crowd into a feeding frenzy, like sharks about to feast on a lifeless carcass. The morbid similarities didn't escape her.

Bright flashes told her journalists were reporting the event for the masses who didn't get to witness it themselves. Her hanging body would be splashed across the front page of every newspaper and televised news report for all to see – and learn from.

The shudders running through her were nearly convulsions. Just beyond Hudson's silhouette was her final podium where only two figures clad in black waited for her. One held the noose, ready to bestow it its home.

"Everything will be okay, Charlie," Hudson told her over his shoulder. "Everything is going to be okay."

The words rang hollow, she knew he meant well but the time for meaningless reassurance had long gone.

As the sound of the jeering crowd swelled, Hudson and Rhett joined shoulders, shielding her from the vile names and condemnations. To the horde, she was an incorrigible young girl, as alone in death as she had been in life. But her ghostly friends walked with her and shouldered the worst of the assault.

It was simultaneously the longest and shortest walk of her life. She wished to be beyond the reach of the growing cacophony of the crowd but, when her feet met the first wooden step, she longed to still be walking across the oval. Hell, she wished she was back in her prison cell with Anna teaching her sign and Denise whispering through the wall. She wished she was back in her cramped, derelict apartment. Anywhere but here.

The Chief Enforcer welcomed her with a predatory leer. A dead-behind-the-eyes man stood behind him, watching her without emotion. He must be the hangman. The wind snagged at their black coats, making them look even larger and more menacing.

Pushed into position beneath the dangling rope, Charlie's toes touched the edge of the waiting trapdoor.

Barron cleared his throat and raised a megaphone to his mouth. "Ladies and gentlemen, it is a fine day for justice." The crowd cheered, chills running down Charlie's spine. "As you may know, this woman, for lack of a better term, believes she can see dead people." On cue, the crowd laughed raucously.

"She believes in ghosts, and probably goblins and unicorns, too. But not only does she so vehemently cling to these aberrations which conflict directly with the State and our guiding legislation, but she attempted to indoctrinate others with her depraved delusions. She attempted to kidnap and manipulate my own son." A ripple of gasps and murmuring ran through the onlookers. "That is why I must see to it myself that this blight on society dies today. Live by the State, die by the State."

He handed the megaphone to one of the guards before draping the noose around her neck. It was unexpectedly heavy and the weight of it sent another round of spasms through her limbs.

She had spotted several blurred figures in the crowd. If she could just get that megaphone... "Do I get any last words?" She jutted her chin out, doing her best to hide her fear.

Barron brought his nose level to hers. "Scum have no rights."

The rope was drawn tighter. Her mind raced; be brave, be strong, find a happy memory – but her scrambling brain couldn't find anything to hold onto. The man in black placed both hands on her shoulders and pushed her forward until she was in the middle of the dreadful square.

He stepped back and her heart thundered, this was it.

Rhett moved to stand in front of her, a mere wisp doing his utmost to shield her from the whooping audience.

"Just look at me, everything's going to be alright. Just look into my eyes." She did, determinedly staring into his face, and waited.

Something in his eyes spoke to her. In them, she saw sadness at the closure of one chapter and maybe, just maybe, hope for the beginning of a new one. Together. Maybe, if Charlie really wanted to, maybe she could stay.

Seconds ticked by with agonising slowness, the crowd leaned forward in anticipation, but the platform didn't drop.

"This won't do," Barron's baritone voice dripped with consternation.

"Bring me my boy," he addressed the hangman. When the man looked at him questioningly, his voice became grossly amplified. "I said, bring me my boy!"

The man jumped backwards, almost falling down the few wooden steps as he half-ran towards the front row of the stadium.

Hudson was there, speaking calmly into Wynn's ear but it was having no effect; the boy's eyes were like saucers and he visibly shrank as the man approached him. Dragged by the wrist, Wynn was wrenched across the oval until he stood quaking at the bottom of the stairs.

Charlie panicked, what was Barron doing?

Rhett, it seemed, already knew. "No, no, no," he began imploring beside her.

Barron watched calmly as his son was bullied into compliance and joined him on the podium, eyes watering and lip quivering. Hudson was still trying to placate the boy, offering words of reassurance which did nothing to calm the child.

"Have you learnt your lesson, boy?" he asked quietly, daring him to say otherwise.

Wynn nodded frantically. "Y-yes."

"Hmmm," Barron walked languidly to the rope which hung around Charlie's neck. He caressed it thoughtfully. "I don't think you have. How can we fix that?"

His footsteps on the hollow wood paced slowly behind Charlie. "I know. You will pull the lever."

"No!" Charlie whipped her head around and was met with a sharp blow to the cheek. The herd jeered.

"You sick bastard," Rhett snarled as Charlie flexed her jaw.

"Please, please, Pa." Wynn began to cry in earnest, attempting to back off the platform but his father's firm hand refused to let him leave.

"Now, now, men don't cry. Stiffen your lip for me, good boy."

Behind her, she heard Wynn being dragged across the platform. "See this here? You just have to pull this lever. That's it. Easy, isn't it?" His voice had raised an octave, as if Satan himself were talking to a puppy. The sound was unnatural.

Apparently Wynn was still refusing to comply because there was a sharp smack and Rhett's jaw tightened.

"You'll do it, boy, when I tell you to."

Barron resumed his position, straightening his coat and taking several seconds to survey the scene before him. The crowd held its breath and Charlie again sought comfort in Rhett's eyes.

"Love you," he whispered, raising a hand to her cheek.

Tears welled as her chest threatened to burst with emotion. "Love you, too."

"Now!" Barron bellowed and the crowd erupted into a roar.

A fraction of a second later, the heavy clunk of the lever followed and Charlie squeezed her eyes shut, waiting for the sharp drop and the crack of her neck which would end the torment. The platform fell away and her feet saw the earth, only the noose around her neck preventing her from hitting the ground.

But she didn't drop. Her feet twitched and felt nothing beneath them. Was she dead?

Charlie opened one eye cautiously. She was still on the platform, Rhett in front of her with an odd expression on his face. A warm tingling sensation spread around her waist and she realised what was happening.

"Just stop!" she cried. "It's over, let me die."

Simultaneously, there were confused cries from the crowd.

"What is this?"

"How is she doing that?"

A woman screamed. People yelled. Guards shouted to try and maintain control but they were fighting a losing battle. Then all hell broke loose. People spilled from their seats and down the stairs of the stadium, falling over each other, out of either the desire to kill her themselves or to run as far away as possible.

The journalists' cameras flashed, desperately trying to capture the unfolding drama.

"What the—" Barron gawked, shaking his head to clear his vision because he couldn't possibly be seeing properly; there was not a woman levitating in thin air.

The guards scattered, backing away in confusion as they tried to make sense of the levitating woman who refused to die as she was supposed to.

"Hudson, drop me!" she pleaded.

"I'm afraid I can't, my lady." His voice was strained but resolute.

With wild eyes she implored Rhett. "There's no point, please!" But he only shook his head.

There was a sharp kick to her calf and Barron's furious, red face appeared beside her.

"Enough of this!" he snapped, spittle flying as he reached within his coat and produced a pistol. He aimed it squarely at her head and she braced herself again, ready for the bullet to pass through her brain.

Rhett launched himself at him, wrapping his hands around the gun and pointing it away from Charlie. In furious confusion, Barron fought to reclaim the weapon from the unseen force that was wrestling him for power. Rhett let out a yell as he used brute force to point the gun towards the other man still on the platform.

The hangman raised his hands and backed away nervously. "Sir, what are you doing?"

Barron grunted in fury as a gunshot rang out. The sudden bang echoed across the oval and the hangman dropped to the ground, howling in pain as the bullet pierced his shoulder. Screams and shouts erupted from the frenzied crowd, many now pressing their faces against the wire fence and demanding for her to be burned.

"Sir, drop the gun!" Guards were edging nervously around the perimeter of the oval, pulling their guns from their holsters and raising them anxiously towards their illustrious leader.

Barron was still bellowing furiously as Rhett refused to let go. Deliberately, he directed the aim towards one of the guards.

"Drop it, sir!" he yelled.

There was another gunshot, followed by several more and Barron fell, as did the guard. Shrieks of pain and terror echoed through the air and Charlie could only watch on in shock.

"Wynn, I need your help!" Hudson growled through gritted teeth as he hauled her backwards until the floor was again beneath her feet.

Wynn snapped out of his terror-induced stupor and began loosening the knot around Charlie's neck. She had the sense to stoop and he slipped her free from the rope which had been meant to end her life. Raising a trembling hand to her neck, she had to feel for herself that it was definitely gone.

"Don't you move!" Barron was on his hands and knees in the dirt, struggling under the added weight of his eldest son on his back.

Some of the guards now pointed their weapons at Charlie, terror in their eyes as they looked from her to Barron.

"Shoot her! Do it!"

Charlie found the last scrap of courage in her gut. "What more proof do you need?" She raised her arms to the guards and began to walk towards them.

"There are spirits here and they're angry, very angry!" Her voice was deeper and more threatening than she had known she could make it.

The men swallowed, sweating profusely as their eyes frantically searched the air for the source of the chaos.

"What do we do?" the youngest guard cried amongst the ongoing din of the panicked crowd.

"She's bluffing!" another yelled. "It was a trick!"

Seeing what needed to be done, Hudson was already in front of him. Extending both arms, he shoved him hard in the chest and the man stumbled backwards with a screech of terror.

"What the— Something— something pushed me!"

"Still think I'm bluffing?" Charlie crossed her arms with a smile.

The man wheeled around to his younger counterpart. "You did that, didn't you?" He pushed his gun into his chest.

"What are you talking about?" he blustered, raising his hands in surrender. "I was nowhere near you!"

"Well then who pushed me?"

As they argued, Hudson struck the face of another who dropped his gun and backed away with a cry of bewilderment. He hit another, and another, and then the circle of guards were pointing their guns at each other, demanding to know what was going on.

Rhett was panting now, clinging desperately to his father's back in a desperate effort to keep him on the ground. Hudson joined him, adding his force and planting the Chief Enforcer's face squarely in the dirt.

Charlie wrapped a protective arm around Wynn and crept slowly down the stairs, expecting a bullet to find her without warning.

"You started this!" The older guard landed a punch squarely on the jaw of his younger counterpart, who staggered backwards, raising his hand to his mouth to pull away a finger covered in blood.

"Hey, don't you touch him!" A sharp jab in the ribs keeled him over in pain but he rose, driving an uppercut into his attacker's abdomen. The guards descended on each other, some attempting to break up the violence but quickly being struck down in the process.

This was their chance. Charlie looked around desperately, seeking a way out, but there were no breaks in the wire fence and the locked gate was groaning under the weight of the teeming crowd.

"What do we do?" Wynn gripped her hand tightly.

She licked her lips, searching desperately.

As if in answer, there was an almighty crash behind them and they turned to find a cherry red truck had reversed full speed through the fence.

She gawked and began to back away, pulling Wynn with her, expecting an angry citizen to emerge with a shotgun pointed at her. But there was something familiar about that truck.

A figure leaned out of the car, waving furiously at her. "Charlie!"

Denise was leaning out of the passenger window of the red Chevrolet coupe she had seen parked out the front of the prison.

"Charlie, get in!" she bellowed, gesturing madly.

She didn't need to be told twice. Gripping Wynn's hand, they ran, full sprint, towards the car. Someone dived for her ankle but she jumped it lithely, gripping Wynn's hand tighter in case someone made a grab for him.

Throwing herself into the trayback of the Chevy, she leaned down to lift Wynn up with her but the boy gasped in pain and fell, scraping his fingernails down her arm as he tried desperately to cling on.

"Wait!" she yelled to Denise, jumping from the car. Wynn's ankle had become ensnared in the razor wire which was biting furiously into his skin.

Trying to extricate him as quickly as possible without causing him further injury, she glanced up to see how much time she had. Still preoccupied with beating each other to bloody pulps, the guards weren't looking their way, but Barron was.

He had risen to his feet, his ruddy face sweating and contorted with anger as he saw what was unfolding. She had to strain her eyes to see Rhett who was lying on the ground, a mere wisp of himself remaining. His eyes met hers and she saw his fear, knowing there was not enough of him left to save her.

As Barron raised the barrel of his gun towards her, she gave a last desperate tug on Wynn's ankle but the shot had already rung out.

She threw herself in front of Wynn and waited for the bullet's impact, but the pain never came. With every morsel of Rhett's remaining strength, he had pushed himself from the ground with a shout and thrown himself at his father so that the man dropped his gun as he fell sideways onto the ground.

In horror she watched as Rhett staggered for a moment, looking from his father towards Charlie and Wynn. He smiled enigmatically as the last of him dropped like grains of sand and nothing remained but empty air.

"No!" Wynn cried, kicking off the last of the wire and trying to run towards where his brother had stood, but Charlie wrestled him back towards the car.

"We have to go, Wynn," she yelled through her own tears. "Don't let that have been for nothing!"

Letting out a guttural cry of defeat, he turned back towards the car and allowed her to help him up before throwing herself in beside him.

"Go!" she yelled to Denise as she pushed Wynn's head down behind the tray wall.

The engine revved furiously and the tyres spun on the dirt before gaining traction and they lurched off the fence, dragging a piece behind them before it fell away. Charlie raised her head to peek at the carnage.

Barron had risen to his feet and reclaimed his gun, running furiously towards them. Realising he had no hope of catching them, he raised his gun and began firing at random. A bullet struck the side mirror of the car but several shots later he was out of ammo.

A few guards emerged from the broken fence and raised their firearms too, but soon they fell away behind them, quickly becoming ants in the distance. They sped into the fading sun, leaving the chaotic aftermath in the rearview mirror.

Twenty-Nine

THE HIGHWAY

The moon was reclaiming the sky before they finally stopped on the side of a dirt highway in the middle of nowhere. They had changed directions so many times to throw off their pursuers that Charlie had lost all sense of where they were.

As Charlie and Wynn had cowered in the back, watching the gradually darkening sky above them, she pulled him close and held him as he sobbed. Biting back her own tears, she stroked his hair, knowing no words could alleviate the pain he was in.

The boy had had to lose his brother twice. This time, he had lost him forever. Whatever pain she was feeling now, it didn't compare to his agony.

The car ground to a halt under the cover of a spreading oak tree even though they hadn't seen another soul for miles. Planting a kiss on Wynn's forehead, Charlie removed herself gingerly and jumped down onto the ground.

Throwing the door open, Denise emerged from the passenger side and pulled her into a hug. "It's good to see you, Char."

"It's good to see you too. How on earth—"

She trailed off as Anna emerged behind her, looking shell-shocked, and wrapped her in a tight embrace.

The driver's door swung open and Tani stepped out triumphantly, letting out a whoop of excitement. "Sweet freedom." She sucked in a deep breath, closing her eyes.

Charlie couldn't believe this was really happening. "Who did you— when did— how?" she spluttered, looking from one victorious face to the next.

"Well, sweetheart, when you put on your little performance, them guards were a bit distracted. I nicked one of their guns and we backed them into one of the cells. Who knows, they could still be in there." She laughed as tears stung the corners of her eyes. They had really made it out.

"Anyway, I've always had a crush on this thing." She patted the shiny red bonnet fondly. "So I grabbed these guys and we got our arses straight to the warden's office. She had no idea what was going on, should've seen her face. Tied her up, unplugged the phone just in case, and the keys were just hanging there."

"So you've been out since yesterday?"

"Yeah. Warden had a paper with your execution details all over it so we knew where to find ya. We just got out of town and laid low for the night. Wasn't expecting you to have caused another bloody brawl!" Denise clapped her back.

Anna made a gesture Charlie now knew to mean "troublemaker".

"Yeah, well, neither was I," Charlie confessed, remembering Wynn was still in the truck. "I'd like you guys to meet someone. This is Wynn. He's—" She reached in and took his hand, bringing him down to join them. "He's family." She wrapped an arm around him and held him tight to her side.

His face was still tear-stained and blotchy, but he looked up at the women and gave a one-sided smile.

"Hey, kiddo." Denise ruffled his hair. Anna gave a small wave.

"Kinda young to be a fugitive." Tani crossed her arms, pretending to scrutinise him. "I say that makes you a badass. Welcome to the club." She punched his shoulder lightly and his smile became a little more genuine.

"So, what's the plan?"

"What plan?" Tani guffawed. "We're on the edge of Lancester Downs right now, so I say we keep heading north-west until we get to the border."

"It ain't gonna be long before our faces are plastered on every shop window across the country. It might not be far enough, but it's a good start," Denise agreed.

Anna was staring at their mouths, doing her best to follow the conversation in the inspid moonlight.

"What about you?" Charlie asked her. "Is family waiting for you?" Anna had taught her the sign for 'family'.

With a sad smile, Anna shook her head, then pointed from herself to the group.

"Look, I think you all need to know the risks of travelling with us." She motioned to herself and Wynn, who was still glued to her hip. "Wynn is the Chief Enforcer's son, and he's not going to stop looking for us."

An uneasy silence fell over the group. Anna placed a tentative hand on his shoulder.

"That's rough. I'm sorry, kid," Tani murmured.

"We won't let him hurt you," Denise added gently.

Charlie's brow furrowed. "Wait, you still want to travel with us?"

"Of course," Tani said easily, leaning against the truck. "We got this far working together. Not breaking up the team now."

Denise nodded. "Ain't no one being left behind just because it'd be easier."

Charlie bit at her lip, not convinced any of them realised the danger she was putting them in. "Okay, but as soon as I think we're putting you in any real danger, we're going our own way."

Denise rolled her eyes. "Whatever. We can fight about this later."

"Time to keep moving?" Tani threw the car keys in the air and caught them.

Charlie looked down at Wynn who was staring blankly at the ground. "Can you just give us a minute? I want to have a chat with Wynn."

Tani nodded. Charlie took the boy's hand and led him towards a fallen tree a few metres away. The pair sat on the thick trunk, staring up at the stars which were decorating the night sky like glittering diamonds displayed on a rich black satin cloth.

"I'm sorry, Wynn. I won't pretend to know how you're feeling, but I know it hurts," she began gently. "And it's okay for you to feel upset, and angry, and overwhelmed, and whatever else it is that you're feeling. Your brother loved you very much. Lots of people would pay dearly for the bond you both had. The more we love each other, the stronger the pain when they leave."

Wynn took a deep shuddering breath. "I just want to give him a hug."

Charlie put an arm around his shoulders, knowing it wasn't the hug he wanted, but he nestled into her side all the same.

She chewed her lip, not knowing how to broach the next subject. "Do you want to go home?"

He sniffled. "I can't."

She relaxed a little that Wynn recognised it himself and she didn't have to explain to him that he probably would never see his parents again.

"I know I'm not Rhett and I'll never pretend that I can replace him, but I promise I'll do my best to keep you safe and make the best decisions I can for you. Okay?"

He nodded into her side. "Is Hudson okay?"

Charlie had been wondering herself but wasn't sure she could handle the possibility of losing him as well. Reluctantly, she called out for him in her mind, terrified there would be no answer.

A moment later he was standing before them, looking a little more hazy than usual, but still very much present. "I am so glad you are both safe."

"I'm glad you are too, Hudson." With her eyes, she asked if there was any chance Rhett had survived but, with a sad sigh, he shook his head minutely.

"Wynn, you have my deepest sympathies for the loss of your elder brother. He was an incredibly brave, kind soul who I will miss profoundly." His gravelly voice was deeper than usual, the day's events evidently having taken their toll.

Wiping his nose on his sleeve, Wynn looked up at the old man. "So he's definitely—" But he couldn't finish the question.

"He's no longer on this earth," Hudson replied tenderly. "But I confess, child, that I do not know all that there is to know. I suspect when we run out of energy in this world, we are reborn in the next. I am afraid it is impossible to know without having been there myself."

Wynn kicked his heels against the trunk. "I think you're right."

"So do I." Charlie rubbed Wynn's back, hoping dearly she would be able to give the boy some semblance of the life he deserved. The thought jogged a memory. "Wynn, did Rhett tell you about my bag?"

He smiled slightly and lifted the back of his shirt to show her a small satchel which was strapped around his middle. "I didn't have a safe place for it, so I was keeping it on me until I could find somewhere. I'm sorry I don't have the rest of your things though..."

But Charlie was already planting a kiss on top of the boy's head. "I knew you were a clever kid."

He seemed to blush and Charlie relished the sight of him feeling something other than intense sorrow, even if just for a moment.

"Are you ready for our next adventure, kiddo?"

Wynn looked up at Hudson. "Are you coming with us?"

Hudson smiled down at the boy fondly. "Young man, nothing in this life or the next could tempt me otherwise."

Charlie rose and took Wynn by the hand, holding out her other to Hudson and feeling the warmth of his energy as he accepted.

Together, the three of them walked back towards the car where Tani, Denise, and Anna were strategising which direction and potential stops would be best to risk.

Charlie gave Wynn another squeeze as their route was decided.

"We'll take shifts in the tray," Denise said. "Anna, feel like some air?" She gestured from Anna to the open back.

Tani stuck her tongue out.

"Yeah, I'll take my turn. Anna, feel like some air?" Denise gestured from Anna to the tray.

Anna's finger pivoted forward from her mouth before she hoisted herself onto the back and held out a hand to help Denise up.

Tani reclaimed her driver's seat, a look of satisfaction on her face as she turned the keys and the engine thrummed to life. Charlie slid Wynn between them both, the leather still warm from the first leg of their trip.

"You ever learn how to drive, kid?" Tani asked Wynn as they pulled away from the tree.

"Um, no," he replied quietly.

"Seems like as good a time as any. Put it into second for me," she told him, pushing the clutch in.

Hesitantly, Wynn reached a hand out and slid the gear stick back into second.

"That's it, you're already a better driver than most of the folks in Blanford. Next I'll teach you about all the different things you can do with spoons."

Charlie relaxed back into the seat, watching the countryside rolling past them. Moonlight grazed the fields of grass, clouds of dirt rising behind them as they shed their old lives and drove determinedly towards the unknown.

Thirty

EPILOGUE

Charlie surveyed the usual black and white photograph of herself, eyes hovering over the open trapdoor with a noose waiting to break her fall. Behind her, Wynn's small hand was on the wooden lever and his eyes were closed, not wanting to watch her drop. Barron was gripping the back of the boy's shirt, his expression just beginning to shift from one of victory to confusion. Given how many newspapers and posters she had now seen it splashed across, it was evidently one of the only clear photographs they'd taken before all hell broke loose.

"SEARCH CONTINUES FOR INCENDIARY KIDNAPPER", the headline read.

"Today marks eight weeks of an extensive investigation into the whereabouts of twenty-one-year-old Incendiary, Charlotte Hall. The self-proclaimed 'Seer' escaped during her execution proceedings in Blanford, also abducting the Chief Enforcer's son, Mr Wynn Barron. Hall was last seen entering a red Chevrolet coupe with the child and three other escapees from Ingbridge Correctional Centre, Miss Denise Thomas, Miss Tani Brown and Miss Anna McKinsey.

"Hall is described as being of average height and build, with a fair complexion and long, black hair. Thomas is tall, lean and of African American descent. McKinsey is caucasian with short, dark hair and of smaller stature. Brown is tall and athletic and also African American.

Anyone with information on their whereabouts is encouraged to notify Enforcement.

"The events of Miss Hall's execution have ignited speculation and unease in the wider community. Protests have gathered momentum across the country, with many now believing the religious abolition movement to have been a means of control."

That was putting it lightly, Charlie mused, though she supposed 'blatant and ruthless authoritarian stranglehold on power by the self-entitled ruling elite' didn't roll off the tongue.

"Enforcement continues to assure citizens that these laws are in place for their safety and the betterment of society. Chief Enforcer Gerard Barron released a new statement on Monday, urging citizens to remain calm and think rationally.

"The past several weeks have been difficult for us all. I, above all others, value justice and peace. Our legislation is in place to maintain that peace and ensure the delinquents who endanger our way of life feel the full brunt of the law. Do not be swayed by their terrorism. Remain strong for the State and the State will remain strong for you."

"Enforcement would like us to remind readers that anyone found to be in breach of the Enlightenment legislation will be arrested and penalised accordingly."

With a satisfied smirk, Charlie folded the paper and dropped it into her bag as she walked. Strands of blonde hair clung to her neck, damp with perspiration from the unforgiving summer sun. Raising a finger to catch her sunglasses which were threatening to slip from their post, she cast a glance to her right where, on cue, Denise emerged from the chemist.

They kept their distance, Charlie on one side of the road and Denise on the other, artfully dodging the full-skirted women window-shopping and loud shopkeepers flaunting their wares. Charlie smiled and shook her head politely to the worker at a fresh produce stall as he held up a carton of eggs.

"Freshest eggs you'll find in town, Miss! My girls lay the largest eggs around for miles."

Charlie had to admit they looked quite hefty, but eggs were one thing she would hopefully never need to purchase again. "Thank you but I wouldn't want to offend my own brood."

He held up a hand in apology before swapping the egg carton for a vibrant eggplant. "How about some juicy veggies?"

Laughing good-naturedly, Charlie shook her head again and left his persistent offerings behind her. Tightening her grip on the bag at her side, she ducked her head as she passed the town's police station. Two officers clad in navy blue emerged as she passed, arguing heatedly about whether turkey or chicken made better sandwich meat. They passed her without a second glance.

Soon, Charlie and Denise reached the end of the main street, continuing well past the midday bustle until they reached more rural surroundings and a disused, long-forgotten barn. Long, dry grass tickled Charlie's elbows as she waded towards the flattened tracks leading to the rickety barn doors. Denise waited by the roadside, inspecting the contents of her own bag in an effort to look as normal as possible.

The pale blue bonnet tied around her chin suited her, as much as she vehemently insisted it would look better buried in manure. With her dark complexion, dying her hair any colour other than black would draw more attention, so her only option was to cover up. Fortunately, hats were very much in fashion in small country towns.

Paint flaked under Charlie's hands as she heaved the doors open, revealing the waiting Chevy. Its cherry red was now a subdued rust colour, owing to the amount of dust it had accumulated during its travels over the long dirt roads.

Climbing into the driver's seat, she deposited the bag beside her and turned the key in the ignition. The engine thrummed to life and Charlie eased out of the hiding place, keeping an eye on Denise in case she gave the signal to wait. All clear.

The car trundled over the tracks it had made in the grass, pausing when the tyres met the road for Denise to clamber into the passenger seat. She kept her bonnet on just long enough to make sure they were beyond the eyes of the township before she hurriedly untied it and threw it at her feet. “I hate that bloody thing.”

Charlie chuckled. “You hadn’t mentioned.”

Denise huffed before turning her attention to the bags between them. “Did you get everything?”

“I think so. Should be more clothes than we can put holes in – this summer, anyway. I bought a couple of sizes up for Wynn. If that kid keeps growing at his current rate, he’ll be borrowing our dresses for shirts.”

Denise snorted, rummaging through their collection and nodding with satisfaction.

Plumes of dust rose behind them as they rumbled along the desolate tracks, occasionally slowing to navigate the larger rocks they had committed to memory after their first unexpected encounter. It was barely wide enough for two cars to pass if they met someone travelling in the opposite direction – which they never did. Sparse vegetation dotted the landscape, occasionally giving way to crops of trees through which filtered shards of golden sunlight. Mountains they never seemed to reach softened the horizon.

The sun beat down on Charlie’s arms, which were more tanned than they had ever been, as her callused hands gripped the steering wheel. She wound down the window a fraction to let in some of the sweet, earthy air without extending the same invitation to the dust.

They sat in comfortable silence for much of the long drive home, stopping halfway to change drivers. With Denise at the wheel, Charlie rested her head back against the seat, allowing the gentle rocking of the car to lull her into a short nap.

She still dreamed occasionally of a noose around her neck and cold, impenetrable eyes condemning her as an invisible crowd cheered. There were nights she climbed quietly out of her own bed to watch Wynn as he slept, just to make sure they both had really made it out alive.

Charlie had stared death in the face now and, sometimes, she worried that would mean he would find her more easily next time. But she wouldn't go easily, not with a child's life in her hands and the price that had been paid for hers.

A vibrant palette of coral and magenta was splashed across the sky by the time their homestead drifted into view, a lone dot exactly halfway between nowhere in particular and the back of beyond. As they drew closer, its white panelling contrasted starkly with the ochre backdrop. Their crops spread out behind the house in an olive rug, the two cows huddling together by the flimsy wooden fence in preparation for the encroaching evening. They could easily walk through it if they wanted to, but they never did.

Denise gave two short honks as they approached. Wynn was the first one out the front – he always was. He jumped the three steps from the verandah to the well-worn path, dirt smeared on his face, which was spread into a wide grin.

They ground to a halt in the driveway, if the dirt patch could be called that, and Charlie stepped into the evening air, relishing the way it filled her lungs. The smell of freshly turned soil, manure and blossoming alfalfa flooded her senses. *Home*, she thought blissfully.

Without warning, a force struck her abdomen, almost winding her. "Wynn!" she wheezed, as he enveloped her in a tight hug.

"You were gone too long," he complained.

Charlie squeezed him back. "Sorry, kiddo. We were as fast as we could be."

He released her to eagerly grab the bags from the car. "Can I come next time?"

She rolled her eyes. "When you're my height, we can talk about it."

"So next month then?" He stuck his tongue out and Denise laughed as Charlie playfully punched his arm.

"I got you some things," Charlie whispered as they made their way inside. From the smell that met them at the door, Anna and Tani had already started dinner.

"You didn't have to," Wynn protested, doing a terrible job of hiding a delighted smile.

Their new home was only just big enough for the five of them and pleasantly rustic and simple. Unvarnished floorboards stretched throughout the modest living space and four bedrooms, one of which Charlie had volunteered to share with Wynn.

It was the third remote property they had staked out, finding a ditch in which to hide the car and taking turns watching the house. After a few days with no signs of life, they had tentatively knocked and the front door plied under their touch. While dusty, it was still fully furnished, complete with framed artwork and a drying rack full of plates and cutlery.

No one had stepped foot on the weathered porch for sometime but, nonetheless, their shifts had continued. One person sat in the front window at all times until, finally, they had accepted no car was going to trundle into the driveway. The house was abandoned and, now, it was theirs.

Lighter coloured windows in the floral wallpaper indicated where photographs had previously been hung. The shelves and wall units looked unnaturally barren without their memory-laden trinkets.

Skirting around the low-sitting burgundy couches with fraying threads at the edges, the trio made their way into the cosy kitchen. As expected, Anna was stirring something as it simmered on the stovetop while Tani leaned against the beaten wood countertop, cloth in hand, drying the freshly washed cutlery.

"The mighty return! Show us your haul, then." Tani smacked her hand on the small, circular breakfast table which stood in the centre of the kitchen. It was empty, ready for their arrival.

The bags were quickly relieved of their contents, spilling across the surface as eager hands inspected the goods; pain killers, bandages, vinegar, cooking oil, an assortment of canned produce and a hamper's worth of clothes. No one seemed particularly interested in anything but the latter, so Anna quietly stored the items in the appropriate cupboards.

"I like these." Tani held up a pair of trousers with leather patches on the knees.

"This is lovely," Denise commented on a navy frock – the only one Charlie had bought. Dresses were impractical for working a farm, but a necessity for occasions like that day when they needed to blend in.

Wynn was pulling on an oversized blue plaid shirt, laughing at the way the sleeves flopped over his hands.

"Look, we'll just turn them up like this." Charlie expertly folded the sleeves to his wrists and gave him an appraising look. "There, now you really do look like the man of the house." He grinned in delight and scampered off to find a mirror.

Propping the wooden spoon over the bubbling stew, Anna raised her hands. "Any trouble?" she signed.

Charlie touched her thumb to her chest. "All fine. Oh." She had nearly forgotten the newspaper which had been bypassed in the frenzy. "Here." She made a clear patch on the table with her forearm and spread the paper for the three to read.

There were a few seconds of short-lived silence as they skimmed. Tani snorted. "Terrorism! They want us all to hang and *we're* the terrorists?"

Anna brought her thumbs and fingers together with both hands, bringing them together twice in front of her. "There are more," she mouthed.

"Just because they're starting to question the State doesn't make them like us," Denise replied.

"The enemy of my enemy is my friend," Tani quipped.

"You really think they want to be pals with fugitives, a witch, and Satan's child? Not my words," Denise added quickly when Charlie shot her a glare. "You know he wouldn't be the most popular boy in school."

"He's cooler than me."

"That's not difficult, Miss Witch." Denise gave her a sympathetic nod.

Quietly, Charlie slipped a dark blue bundle from the pile and left the three of them to speak about the horrible and fantastical things people had been saying about all five of them. She peered into their shared bedroom. Wynn was sitting cross-legged on his bed, staring at himself in the streaky mirror in the corner. In the few short months she had known him, the boy's face had already begun to change. His jaw was ever so slightly more angular, his nose broadening just a little.

He had known more fear and loss than any boy his age should have to. Their first few weeks on the road had been hard, often resorting to sleeping in the car and freshening up in public restrooms. His life and the only person who had truly cared for him had been taken from him in one brutal minute, yet he stiffened his lip and did his best to pull his weight without getting in their way. Sometimes he still stole away to be alone with his thoughts. Charlie knew all too well how grief came in waves; a fresh flood of consuming sorrow could emerge from nowhere.

"You look more like him every day, you know."

He lowered his eyes as Charlie sat beside him, fiddling with the final button on his shirt. "I hope I can be like him, too."

"You're more like him than you know. You're strong, resilient and you think of everyone else before yourself. Not to mention being painfully stubborn. God help me when you get older." His lips tweaked upwards but the humour didn't reach his eyes. "I saw something today that reminded me of him."

Charlie placed the bundle of material in his lap. He unfolded it carefully and held up the dark blue overalls to let them unravel to the ground. They were virtually identical to the pair Rhett had donned during his earthly existence, sans the oil stains which Charlie was sure Wynn would see to in no time. "They're just like his!"

"I know." She smiled at his delight. "Put them on, see if they fit."

She turned her back as Wynn wiggled his legs into the pants and hoisted the straps over his shoulders. Her breath stuck in her throat when she turned back to him. If Rhett could have been plucked from the past, she would have been sure she was looking at his teenage self.

He ran his thumbs along the shoulder straps and Charlie smiled as he admired himself in the mirror. "They suit you." He nodded, eyes glistening. His silence said more than words could. "Let's go visit him."

Taking him by the hand, she led him through the house and out the back door, privately wondering how much longer it would be before he was too embarrassed to let her. The sky's magenta had faded to a gentle apricot as the last of the sun's rays slipped over the mountain range. From the dusty coop came the clucking of hens negotiating the sleeping arrangements for the night. There was still just enough light to navigate the cow scat as they trotted across the yard towards their small dam, partially shaded by a flowering dogwood.

They took a seat at its base, between the lilies which were beginning to flourish under Charlie's ministrations. Above them, a carved inscription read '*Rhett Barron - 1930 - ∞*'. Although the other girls had never known him, they knew of his sacrifice and that they were only there because he had paid the ultimate price. Often, they would sit with Wynn beneath the shade of the ample branches and ask him to regale them with the happiest memories he had with his older brother. With him, they laughed and cried and immortalised his spirit in their little slice of freedom.

"Good evening to you both. I do hope I am not intruding." Hudson appeared from behind the trunk.

"Hey, Grandpa! Look at my new overalls." Wynn leapt to his feet, turning so the elderly man could admire him in full.

When Charlie had explained to the boy that Hudson was her great-grandfather, she hadn't been sure how he would receive the news. She certainly didn't expect the unbridled enthusiasm which had lit up his dejected face. "Well, if you're Charlie's grandpa then you're my grandpa, too," he had promptly replied. Charlie had almost been able to see Hudson's heart swell.

"My word, who is this handsome chap?" Hudson lowered himself to one knee and adjusted his glasses for a closer inspection. "If I didn't know better, I'd think I was looking at an equally fine man by the name of Rhett."

Wynn's face spread into a true smile and he dropped again next to Charlie, wiggling himself into her side. "She found them for me."

"You are fortunate to have someone who cares for you so deeply." His eyes twinkled. "Both of you."

Charlie threw an arm around the boy and kissed the top of his ruffled head. "We know."

They sat like that for a while, Hudson humming gently, until the fields were cloaked in darkness and the chickens fell silent for the night.

"Come on, you lot. Time for dinner!" Tani's robust voice broke the perfect silence.

Climbing slowly to their feet, Hudson paused. "Charlie, a moment if you don't mind?"

"Of course. Go on, kiddo." She pushed Wynn lightly. He looked like he was about to argue, but the aroma of dinner wafted down the yard and his stomach overruled his mind. He trotted back up to the house, leaving Hudson and Charlie alone.

"What's wrong?" It was odd for him not to speak freely in front of Wynn.

He took a few moments to choose his words. "People are looking for you, my lady."

"No, really?" she scoffed.

"Not the Enforcers. And not just Seers, although they would most certainly be among them. Ordinary people. They think you hold answers."

"It's started, hasn't it? The uprising?" Charlie kicked at the dirt, not needing an answer. "People are going to die, aren't they?"

"I believe the worst of the suffering is coming to an end. For the first time in decades, people have hope. The question is now if you will join them."

There was a heavy silence as they began to pace slowly towards the house. The storm had been growing for some time and she had known, deep down, she would have to weather it before long. But, for the first time in her life, she would face adversity knowing she was not alone.

Charlie stopped abruptly, turning to face Hudson. "You'll take care of him, won't you? If something happens to me."

"My dear," his gaze softened. "I do believe that is what family is for."

A note from the author

Did you enjoy *Incendiary*? I hope you loved reading it as much as I did writing it.

If you did enjoy this book, I'd really appreciate it if you left a review on GoodReads and/or the etailer of your choice. Reviews are game-changers for authors and your support would be invaluable.

I'd love to keep you updated with future releases and take you on as many adventures as you'll allow me.

Visit www.clairedowler.com to subscribe to my newsletter.

I'll also share excerpts, exclusive content and give away Advanced Review Copies (so you get to read it before anyone else!)

Until next time,
Claire

www.ingramcontent.com/pod-product-compliance
Lightning Source LLC
Chambersburg PA
CBHW060809310726
48980CB00002B/281

* 9 7 8 0 6 4 5 3 8 0 3 1 6 *